*Fields in the Sun*

BY THE SAME AUTHOR
*The Quiet Earth*

# FIELDS IN THE SUN

*Margaret Sunley*

ROWAN

A ROWAN BOOK

Published by Arrow Books Limited
20 Vauxhall Bridge Road, London SW1V 2SA

An imprint of the Random Century Group

London Melbourne Sydney Auckland Johannesburg
and agencies throughout the world

First published by Century Hutchinson 1991
Rowan edition 1991

1 3 5 7 9 10 8 6 4 2

Printed and bound in Great Britain by
Cox & Wyman Ltd, Reading

ISBN 0 09 972130 9

## ACKNOWLEDGEMENT

With thanks to Mrs Knock of the Little House, Howsham, for her kindness in allowing me to see the interior of Howsham Hall

# CHAPTER ONE

Elizabeth Oaks passed the back of her hand across her dripping brow, leaving a floury streak. She had been up since half-past five, when her husband rose to go to his father's farm, where he worked. As soon as the fire was drawing and the oven was hot, she had started to bake. Now, as she stood back and surveyed the array of cakes and pies spread across the dresser and over one end of the kitchen table, she felt a glow of satisfaction. Crossing to the range, she opened the oven door and passed her hand quickly across the inside. It was still too hot for the pork pies, so she left the door ajar and picking up the coal-rake, drew out some of the fire from beneath the oven. 'There,' she murmured to herself. 'By the time they're ready for in, it should be just about right.'

Since her marriage to George Oaks almost seven months before, she had stood the Wednesday market in the nearby town of Kirkbymoorside with her mother-in-law, Annie Oaks. At first, she had not had sufficient in the way of eggs and dairy produce to bring in enough money to eke out her husband's wage from his father. She had decided then to stretch her farm produce by baking, and had gradually built up a number of regular customers for her cakes and pies.

Elizabeth soon realised that her venture was unpopular amongst the bakers and publicans of the little town, who expected to supply food for those attending the weekly market. However, she was quite happy with the success of her business and knew that both her own family – the Butlers – and George's family – the Oaks – were too highly thought of in the area for any of the innkeepers to complain aloud that she was taking their trade. They preferred to dismiss it as a woman's fancy – of little importance. Elizabeth, however, knew that her experiment was already earning more money than her mother-in-law had ever made on her market stall. She managed the home thriftily and put her earnings into the bank each Wednesday, to add to the nest-egg which she and George were building up.

While the pork pies were baking, she packed the rest of her produce into large flat baskets, covered with clean white cloths. Putting on her cloak ready to face the cold March day in the market place, she glanced out of the window across the garden towards the lane, which wound through the little valley of Sleightholmedale.

'Where's that lad?' she muttered anxiously. On Wednesdays, when she left Cherry Tree Farm to attend the market, either her husband stayed behind to work or her father-in-law sent Ned Blake, one of the farm lads, to work on hedging and ditching and to keep an eye on the stock and farmhouse. She moved the trays of pork pies from the oven and placed them on the table before packing them into the last of her baskets, and then crossed to the kitchen mirror to put on her bonnet.

As she went to open the door, there was a crisp knock on it, and the cheeky grin of Ned was revealed. 'Noo then, missus. Aah've yoked Bella up ti t'trap for thi. Gimme some o' thi baskets an' Aah'll stow 'em in t'trap,' he offered.

'Oh, bless you, Ned.' Elizabeth smiled at the lad's eagerness. 'I thought you were late – I should have known better.' He flushed with embarrassment at the compliment. Mrs George, as she was known to the workers on the Oaks' farm, was a firm favourite with the men, treating them as human beings, rather than merely a source of labour.

When the trap was loaded, Elizabeth Oaks banked up the kitchen fire with peat turfs and left the house. Entering the trap, she clicked her tongue for the pony, Bella, to walk on. She turned out of the yard gate and set off down the lane towards Aumery Park Farm. Here her husband's mother Annie would be waiting with her own pony-trap laden with dressed chickens, eggs, butter, curd and any other farm produce which she had managed to collect up for market. At Kirkbymoorside the farm-wives sat on chairs, their produce spread around them, and chatted to each other between serving customers. Many of them, like the Oaks, lived in isolated valleys and dales and attendance at the market was the highlight of their week. Here, news was exchanged and friends and families encountered from more distant moorland farms and villages. Although she knew that her parents, John and Ann Butler of Fadmoor, disapproved of her selling goods at market, Elizabeth enjoyed these days. She felt that the shared outings had created a bond between herself and George's mother, who at first had resented that fact that Elizabeth was seven years older than her son. However, the two women had drawn closer during the months since the wedding.

Elizabeth's lips curved in a slow smile of satisfaction as she climbed down to open the gate which barred the track before the approach to Aumery Park Farm. By now she was certain of her pregnancy. She did not intend to share the news with anyone until she had confided in George, but she knew that Jonadab and Annie Oaks would be pleased. She fastened the gate and re-entered the trap, to cover the last few yards to the Oaks' farm. 'That's odd,' she thought, noticing that her mother-in-law's pony and trap were not waiting by the door. 'I wonder why Ma's not ready?'

Dismounting, she tied up Bella and then entered the kitchen where her sister-in-law Martha was standing by the stone sink, filling the large black iron kettle. As she turned to Elizabeth, she wiped away tears with the back of her hand. 'Whatever's the matter?' Elizabeth crossed the kitchen and placed a comforting arm round the girl's shoulder.

'Oh, Elizabeth.' Martha swung round and threw herself into Elizabeth's arms, sobbing convulsively.

'Where's Ma?' asked Elizabeth, rocking the girl and patting her back rhythmically in a comforting gesture. At that moment Lydia, the little maid of all work, came running through from the parlour.

'T'missus is upstairs wi' Miss Tamar,' she announced. "Er time's come – an' a bad time it is an' all,' she added, as she lifted the kettle on to the reckon, over the fire.

Elizabeth ran through the parlour and up the stairs. When she entered the bedroom Annie Oaks was wiping her daughter's brow with a cloth wrung out in vinegar and cold water. Tamar's vibrant beauty had vanished: she lay on the bed completely exhausted and barely conscious. Her face was sallow and drawn, her forehead and upper lip beaded with perspiration. Her usually lustrous, curly black hair clung in tendrils to her damp forehead and cheeks. As she turned her face towards the door and opened her eyes to see who had entered, she gave a sudden gasp and her knees involuntarily drew up in a spasm of agony.

Elizabeth looked from the rail at the head of the bed, to which Tamar was clinging with whitened knuckles, towards Annie, whose whole attitude mirrored her daughter's fatigue and fear. 'She needs a doctor,' the mother whispered. 'Aah don't know what's wrong. She's been like this all night.'

Elizabeth pressed her arm. 'I'll call at Dr Dawson's in Kirkby,' she promised. 'He'll come straight away.'

'No! No!' Her mother-in-law pulled her back from the door. 'Her faither won't let anybody know. We can't 'ave t'doctor.'

Elizabeth was incredulous. She knew her father-in-law to be a proud and stubborn man, but surely he would not let his own daughter die in childbirth for want of a doctor! That Jonadab had not addressed a single word to Tamar since her pregnancy had been revealed to them the previous autumn, Elizabeth well knew, but she refused to believe that he would still harden his heart now that Tamar's condition was so desperate. 'Where's George?' she demanded, thinking that if they all faced Jonadab, he must capitulate.

Annie, however, shook her head. ''E's taken Violet and Rosie up ti t'farrier's in Fadmoor ti be shod,' she answered.

Elizabeth bit her lip. 'Shall I stay here to help you?' she suggested.

'Nay – get thissen off ti market. Will you tek little Molly out o' t'road?' Annie asked.

'Of course, and I'll tell you what,' suggested Elizabeth, 'if Martha packs the trap and comes up to Kirkbymoorside after me, I'll have a chair ready next to mine and she can sell what she can. I'll see she's all right and give her a hand.' She went to the bed and kissed Tamar's damp cheek. 'Gather your strength, love. It'll be over soon,' she whispered, adding to herself, 'one way or the other.'

Tamar's eyes flickered open and she forced her lips into a painful smile. 'Never fear,' she croaked dryly, 'Aah'll come through. Aah'll best yon devil, yet. Faither may not want

12

this bastard, but 'e'll 'ave it ti put up with.' Her lashes then drooped over her amber eyes and she seemed to sink once more into a stupor, as Elizabeth turned away from the bed.

She pressed her mother-in-law's hand. 'I'll go if you're sure,' she said. 'Try not to worry – I think perhaps she's right and she will pull through.'

When Elizabeth had gone, Annie looked at her daughter and shook her head sadly. The labour had already lasted several hours and she feared for the baby, as well as the mother. Wiping the burning face gently once more, she made her way downstairs. Martha and Lydia were busy packing the trap and Annie was too worried to ask if her youngest daughter could manage all the way to Kirkby alone. Martha had never actually driven the trap before, but knew the pony well and had ridden as a passenger all her life.

Annie took a pan of finely chopped beef out of the side oven and poured some of the beef tea into a mug. Before going back upstairs, she spoke to Lydia. 'Run down ti t'Blackgate Field and ask t'maister if 'e can spare me a minute. Aah know 'e's sowing oats there wi' Bert, but say as 'ow it's important.'

While Annie waited for the beef tea to cool sufficiently for Tamar to drink it, she sat in her chair before the fire and leaning her head wearily upon the high back, rocked gently to and fro. Although she had delivered several babies including little Molly, her daughter Ann Waind's child, all had been fairly short and trouble-free labours. She had never had to deal with one so long, exhausting and complicated. Tamar was worn out and now had no strength left to push her child out into the world.

At the sound of the door, Annie opened her eyes and looked up at her husband. Now in his early fifties, Jonadab Oaks was as upright as ever. A broken thigh from an accident a few months previously had left him with a slight limp, but with the passing of time this was scarcely noticeable. His black hair was now touched with a wing of silver at each side, yet his vivid blue eyes, unfaded with the years, burned fiercely from a face tanned by daily exposure to the weather.

Annie rose stiffly to her feet. 'Jonadab, we must 'ave a doctor for oor Tamar,' she protested.

'*What?*' he thundered. 'Is this why you've brought me from mi work? We 'ad this out during t'night and Aah made it clear then: Aah'll *not* 'ave a doctor down in this vale ti spread t'word of oor shame.'

Annie looked at him in disbelief. 'Art thoo willing ti se thi bairn, not ti say 'er bairn, die?' she demanded.

Jonadab drew a deep breath. 'The Lord's Will Be Done,' he announced heavily. 'She's a sinner and the child is t'result of sin. Whatever the Lord decides must be right.'

Annie picked up the beef tea and crossed the kitchen. 'If they die because you're too stubborn ti 'ave t'doctor, Aah'll never ever forgive you, Jonadab Oaks, as long as Aah live,' she said with quiet intensity, as she passed through into the parlour and off up the stairs.

Jonadab had never seen his wife in such a defiant mood. Normally Annie was placid and obedient to his every wish. He stared at the door after it had closed behind her, feeling bewildered and uneasy. How could she threaten him in such a way, he wondered. He knew that his attitude to sin was correct. He lived by his Bible and had brought up his family in the ways of the Lord. Before going back to his work, he closed his eyes and his lips moved silently. 'If it be Thy will, oh Lord, save t'lass and 'er bairn,' he mouthed silently. Then, watched by Lydia, who stood unobserved in the deep shadow by the dairy door, he swung on his heel and went out.

Lydia scurried upstairs to see if she could be of any help to her beloved mistress. Since her arrival from the workhouse to work for the Oaks, she had adored the motherly Annie, who had given her the only real home she had ever known. Now, knowing how drained Annie must feel after her night's vigil, she tiptoed into the bedroom carrying a mug of strong tea.

Annie glanced up with a tired smile. 'Thank you, love,' she half-whispered. 'Can you give me an 'and to lift 'er up.' Lydia knelt on the bed and raised Tamar's head. 'Come on, pet,' urged her mother, as Tamar's eyes opened wearily. 'Drink this. It'll give you strength.'

Supported by her mother and Lydia, Tamar allowed the warm sustaining liquid to trickle down her throat. 'Thank you, Mam, that's grand,' she tried to smile. 'Will it take much longer?'

Annie placed her hand on Tamar's body. 'T'bairn's moving, so it's still all right,' she assured her daughter. 'Rest a while and when it starts to come again, you'll be strong enough to bear down.' She fluffed up the pillows so that Tamar could lean back, and sat drinking her tea while holding her daughter's hand with her free one.

Just after Lydia went down to start the preparations for midday dinner, Annie felt Tamar's hand tighten on her own. The girl's eyes widened with fear. 'Oh, Mam! It's starting again,' she gasped.

'Hang on to t'bedrail and be ready to push when Aah says.' Annie spoke calmly although her heart was racing. 'Now you've had a rest, you'll be stronger, lass.' Annie was proved right – Tamar had gathered up her last reserves of strength and was determined that both she and her child would survive. She had no idea of her father's whereabouts on the farm, but had made up her mind that Jonadab would not hear a single groan or cry of pain from her lips. Consequently, she gritted her teeth and followed her mother's instructions. Just when she felt she could bear no more – it was all over. As she sank back on the pillows, exhausted, Annie held up the baby. 'It's a lass!' she sobbed. 'A lovely little lass. And she looks just like you.'

As Tamar slipped into the luxury of sleep, Annie poured warm water from the bedroom pitcher into the earthenware bowl and bathed her latest grandchild. She dressed the baby in one of the gowns sent over by her daughter Beth, who was married to a neighbouring farmer's son and had given birth to her first child a few months before. She quietly tidied the bed, where Tamar now lay in the deep sleep of utter exhaustion and closing the door softly behind her, carried the newborn child downstairs. As she sank into the rocking-chair by the kitchen fire, nursing the little bundle, Lydia came and stood beside her.

'Eeh, but it's lovely. What is it, missus?' she breathed, gazing at the doll-like features.

15

'A little lass, Lydia,' smiled Annie.

By the time the men came in for their dinner at noon, Annie had taken up more beef tea and Tamar had fed the baby, who was then placed in the cradle beside her bed. Mother and child had drifted again into sleep. Jonadab strode through the door but before washing his hands at the sink, looked questioningly across at his wife. 'Well?' he growled.

'It's all over – a little lass.' Annie answered his unspoken question, then swung round to face him. 'Both are well, but wi' no thanks to thoo!' she spat out as tears of weakness and fatigue welled up. Jonadab was lost for words and George and young Jonna were dumbfounded at their mother's outburst. They sat uncomfortably at the table while Lydia served them their dinner and Annie just rocked in the chair by the fire, sobbing. Once begun, her sobs were uncontrollable, stemming as they did from hours of anxiety and tiredness.

'Nay, Mam, it's over and all's well.' George spoke compassionately.

Annie, however, would not be consoled. 'Nay, nay. Your faither wouldn't have t'doctor. We could've lost 'em both,' she wept.

Lydia had hung back, unwilling to push herself forward into what she realised was a private family matter. Now, however, she came shyly towards her mistress and touched Annie's shoulder. 'Nay, missus. T'maister offered up a prayer for 'em,' she faltered, glancing back at Jonadab, uncertain of his reaction. He was taken aback, unaware that the girl had been present during what he now regarded as a moment of weakness. His forehead was furrowed by a frown as the heavy black brows met above the piercing blue eyes.

Before he could speak, however, Annie looked across at him, her expression radiant through the tears. 'Oh, thank you, Jonadab. Thank you. Your prayers were answered,' she cried.

Jonadab shifted uncomfortably. 'The Lord has preserved them both,' he acknowledged, 'but that doesn't absolve her from sin.'

Annie found great solace in the fact that her husband had prayed for Tamar and her child. She knew how Jonadab struggled to instil his own standards into his flock and how deeply wounded he felt when they let him down. Tamar was not the first of his children to fall by the wayside. His eldest son Joseph had married Mary Butler when she was pregnant: this had been a bitter blow to Jonadab, but at least the couple, deeply in love, had been able to marry before the child was born. Tamar's shame, however, had been brought about by her secret liaison with Sir William Forster, a member of the aristocracy. There had been no possibility of marriage to save *her* from disgrace.

During the long winter months of Tamar's pregnancy, the harsh weather of the Yorkshire moors had kept the family confined to the isolated valley of Sleightholmedale; no one, apart from the immediate family, knew the secret of her condition. Jonadab had determined that neither Tamar nor her child should leave the valley. He was unsure how to accomplish this, but was convinced that he would succeed. 'She'll not leave this dale,' he frequently told himself, ignoring the fact of Tamar's rebellious and fiery temperament.

Now, sitting at the head of the table, he closed his heart to the fact of the child's existence. Since he had discovered that Tamar was pregnant, he had not addressed a single word to her: he refused to acknowledge her presence in the house. The child of Tamar's sin was also non-existent in his eyes. Sighing deeply, he pushed away his plate, the meal only half-eaten. His chair scraped on the flagged stone floor as he rose to his feet.

'Nay, maister,' protested Lydia. 'Thoo can't 'ave 'ad enough, surely. What about some pudding?'

Placing both hands on the table, Jonadab gazed sadly from one to another. 'Enough?' He smiled grimly. 'Aah've 'ad more than enough, lass. Them 'as sups sorrow 'as no need o' meat.' So saying, he strode gloomily to the door, put on the heavy coat which hung on a nail and strode out into the bleak March day.

Once the constraint of his dour presence was removed, those left in the kitchen began to talk almost animatedly.

17

George had spent most of the morning at the blacksmith's forge in Fadmoor and had returned with snippets of news for his mother. Both he and his seventeen year old brother Jonadab junior, wanted a full description of the baby and reassurance that Tamar had come safely through her ordeal.

As the two brothers downed their mugs of steaming tea, George was concerned to notice the lines of strain on his mother's face and the weary slump of her shoulders. 'Come on, oor lad.' He nodded his head towards their mother as he spoke. Jonna took his point and rose from his seat at the table. As they approached the door, George looked back at Lydia. 'See that she puts 'er feet up and 'as a minute, this afternoon,' he said.

'Aye, Aah will an' all,' she assured him.

By early afternoon, Elizabeth and Martha were ready to come home from Kirkbymoorside. Although they had not quite sold up, both were chilled to the bone. Their heavy winter cloaks had long since proved no match for the bitter north wind which swirled down the main street of the little town. The chairs of the farmers' wives were placed on the cobblestones which skirted the road on each side. They had no stalls to shelter them, for these were strung out together lower down the street.

Elizabeth had explained Annie's absence to the other women by saying that she had a severe cold, but she knew that many of them were curious as to why little Molly Waind had come along, especially on such a raw day. At first, the little girl had been excited by the visit to town, chattering animatedly about all she saw but gradually, boredom overtook her and the piercing wind caused her to shiver. Eventually, all pleasure in the day deserted her and she began to whimper, her teeth chattering with cold. 'Let's go 'ome, Auntie Lizzie,' she implored.

Neither Elizabeth nor Martha's hearts were in the task and they needed no urging from the child. 'Come along, Molly.' Elizabeth spoke briskly. 'Auntie Elizabeth will give you one of her pork pies and when you've eaten it, you can help to pack up what's left. I'll go and harness the ponies and then we'll go back home.' Molly brightened immediately and scuttled about, shaking cloths and helping Martha to fold them into baskets.

Elizabeth went to the Black Swan yard and paid for the stabling of the ponies. When she had the traps ready, she quickly crossed the street again to where Martha and Molly were waiting. 'We'll take the chairs back, and then get started,' she said.

Although Tamar had been heavy on their minds the whole day, the presence of little Molly and the other farm-wives had prevented the two women from giving voice to their fears. Now, driving separately, they were still unable to share their worries. Elizabeth felt a cold sickness in the pit of her stomach as she pictured Tamar as she had left her that morning, practically at the end of her endurance. She regretted bitterly now that she had not called on Dr Dawson in defiance of her father-in-law's wishes. Although she knew that Jonadab was fond of her in his own way, she felt that he was far too rigid in his discipline over his family.

Yes, Tamar had done wrong, but Elizabeth knew in her heart that had she been younger and not so strong in self-control, she too would have given in to the demands of George's love before their marriage.

When they reached Aumery Park Farm, she tied up her pony and lifted little Molly down from Martha's trap. As she ran to the door, she called to Martha to follow her in. 'Leave Topper and I'll get one of the men to see to her,' she called. 'I must get Molly into the warmth. The poor bairn's frozen. I can't stay long – it's drawing in dusk,' she said to her mother-in-law, as she entered the kitchen. 'How is she?'

Annie had shed her despair and dejection. Now she was her normal rosy self, bustling about her kitchen. 'It's a lovely little lass,' she announced. 'They're both all right, the Lord be praised.'

'No thanks to *him*,' hissed Elizabeth, as Jonadab passed the kitchen window.

'Now, lass. That'll do.' Annie put one hand on Elizabeth's arm and a finger across her own lips, as the door opened to admit her husband. His accusing look bored into Martha.

19

'Thoo 'asn't seen ti t'pony.' He spoke sharply and Martha flushed and made for the door.

Elizabeth, however, faced her father-in-law calmly. 'I'm afraid that I'm to blame,' she smiled placatingly. 'We were all so cold and I realised that it was time for afternoon drinkings, so I knew one of the lads would be free to see to Topper.' As her husband followed his father into the kitchen, she turned to him. 'Slip your boots off, George, and we'll go up and see Tamar and the baby before I go home.' She could see that her mention of Tamar and the child had annoyed Jonadab. He did not speak but his lips set in a thin line, and a pulse in his temple throbbed.

When George and Elizabeth entered the bedroom, she marvelled at the change in Tamar. That morning, she had left her sister-in-law at the very brink of death. Now, although obviously still frail and lying back on the pillows, Tamar was filled with a new luminosity which enhanced her vivid beauty. She indicated the cradle, proudly. 'Pick 'er up if you want,' she said to Elizabeth.

As Elizabeth held the baby in her arms, she looked down at a miniature edition of Tamar. The infant had quite a mass of dark curls and Tamar's topaz eyes looked up from between long black lashes. 'Have you thought of a name yet?' she asked.

'Yes,' Tamar smiled. 'Victoria – because she's my little queen.' She considered for a moment and then confessed, 'Many's t'time that Aah've wished she'd never 'appened and the Lord forgive me, if Aah'd known 'ow ti, Aah'd 'ave gotten rid. Now she's 'ere, though, she's my life.'

George cleared his throat, feeling rather embarrassed at his sister's intensity. 'You'll have a hard row to plough, lass,' he reminded her. 'I know I speak for Elizabeth as well so if there's owt we can do to help you, you've only to say.'

Tamar smiled. There was a new maturity about her. 'Thank you. I'll remember that,' she promised.

On the landing, Elizabeth drew George to her. 'George, dear,' she whispered. 'I'm expecting, too.'

George was overcome with joy. Picking up his wife, he swung her round, his lips closing on hers in a passionate kiss. 'Oh, my little love,' he beamed. 'That's the best news I've heard since you promised we'd be wed.'

'Yes,' she smiled. 'It will complete our happiness. I only wish that poor Tamar's bairn could have been welcomed with the same joy.'

As she drove down the little valley in the gathering gloom towards the solid, stone-built farmhouse which was their home, Elizabeth reflected on how lucky she was. She compared her own lot with poor Tamar's, who faced an arid and sterile future under the domination of her stern and rigid father.

# CHAPTER TWO

As soon as Annie Oaks was told of Elizabeth's pregnancy, she adopted a protective and maternal attitude towards her daughter-in-law. 'Now, start on raspberry vinegar straight away,' she advised. 'Taken daily while you're carrying it makes for an easy labour.' She glanced across at Tamar, who was sitting at the table, knitting a dress for Victoria. 'Our Tamar nivver took it, an' that's why she 'ad such a bad time,' she added with conviction. She knew that, in Jonadab's eyes, Tamar's difficult labour was a punishment from God for her transgression, but she, herself, refused to believe such a thing. All her other girls had taken their mother's raspberry vinegar during pregnancy and all had had straightforward labours.

Elizabeth dutifully took daily doses of the concoction, but she also called in to consult the doctor on one of her weekly visits to Kirkbymoorside. He assured her that she had nothing to fear from a first pregnancy at the age of over thirty, so she settled down happily to look forward to the coming of their baby.

George underwent the usual chaffing from his father's farm-workers. 'Thoo's proven thissen a man then,' was his father's only comment, but George knew he was pleased and relieved that another Oaks was on the way. Jonadab's eldest son, Joseph, had emigrated to Canada a few years before, taking with him young Georgie, his son. Although Jonadab had washed his hands of Joseph when he had first got Mary Butler 'in t'family way', as he put it, he had come part-way to accepting the child, once they were married. Consequently he was devastated when the pair had emigrated, taking away to foreign parts the only grandson to bear the name Oaks.

Soon, however, God willing, Elizabeth would bear a son and there would, once again, be an Oaks man-child to take over the farm eventually. Although Jonadab was only a tenant-farmer, the land had been worked by his forbears for as long as anyone knew. This land was his life and he wished to ensure that the Oaks family farmed it for the foreseeable future, long after his own lifetime. Even though his attitude to Tamar had not softened, Elizabeth's pregnancy had given him hope and the feeling that his God had not forsaken him.

Elizabeth looked far younger than her years. Her olive skin was unlined and her eyes were dark and expressive. When she laughed, as was frequent, her lips parted to show small, but even, white teeth. She had what George referred to as 'sparkle' and the burgeoning of her pregnancy had increased her innate vivacity.

So it was, that as she drove towards the Oaks' farm one Wednesday morning, she hummed to herself as she went down the valley. The April sky was a clear, azure blue with puffs of white cloud scudding across it in the light breeze. Elizabeth felt a glow of contentment as she reflected that life had been good to her and George. Upon rounding the final bend, which brought Aumery Park Farm into view, she screwed up her eyes against the sun to bring into focus the horseman who was approaching it from the other direction. Surely it was her father – but John Butler gave no wave of recognition as he dismounted and strode to the door.

By now, Elizabeth was almost up to him. She was uneasy about the purpose of his visit, especially so early in the day. Mr Butler was always florid, but now his face was verging on magenta, with veins of purple mottling the cheeks. She drew level with him as he raised his fist and banged vigorously on the door. 'Whatever's wrong, Father?' she cried, as she seized hold of his upraised arm.

John Butler had been so intent upon his mission that he had not noticed his daughter until that moment. He whirled round to see who had interrupted him. 'Wrong? *Wrong*?' he shouted. His eyes, which were usually so good-humoured and merry, protruded in anger from the blood-red face. Before he could utter another word, however, the door was flung open by Jonadab Oaks, affronted at the assault on his door and curious to know the cause.

Upon seeing Elizabeth accompanied by her father, he stood aside. 'Come in, John. Come in,' he invited, looking from one to the other. 'What can Aah do for thi?'

'Do? Oh, there's nothing you can *do*.' John Butler was struggling to control his voice, but it was apparent to those in the kitchen that he was both distressed and angry.

Annie spoke first. 'Lydia, pour Mr Butler a cup of tea and then tek oor Molly and collect t'eggs,' she said. Although it was time for her and Elizabeth to set out for market, she was curious to know why John Butler had come. He took out a kerchief and wiped his damp brow and mopped his neck, before taking a great swig of tea.

Jonadab sat opposite, assessing the other man's mood. Something had certainly upset Butler, but his host waited patiently for him to recover his composure. Having swallowed the first mouthful, Butler expelled his breath in a great gust. 'That's better,' he sighed, as he drank more of the hot, strong brew.

'Whatever is the matter, Father?' asked Elizabeth, solicitously.

Butler looked searchingly from one to the other. 'None of you knows, then? You're not deceiving me?'

Jonadab Oaks' startling blue eyes turned glacial as he stared across the table. 'Deceiving thee?' He was incredulous that one who knew him so well could even consider that he could be guilty of deceit. 'What dost thoo mean?'

John Butler took a deep breath but his voice trembled as he spoke. 'It's our Jack. He's gone.'

Elizabeth's gasp was audible throughout the kitchen. 'What do you mean, gone?' she demanded.

Her father's voice began once more to rise. 'Gone to t'Canadas! Gone on a ship! Sneaked off in t'night!' With each explosive exclamation, the volume increased until he was shouting.

'Nay, nay, Mr Butler. Calm thissen down.' Annie Oaks tried to soothe him, as Elizabeth rose and went to stand by her father, putting an arm round him.

'Now, Father, you'll make yourself ill. Please try to explain calmly what has happened,' she urged.

He sprang to his feet and began to pace up and down.

'It's all your Joseph's fault!' He pointed accusingly at Jonadab, who was taken aback at this verbal attack from the other man. His eldest son Joseph had emigrated almost five years before, much to the family's sorrow; how he could be blamed was a mystery to his father.

As John Butler continued his pacing to and fro across the kitchen his voice grew more accusing. 'Your Joseph's been writing to our Jack every few months, filling his head with daft ideas about life out there!' he spluttered. 'My lad hadn't the guts to come out with it and tell us. He's been planning it for months, it seems. Any road, off he went in t'night.'

This was like a bombshell to the Oaks. 'Nay, John. Thoo can't blame oor Joe,' remonstrated Jonadab. 'We've 'ad regular letters but neither o' my other lads 'as took it into their 'eads ti go.'

Elizabeth could see an irreparable rift developing between the two families, if nobody intervened to heal it now. She spoke soothingly. 'Now, Father, this has been a shock to us all, but you can't blame Joseph – you must see that. Mary has written, too, with glowing accounts of life in Canada and, after all, Jack's a grown man. He's old enough to make his own decisions.'

'Old enough?' Her father's lip curled and he almost snarled the words. 'He's old enough to wed and father a son, but he refused to settle down! He's old enough to come out in t'open like a man and discuss his plans, but he didn't. No!' He wiped away the sudden tears which sprang to his eyes. 'No!' he repeated. 'He hadn't the pluck to tell us openly. Off he sneaks like a thief in the night, leaving a letter to say his horse'll be stabled at Whitby, if I'll send somebody for it.' He turned and gazed sadly at Elizabeth, who stood beside him with a grave face. 'That's the sort of man I've raised.' He spoke so sorrowfully that Elizabeth felt the tears prick behind her eyes. She squeezed his shoulder.

'Try to keep calm, Father. What's done is done and we must cope as best we can.' She turned to her mother-in-law. 'We'd best be off, Ma, or we'll have no customers. George and I will come up tonight and have a word with you and Mother,' she added to her father, as she and Annie Oaks made for the door.

When the two women had left them, Jonadab cleared his throat. 'If t'ship's sailed already there's nowt ti be done, John,' he ventured, 'so thoo mon mek t'best on it.'

Butler sighed heavily. 'As far as I can see, there *is* no best,' he protested. 'I've not been feeling too well lately, and how we're going to get through all t'work without our Jack, I just don't know.'

His resentment of Jonadab Oaks had always lurked just beneath a veneer of easy camaraderie. He felt bitter that the other man's farm seemed to prosper when all around him were struggling. The two families were inextricably bound together, so there was no way that he could avoid meeting this man, whom he regarded with an implacable hatred. He had only ridden down to Sleightholmedale this morning because he was certain that if his son had confided his plans to anybody, it would be to the Oaks. He now regretted that he had come down to the valley and disclosed what had happened.

He looked across the kitchen at Jonadab, who was sitting ramrod-straight in his chair, his face filled with compassion. 'If there's owt we can do, John, thoo's only ti say,' Jonadab offered, although he could not really spare any of his work-force to lend a hand during haytime and harvest. With his only son lost to him and to his farm, he realised that Elizabeth's father faced a worrying time.

As John Butler rose to take his leave, the parlour door opened and revealed Tamar, carrying her baby. She stepped into the kitchen before realising that her father and John Butler were still there. Normally she tried to keep herself and Victoria out of Jonadab's way. Now she hesitated, wondering whether to retreat, but as both men were looking at her, she decided to stay where she was.

Comprehension dawned on John Butler's face. 'So this is why nobody's seen yon lass for going on a year!' he exclaimed. His gaze swept from Tamar to her father. 'My God! What a hypocrite you are!' he threw at Jonadab. 'Always at chapel – looking down at other folk, putting yourself up to be on a level with God Almighty.'

Jonadab interrupted him. 'Nay, John. That's not so, and thoo knows it.'

John Butler would not be silenced, however. Tamar stood, her face scarlet and her amber eyes downcast. She dared not look up, knowing how keenly her father would feel the shame of John Butler's discovery. 'What a brood you've raised, Jonadab Oaks.' He almost spat the words, allowing his true feelings full rein at last. 'Your Joseph seduced our poor Mary and then took her and her bairn across the other side of t'world.'

Jonadab had no chance to remonstrate that his son was also lost to his family and that Georgie was their grandchild, as well as Butler's. Now that the flood-gates were opened, there was no stemming John Butler's torrent of resentment and condemnation.

'Your George is a jailbird. I can't understand our Elizabeth marrying him. She's had many a chance to wed – gentlemen, and all – but she was trapped by that lad o' yours, because he thinks she's likely got a bit o' brass coming from t'missus's brother in Leeds. I could wish the bairn she's expecting had any blood but Oaks'.'

As Butler paused to draw breath, Jonadab opened his mouth to refute his allegations but then looked more closely at the other man and bit back the words. Butler's eyes were protruding from a face suffused with blood. The veins in his neck stood out like ropes and the throbbing of the pulse in his temple was clearly visible. Jonadab took a step forward, concerned at the man's appearance but before he could reach him, John Butler swung towards Tamar.

'And now we've another of your precious family who's brought discredit to your name,' he sneered, curling his lip as he looked at her. Tamar's flush deepened but she kept her eyes cast down, as his voice once more began to rise. 'By God! My lad may be weak, but he's done nowt for me to be ashamed of,' he roared. 'My lad . . .' his voice was choked in mid-sentence and a terrible look of comprehension dawned in his eyes as his hands tore at his neckerchief, trying to find breath to fill his lungs. It was a vain effort, however. As Jonadab reached him, he sagged forward to be caught in his arms and lowered gently to the floor.

Kneeling beside him, Jonadab placed an ear to his chest, but could hear no heartbeat. Addressing Tamar for the first time in months he threw over his shoulder, 'Bring t'looking glass!'

Swiftly she placed the baby in the cradle, which stood by the fireside and lifted down the mirror from above the sink. Rubbing it with her sleeve, she ran and handed it to her father. 'Is he dead?' she breathed.

'Aah'm afraid so,' answered Jonadab, placing the mirror above the blue lips. There was no tell-tale misting of the glass and he sighed as he rose to his feet. ''E's gone,' he pronounced. ''E's a big chap – canst thoo 'elp me ti carry 'im into t'parlour, before Lydia gets back wi' little Molly?'

'Aye, Faither. Aah'll tek t'legs, if thoo'll carry 'is shoulders.' She was only too relieved that her father was speaking to her, even though it had taken this tragedy to bring it about. When they had lain the body on the parlour sofa, Tamar brought a sheet and draped it over him. She was shaking from the shock and felt quite faint. Back in the kitchen she went towards a chair, but her father had more for her to do.

'Go and bring oor George and young Jonadab,' he instructed. 'Tell 'em ti saddle their 'orses.' As she made for the door, he spoke her name. 'Tamar!'

'Aye, Faither?' she answered.

'The things 'e said,' he paused uncomfortably. 'There's no need for anyone else ti know. 'E was upset over their Jack and got carried away. T'chap was poorly and not responsible for 'is words. Any road, he knew why oor George 'ad spent a night in jail. When he struck Sir William Forster, it was for their Elizabeth, as well as oor Beth.'

Left alone with the sleeping child, Jonadab stood over the cradle and looked down at the baby. She was a miniature edition of her mother, having inherited all Tamar's beauty. Searching her features, he could find no trace of Sir William Forster and for this he was relieved.

Tamar and his sons returned to the house just as Lydia came back with little Molly and the basket of eggs. She had kept the child out of the house as long as possible but had not seen John Butler ride away out of the valley. As Molly was growing fretful, Lydia had decided to bring her back to the farm.

When they entered, Jonadab was seated in his Windsor chair by the hearth. His elbows rested on his knees and his head drooped in his hands. He looked up and sighed deeply when they came into the kitchen. 'No doubt oor Tamar's told thoo what's amiss,' he began.

George was stunned. 'She says Mr Butler's dropped dead. I can't believe it,' he blurted out.

'Aah'm afraid there's no doubt,' his father answered. 'Their Jack's sneaked off in t'night and sailed ti Canada, ti join Joe and Mary. It was such a shock ti poor John that 'is heart must 'ave give out.'

George digested this information, finding it difficult to grasp. Jack Butler had given no indication of his intentions when he had last seen him at Easter. 'How am I going to break the news to Elizabeth?' he wondered aloud.

'You're not,' his father answered. 'Aah wants thoo ti go ti Fadmoor and tell Mrs Butler. You'll do it better than Jonna, being as 'ow you're older.'

George's heart sank. It would be hard enough to break the dreadful news to his wife, but to have the task of telling Ann Butler was utterly daunting. Although she was his mother-in-law, he sensed her dislike of him. She had always made it clear that she thought that Elizabeth had married beneath her! His sensitive soul shrank from the task, but he accepted his father's decision without question.

Jonna was dispatched to Kirkbymoorside to fetch the doctor and call at the Police House to ask Sergeant Bannister whether or not the Coroner would need to be notified. Only when these errands were done was he to go to the market and tell his mother and Elizabeth what had happened.

The two brothers rode together up the steep hill out of the valley, discussing the tragedy. 'At least oor Joe told us 'e were going, but ti do it like that, giving t'Butlers no chance ti say goodbye was bound ti be a shocker.' Jonna ruminated on the situation.

'Aye,' George reflected. 'Thoo'd think he'd have talked it over with his family.'

'It's not as if 'is faither was strict, like oors,' Jonna continued. 'It took guts for oor Joe ti stand up against 'im.' By this time the brothers had reached the parting of their ways. Jonna turned towards Kirkbymoorside, saying, 'Aah'll see thi later, then.'

'Aye,' said George heavily, as he made for the village of Fadmoor, his heart sinking at the thought of his errand. He wondered what his mother-in-law would do, losing the farm's two key workers at one blow. Jack Butler had acted as his father's foreman and, as far as George could remember, the rest of the men were incapable of taking charge. Although Jonadab Oaks had two capable sons of twenty-three and eighteen, he also employed a farm foreman, or hind, as they were known locally. Apart from the two Butlers, the farm George now approached had no continuity of labour, relying on annual recruitment at the Martinmas hirings. George had always considered this to be a mistake, as the men did not build up a loyalty to their employer, nor an interest in the farm.

With a slow step George approached the back door. He had never felt sufficiently at ease with Elizabeth's family to walk in unannounced and now he brought his knuckles down on the door panel with a couple of resounding knocks. It swung open to reveal his youngest sister-in-law, Sarah Butler. George was struck yet again with her striking resemblance to Elizabeth. Although only thirteen, Sarah grew more like his wife every time he saw her.

As she stood aside for him to enter the kitchen, Sarah's face lit up with the familiar sparkle which had always entranced him in her sister. Seeing his grave face, the radiance faded and she frowned. 'Is summat up, George?' She looked up at him uncertainly.

'Where's your Mam?' he asked, with such a wealth of compassion in his voice that she blanched.

'Mam, Mam!' she called up the stairs. 'George 'as come. What is it? – what's up?' The girl turned to him again, her face mirroring her apprehension. Before he had time to reply, his mother-in-law came into the kitchen.

George looked at her in silence. Even though the problem had occupied his thoughts all the way to the village, he still had not found the words to break the news to the newly-widowed woman. Sensing his distress and realising that his presence there on a workday morning must presage bad news, she halted by the stairs door. Her hand strayed to the base of her throat, and she whispered, 'What is it, George? Is it our Elizabeth?' George shook his head mutely. 'John, then? Nowt's happened to John?'

George cleared his throat. 'Aye, Ma. Your Jack going like that was such a shock to him, that . . .' His voice trailed off.

Sarah interrupted, 'What do you mean? Where's our Jack gone?'

Her mother silenced her with an upraised hand. 'Hold your tongue and let George finish.' She fixed her eyes on George's face, which was grave and filled with pity.

George took a deep breath and proceeded, 'I'm afraid he's gone.'

'Gone?' Her voice was hoarse; her tone incredulous. 'You can't mean that he's dead. There's some mistake.' She spoke pleadingly, but George shook his head in silence. Both Sarah and her mother began to cry. Sarah rushed into Ann's arms and the two clung together. As the child sobbed hysterically, her mother rocked and patted her, tears coursing down her cheeks in silent grief.

George pressed his mother-in-law's arm. 'I'll go and harness t'pony and trap,' he murmured. 'You'll want to come down with me.'

As the sad little procession wound its way down the hill into Sleightholmedale, young Jonna was making his way towards the market place, where his mother and Elizabeth were sitting. He had called on Dr Dawson and reported the death to the Police Sergeant. Now, he realised with reluctance, he must break the news of her father's death to Elizabeth.

As he approached the section of the market occupied by the farm-wives, Annie Oaks caught sight of him. 'Why, whativer's oor Jonna doing 'ere?' she said to her daughter-in-law, noting his serious expression. 'What's up, lad?' she queried. 'There's nowt wrong, is there?'

He nodded miserably, unable to speak. Elizabeth knew intuitively that the bad news concerned her father. 'It's my father, isn't it? He's been taken ill.' Jonna nodded mutely. 'Is he very bad?' she pressed. Before he could answer, she knew by his stricken face what the reply would be.

'Aah'm afraid 'e's dead,' he gulped, staring at the ground, unable to meet Elizabeth's eyes.

The news was confirmation of the feeling of impending doom which had haunted her all morning like a leaden weight, since she had seen her father riding towards Aumery Park Farm. She could not speak, but began to pack her baskets automatically while Jonna went across to the inn yard to bring the two traps.

Annie Oaks was concerned by Elizabeth's pallor and the fact that she did not utter a word. She put an arm round her daughter-in-law's shoulders. 'All right, lass?' she asked compassionately. Elizabeth nodded speechlessly as they set off for home.

This was the blackest day of Elizabeth's life. She had lost her only brother and would probably never see him again, and now the shock of Jack's departure had resulted in her father's death. She was convinced, moreover, that there was yet another blow to come. 'Never two, but three,' she thought to herself as she urged the pony on to full speed. She felt that she needed the comfort of her husband's strength on this darkest of days.

# CHAPTER THREE

The precipitous road which led down into the valley of Sleightholmedale clung to the steep face of the escarpment, forcing their pace to a crawl. Once on the level valley bottom, and to her mother-in-law's concern, Elizabeth Oaks urged her plump little pony into unaccustomed exertion. 'Come on, Bella! Get on,' she cried, flicking the long carriage whip at the animal's neck. Bella was so unused to this treatment that with a whinny of protest and a snort of dismay, she set off at such speed that the trap was tossed and jolted along the bumpy track.

'Catch 'er up, Jonna,' Annie called to her son. 'She mustn't be shaken about like that in 'er condition.'

A look at his mother showed that her normally pleasant features were twisted into an anxious frown. Digging his heels into his horse's sides, Jonna broke into a gallop. As he drew level with Elizabeth, the youth turned his head sideways towards her. 'Slow down!' he shouted, but her lips were pressed tightly together and her whole body strained forward as she concentrated upon getting the last ounce of speed out of the pony. With a final effort, Jonna surged past the trap, and drew alongside Bella. Once in this position, he reached over and seized the pony's bridle.

As they drew to a halt, Elizabeth gave a shuddering sigh and passed a hand across her forehead. 'What is it? Why have you stopped me?' she demanded, looking around.

'Mam was worried,' he replied breathlessly. 'You were going too fast and being banged about.'

'Oh!' She came back to the present with difficulty. 'I didn't realise. I wanted to get back as soon as possible.' To Jonna's embarrassment, her eyes filled with tears as she spoke.

'There's no rush, lass,' Annie said, as she drew alongside. 'What's done's done and there's nowt thoo can do ti alter it.'

Elizabeth nodded miserably. She had lost two of her family on this day, but she could not put into words her overwhelming certainty that there was another blow still to fall. She chided herself that the feeling was merely superstition, yet could not shake it off. Aumery Park Farm was now in sight and in a few minutes she would be in the comfort of George's steady strength. With this thought, she jerked the reins and they all moved forward at a more sedate pace, arriving at the farm without indulging in any further conversation.

As the two women entered the kitchen, Annie Oaks glanced swiftly round. The cradle had been moved from its customary place by the fireside and there was no sign of Victoria. Good! At least Jonadab had not had the embarrassment of the Butlers seeing the baby, she thought.

Ann Butler sat at the kitchen table, a mug of tea before her. Annie bit her lip in vexation. How many times must she try to din into Lydia the fact that visitors should be given a cup and saucer! She then mentally shook herself – as if this little detail was important under these tragic circumstances. She quickly crossed to Ann Butler and took her hands. 'Eeh, Aah'm that sorry,' she murmured.

'Aye.' The other woman's voice trembled as she dabbed at her eyes. 'It's hard to take in. He was such a big, strong man,' she sobbed.

Annie looked at her curiously. She could not believe that John Butler's increasing weight and breathlessness had escaped his wife's notice. She glanced across at her own husband. Surely she would recognise any change or deterioration in his appearance, she thought, assessing him fondly.

When they entered the kitchen, Sarah Butler had run to her sister in tears. Elizabeth now sat with her arms round the girl, patting her back and whispering soothingly to her. George stood in silence behind his wife's chair, one hand resting on her shoulder to reassure her of his presence and support. He felt fiercely protective towards her. She was so slight and finely boned that now she was robbed of her normal vivacity, she appeared frail and vulnerable.

Ann Butler drained her mug and placed it firmly on the wooden table top. She seemed to have put away her grief and pulled herself together. 'Now, Sarah,' she said decisively. 'Stop leaning on our Elizabeth. She's got some letters to write.'

'Letters?' Elizabeth raised her brows questioningly.

'Aye,' her mother replied. 'You must write to your Uncle Nathan and our Christiania straight away. Then, if Mr Oaks'll be so kind as to let one of his lads ride up to Kirkby, they'll catch tomorrow's mail coach.'

A shadow crossed Elizabeth's face. She felt too sick and weary to tackle the letters just yet, but knew that her mother was right. They must be done immediately. George drew a breath to protest but bit back the words. His mother-in-law had suffered the loss of both her husband and her only son in the one day and, although he sensed that Elizabeth was both emotionally and physically exhausted, he was reluctant to intervene.

As he moved away from her and lowered himself on to one of the wooden chairs which surrounded the deal table, Elizabeth's eyes met his and she gave a faint smile. 'I'm all right, love,' she whispered reassuringly. Low as her voice had been, however, her mother's sharp ears caught the remark.

'Why shouldn't you be all right? What's up?' Her tone was sharp, but whether through concern or impatience was not clear to those in the kitchen.

'I've a bad back. It's nothing.' Elizabeth rubbed her lower back as she spoke.

The Butlers had expected Elizabeth to remain a spinster and look after them in their old age. They had been none too pleased when she had, in their opinion, made a fool of herself by marrying a man seven years her junior. Despite her apparent control, Ann Butler was devastated by the day's events. She had managed thus far to mask her emotions with a veneer of efficiency but now, for a moment, the veil was lifted and she turned on her eldest daughter using a tone that was almost vicious. 'If you expect to carry a bairn for nine months with no discomfort, you've another think coming,' she snapped. 'You'll know better when you've had seven like us, won't she, Mrs Oaks?'

Annie did not reply. Although she had seven living children, she had borne eight. She was hurt that Ann Butler seemed to have forgotten little Maria, who was drowned in Hodge Beck at the age of eleven. Putting herself in the other woman's place, however, she realised that Ann Butler's mind was probably in turmoil and that she was hardly responsible for her words.

These thoughts were confirmed by Ann's contrite apology when Elizabeth's eyes brimmed with sudden tears. 'Eeh, I'm sorry, lass, for taking it out on you.' She reached out and pressed her daughter's hand as it lay on the table. 'You've lost a father and brother, while I've lost a husband and son.' She bit her bottom lip and then pressed her lips firmly together again.

Jonadab had brought the writing materials from the parlour and placed them on the table in front of Elizabeth. She was just about to start writing when there was a knock on the door. Lydia ran and opened it, to reveal the Police Sergeant standing on the step. He ducked his head and entered the kitchen. Sweeping his eyes over the two families, he cleared his throat and approached Ann Butler. 'I'm very sorry to intrude on your grief, Mrs Butler,' he said, 'but cases of sudden death 'as to be looked into.' Turning to Jonadab, he went on, 'Can I see the body, Mr Oaks? It hasn't been moved, 'as it?'

'Aye, Sergeant, Aah'm afraid it 'as,' explained Jonadab. 'It 'appened in 'ere, thoo sees, so we moved 'im into t'parlour.' Indicating the door, he rose and led the way through. Before the policeman could follow, however, there came another tap on the door and Dr Dawson hurried in.

'Sorry to take so long, but I was out on a call,' he explained. 'My condolences, Mrs Butler.' Ann nodded wordlessly and the doctor followed Sergeant Bannister, closing the parlour door behind him.

An uneasy silence fell upon the kitchen, broken only by the scratching of the pen as Elizabeth wrote to her mother's brother, her Uncle Nathan, who lived in Leeds. Upon Elizabeth's marriage to George, her place as Uncle Nathan's housekeeper had been taken by her younger sister, Christiania, and there was also a letter to be written to her, explaining what had happened, so that she would return home for the funeral.

Elizabeth laid aside the letter to her Uncle for the ink to dry, but before beginning on the second one, she had a sudden wave of nausea and half-rose from her chair. The feeling passed and she sank back. George had seen the movement and looked across at her, disturbed by the pallor which drained his wife's face of all colour, making her appear sallow and wan. She saw the concern in his expression and smiled, with an attempt at her usual vivacity. 'Don't look so long-faced, love. I'm all right, really,' she assured him. 'Bella gave me a shaking up on the way back. She seemed to choose the roughest bits of road.'

Not entirely satisfied, George pushed back his chair, scraping it on the flagged floor with a jar which tore at their ragged nerves. 'I'll be off back to work, then,' he said to the room in general as he went out.

Elizabeth resumed her writing and the others sat in silence, each busy with her own thoughts. Annie Oaks studied Ann Butler surreptitiously, reflecting on how little they had in common. They were related twice over by marriage: there the resemblance ended. The other woman had an air of self-assurance lacked by the diffident Annie and bore a reputation in the surrounding villages as considering herself a cut above the rest. Her husband had owned his own farm and she felt that this set them above the more usual tenant-farmers.

'You and Sarah'll stop and 'ave a bite of tea with us?' she suggested.

Ann Butler hesitated. 'No, thank you all the same. There's plenty to do up at home, and who's to run the farm and direct the men, I really don't know.' She shook her head as the enormity of her loss swept over her. There was not only the personal tragedy of the loss of the two men in her life, but she could not imagine how she would cope with the day-to-day running of the farm. Deciding that she could not face this problem yet, she pushed it to the back of her mind and concentrated on the two letters which Elizabeth had completed. Though by no means a fluent reader, she gathered the gist of them. 'Aye, they'll do,' she sighed.

As she spoke, the parlour door swung open and Jonadab escorted the doctor and the Sergeant back through the kitchen. 'It was a heart attack, Mrs Butler.' The doctor spoke gently. 'If you'll give me his age, I'll make out a death certificate and you can send one of your men for it in the morning.'

When the two men had left, Ann Butler rose from her chair. 'Come along, Sarah. We'd best be getting home.' She had tried to speak briskly but the words came out dispiritedly.

Elizabeth also rose to her feet. 'I'll drive up in the morning, Mother, and give you a hand,' she said, kissing her mother's cheek and patting her arm.

'Aye.' The word came out as a sigh. The fortitude which had carried Ann along throughout her ordeal had now deserted her and she seemed to have shrunk to a shadow of her former self as she turned to leave. At the door she looked back, her eyes on Jonadab. 'Will you send him home, Mr Oaks?' She stumbled over the words.

'Of course, Mrs Butler. Oor George'll bring 'im.' He spoke gruffly, his heart going out to her. Jonadab knew that time would blur the edge of her grief but he could not envisage how she would manage to keep the farm going. ''E'll tek yon letters up ti t'post office an' all,' he added.

With Mrs Butler's departure, some of the tension left Elizabeth. While she understood that her mother's brittle manner was a defence used to protect her raw feelings from the sympathy which would reduce her to tears, she had felt it grating on her own taut nerves. George's family respected her silence, as she sat by the table, her head resting in her hands. Although they presumed her to be praying, in reality Elizabeth was picturing the father of her childhood – big, strong and jolly. He had always been one for a childish romp or joke, making their lives carefree and happy.

She realised that Jack, his only son, had been a great disappointment to their father. She could hear him saying regretfully, as he had done so often, 'Your mother put all t'spirit into t'lasses and none into t'lad.' Jack had shown no interest in the farm, which was his destiny. He had always chafed at the dullness of life in the quiet moorland village which was his home. What Elizabeth found difficult to grasp, however, was that he should steal away in the night, with no warning to any of the family. With a deep sigh, she raised her head and moved her hands to massage her aching back. 'I'd best be off, Ma,' she commented.

Annie came over from her seat by the fire and looked anxiously into her daughter-in-law's face, which was pale and strained. 'Take care, lass. Thoo's had two bad shocks in one day, and thoo looks a bit peaky. Is thi back very bad?'

'Yes, it is.' Elizabeth grimaced ruefully as she kneaded it with her clenched fist. 'You were right, Ma. I must have jolted it when we came back from Kirkby. Anyway, I'll get going. I'll call in tomorrow on my way back from Fadmoor.'

'Right, lass.' Annie gave an anxious frown as Elizabeth went out. 'Aah dissent like 'er starting with backache at this stage,' she confided to Tamar.

'She'll be all right,' her daughter answered as she made her way towards the bedroom, where Molly Waind and Martha were playing with baby Victoria. Although Tamar had grown fond of her sister-in-law, she felt she had troubles enough of her own without worrying about anyone else. In her heart she was convinced that Jonadab would secretly blame her for John Butler's death. 'Anyroad,' she thought, 'he had to speak to me – I've bested 'im over that. He 'ad to say t'first word that's passed between us for months.' The reflection gave her great satisfaction. She picked up the baby and cradled her close. No matter what her father thought, she was glad she had Victoria. She adored the baby and her whole life centred around the child.

On the morning of John Butler's funeral, they awoke to find that the newly-washed brightness of April had fled and the gloom of the day reflected the solemnity of the occasion. As Elizabeth dragged herself through the morning's tasks of milking, egg-collecting and pig-feeding, the dull, persistent pain in her back mirrored the ache in her heart. The death of a parent, she thought sadly, was surely one of the most poignant wrenches that life could hold in store –

except, perhaps, the death of a child she added anxiously to herself, placing a hand on where her unborn child lay.

When George came back at mid-morning, she had already changed for the funeral. Seeing her dressed in unrelieved black, he was struck again by the change in her appearance since her father's death. Elizabeth's face was pale with fine lines of strain and her eyes, normally so merry and luminous, were dull and lacklustre. Placing his hands on her shoulders, he did not draw her into his arms as he yearned to do, conscious of the farm smells that hung about him and the fact that she was dressed in her funeral clothes. Instead, he brushed his lips across her hair. 'Once it's over, you'll feel better,' he comforted. He recalled from the death of his grandparents and also, when his little sister Maria was drowned, the feeling of release once the funeral rites were completed. Grief persisted, but life went on.

Elizabeth had sewn a black armband around the sleeve of his Sunday jacket. Once he was washed and changed, she produced a square of fine black cotton which she draped round his neck, tucking the ends under his lapels, to cover the light colour of his shirt. He raised her hands to his lips and kissed them. 'Always prepared for everything, aren't you?' he teased gently, hoping to lighten her mood.

'I wasn't ready for this day,' she answered despondently, as they left the house.

As they took their seats in the trap, George studied his wife. Since John Butler's death her radiance had been extinguished and even her movements, normally so light and graceful, had become heavy and laboured. Trying to bring her thoughts back from the ordeal which faced her, George remarked, 'I didn't know you had a black gown.'

Elizabeth glanced down at her skirt and passed her hand over the folds of material. 'It was my everyday gown when I lived with Uncle Nathan,' she explained.

Not for the first time, it occurred to George how little he really knew of his wife. He had no recollection of her before their meeting at her sister Mary and his brother Joseph's wedding five years before, when they had been the best man and bridesmaid. A whole section of her life had been spent in Leeds acting as housekeeper to her Uncle, the owner of a large draper's shop in Briggate. The biggest town ever visited by George was Whitby. He had so little experience of life beyond the tiny valley that was his home, that he had no means of imagining Leeds nor what Elizabeth's life there had been like. That she should love him, as deeply and passionately as he loved her and that she should have settled so contentedly in the tranquillity of Cherry Tree Farm, so far removed from the bustle of the outside world, never ceased to amaze him. Every night as he knelt by his bedside, he gave thanks for the sheer joy of having Elizabeth to share his life.

When they reached Aumery Park Farm, he had no need to halt the pony as his parents were already seated in their trap. Before they drew alongside Jonadab Oaks clicked his tongue to the pony and set off to lead the way up to Fadmoor. It was typical of his father, thought George: even though Elizabeth and George were family mourners at John Butler's funeral, it never occurred to Jonadab to allow them precedence.

Upon arriving at Fadmoor, they found the hearse already drawn up in front of the Butlers' farmhouse; the four black horses were pawing the ground restively and nodding their sable-plumed heads. While their two menfolk took the ponies and traps into the yard at the back, to join several others under the care of the Butlers' waggoner and his lad, the two women entered the house by the front door, which was propped open. As they walked in, Ann Butler came across from where she had been talking to her brother, Nathan. 'You're late,' she said reproachfully to Elizabeth, her voice low.

'I'm sorry, Mother. There was a lot to do.' Elizabeth reached up to kiss her mother's cheek.

'There was a lot to be done here, as well.' Her mother dabbed her eyes with a handkerchief as she spoke. No more was said between them, as Nathan came across and embraced Elizabeth.

'Now then, lass. How are things with you?' He spoke solicitously, alarmed at the haggard appearance of a once lively and vivacious young woman. Was this what marriage had done to his niece, he wondered. Before she could answer him, George and his father walked through from the back of the house. When Nathan saw how tenderly Elizabeth's eyes met those of her husband and the look of relief on her face when George came to her side, he recognised that whatever was wrong with Elizabeth, it had nothing to do with her marriage. Perhaps it was the shock of John Butler's death and Jack taking himself off to foreign parts, he thought to himself.

As the cortège assembled, Elizabeth dreaded the slow walk of over a mile to Gillamoor Church. The dull ache in her back had developed into a throbbing pain, at times so severe that it made her bite her bottom lip. According to protocol, she and George fell in behind Ann Butler who, in the absence of her only son, was accompanied by Nathan. The rest of the mourners followed in a long procession, each couple taking their proper place as custom dictated.

Ann Butler had been determined that John should not go on his last journey borne on one of his own flat carts, hauled by a couple of work-horses, as did many of the local farmers. He had been a man of some standing in the local community and even in the midst of her grief she was secretly gratified that his funeral was an impressive one. All the way along the route, there was not a house in either Fadmoor or Gillamoor where the curtains were not drawn out of respect for Farmer Butler.

After her father had been laid to rest in Gillamoor churchyard, which held Oaks and Butlers from as far back as anyone knew, Elizabeth took George's arm for the return to the house. The further they walked, the more she leaned on him and the slower was her pace, even though the rain was now falling steadily.

'Come on, love,' he urged, as the gap between them and the couple in the lead grew so great that they were scarcely visible through the grey curtain of rain.

'It's no good, George. I just can't go any faster,' she faltered, leaning forward to try to ease the pain, which was suddenly sweeping through her. It was now patently clear to George that it was not only the shock and grief of her father's death which had drained Elizabeth over the last few days, but that she was ill.

As this realisation dawned, Elizabeth suddenly began to stumble. She crumpled, and George scooped her up into his arms as though she were a child. He strode out purposefully, quickly closing the gap so that he caught up with his mother-in-law just as she reached the front door. 'Elizabeth's fainted!' he said tersely. 'Where can I put her?'

Ann thought quickly. 'Take her up to that little room that Mary and Joe used to have,' she instructed. As he mounted the stairs, those mourners who had been invited back began to enter the house, most of them unaware of Elizabeth's collapse.

Annie Oaks, looking round anxiously for Elizabeth as she came in, saw George disappearing up the stairs with his burden. Quickly, she slipped her way as unobtrusively as possible through the Butler relations, to Ann's side. 'Your place is here. Aah'll see to 'er,' she assured the other woman, as she passed into the hall and followed George up the stairs. When she reached the bedroom, George had already tenderly placed his wife on the bed and, after removing her bonnet, was gently stroking strands of damp hair from her forehead.

Annie patted her son's arm. 'Go fetch some towels while Aah get 'er boots off,' she instructed. When he came back, his mother had already removed most of Elizabeth's outer clothing. 'Get thissen downstairs, lad,' Annie said. 'There's nowt thoo can do 'ere. It's woman's work.'

'Is it to do with the bairn, Mam?' he asked anxiously, his heart going out to the figure on the bed which looked so frail and defenceless.

''Appen it is. Aah'm afeared it may be,' his mother answered. 'Any road, we sh'll see.'

Downstairs, George mechanically drank tea and ate the little funeral cake passed round by Elizabeth's sisters. Although he chatted in a desultory fashion to various groups, his thoughts were upstairs with his wife. As the guests began to drift away, his mother appeared at the door into the hall and beckoned to him. 'She's come round. You can go up, but . . .' she grasped his arm and drew him back as he began to hurry towards the stairs. 'George, lad,' she looked at him sadly, 'Aah'm afeared she's lost t'bairn.'

George paused outside the little room which was situated halfway up the stairs in the Butler house. He needed time to pull himself together before going in to his wife. The only other time he had been into this room was to see Joe and Mary's newborn son, Georgie, who was his godson. His feelings on that day contrasted keenly with the grief which now overwhelmed him.

# CHAPTER FOUR

When Annie Oaks had left her, Elizabeth lay in her bed, her eyes wandering round the room. This was where her sister Mary had given birth to her firstborn and this was where she had lost hers. She closed her eyes and her lips moved in silent prayer, 'Dear Lord, let there be other children.' She heard the sound of her husband's steps on the stairs and registered the fact that he had paused on the landing. As the door swung open, she watched him cross to the bed. He almost leapt the last couple of steps and bent over her, tenderly. Tears coursed down her cheeks, as she searched his face. 'I'm sorry, George,' she whispered.

He sat on the side of the bed and raised her in his arms. 'As long as you're all right, little pet, that's all that matters to me,' he reassured her, gently wiping away her tears.

'What a dreadful week,' she murmured. 'It's been the worst in my life.'

'There'll be other weeks and other bairns, too,' he comforted her. 'We must look ahead. Try to get some sleep now. I'll go back down and see what's to do.'

Downstairs, Ann Butler spoke to Jonadab as he and Annie prepared to take their leave along with the other mourners. 'Sit down again please, Mr Oaks. I'd like a word,' she said. Jonadab and his wife looked at each other in puzzlement, but took their places on two hard-backed chairs. There they were sitting, unspeaking, when George joined them.

'She's sleeping now,' he informed his mother. 'Does she need a doctor?'

'Nay, Aah shouldn't think so, lad,' she replied. Calling in the doctor was an expensive luxury to be avoided in all but the direst of circumstances. Countrywomen had a stock of home-brewed remedies which usually coped with most illnesses and accidents.

When Ann Butler came back from bidding farewell to

the guests, Jonadab took his watch from his pocket and consulted it. 'Time's pressing, Mistress Butler,' he said. 'There's a lot ti be done.'

'Aye, and there's a lot to be said,' she answered in a determined tone. He frowned: did she want more details of how her husband had died, he wondered. 'It's a shame about the bairn,' she went on, 'but it does make what I've to say easier.' Jonadab eyed her speculatively. He had never paid much attention but now, assessing the firm set of her lips and jaw, he realised that he had underestimated her. Beneath the affable exterior lurked a strong-willed woman. He recalled the day his eldest son Joseph had poured out to his family the reasons behind his decision to emigrate. His grievances had been focused on his mother-in-law and Jonadab suddenly knew in his heart that she had been the driving force behind John Butler.

She broke the silence in which the other three sat regarding her, and leaned forward in her chair. 'Now, Mr Oaks. I'm left in difficult circumstances with no menfolk of my own and a farm to run. Elizabeth will have to stay here in bed until she's stronger and I shall need your George up here to run the farm for me.'

This statement, coming out of the blue, startled and alarmed them all. George darted a pleading look at his father but Jonadab's steely eyes were staring from beneath drawn brows into Ann Butler's icy grey ones. He wondered why he had never before noticed their coldness. 'Nay, 'e's needed at home,' he expostulated. 'There's 'is own sheep as well as ourn ti see ti, wi' lambing, shearing and dipping coming on.'

Her eyes bored into his as though to wear him down, but Jonadab was a master of the tactics of the wordless battle. He sat on his chair, ramrod-straight, one hand on each knee, his vivid blue eyes fixed implacably on the woman who faced him. Realising that he could not be overcome by the strength of her character alone, she abandoned this ploy and changed her strategy.

Taking a handkerchief from her sleeve, she lowered her lids and dabbed at her eyes. With a catch in her voice, she spoke pleadingly. 'Don't be hard on me, Mr Oaks,' she begged. 'I'm a poor widow-woman with no one to turn to. This week I've lost my husband, my son and a future grandchild. I've no man left to run the farm.' She turned her attention to Annie and said beseechingly, 'As a woman, you can put yourself in my place, can't you? If you suddenly lost your husband and sons, how would you manage unless one of your daughter's husbands came to give you a hand?'

Faced with this picture, Annie's soft heart was touched. With tear-brimmed eyes, she clutched Jonadab's arm. 'Oh, Jonadab! It'll only be for a little while,' she urged. 'We can manage both places for a time.'

He was speechless at what he considered to be her perfidy. He and George exchanged disbelieving glances above her head, as Annie leaned forward to clasp the other woman's hands. 'Of course George will stay till you're sorted out. He'd want ti be wi' Elizabeth any'ow,' she comforted.

Ann Butler sighed with relief. 'Thank you so much. I knew I could rely on you,' she smiled tearfully.

Contrition swept over Jonadab in a wave and he crimsoned with shame at his previous resistance to her request. Dalesfolk were noted for their hospitality and the way they rallied round those in trouble, but he had been reluctant to offer a hand of friendship to a bereft woman. He rose to his feet and shook her by the hand. 'Don't thoo worry, Mistress Butler,' he said gruffly. 'We'll do all we can to lift the burden off your shoulders. Shall George stop with thoo now, or will tomorrow do?'

'Perhaps if he has a word with Elizabeth as to what she wants him to bring, and then he can come back tomorrow, to take over as foreman,' she replied.

On the way home, George brooded upon the path that had suddenly been mapped out for him. He realised his mother was right: he was duty-bound to help Elizabeth's mother, but he could not forget that it was his mother-in-law's interfering ways that had driven Joseph and Mary to Canada.

The following day dawned clear and sparkling. Although there was a nip in the air, the sky was a cloudless, deep blue and the sun caught the swelling buds on the orchard trees. George had packed enough clothes for both himself and Elizabeth for what, he hoped, would be a short stay with her mother. 'Mebbe she'll sell and move out before long,' he thought to himself as he looked round the bedroom regretfully. One of his father's favourite maxims came to him: Pride goeth before a fall. Jonadab frequently reminded his family of this and the words re-echoed through George's mind as he crossed to the window and looked out over the sunlit garden.

He had been proud enough, he thought ruefully. 'Aye,' he reflected, 'I was proud to win Elizabeth and proud to have our own home. Now I'm paying for that pride.' He turned away with a sigh and went over to the bed where the two baskets of clothes rested. He placed over each a larger basket, which served as a lid, and fastened leather straps round them. Again, he crossed to the window, reluctant to leave the view of the garden at the front of the house and the land which fell away towards Hodge Beck. Tearing his eyes away from the little stream which rippled over its bed of stones, he saw his Uncle coming down the lane, towards Cherry Tree Farm.

His father's younger brother, after whom George was named, had been told by Jonadab Oaks upon his return from Butlers' that he would be needed to live in the house at Cherry Tree Farm. 'Ti keep an eye on things,' Jonadab had told him. He had given a lifetime of work to the family farm and a lifetime of obedience to his brother, who had inherited the tenancy of it. Now, here he came as directed, trudging down the lane to take up his new duties, unquestioning and faithful to Jonadab's will. Seeing him from the bedroom window was like seeing him anew. Suddenly George saw how frail and old and weary he looked. 'By – he looks years older than mi faither,' he thought to himself. 'Poor owd Uncle George. I don't suppose he's ever done owt that he wanted to, only what he's been told.'

Turning away, he swung a basket in each hand and went downstairs. Placing the baskets on the kitchen floor, he went out into the yard to greet his Uncle. The older man's face brightened upon seeing him. 'Noo then, George.

Thoo'd best be off up ti Butlers' or Elizabeth'll be frettin',' he said.

'Nay, Uncle. There's time enough! I'll just show you where everything is,' he answered, leading his Uncle towards the range of buildings. The tour of inspection took longer than George had anticipated. His Uncle was so pathetically eager to carry out his duties as George wanted them done, that he asked the same questions again and again. Eventually George fished out a big turnip watch, which had belonged to Grandad Oaks. 'I must be off,' he said. 'Elizabeth is expecting me by noon.'

'Aye, get thissen off, lad. Aah'll see ti everything. Don't thoo worry,' his Uncle assured him.

As George drove down the narrow winding road towards his parents' farm, he glanced back with regret at Cherry Tree Farm. He and Elizabeth had lived there for only a few months and the need to leave came as a bitter blow.

He called in to tell his parents that he was on his way. His mother felt the tears pricking behind her eyes as she looked at him. Her eldest son Joseph had been driven to emigrate through the domineering attitude of his mother-in-law, Ann Butler. Now her second son was being placed in a position that seemed almost similar. She swallowed a lump in her throat and gave voice to her fears. 'Thoo won't do owt daft, lad?' It was a question rather than a statement.

'What sort o' daft?'

She hesitated and bit her bottom lip before answering. 'Thoo won't let her drive thi away, like she did oor Joe and their Mary.'

Before George could reply, his father broke in sharply, 'It's thoo who's being daft, Mother. Oor George is made o' sterner stuff than Joseph. Anyroad, they won't be up there for long. Aah'll see ti that.'

George let out a faint sigh of relief. If his father was determined to get him and Elizabeth back to Cherry Tree Farm as soon as possible, he felt that he could go and give a hand on his mother-in-law's farm for a few weeks. He had implicit trust in his father's ability to deal with any crisis.

It was with a slightly lighter heart that he mounted the

trap and urged the pony along towards the foot of the steep hill which led up from the valley. As he rounded a bend in the road, he was surprised to see his sister Tamar leaning against a tree, clutching her baby in her arms. As George came into view she ran into the road, her outstretched hand drawing him to a halt. 'Oh, George! I thought thoo was never coming,' she cried.

'What's up?' George was anxious to return to Elizabeth, but first one person amd then another seemed to stop his progress. Tamar's face was pale and she looked at him in desperation.

'Don't stay at the Butlers',' she pleaded. 'Aah can't stop down in this valley if thoo and Elizabeth leaves. Aah'll go mad! Aah'll kill missen.'

George got down from the trap and put an arm awkwardly round her shoulders. The Oaks were not a demonstrative family but his sister was becoming distraught. 'Now, now, lass,' he soothed. 'We sh'll not be gone long. Don't worry.'

Tamar, however, was not to be consoled. 'Aah might as well be dead,' she cried. 'Oor Faither never speaks ti me. In fact, 'e doesn't look at me if 'e can help it. Aah thought when Mr Butler died that Faither would change. 'E spoke ti me then – when 'e needed me – but now 'e's gone back to 'ow 'e was. Aah can't stand it.' she ended on a high note. 'If Aah can't go down ti Cherry Tree Farm, out of 'is way, Aah'll do missen in.'

George realised that this was no idle threat and although he was eager to get back to his wife, he must take time to calm Tamar. He patted her shoulder. 'You're not t'first lass to get a bairn before you get a wedding ring,' he comforted. 'It was a shock ti Faither, but look how he went on about our Joe, and he's all right now.'

'Joe and Mary got wed. There's no chance of that for me,' answered Tamar dispiritedly. 'Nobody wants damaged goods.'

George gave her a little shake. 'That's enough of that kind of talk,' he said. 'You're a fine-looking lass, our Tamar, and there'll be a man for you, don't worry.' He fished his watch out of his pocket and looked at the time. 'I must get back to Elizabeth,' he apologised, 'but stick it out, lass.

When we get back to Cherry Tree, you and Victoria can come down and stay with us if things is no better. When Elizabeth's up and about, we shall come down once a week and you can come to Chery Tree Farm to give her a hand.'

'Thank you, George.' She smiled up at him, tremulously. 'It's the first bit of hope I've had for a long time. It gives me summat to look forward to.'

'Well, buck up and don't think things like that again.' As he remounted the trap and took up the reins he looked down at his sister. 'What you've got in your arms is summat we'd give owt in the world to possess,' he said sadly. 'We've lost our bairn – don't let your bairn lose her mother.'

Tamar clutched the child to her in a protective gesture. 'Don't worry, George, she means more to me than all the world,' she answered earnestly.

As he jerked the reins and moved away, Tamar stood and watched her brother out of sight, before beginning to walk slowly down the road towards home. At least, she thought, there was the glimmer of hope that her circumstances would improve, once George and Elizabeth came back.

After the slow and laboured journey to the crest of the hill, George gave the pony her head and let his thoughts drift. He was anxious to get back to his wife, although he knew full well that if there had been any deterioration in her condition, his mother-in-law would have sent one of the farm lads down with a message. Now there was the added complication of Tamar's state of mind to occupy his thoughts. Looking back to the previous year, he recognised the extent of the change in his sister. Tamar's former turbulence was quelled and the inner radiance which had raised her elfin features from mere prettiness to beauty was now dimmed. Last year, her movements had been quick and lively but now she walked slowly, the picture of dejection. Tamar was only a year younger than George, so that she had always been closer to him than the rest of his sisters, even though she had always been spirited and rebellious – until her shaming by Sir William Forster. As George turned over the problem in his mind, he was suddenly hit by a solution. 'By gum, that's it!' he thought. 'That'll sort out two birds with one stone.'

By this time, he had reached Butlers' farm and leading the pony round the back, he handed her over to Sam Sturdy, the second waggoner. 'Rub her down and feed her, will you, Sam? I'll need her again after dinner,' he said crisply, as he strode indoors. His father's advice of the previous day rang in his ears: 'Start as thoo means ti go on – both wi t'men and wi' 'er.' By her, he had of course meant Ann Butler, remembering the hardness behind the affable exterior.

Now, as George entered the kitchen, his mother-in-law came down the stairs. 'You're late,' she said in an aggrieved tone. 'Your dinner's keeping warm.'

'Aye, well, I'll just go up and see Elizabeth and then I'll have it,' he answered calmly.

Elizabeth was sitting up in bed and although she still looked tired, her colour was returning and she looked more like her old, lively self. 'George,' she smiled, holding out her arms to him. 'I've had time to think while you were down at home. Of course it's a blow to lose the baby, especially our firstborn, but it's not the end of the world. As you said yesterday, we've still got each other, and there'll be other babies.'

As he bent over her and took her in his arms, George felt a lump rising in his throat. He spoke huskily. 'It's you that matters, little love. As long as I've got you, nothing and no one else matters.' He straightened up and went towards the door. 'I'll have some dinner and then I've to go back to Aumery Park,' he said.

Elizabeth's eyebrows raised. 'I think Mother's expecting you to start work today,' she reminded him gently.

'Aye, well, she'll just have to expect,' he answered firmly. 'They've managed without me this morning and they'll have to manage this afternoon.' So saying, he turned on his heel and left the room leaving Elizabeth wondering what had got into him. He was not the gentle, easygoing George whom she had married and yet she could not help but like the change. His inner strength had always been hidden behind his eagerness to please but she could see a new George emerging. Perhaps he had inherited more from his father than anyone had realised . . .

# CHAPTER FIVE

As George rode back down into Sleightholmedale, he smiled to himself at the recollection of the scene in Mrs Butler's kitchen. Upon finishing his meal, he had thanked his mother-in-law and then delivered the news that he was returning to his father's farm. At first, she had tried domination but George was assertive – without being aggressive. He had business to attend to – and attend to it he would. He made it quite clear that he would run his mother-in-law's farm to the best of his ability but if there was a clash of interests, his own home and stock would come first. Now, reflecting on the scene, he chuckled. 'It's easy,' he marvelled. He was now convinced that with his newfound confidence, he would prove a match even for his father.

Jonadab was burning piles of thorns in one of the roadside fields when he saw George riding along the road towards the farm. He paused and looked towards his son. 'Aah wonder what 'e's doing back again?' he thought. As George slowed the horse, his father walked towards the hedge. To his surprise, however, George did not draw to a halt. He merely called across, 'Can I have a word, Father?' and went on his way towards the farmhouse.

Jonadab scratched his head in disbelief: that one of his children should treat him so casually was incredible. He considered it his due that they should respect him and defer to him. Perhaps George was getting too big for his boots, he reflected. 'Aah'll keep an eye on 'im,' he promised himself, as after casting a glance along the little fires that were burning in the field to assure himself that they could be safely left, he made his way along the road in his son's wake.

As Jonadab entered the kitchen, Lydia was carrying the big black iron kettle from the fireplace to the table. Though she had blossomed and was no longer the undersized little workhouse waif that she had once been, she needed both hands to carry the heavy kettle. When she had tipped the boiling water into the large brown teapot, she gave it a stir and replaced the teapot lid. 'There! It'll be mashed in a couple o' ticks,' she remarked to the room in general, going into the pantry for a plate of buttered scones.

Jonadab leaned back in his Windsor chair, beside the fire, holding his pint pot of tea in his hands. Though the day was bright there was a sharp wind, and the warmth from the mug was comforting to his cold fingers. As his wife questioned George about Elizabeth, he studied his son from beneath drawn brows. George took after his mother's side with wayward chestnut-coloured hair which would not lie flat, no matter how much he tried to comb it down with water. His dark brown eyes were sensitive and gentle, while his tanned face possessed a frankness and openness which mirrored his nature. As Jonadab allowed his gaze to pass over his son, however, he recognised something new. It was more than firmness and yet not hardness. 'Marriage 'as changed 'im,' thought Jonadab. Whether it was a change for the better or worse, he was uncertain.

As though feeling his father's eyes upon him, George paused in his conversation with his mother and turned towards Jonadab. 'You haven't asked what I'm doing back again,' he observed.

'No doubt thoo'll tell me when it suits thoo,' his father replied quizzically.

'Aye.' George looked round the kitchen. 'Where's our Tamar?'

There was a slight pause before his mother answered. 'Aah think she's upstairs, putting t'bairn down for a nap.'

It was not lost upon George that his mother looked nervously at her husband as she spoke, and that his father's brows drew together in a frown and his lips were pressed tightly at the mention of Tamar and her child. For a moment George's newfound resolution deserted him. He felt that he had endured enough this week without incurring his father's wrath. However, he recalled how he had already successfully defied his mother-in-law and realised that, by facing up to his father, he could lighten the atmosphere of the whole house, as well as improving Tamar's lot. He hesitated momentarily – a fact which Jonadab noted – but it was a mere fraction of a pause before George continued, 'Well, as what I've got to say concerns our Tamar, we'd best have her here. Go and fetch her down please, Lydia.'

As the maid scurried away, there was a tightening of the tension in the kitchen. George noted the way his mother's hand strayed to the base of her throat and rested there – a sure sign that she was disturbed. His sister Martha halted her vigorous polishing of cutlery over a newspaper spread upon the kitchen table, but she did not raise her head.

Jonadab's fingers began to drum out a tattoo on the chair arm. George risked a quick glance at him: his father's vivid blue eyes were staring into the distance, unfocused on the kitchen or anyone within it. His face was a grim, expressionless mask. All those in the kitchen seemed to be in suspended animation, until the door opened to reveal Tamar. She hesitated in the doorway, looking from one to the other.

'Come in, lass,' said George. 'I've summat to ask you.'

As she took her place at the table, Tamar kept her eyes on her brother, not looking towards her father, who now sat forward in his chair glaring at George. 'As thoo finished givin' thi orders in my home?' he queried with cutting sarcasm.

George turned towards him, the steady brown eyes challenging his father's icy blue ones. 'I once told you, Faither, that there's only one boss here, and that boss is you. Anyroad, I've given a lot of thought to life in this house. Until I got wed and had my own home, I accepted your word and thought you were always right.' He paused to try to sort out his thoughts, before putting them into words. 'Now, I'm . . .' He hesitated before continuing. 'Now I've moved away, I can see you from outside. I realise that you can be intolerant, Faither.'

Jonadab was stunned that one of his children should criticize him. He sat in silence, his hands gripping the chair arms. The telltale pulse throbbing in his temple was the sole indication of the rage which swept through him. Only the ticking of the grandfather clock in the corner broke the silence as those in the room held their breath, waiting for the torrent of his anger to spill out. His voice, when eventually he did speak, was deadly cold. 'Intolerant, am Aah? Is that all t'thanks Aah gets for all Aah've done for thoo? Who bred and raised thoo? Who learned thoo thi trade? Who set thoo up at Cherry Tree Farm?' On each question his voice increased in volume until it seemed to roar through the kitchen with his final outburst: '*Oh, Lord, have I nourished a viper in my bosom?*'

As he raised his eyes heavenwards, George quailed inwardly but gritted his teeth and rose to his feet instinctively, to put himself in the commanding position. He raised his hand to check Jonadab's flow of words. 'Faither, I'm grateful for all you've done for me, but I'm not a child any more. I've come down today to make a suggestion which I think will help us all.' He looked towards Tamar and continued, 'Our Tamar's done wrong. Nobody can deny that, but none of you can live in this atmosphere. If she's willing, I'd like her to come down to Cherry Tree Farm to live.'

Jonadab's first reaction was annoyance that anyone but himself should interfere in the running of their lives. He was the head of the family and as far as he was concerned, he was the one who made the decisions. He was slow to reply, turning over in his mind all sides of the proposal. George pressed home his advantage, encouraged by the look of relief on his mother's face and the sudden joy which flooded Tamar's expression. 'I'm sorry if I've upset you, Faither. Mebbe "intolerant" was too strong a word. What I really meant was that your standards are high and you can't abide lower ones.'

'That I can't and that I won't,' his father interpolated.

George sighed. It was difficult to say much when dealing with his father. However, seeing that the older man was slightly mollified, George began to unfold his plan. 'Although it's kind of Uncle George to go down to live at Cherry Tree, he can't look after the house as a woman would,' he began. That Uncle George had had no choice was known to all his listeners, but George was trying to be tactful. 'Besides which,' he added, 'he can't trail backwards and forwards to have his meals here. It's a waste of both time and effort.' He knew that time-wasting was an anathema to his father, who demanded that every minute of the working day should be accounted for.

Glancing round, he saw that he had everyone's attention, including his father's. George had had plenty of time to plan his arguments, both on the way to Fadmoor that morning and on the way down again after his midday meal. Now he warmed to his theme. 'If Uncle has his meals down there, he won't get proper ones. Likely he'll live on nowt but bread and cheese. A working man needs plenty of good fodder, but he won't have time to do any cooking.'

Annie shook her head. ''E's nivver 'ad ti cook owt in 'is life,' she agreed. 'A working man needs meat three times a day,' she added.

George drew a deep breath. His mother was on his side, he realised. However, he knew that the final decision would be his father's.

Jonadab's anger had subsided. There was no trace, now, of the pulse beating beneath the taut skin of his forehead. He sat in his chair by the fireside, his eyes fixed on his son, his face totally devoid of expression. He was a master at masking his thoughts if he so chose and he now gave no clue as to what he was thinking. 'Is that it, then?' he demanded, with exaggerated patience. 'Is that what's kept thoo from thy work up tops and me from mine down 'ere?'

'No, Faither.' George searched for the right words, not wishing to rouse his father to anger once again. 'If Tamar goes to live down at Cherry Tree, she can cook for Uncle George, look after the dairywork and see to the house. I know she'll keep it as Elizabeth would want.' He glanced over at Tamar, who nodded without speaking. 'Besides,' he continued, 'we get no visitors at Cherry Tree who'd be likely to spot Victoria, whereas here you get horse buyers, corn dealers and all sorts of folk.'

Jonadab nodded, stroking his chin reflectively. 'Aye, that's true,' he conceded.

George could see success within his grasp. He knew his father too well, however, to be tempted to rush things. 'Anyroad, Faither,' he continued, 'it's plain that our Tamar and t'bairn upset you. They're a constant reminder of what has happened. If they went down to Cherry Tree Farm, they'd be out of your way and out of your thoughts. You'd feel better with them safely tucked away down there.'

'Aye. They're a thorn in my flesh, Aah must confess.' Jonadab spoke as though his daughter was not present. Tamar swallowed hard and pressed her lips together to prevent an outburst. She had inherited her father's fiery temper but knew that any words from her could upset the delicate threads of the plan being woven by her brother.

Jonadab considered the suggestion put forward by George: he could find no fault with it. He was determined that none outside the family should know of Tamar's shame, even if it meant keeping the child down in the valley for years. The more he thought about the plan, the more he liked it. It would solve several problems with one stroke. 'What about when you and Elizabeth come back? Aah don't want that ti be too long. We're stretched for workers down 'ere as it is.'

'We'll deal with that when the time comes,' was George's reply. He had thought that on her return to Cherry Tree Farm, his wife might be glad of Tamar's company. However, not wishing to raise his sister's hopes for the longer term, he kept this thought to himself.

'Aye,' Jonadab said thoughtfully. 'Aah'll give thoo credit, lad. It's a good plan and ties up a lot of loose ends.' George let out his pent-up breath in a long sigh and his forehead broke out in beads of perspiration, so great was his relief. He caught the sardonic gleam in his father's eye as he noted the release of tension in his son. 'Aah would 'ave rather thoo'd 'ave talked it over wi' me first, instead of blurting it out in front of everybody, afore Aah'd time ti consider it. 'Owever, what's done's done.'

Now that he had got his own way, George could afford to be magnanimous. Besides, he thought with pride, it wasn't often someone got his father to agree to a plan which Jonadab himself hadn't conceived. 'I'm sorry, Faither,' he apologised. 'Aah've not even told Elizabeth. I only thought of it on my way up to Butlers', so I came straight back to tell you.'

Jonadab let this explanation pass, not reminding his son that it could have been discussed out in the field when

George first saw him. He was well-versed in the manipulation of other people and realised, in grudging admiration, that this was something George had recently acquired. "E's got it from me,' he told himself philosophically.

George offered to drive Tamar down to her new home straight away. 'I've not started work up at Butlers' yet,' he told his father with a grin, 'so Mistress Butler can wait one more day for her new foreman to start.'

'She's lucky ti get thoo,' his father said. 'She'd better mek other arrangements afore long. Aah appreciates she can't get a full-time hired man afore Martinmas, but Aah've lost a man an' all now, and can't replace thoo, either.'

As soon as he went back to work, those left in the kitchen looked at each other in delight. 'Eeh, lad,' said Annie, 'Aah nivver thought ti see thoo 'andle 'im so well.'

Tamar's tawny eyes danced with amber lights and her face was lit up with the old radiance. She clapped her hand over her mouth to stop herself laughing out loud. 'Oh, George! Aah'll never be able to thank thoo,' she cried. Looking across at her mother she said, 'It's not that Aah want ti leave thoo, Mam, but 'e's made my life Hell, thoo must admit.'

Annie would not be drawn into criticising Jonadab, no matter what she thought in private. 'Your Faither's standards are 'igh, Tamar, and 'e can't abide wrongdoing,' she replied.

'Aye, well! His standards towards me and mi bairn 'asn't been so 'igh,' Tamar said bitterly.

George broke the awkward pause. 'Come on, then. Let's have your things gathered up. I'll go and harness the pony and trap, while you collect your stuff.'

While Tamar ran upstairs to tell Lydia the news and tie her few personal belongings into a shawl, her mother went into the dairy and brought out a cheese and a couple of pounds of butter. 'This'll put her on till she gets settled and gets some of her own made,' she observed to Martha. The whole plan seemed to have been proposed, agreed and was now being implemented, so quickly that Annie felt bewildered, as though her thoughts were lagging behind events. 'It's all so sudden!' she exclaimed aloud, but realised that Tamar's presence in the house since the birth of her baby had acted as a goad to Jonadab. His resulting brusqueness and short temper had cast a cloud of gloom over the whole family so that, although Annie was sorry to see Tamar go, she could not but feel that her departure would make for a happier atmosphere in the house.

When George came back, he carried the cradle downstairs and placed it on the floor of the trap. Tamar followed him out, her bundle in one hand and the baby in the other arm.

'There'll be plenty of flour down there?' Annie asked anxiously.

'Don't wory, Mam, there's all she'll need,' George answered. 'There's bacon, eggs, plenty of jam and everything. Anyway, if she runs short, she's not much more than a mile away,' he comforted.

As the pony trotted along the valley road, George laughed out loud. 'By 'eck, our Jonna'll get a shock when he goes home at tea-time,' he said. 'It's all happened so fast and he knows nowt about it.'

A shadow passed over Tamar's face. ''E's a chip off t'owd block,' she observed. ''E's Faither over again – in more ways than one, an' all.'

George leaned over and patted her shoulder. 'Uncle George'll be glad to see you,' he said, 'and you'll be your own boss.'

Tamar looked up at him. 'Thank thoo, George,' she said huskily. 'It's like a new life beginning and it's all due ti thoo.'

# CHAPTER SIX

By the time Elizabeth was out of bed and had regained her strength, George was already heartily sick of life up at the Butlers' farm. As April progressed, lambing was in full swing and George's heart was with his own flock down in Sleightholmedale. Since his childhood, his father had constantly instilled into him, 'Know thi sheep, lad.' Jonadab had taught him to stand in front of each lamb, as soon after birth as practicable and gently take its face in both hands. 'Study its face, George, till thoo'll know it again and again. Wool grows and is shorn: shapes and outlines change, but faces remain the same. Every sheep is different, just as is every human. If thoo wants ti be a good shepherd, not only must thi sheep know thoo, but thoo mun know them.'

So George had grown to manhood able to recognise his father's sheep as individuals and, since he had founded his own herd the previous spring, each of his flock was unique to him. He knew them all: their characters, mannerisms and appearance. Faced with a whole new herd, en masse, they were merely sheep to him. Although he supervised the lambing along with Tim Wood, the Butlers' shepherd, the sheep meant nothing to him, apart from a job done to the best of his ability.

The dogs he worked with were strange, unused to his commands and his gestures. The workforce, too, did not work willingly for him. John Butler had been too easygoing with his men, eager for popularity while his son Jack had lacked interest in the farm, so that the men had become slovenly in their attitude. George had been tutored in a hard school, with his father as a strict task-master. Here, when he tried to bring the standards up to those down at home, the men were grudging and resentful at his suggestions for improvements. Although there was no open hostility to his face, behind his back the men were not slow to grumble.

'Same as all t'Oaks. 'Is faither thinks 'e's better than t'rest on us and this'n's in t'same mould,' muttered Sam Sturdy.

'Anyroad,' took up Joe Last, the waggoner, 'there's nowt ti be done till t'Martinmas Hirings. We're stuck wi' 'im till then.'

'We 'aven't a deal o' choice then either, as far as I can see,' answered Sam. 'If we stands for 'iring, we can get a worse place. On t'other 'and, t'missus might sell up, in which case we'll 'ave no choice but ti go. 'Appen George Oaks'll be t'best bet in t'long run.'

'Aye. Forecmeat is no choice,' put in one of the others.

Although his father was a hard man, demanding implicit obedience and the maximum of effort from both his sons and farm-workers, he was just in his dealings with them. This facet of his character inspired their loyalty and they worked in harmony with him. George tried to run Butlers' farm as his father ran Aumery Park Farm, and was at a loss to understand the difference in these men's attitudes. There was no pleasure in working alongside morose and sullen men, who contrasted sharply with the cheerful and willing workforce on his father's land.

When he returned to the farmhouse at the end of his day's toil, George was not only physically tired, through a different routine, but mentally exhausted from the constant efforts to get on a more friendly footing with the men. As soon as he drained his mug and pushed his plate away, however, there was no relaxation. His mother-in-law would begin a gruelling interrogation to find out exactly what had been done that day and how things were going on the farm. Although George tried to tell himself that she was only interested in the day-to-day running of the farm, he could not help but feel that she doubted his ability to cope.

The only person to whom he could pour out all his feelings was Elizabeth, and then only in whispers when they were in bed. Although she did her best to comfort him, Elizabeth felt that he was exaggerating the situation. 'It won't be for long, George,' she promised. 'I keep telling Mother how happy she'd be in a private house in Kirkby.

We only have to see one she fancies and I'm sure she'd sell up for next Lady Day.'

She had no way of knowing how bitterly resentful and deeply unhappy her husband felt at this enforced exile from his home. Now, as he stiffened and turned over in bed to face away from her, she realised that he was truly disturbed. Placing an arm around him, she whispered to his unresisting back, 'It will pass quickly enough, George. Try not to get upset.'

'Quickly?' He forced the word out. His jaw was tense and his throat ached as he strained to control his pent-up emotion. 'I expected to be here a few weeks at the most and you're talking about months – almost a year.' He turned to face her and raised himself on one elbow. In the dim light from the window, she could just make out the hardness of his expression. It was brought home to her yet again how changed he was from the tractable, easygoing George whom she had married.

'Your mother hates me,' he whispered hoarsely. 'She never wanted you to marry me and now she's only too glad to have you back up here. Well, your place is with me down in our own home, and if she doesn't do summat soon about either getting a foreman, or selling up, I sh'll have it out with her, I can tell you that.'

Elizabeth sighed, as she patted his shoulder. 'Something will be done, that I promise you,' she murmured. 'Go to sleep now, George. We'll work something out, don't you worry.' With that assurance George had to be satisfied.

Before many days, an event occurred which was to improve his relationship with the farm-men. It was a Wednesday in mid-May and George was returning from Kirkbymoorside market. Elizabeth and her mother had taken the trap so George was coming home alone, on horseback. As he was in the stable attending to the horse, he heard a shout from the direction of the cow-house. 'Come back, Billy!'

George recognised the voice of Clem Magson, the cowman. Billy was the bull, purchased by John Butler only a few weeks before his death. A massive specimen, he was docile enough in the company of the cows. Once before, however, when he had become separated from them, he had turned nasty: only the fact that Clem was carrying a muck-fork, with which he warded off the bull, had saved him from being attacked.

Consequently, when George realised that Billy must have missed the door to the cow-house and become separated from the herd, he quickly left the horse and picking up a hay-fork, went in search of the bull.

Later, he learned that Clem had not at first realised that the bull had failed to follow the cows and had wandered up into the stackyard. Clem had fastened up several of the cows by their neck-chains before glancing across at the standing normally occupied by Billy, and finding it empty. 'Fasten t'rest up, Tommy,' he called urgently to the 'Tommy Owt', the lad on a farm who was expected to be anyone's labourer, then Clem ran out into the stackyard to find the bull before he got far away.

The nearest stack to the cow-house was a partly-used one, and as Clem hurried round the corner of it, he came face to face with the bull. As he looked into the glaring red eyes he felt a stab of fear, but recovered his calm and reached out to seize the ring in the bull's nose. Billy was not going to give up his freedom so easily, however, and twisted his head away and then hunched his massive shoulders, so that his nose was at ground level, out of Clem's reach. With a trumpet of rage, he began to paw the ground and rub his horns against and into the stack, hooking out clumps of hay.

This was the scene which met George's eyes as he came from the stable and into the stackyard. He approached the tableau from the rear of the bull, to see Clem snatch a stake which was propping up the side of the stack. Clutching it in both hands, the cowman brought it down between the bull's horns with full force. To his horror, it snapped into fragments, having no effect on the bull except to enrage it even further.

Clem seemed rooted to the spot as the huge beast bellowed and snorted, tossing up lumps of earth while it pawed the ground ominously. George was conscious that the situation was worsening. The animal was working itself into a frenzy and there was no help in sight. If Clem took even one step back, the spell would be broken and the bull would charge – tossing him into the air like a straw scarecrow. As Clem stood as though paralysed, his eyes, wide with terror, held those of the bull and kept it at bay.

Glancing round, George was relieved to see that the ladder which leaned against the stack was at the opposite side to where Billy stood. Still grasping the hay-fork, he quickly shinned up the ladder to the top of the stack. Quietly crawling across the top, he found himself looking down on the scene and was pleased to see that, as he had hoped, he was in a position immediately above the bull. He carefully slid the fork handle through his hand, until he was grasping it near the top. Once his grip was firm he leaned precariously over the edge of the stack and drove the fork into the bull's neck, at the same time shouting loudly, 'Yarroo, Yarroo! Up there!' Startled by the sting of the fork and the cries the bull took its eyes off Clem and looked round, shaking its head. 'Grab his ring,' shouted George, but the cowman was rooted to the spot, shaking and sweating.

George leapt from the stack, fortunately landing on his feet. Seizing the ring, he prepared to twist it, to give himself mastery over the animal. Once his concentration on his intended victim was broken, however, Billy was once more his old docile self, allowing George to lead him into his standing and fasten him up. 'Tommy Owt' had begun the routine of milking the cows. When George had tethered the bull he called to the lad, 'Carry on, Tommy. Clem won't be long,' and went back to find Clem leaning against the haystack, vomiting.

'Come on, man,' said George kindly. 'Come to the house and I'll make thoo a cup of tea.'

'Aah'll nivver be able to repay thoo.' Clem had got his voice back and was profuse in his thanks. 'Thoo saved mi life, George,' he repeated again and again.

'Nay, nay.' George was embarrassed. 'You'd 'ave done t'same for me if it 'ad been t'other way round.' He realised that if he had been a few minutes later returning from the market, Clem might indeed have been badly gored or even killed.

George made a pot of strong tea and when he and Clem

sat down at the kitchen table, he found that he too was shaking.

'Aah've allus thought 'e was a bad old beggar underneath,' Clem stated, as they discussed the bull's behaviour. ''E's quiet enough when t'cows is with 'im, but once 'e gets separated from them 'e plays up. Mind you, 'e's never been like 'e was today.' He sat staring into the fire and then warmed to his theme. 'Aah telled t'Maister when 'e bought 'im that 'e 'ad a look in 'is eye that Aah didn't fancy, somehow. T'Maister wouldn't tek no notice, though. 'E were fair capped wi' 'im, an' all.'

'Well,' answered George, 'I can see his point. Billy's a proven stock-getter, not only for Mistress Butler's own cows, but for the money he brings in for stud fees. Mind you, now we know he's dangerous, he must be sold.'

As Clem was about to add his approval to this statement, the door opened to reveal Mrs Butler, closely followed by Elizabeth and Sarah. When she saw the two men seated at the kitchen table, each holding a pint pot, her lips tightened into a thin line and her face was suffused with colour. Her eyes fixed accusingly on George as she demanded, 'Is there no work to be done, then?'

Clem leapt to his feet, saying, 'Aah was just off, missus,' as he placed his mug on the table and scurried out through the back door.

His mother-in-law never took her cold grey eyes off George as she sat in her chair by the fire, drawing off her gloves. Elizabeth and Sarah busied themselves unpacking the baskets and putting away the shopping, recognising the signs of their mother's anger. When at last she spoke, Ann Butler's voice was icy. 'As soon as my back's turned, I don't expect you to be entertaining the men to tea in my kitchen. How you conduct yourselves down in Sleightholmedale is your business, but how things are conducted on my farm is mine.'

George looked at her for a moment without speaking. When he did answer, it was with no hint of apology. 'Clem had a nasty experience with the bull, which shook him up. He could have been killed, so I made him a pot of strong tea to pull him round,' he said.

'Nonsense,' she snapped. ' He's been scared of the animal since Faither bought him. No doubt he's trying to pull the wool over your eyes, to get out of some work.'

George ignored her outburst, turning instead to Elizabeth, who stood at the table with Sarah at her side. Briefly he described the episode with the bull. When he told them how he had come over the top of the stack to attack Billy Sarah clasped her hands together, her eyes shining with admiration. 'Oh, George,' she breathed. 'How brave.'

Elizabeth turned pale. 'You could both have been killed,' she gasped. 'Thank God you're all right.' Her mother made no comment and her face was still hard.

'So you see, Ma,' George concluded, turning to her, 'he'll have to go.'

'Go?' She looked at him in amazement. 'Go where?'

'He must be sold,' George answered decisively.

Mrs Butler rose to her feet. 'Are you out of your mind?' she demanded with incredulity. 'That bull is the last animal that my poor late husband bought! He's a magnificent animal and here he stays.'

George heard Elizabeth's gasp of dismay, while Sarah looked from her mother to him, wide-eyed and apprehensive. He took a deep breath to steady his nerves, but his hands were clenched as he faced his mother-in-law. 'You didn't see him,' he said, quietly but firmly. 'He'll kill somebody before long. Clem was lucky, but the next one may not be.'

Her jaw was set and her face paled with anger. 'That bull brings in a good income in fees from other farmers, as well as folks in the village with just one house cow. If Clem Magson has grown scared of him, the bull'll sense it. I'd rather get another cowman than another bull.'

George stood in silence for a moment but though the cold grey eyes bored into his, he refused to look away. When he spoke, Elizabeth had never heard such an uncompromising tone from him. 'There can only be one boss on a farm. If the boss here is going to be you, you've no need of me. I'll be better served down in t'dale, caring for my own stock and mi' faither's.' For a split second a flash of uncertainty crossed his mother-in-law's face, but she rapidly regained her composure and her lip curled in a scornful smile. Before she could speak, George swung on his heel. 'Go up and pack, Elizabeth. I'll go harness Bella to the trap. We can be down home for tea-time.'

Ann Butler was dumbstruck by this stand from George, who in her own mind she had classed as far too spineless to make a suitable husband for Elizabeth. Groping behind her for the rocking-chair, she lowered herself into it. She leaned her head on the back and closed her eyes. As the other three watched in silence, two tears squeezed out from under her eyelids and coursed unchecked down her face.

Elizabeth made a move to go round the table to comfort her mother, but George's upraised hand stopped her. 'If you go to her now, Elizabeth, I shall take it that you're siding with her against me,' he said in a low voice.

'Never! I would never do that, George,' she protested.

He looked at her gravely. 'This is the turning point,' he announced. 'My authority on this farm is in question. If your mother overrides me, when I've given my word to Clem that the bull will be sold, I'll never get the men on my side. I can't work with them, if they won't trust my word.'

Drawing a stool from under the table, George placed it before his mother-in-law. Picking up the hands which lay loosely in her lap, he held them in both of his. 'Look at me, Ma,' he insisted firmly. Slowly, she opened her eyes and looked at him. George fixed his gentle brown eyes on hers. 'I'm sorry to upset you but please see this from my point of view.' He decided to put all his cards on the table and went on, 'I promised that the bull would be sold. If I don't keep that promise, I might as well pack up and go home.'

Ann Butler drew a shuddering breath and then gave a sniff. 'But Billy's a good bull,' she protested.

George hesitated, not wishing to criticise a dead man's judgement, but then decided that he must press on. 'Didn't you, or for that matter Mr Butler, even question why anyone would sell such a magnificent creature at only three years of age? Billy is in his prime and nobody would part with him unless he had a fault. He hasn't got a physical fault, so it must be a hidden one.'

She thought for a moment. 'John *was* surprised that his owner wanted to sell him,' she admitted.

'Where did he get him?'

'Somewhere near Malton.' She seemed to be coming round to George's opinion. 'He was advertised in the paper. He didn't come from anyone we know.' She paused for a moment, reflecting. 'There was one odd thing,' she went on. 'John noticed that two men brought him. As well as the one with the rod attached to the ring in his nose, there was a man at the other side holding a rope looped round his horns and running down his face through the ring, as well.'

'Did he ask why?' George could not imagine his own father taking on a strange bull which took two men to control it.

She hesitated. 'No,' she confessed. 'We thought it was because he was so valuable.'

George sighed. It was typical of John Butler to want to own the best animal in the district. He'd been given to flaunting his money and possessions. Ann Butler eyed him speculatively and couldn't help but feel less hostile as she looked into his dark sympathetic eyes. 'Perhaps I was a bit hasty, George,' she conceded. 'He does sound to be a handful. What do you suggest?' During her husband's lifetime she had always found it best to let him believe that she deferred to him, and that he made the decisions.

'All our cows are in calf, so he'll be no loss if we put an advertisement in the paper,' George replied. 'Even if you lose a bit on him it won't be more than you'd have had to pay in stud fees for somebody else's bull.' He studied her for a moment, considering whether or not he should press home his advantage. He rose to his feet and pushed the stool back under the table. 'I'll go and see how the men are getting on, and we'll advertise Billy next week. Make no mistake, though, we shall need to sit down and have a talk. I don't intend to stay here any longer than is absolutely necessary, so you must begin to think about selling up.'

Her eyes widened and she made to speak, but he broke in, determination making his voice hard. 'Elizabeth and I have our own home and I have my own stock. Faither needs me down in the dale, so you must think on the future. You and Sarah are very welcome to come and live down at Cherry Tree Farm with us until you find a house to suit you, perhaps in Kirkby.' As he opened the door, he looked back. 'You must see that I'm right.'

She sighed deeply. 'Aye. I don't suppose things can stay as they are, now John's gone.' She looked at him, beseechingly. 'But give me time, George!'

'Right. We shan't rush you.' As George went out he thought that perhaps he'd made a mistake, allowing her to wring this promise from him. His mother-in-law was not a woman he felt able to trust.

# CHAPTER SEVEN

Tamar Oaks was happier living at Cherry Tree Farm than she had ever believed possible. Removed for the first time in her life from the constraints of her father's iron discipline, she revelled in her freedom, although deep in her inmost core she recognised that her present life fell far short of what she once hoped for. From earliest childhood she had been rebellious and turbulent. Annie, her mother, had often complained to the rest of the family that Tamar delighted in creating turmoil around her. 'She'd tek a stick ti stir mud from t'bottom of t'clearest pool,' she was often heard to say.

Tamar was forced to acknowledge that her mother's summing up of her character held some truth. Ever since she could remember she had chafed against the rigid rule of her home life. Although she loved her brothers and sisters, she was unable to comprehend how they could placidly accept their fate. They were willing to plod through life following the farming traditions of their ancestors and apparently, wanting no more.

'Not for me,' Tamar often told herself. She was aware of her beauty and during her brief but passionate affair with Sir William Forster, had believed that this was the key which would unlock the door to a more satisfying future. She had been devastated by the way he had abandoned her when she was pregnant, and the humiliation that had followed. Now, freed from the daily evidence of her father's rejection, she revelled in the mundane tasks she had found so irksome under her mother's direction. Then, she had tackled the housework and dairywork in a splapdash and haphazard fashion, but now she took pleasure in doing them with care, as a repayment to George and Elizabeth for the change in her circumstances.

Although she realised that her brother and his wife would one day come back to their own home, Tamar lived one day at a time. The morrow could look after itself and she pushed to the back of her mind speculation as to what would happen to her and Victoria, when they returned.

Whereas, previously, she had ignored her Uncle George, accepting him as just another worker on the farm, she now found him to be a kind-hearted and sensitive man, who appreciated the sights and sounds of nature for their own sake, not merely for the effect they had upon the farming day. When their day's work was over, the two would often sit for an hour while she read extracts to him from the weekly paper. Not only was she trying to improve her reading ability, but she was also practising a more refined way of speaking. A born mimic, Tamar was deliberately modelling her speech on Elizabeth's and trying to lose her country accent. Knowing that she could never again be happy under her father's roof, and that he would never want her back, she hoped that she could find a home, working as a cook or housekeeper, in a farmhouse away from the area.

One stifling hot day in mid-June, her Uncle pushed back his chair after the midday meal. 'Aah'm just going across t'beck ti Stone Ruckles,' he announced. 'Aah'll check over George's sheep and lambs ti mek sure they're all right.' At the door he paused. 'Doan't worry if Aah'm a bit late. Some might have strayed as far as Skiplam Moor,' he added.

'Yes, all right Uncle,' she said, as she carried the kettle of hot water from the stove to the enamel bowl which stood in the shallow stone sink. When she had finished the washing up, she took the cushion from the rocking-chair and tossed it on to the step at the kitchen door. Picking the baby up from her cradle, she carried her out and sat on the step with her. Undoing her bodice, she leaned against the jamb in the sunshine to feed Victoria. Her mother would be scandalised if she could see her, Tamar knew. Annie Oaks believed that sunshine damaged a baby's eyes and none of her children had been out in the fresh air for the first year of life.

Tamar raised her face to the heat of the sun and closed her eyes, lulled by the murmurous drone of the bees going heavily about their work among the roses in the front garden. 'I'll gather some rose-petals and make some jam for Elizabeth to take to next week's market.' The sleepy thought drifted through her consciousness. The rhythmic sucking of the baby soothed her and she luxuriated in the warmth and enforced idleness which the period of breast-feeding brought.

So it was that the stranger saw her. He had come striding down the track from Pennyholme, the farthest farm down the valley. He had been about to press on towards Aumery Park Farm, but had turned aside to try his luck for a casual-labourer's job at Cherry Tree Farm. He paused at the sight of the mother and child, savouring Tamar's beauty. Although caught into a bun at the nape of her neck, the black hair was as wild and untamed as Tamar herself. Clusters of curls brushed her forehead and dark tendrils framed her cheeks. The man's eyes travelled over the exquisite, heart-shaped face, now brushed by the sooty lashes, which hid eyes of a colour he could not have imagined. The child, sated, had fallen from the nipple and now lay asleep on the crook of her mother's arm, her head back, lips apart and a trickle of milk beading her chin.

He passed his tongue over his lips as his eyes raked her creamy breast, culminating in the rosy nipple, raised by the child's feeding. He drew back into the trees out of sight as Tamar stirred and spoke to the sleeping child in a voice which was itself heavy with sleep. Slowly she stood up and gently carried the slumbering baby and laid her in the crib. She stood, smiling down at the child, as she slowly buttoned her bodice. Although her back was to the kitchen door, she was suddenly aware that the light through it was shadowed. She swung round, to find the doorway filled by a stranger, who stood eyeing her.

'Afternoon, missus,' he grinned, as he saluted cockily.

'Yes? What do you want?' she answered in a brusque tone, annoyed that he had not knocked on the door. She felt, uneasily, that he had been observing her from the doorway, unbeknown to her. Why hadn't the geese given warning of his approach, she wondered. They were usually better than the keenest dog in their reaction to visitors. Not only were they vociferous in voice, but especially at this time of year when they had goslings, the gander would hurl himself at strangers, wings flapping and neck outstretched.

One blow from his mighty wings could break a man's leg. Now, however, though Tamar could not know it, they had ushered their flock of young down to the beck, to enjoy a swim in the heat of the day. She stood and stared at the intruder, taken aback by his sudden appearance.

He took a step inside without invitation, and she could study him in more detail in the light of the kitchen. He was a bulky man of about thirty, tall and broad. His corduroy trousers were tied below the knee with coarse bands and the sleeves of his union shirt were rolled up above the elbow, baring arms that were heavily muscled and burnt brown by the sun. His face, too, was deeply tanned except for a scar which stood out stark-white in a vivid gash from eye to mouth corner, down his right cheek. The impudent eyes were brown – not the velvety brown of her brother George's, but hotly brown, of the kind that often goes with red hair. This he had in plenty, curling crisply on top of his head and down to the shirt collar at the back.

As her eyes moved up him, the full beauty of them made him catch his breath for a moment. He had presumed they might be dark, to match the blackness of her hair but instead he was confronted by large eyes of a tawny-topaz, lit with golden glints and fringed by long lashes of an inky blackness.

Neither spoke for a moment. Tamar took in the casual insolence of this man, who had intruded into her sunlit dream. Was he a gypsy, she asked herself and then wondered why she had presumed this. Of course! It was the gold ring he wore in one ear. Not a gypsy, perhaps – maybe a seaman?

He it was who first broke the silence. 'Is t'maister in, missus?' he queried.

'No! He's about the buildings,' she answered, conscious that she must not let him know that she was alone. Quickly she slipped her left hand under her apron, to hide its ringless state. As he looked from her to the sleeping child, however, she knew that he was not deceived.

He took one more step into the kitchen. 'I'm looking for work for a week or two,' he said. 'Does 'e want a man?'

'No,' she answered. 'It's a bad time of year, with haytime not started yet.'

'Could you spare me a cup of water then, missus?' he asked. 'I've walked over t'moors from Rosedale and it's thirsty work on a day like this.'

Tamar hesitated. To cross to the water barrel and fill a mug for the stranger would bring her closer to him. As they were now, the table was between them and this gave her a feeling of security. For all his apparent affability, she felt a menace emanating from him and was only too aware of his open admiration as his eyes moved over her. Realising, however, that she could not refuse his request, she went to the dresser and lifted down one of the mugs that hung there. As she lifted the lid of the water-barrel and filled the mug, he took a step towards her. Swiftly she placed the pint pot of water on the corner of the table nearest to him and moved back to her previous position at the far side of the table.

'There you are,' she said. Glancing at the grandfather clock which stood in the corner of the kitchen, she observed, 'My husband will be in before long, but he's no need of a man.'

Throwing back his head, the stranger drained the last drop of water and sighing appreciatively, passed the back of his hand over his wet lips. 'Thank you – that was grand. You must have a good deep well,' he observed.

'Yes.' Tamar tried to keep the conversation as brief as politeness allowed, wishing that the man would go. He made no attempt to move however, but stood and let his gaze wander over her as though savouring the look of her.

'Perhaps *you're* in need of a man,' he said, stressing the pronoun and the leer on his face emphasised his meaning. For a second Tamar thought she had misheard him. Apart from her tempestuous affair with Sir William she had led a sheltered life in the little vale, and was unsure how to deal with this interloper.

Mistaking the reason for her hesitation he gave a chuckle. 'Wondering where we can go – out of t'maister's way? There's plenty of time. 'E's away over t'moor top, as well you know.'

Tamar knew then that he must have seen her Uncle setting off to make his rounds of the sheep. She tried to maintain an air of dignity, drawing herself up and looking him straight in the eye. 'You'd better go,' she announced in a firm voice. 'We don't need a man for any purpose.'

To her dismay, the stranger made no attempt to leave the kitchen. Instead, he dropped his jacket on to a chair by the table and hooked both thumbs into the wide leather belt that encircled his waist. He was cocksure in his vanity. Women fell easy prey to him and he could see no reason why he should not make a conquest of this delectable creature. Her apparent reluctance only served to inflame his lust even more. 'Easing your conscience by pretending to be hard to get, are you?' He took a step forward as he spoke, then cocked his head on one side and gave her a wink. 'Come on! You know you'll enjoy it.'

Tamar wanted to step back as he came forward, but was unwilling to show her fear. She stood her ground and her amber eyes held his steadily. 'Get out of this house.' She almost hissed the words.

'Are you going to make me?' As he spoke, he advanced another step. He was taunting her now, willing to take his time over what he realised was going to be a rape, not a seduction. The anticipation of a struggle and the taking of her by force roused him even more and he smiled cruelly, his teeth white against his tanned face.

Tamar would not remove her eyes from his. She was sick at heart with the fear that he might touch her baby, if only to gain his way with the mother by threatening to harm the child. As she fixed his gaze with hers, she was aware that his smile had vanished and his hot brown eyes had darkened and suddenly narrowed. The face that closed on hers was no longer handsome, but cold and hard. The speed with which he moved took her by surprise. Before she could dodge round the table, he was upon her – one arm like an iron bar across her shoulders, pressing her back across the table, the other hand fumbling with her skirts. Now that he could see his prey within his grasp, he gave an exultant laugh which rang round the kitchen.

Tamar exerted all her strength in the struggle to escape,

but was powerless against his brute strength. His lips found hers and, as the probing tongue sought to open her mouth, she pressed her lips together and moved her head this way and that in an effort to evade him. She gasped in pain as she felt the sharpness of his teeth against her bottom lip. She knew that she was no match for him and could feel her strength ebbing and feared he would gain mastery over her.

The combination of the throbbing heat of the day and her frenzied attempts to fight him off caused rivulets of perspiration to course down between her breasts. The face which gloated inches from hers was blood-red and she could see the sweat standing out on his forehead. With revulsion, she felt drips of it falling on to her own face, mixing with her sweat, causing her to feel defiled.

With one last, desperate effort she swung her leg backwards under the table and then brought her knee up into his groin, thrusting with all her might. With an oath he took a half-step back and the weight of his arm was slackened from across her chest. Exerting all her remaining force she caught him off-balance and slipped from his grasp.

Her eyes darted wildly round the kitchen, looking for a weapon before he could catch his breath and renew his attack. Just as he straightened up and lunged towards her with a roar, she spotted the big black iron potato pan, which she had left by the sink after the washing up.

'You bitch!' came the yell as he rushed round the table towards her, arms outstretched.

Quickly she grasped the pan in both hands as he was almost upon her, then swung round and brought it across the side of his head with all the might she could muster.

He went down as though poleaxed. Still grasping the pan, Tamar leaned against the table, panting, and eyed him warily. She could not decide whether she had, in truth, knocked him unconscious or whether he was feigning, prepared to grab her ankle if she approached him.

Craning towards him, she saw a gash in his temple which was bleeding copiously. She put the pan down on the sink and going to the table-drawer, took out the carving knife. Filling a mug with cool water from the barrel, she drank deeply, the pot rattling against her chattering teeth. When she had applied a damp cloth to her own bleeding lip, she went and sat in the rocking-chair by the fireside and regarded the man.

What if he died? The thought roused no feeling of compunction in Tamar. Her main concern was to rid herself of him, before her Uncle's return from the moor. She was terrified that the news of the attack would get back to Jonadab. Since her arrival in Cherry Tree Farm, Tamar had recovered some of her self-esteem and had no wish to appear to invite trouble. Her father and even her Uncle might misconstrue the reason for the man's presence in the house.

The need for a decision was removed from her mind, however, by the man's return to consciousness. With a groan he opened his eyes and raised a hand to his bleeding head. He stared at his hand in a befuddled state. 'What happened?' he demanded.

Still clasping the knife, Tamar rose from the chair and stood over him. 'Get up!' she said in a hard voice.

Recollection dawned in his eyes. 'You're mad, bloody mad!' he gasped, as he pulled himself up by the table and stood leaning against it, eyeing the knife in her hand.

Indeed, Tamar did look like a madwoman. During the struggle she had lost some of her hairpins and her hair now hung below her shoulders in a night-black wild tangle. Her face was as pale and cold as alabaster and her tawny eyes blazed with rage. Looking into them, he recalled a lioness he had once seen in a Wild Beast Show. Here he could see an identical golden shaft of disdain and hatred. 'Get off this property or I'll slit your throat.' She spoke in a low voice, vibrant with emotion.

Unsteadily, he walked towards the door, retrieving his jacket on the way. As he opened the door, he turned to look at Tamar. 'I'm going, but you'll see me again, never fear,' he snarled. 'I'll get even with you, you bitch.' As he stumbled out into the sunlit yard, Tamar ran and banged the door and shot the bolt.

Now that her ordeal was over, she began to shake uncontrollably but went to the kitchen window, peering from behind the curtain to make sure that he had gone. To her disquiet, she could not see him making his way down the lane towards her father's farm. Could he be hiding in the buildings, waiting for her to collect the eggs or do the milking, she wondered.

Swiftly, she mounted the stairs and went to look out of a bedroom window. Thankfully she saw him walking across the fields towards Hodge Beck. There, he lay on his stomach and rinsed his wound in the cold water. Wringing his neckerchief out in the stream he bound it round his forehead and then crossed the stepping stones and headed for the moor top. Only when he was out of sight did she feel really safe.

Before going back downstairs, Tamar brushed her hair and pinned it up. She noticed in the mirror that, though the bleeding had stopped, her lip was still badly swollen. Once downstairs she must bathe it to reduce the swelling, she decided, not wishing to upset her Uncle. She had already come to the conclusion that she would not tell him about the stranger. She hoped that the episode was over and in any case, even if her attacker returned, there was nothing that the frail old man could do to protect her.

The following Wednesday, when Elizabeth came down to collect her produce for the market, she was accompanied by George. 'I've come to have a look round, Uncle,' he said, 'before we get too busy with hay-making up at Fadmoor.'

'Aah checked all t'sheep and lambs last week, George,' his Uncle answered, 'so Aah reckons thoo'll find 'em all right.'

When Elizabeth went into the dairy with her to collect up the market goods, Tamar poured out the whole story. 'I was so happy here and so peaceful,' she gulped, 'but now . . .' Her voice trailed off. She could not put into words how the security she had once felt in her isolation at Cherry Tree Farm had now turned to fear. The farm's very remoteness seemed charged with menace and she no longer enjoyed being there.

Elizabeth considered for a moment. 'I must be off, but I'll think about it during the day,' she promised. 'Don't worry – we shall not allow you to stay here alone.' Once the trap was packed, she drove off down the valley to meet her mother-in-law.

Tamar studied her remark. Had Elizabeth meant that they would send her back to her parents, she wondered, biting her lip. She determined that there was no way she would go back to live under her father's roof. 'I'll get a job somewhere. There are plenty of elderly men who want housekeepers,' she told herself as she set about the preparations for dinner.

She had hoped to catch George on his own and tell him the tale, too, but their Uncle was pathetically eager to show George all that he had done, both on the farm and in the garden, so that Tamar was frustrated. When the midday meal was finished, the two men went to look over the sheep, giving George the satisfaction of working among his own flock for a time.

Tamar fed Victoria and put her down into her cradle. She then moved restlessly round the kitchen, unable to settle. There was enough cream separated to make a batch of butter, but she felt too finely-tuned to tackle the sheer hard work of churning.After a few minutes' thought, she sat down at her spinning wheel. Her Uncle often kept her company in the evening, carding wool for her and so there was a large basket full of rollags already made. She was able to sit peacefully at the wheel, treadling automatically and drawing the wool through her fingers while her thoughts strayed to her future.

When Elizabeth came back from Kirkby market, she said, 'I've thought up a plan, Tamar, but we'll wait until George gets back before I say anything.'

'I shall not go back home,' Tamar insisted, with a flash of her old spirit.

Elizabeth held up her hand. 'This is your home now,' she said in a soothing tone. 'You'll stay here for as long as you wish.'

When tea was over Elizabeth recounted to George the story of the attack on Tamar. She herself was disturbed, not only by Tamar's ordeal, but also by revulsion at the thought of the man entering the home which she and George had created. They had provided what they had believed to be a safe haven for Tamar, only to discover that it was not so.

George heard the tale through in silence, but his anger showed itself in the throbbing of a pulse in his temple. 'Would you know him again?' he demanded.

Tamar gave a bitter laugh. 'That I would! Every line of his face is imprinted on my memory. He said he'd be back an' all, for what I'd done to him.'

'If he shows his face here again, I'll swing for him.' The statement was made in a flat, unemotional voice which only served to emphasise George's intensity.

'There's one thing,' put in Elizabeth. 'This will cut the ground from under Mother's feet. She'll soon see that she *must* sell the farm when we move back down here.' She turned to George. 'This proves we must move back, George. You'll agree with me, I hope?'

George's face broke into a huge smile. 'Oh, yes, love! There's nowt I want more than to come back to our own home,' he said delightedly.

'That's settled, then.' Elizabeth smiled across the table at Tamar. 'You won't be alone here any more. We shall come back at the weekend and George can ride up to Fadmoor daily – until the farm's sold.'

Tamar's face was radiant as she shook her head, unable to utter her thanks, so near to tears was she.

# CHAPTER EIGHT

Ann Butler took Elizabeth and George's move back to Cherry Tree Farm as a personal affront. She had persisted in her belief that she was more than a match for George and had hoped that he and Elizabeth would eventually give in to her pressure and make their home with her.

Although loath to do so, she was forced to concede that George was as conscientious and hard-working as ever. He rode up from the dale each morning, arriving punctually and working without stint on her farm. However, when each day's work was over, he popped his head round the door to make his farewell and then rode off again down into Sleightholmedale, leaving her to the sole company of her youngest daughter, long evening after long evening. 'They've no thought for me,' she would complain bitterly to Sarah, but no matter how hard she tried, with blandishments, wheedling or sulks, nothing had any effect. Her daughter and son-in-law made it plain that they expected her to sell her farm in the autumn and let the men go to seek work at the Martinmas Hirings.

Tamar wondered at first how she would get on sharing a house with Elizabeth, especially as she had become used to treating it as her own. However, Elizabeth was tactful in her dealings with the younger woman and Tamar soon found herself revealing to Elizabeth her ambition to become a housekeeper. 'For somebody a bit better off,' she confided. 'Like you were for your Uncle in Leeds.'

'Ye-es.' Elizabeth looked the girl up and down. She could quite see many men being only too willing to take Tamar on as their housekeeper. The trouble would be in finding someone who wanted her for more than her exotic beauty. Her thoughts went to Uncle Nathan, but her own sister Christiania was comfortably ensconced in his home in Leeds. Once she had overcome her reluctance to replace Elizabeth as their Uncle's housekeeper, Christie was enjoying city life – the hustle and bustle, the trips to the theatre and her position running a wealthy man's household.

At that moment, Elizabeth came to a decision. If Tamar would allow her, she would groom her sister-in-law to take a place in a better-class household. Reaching forward, she took Tamar's hands in hers and turned them over. 'We'll start with these,' she smiled, examining the rough reddened hands.'Rub them with a mixture of lard and sugar every time they've been in water. Once they've improved, a little glycerine and rosewater will keep them soft and white. I'll bring some back from Kirkby, next market day.'

Tamar's eyes shone. She took care of her complexion, never using soap on her face, preferring instead to wash it with a muslin bag filled with oatmeal. She had, however, accepted that her rough red hands, chapped in winter, were a natural consequence of her way of life. In Tamar's eyes, only ladies of leisure had soft white hands.

Elizabeth warmed to the idea. 'I'll teach you how a table should be laid, how to deal with servants and how to converse,' she said excitedly. 'We'll practise every evening and keep at it until you're perfect.' She was as good as her word, and started the task that very day. She was determined to make Tamar fit to mix in any society and the girl herself was an apt pupil, making rapid progress.

July was a hard month for George. He knew that his father needed his extra pair of hands for their own hay-making, but Ann and Sarah Butler did not work in the hayfields as did his own mother and sisters. He still rode up daily to the Butler farm in Fadmoor and after working from dawn till dark, had the weary ride back down to Cherry Tree Farm. Often half-asleep, he allowed the horse its head to find its own way home.

In vain his mother-in-law urged him to sleep up at the farm until all the hay was in. George was adamant that his decision to go home each night was the right one. 'Give her an inch and she'll take a yard,' he told Elizabeth. 'Once I sleep up there, she'll have you there too, and we'll be up there for good.'

Elizabeth sighed. They only saw each other for any length of time on Sundays and once haytime was over, the whole arduous business would begin again with the coming of harvest. Her father-in-law, too, did not attempt to hide his impatience and exasperation with the situation. Jonadab reproached Annie with great regularity. 'Thoo persuaded me!' he would say accusingly. 'It was only ti 'elp 'er out for a week or two, but when will it end? We can do wi' oor George down 'ere.' Annie, wisely, made no reply to his rantings. She could see both sides of the coin, but dare not say so to her husband.

In the lull between haytime and harvest, George had the chance to talk to his mother-in-law. Ann Butler was seated in her rocking-chair by the fireside when he popped in to say 'Goodnight' one evening in early August. Sarah was out gathering eggs. 'Now, Ma,' he began, closing the door behind him. 'Time's getting on. Have you done owt about selling?'

He had caught her at a bad moment, though he was not to know it. While sitting over her sewing, Ann Butler had allowed her mind to drift back to the early years of her marriage, when the house had been filled with the laughter of her children. George's question seemed to be an unfeeling intrusion into her thoughts of the past. Brought back so abruptly to her present changed circumstances, to George's consternation and her own surprise, Ann Butler burst into tears.

Having always regarded his mother-in-law as a self-controlled, almost hard woman, George was taken aback. Noting that the kettle was singing on the hob and that the teapot was warming on the hearth, he hurriedly made a pot of tea, giving her time to recover her composure. 'Now, then – what's up?' he asked gently, as he stood before her with a steaming mug.

'Thank you, lad,' she said, taking a long drink of the reviving brew. Haltingly she explained the reason for her tears. 'I suppose I really wanted everything to go back to what it was when our Jack was here and John was alive,' she admitted, with a shamefaced glance towards him.

'You must see that my duty is to Faither and our own farms,' George said. 'If you want to carry on here, you'll have to find a good, live-in foreman. If you want to sell, I

85

can ride into Pickering in the morning and have a word with Mr Boulton, the auctioneer.'

When George swung on to his horse for the ride down into Sleightholmedale, it was with a much lighter heart than he had had for several months. Ann Butler had agreed, albeit reluctantly, that George should ride into Pickering the following day and ask the auctioneer to call and value the farm. As the majority of farms changed hands on 6 April, George could see no difficulty in arranging the auction for late October. In that way, the workers could find new jobs at the Martinmas Hirings in early November.

Now that George could see an end to his work for Ann Butler, he was determined to see that her farm was in as good shape as possible for the day of the sale. It was with an almost proprietary air of pride that he conducted Mr Boulton over the fields and through the buildings. They decided that after the auction of the farm, the live and dead farmstock would be sold on the premises, in order to give the new owner a chance to buy.

'What about the outgoing owner's crops?' asked the auctioneer. 'It's not likely that any buyer will want to take possession before April.'

Not wanting to hold up the sale in any way, George answered, 'I'll see to them. I've been coming up from Sleightholmedale for months now, so another few weeks'll make no difference.'

To his consternation and the auctioneer's thinly veiled annoyance, Ann Butler refused to accept the valuation. 'Nay, it's worth more,' she insisted. Although both men tried to point out that it was an inconvenient time of the year to sell and a potential purchaser was unlikely to be able to move before April, she refused to budge. 'This money must last me for the rest of my life,' she insisted. 'I want the best deal I can get.'

As George saw Mr Boulton to the gate, the auctioneer gave him a quizzical glance. 'Your mother-in-law seems a very . . .' he paused '. . . a very stubborn lady, doesn't she?'

'You could say a pig-headed one,' sighed George. 'If she's made up her mind she'll tek some moving.'

In the weeks that followed Ann Butler did indeed prove

to be obstinate. She refused to budge from her assessment of the farm's value, and neither would she look at a house in Kirkbymoorside for her and Sarah. 'I'll come down to you, over the winter,' she told Elizabeth. George and his wife exchanged glances, knowing full well that if she came to live with them, it would be for the rest of her life.

'You'll have to tell her about our Tamar and the bairn,' said George. He found it hard to believe that they had managed to keep Victoria's very existence a secret but once his mother-in-law knew, he was afraid that the story of Tamar's shame would spread round the district.

When Elizabeth confided the story to her mother, however, she stressed the fact that the man responsible for Tamar's downfall was the same one who had made advances towards her and also attacked George's other sister, Beth. Without telling a blatant lie, she implied that Tamar had been taken against her will, so that Ann Butler was filled with compassion towards the girl. 'Don't worry,' she assured them. 'Not a word'll pass my lips. Nor our Sarah's, either,' she added, glaring challengingly at her youngest daughter.

'No, Mam, I'll not say a word,' promised Sarah.

'Heaven alone knows how long we can keep it a secret,' sighed Elizabeth. 'We can't keep them both down in the dale for ever.'

October was a golden month, free of the autumn mists which often hung in the dale. The purple of the moors had faded and they swept down to Hodge Beck in sable folds, studded here and there with clumps of rust-brown bracken.

Joe Last, Ann Butler's waggoner, made several trips down to Cherry Tree Farm. In addition to all the furniture from her bedroom, Ann found all manner of oddments with which she could not bear to part. Seeing the dale in its autumn splendour, she found it welcoming and hospitable and was pleased with her scheme to make her home there, though the fact that this was to be permenant had not yet been disclosed to George and Elizabeth. Ostensibly, her move down into the dale was merely until spring, although she was determined not to waste her money on a house in Kirkby. The house at Cherry Tree Farm was a good, solid four-bedroomed one, far preferable to a smaller house in the town and with two daughters to pander to her wishes, she could see herself leading a very comfortable life there. George and Elizabeth were well aware of the way her mind was working, but it was the custom for widowed parents to make their home with married children and they accepted the fact philosophically.

When the day of the sale came, Ann sat in the kitchen looking round for the last time, while she waited to sign the contract. Mr Boulton came with a final plea. 'Farms are difficult to sell, Mrs Butler. Won't you lower your reserve price?'

'That I will not,' she snapped, pressing her lips together. 'It's a good farm. My husband always said so, and it'll sell.' He sighed and shrugged his shoulders before motioning George to go into the yard, where the sale was to take place.

'I doubt she's too high in her price, Mr Oaks,' he said gloomily.

His forecast proved correct and when the bidding began to falter, George hurried into the kitchen. 'Lower your price, Ma,' he urged. 'The bids are flagging.'

'No! That I won't,' she insisted stubbornly. No matter how Mr Boulton chivvied and cajoled his audience, the last bid was fifty guineas short of the reserve, and he could raise no further interest.

When, at last, all the livestock and implements had been disposed of and the porters began to carry out the surplus furniture, George had the chance to break the news to her. 'I'm afraid it didn't sell, Ma,' he told her.

'Didn't sell?' She echoed the words incredulously. The colour drained from her cheeks and her lips quivered. She could not speak for a moment and then she said, 'What's the matter with them? Was it a poor turn-out? I couldn't bear to go out and watch.'

George shook his head. 'No, there was plenty of interest. They just thought the reserve was too high, Ma.'

Her face flushed with anger. 'Nonsense! It's a good farm. Did the auctioneer push it? Did he make clear all its good points?'

George nodded slowly. 'Mr Boulton's a well-respected

auctioneer, Ma, as you well know. He did his best, but folk had reached their limit.'

She considered for a moment. 'I need the money. I suppose I must take less.'

'Nay, they've gone, now,' he answered. 'The ones who are left are only staying for the household goods.' George felt his resentment rising. His mother-in-law seemed intent on twisting the screw, he thought bitterly. Since her husband's death he had acted as foreman for her, despite the demands of his own stock and the protestations of his father. Now, just when he thought his servitude was at an end, she had obstructed his plans through her foolish obstinacy. He needed no telling that he and Elizabeth would be saddled with her at Cherry Tree Farm for the rest of her life. That, however, was preferable to trailing up to Fadmoor every day to work the farm.

When the sale was over, the auctioneer came in to settle up. 'I'm sorry, Mrs Butler,' he said. 'I did my best, but I'm afraid the asking price was just too high.'

Eventually, she gave in to their arguments but with bad grace. With an audible sniff, she apologised to the auctioneer and agreed that if he would approach the last bidder on her behalf, she would accept his offer. She had to be satisfied with this arrangement and it was in comparative silence that she and George drove back down to Cherry Tree Farm.

True to his word, Mr Boulton sent a messenger down only about a week later, to say that he had managed to get a sale and that the purchaser's solicitor would come down with a contract the following Thursday afternoon. Ann sank back in her chair, fanning herself with her hand. 'Praise be for that,' she murmured. 'What a relief! And yet I'm heartbroken to have to leave the farm. It's been my home for over thirty years, but I'd no alternative.'

The fine weather held out over the next week. On the Thursday, when the dinner-table had been cleared and the pots washed, Tamar took little Victoria, who was now toddling, for a walk along the bank of Hodge Beck in order to give Mrs Butler privacy to conduct her business. As she set off, Tamar mused. She had felt dismayed on learning that Ann Butler was to make her home with George and Elizabeth but the woman was not as domineering as she had been when mistress in her own home, from what George had said.

A fire had been lit in the parlour and Elizabeth set out a tray with her mother's best china. This done, she put the teapot to warm and they sat down to wait. When the sound of a horse's hoofs were heard in the yard, Sarah ran to the window and peered from behind the curtain. 'Ooh, what a lovely horse,' she breathed. 'It's jet-black and shines like a piece of coal.'

'Come away,' hissed her mother. 'He might see you.' Indeed, as she spoke and as Sarah hurriedly dodged back, the rider dismounted. As he tied up his horse his eyes swept the house.

Sarah swung round to face her mother and sister. 'He isn't old, like a lawyer should be. He's quite youngish. Handsome an' all,' she said excitedly.

Elizabeth laughed as she went through to the front door to admit the visitor. 'Not all lawyers are old, you goose,' she said. 'They all have to start when they're young.' When she opened the front door to his knock, she saw that he was, indeed, youngish, as Sarah had labelled him. She placed him as being in his late twenties. She surveyed him frankly, as he removed his hat with a flourish and gave a half bow.

Standing a little under six feet tall, he deserved the label 'handsome', bestowed upon him by Sarah. He was lean, with an upright stance, and his hair was of an almost silvery fairness, unusual in an adult; more a hue of childhood, which looked incongruous on a grown man. It clung to his head in soft waves and was matched by the moustache which graced his upper lip. This, too, was silvery and soft, as though his top-lip had never felt a razor. His eyes were a clear, deep blue, but the lashes which fringed them were brown, as were his eyebrows. Elizabeth felt pleased at this, remembering a saying of her father's: 'Never trust a man with sandy lashes'.

When he spoke, his voice was low, but clear, beautifully enunciated with no trace of a north-country brogue. 'Mrs

90

Butler?' he asked. 'My name is Stephen Lassiter, solicitor of Helmsley.'

'Do come in, Mr Lassiter.' Elizabeth stood aside for him to enter. 'I am Elizabeth Oaks, Mrs Butler's daughter.' When she had introduced him to her mother, Elizabeth asked, 'You'll take a cup of tea with us, when your business is concluded, Mr Lassiter?'

'Thank you, Mrs Oaks. That would be most kind,' he answered.

With an imperceptible motion of her head, Elizabeth signalled to Sarah to follow her to the kitchen. There she arranged a plate of scones and another of fruit cake, on a separate tray to the cups and saucers.

'Isn't he lovely?' demanded Sarah, excitedly. 'He's so handsome and his clothes so elegant.'

Elizabeth smiled at her sister's enthusiasm. Poor Sarah had led such a sheltered life, as the youngest daughter of a family living in a small village. Whereas Elizabeth, having spent several years living in Leeds with her Uncle Nathan, had met many men of Stephen Lassiter's class, although not, she had to admit, of his striking good looks.

When they carried the tray into the parlour, the contract was signed and witnessed and Elizabeth dispensed tea and cakes. If he was surprised to find fine china and refined manners in a Dales farmhouse, Lassiter gave no indication of it.

'How pleasant it is to be sitting here in charming female company,' he smiled, settling himself comfortably in his chair. 'And what a lovely setting your home has, Mrs Oaks. I've never been down into Sleightholmedale before and found the scenery breathtaking as I rode through.'

Elizabeth smiled. 'Yes. It's a little Eden, so sheltered and peaceful,' she said, closing her mind to the isolated incident of the stranger who had attacked Tamar. Fortunately, there had been no sign of him since and the valley once again seemed a haven.

Ann Butler was not content to be shut out of the conversation. Her husband John had been one of the leading farmers in the district and she considered herself as good as anybody. 'Do feel free to call on us whenever you wish,

91

Mr Lassiter,' she gushed. 'We'd be pleased to see you, and your wife of course, if she would care to come.'

'Thank you, Mrs Butler. I may ride down one day when the spring arrives. However, there is no Mrs Lassiter, so I should be alone. I have quite a lot of work in the foreseeable future, so it would not be for a while.'

Ann was an insensitive woman in many ways. One of her favourite sayings was, 'If you don't ask you never get to know.' Now her probing went beyond the bounds of courtesy. 'Perhaps you have a sister who sees to the smooth running of your household?'

He stared for a moment into the fire and took a sip of tea before answering. The woman was asking for a snub, but he caught sight of the elder daughter's face, showing obvious embarrassment at her mother's tactlessness. 'No, Mrs Butler, I have no sister,' he replied courteously. 'I am at the mercy of housekeepers. And now I must take my leave,' he added, rising from his chair and placing his cup and saucer on the table.

Elizabeth hesitated, reluctant to press the point after her mother's rudeness. However, this might be a chance which would never arise again. 'Have you someone in your employ at present?' she asked, as he picked up his hat. She found herself holding her breath, waiting for his reply. 'I'm not asking out of idle curiosity, Mr Lassiter,' she added.

He looked surprised, but paused, while she stood and waited.'No, as a matter of fact I have not,' was his answer.

With a quick glance at her mother and sister, Elizabeth weighed her words before saying hesitantly, 'I may know of someone who would like to apply for the position.'

'Oh?' Stephen Lassiter looked at her with quickening interest. 'Could you recommend this person?'

'Well . . .' Elizabeth could see the frown of disapproval on her mother's face. 'It would not be proper for me to recommend her, as she is a relative of mine.'

He smiled. 'In my opinion, that is a recommendation in itself,' he said.

'She is my sister-in-law – a young widow with a small child.' Elizabeth had burned her boats now. She could feel silent reproach emanating from her mother as an almost tangible thing. She pressed on, however, determined to obtain a chance for Tamar's future, if at all possible. 'I could bring her next week for an interview, if you wish,' she offered. 'There would be no obligation for you to employ her, unless you thought she would be suitable. I realise,' she added, 'that the little girl may not be welcome, but she could always remain here, if my sister-in-law were satisfactory in other ways.' Although Elizabeth would be only too eager for Victoria to remain with her, she knew as she said this that Tamar was devoted to the child and would never take a job which would mean being parted from her.

Before the solicitor left, they had arranged for Elizabeth to drive both Tamar and Victoria over to Helmsley on the following Tuesday to meet him. As Stephen Lassiter shook hands all round, he smiled at Elizabeth. 'See that your sister-in-law and the child bring their belongings, Mrs Oaks,' he said. 'If she is suitable, I would want her to take up her duties immediately.'

Elizabeth now began to have qualms, fearing that she had cornered him into taking a step he might regret. 'As I said, Mr Lassiter, there is no obligation to engage her. I can guarantee her honesty, but you must see what you think of her suitability for a gentleman's housekeeper,' she said, as he mounted his horse and, raising his hat in farewell, rode out of the farmyard.

Elizabeth turned back into the house, to be met by her mother's accusing glare. The cold grey eyes were as icy as she had ever encountered them. 'Well, I'm utterly speechless!' Ann Butler began and then went on at great length to tell Elizabeth what she thought of a daughter who could tell such lies.

At last, Elizabeth held up her hand to interrupt the flow. 'That's enough, Mother!' Her mother stopped in midsentence, dumbfounded that one of her children should speak to her thus. 'The only lie I've told is to invent a mythical husband, now conveniently dead, for Tamar. It's a small thing to do, to protect both her and the Oaks' name. Besides,' she went on, 'Helmsley's about seven miles away and not many folk from hereabouts go that way. Most prefer to go to Malton. It's the chance of a new life for Tamar

93

and you can't say she doesn't deserve it, after the way her father's treated her.'

Her mother sniffed. 'I don't suppose she's a bad lass, even though she was taken advantage of,' she admitted reluctantly. 'But that doesn't excuse lying for her. If she goes there, somebody'll no doubt find out in time. You mark my words,' she added ominously.

Elizabeth turned to Sarah. 'Don't you say anything about Mr Lassiter being young and good-looking,' she cautioned. 'We don't want to encourage her to take the job for the wrong reasons.'

A few moments later, Tamar came through the back door carrying Victoria. 'It's turning quite chilly,' she observed, 'so I brought her back. I take it he's gone by now?'

Elizabeth's eyes were dancing with excitement.'Yes, and guess what?' she laughed. 'He wants a housekeeper! I've to take you next Tuesday for an interview.'

Tamar looked from one to the other. 'You're having me on,' she gulped, her hand going to her throat to calm the pulse that was racing there. When Elizabeth persuaded her that it was true, she became panic-stricken. 'I daresn't go,' she protested.

'Daren't,' corrected Elizabeth automatically.'You must be careful with your speech, love.'

Eventually, Tamar was persuaded that this was a chance in a lifetime, and the weekend was spent in checking her meagre wardrobe. She and Elizabeth were much of a size, so the latter passed on a gown she had often worn at her Uncle's house. Even Mrs Butler donated a shawl. When all was ready, Tamar felt that if she succeeded in getting the job she would at least look reasonably dressed, in keeping with her position.

Was she to have the chance of a new life, she wondered, away from the dale which had begun to seem like a prison?

# CHAPTER NINE

By the time that Tuesday morning arrived, Tamar was a bundle of nerves. On the one hand she was thankful to be given the opportunity of starting afresh but on the other she faced the ordeal of her interview with apprehension. 'What if he doesn't like me?' She had asked the question time and again over the weekend.

'Then you're no worse off,' came the sensible reply.

When he went off to work that Tuesday morning, George put his arm round his sister's shoulders and gave her a squeeze. 'Look, love – this door will always be open to you,' he promised.'If you get the job, take it. If you don't settle, you can always come back and nothing will have changed.'

'Thanks, George.' She managed a little smile. 'I don't know whether I want t'job or not. Anyroad, if he offers it I sh'll take it and we'll see how I gct on.'

'That's the spirit!' George gave her a little pat and bending to lift Victoria on to his arm, he gave her a kiss. 'You be a good girl,' he admonished.

Once their scanty belongings and the cradle were stowed in the trap, Tamar glanced round in a final farewell. There had been heavy rain in the early morning and the sky was still overcast. In summer, under blue skies and with the trees clothed in their verdant green, the valley was beautiful but now the house looked grey and dark beneath lowering skies. The moor, which rose beyond the beck, was bleak, almost threatening with its sombre heights veiled in mist. Tamar shivered as she wrapped her cloak round both her and Victoria. 'I'm glad it's a dull day,' she said. 'If I was going in the summer I'd be sorry.'

Elizabeth had had a word with Annie Oaks after chapel on the Sunday, and now drew the pony to a halt outside her father-in-law's farm.

'I hope Faither's not in,' murmured Tamar as they went

into the kitchen. She breathed a sigh of relief to see that her mother was alone.

'Oh, lass.' Annie gathered her wayward daughter into her arms. She had seen little of Tamar since her move down to Cherry Tree Farm and appeared, now, to be losing her altogether. She could not help the tears which slid silently down her cheeks, as she kissed both Tamar and her child.

'Don't worry, Mam. We sh'll be all right,' Tamar assured her. 'I'll find some way to keep in touch, and let you know how we are.'

Since Victoria's birth, Tamar had ripened in maturity and had lost the edge of her sharpness. The girl, who had tended to be pert, was now a woman of gentler curves and a softer nature.

'We must be off, Ma,' Elizabeth reminded. 'It's over seven miles, even when we get up the hill.'

As they turned to go, Annie put her hand into her apron pocket. 'Eeh, Aah almost forgot,' she said, holding out her hand. There on the roughened, work-worn palm lay a gold wedding ring. 'Go on, tek it,' she instructed Tamar. 'It was your Grandma Oaks'. Faither give it ti me, when she died.'

Tamar hesitated. It would solve a problem which had been nagging. She held back, however, and did not immediately take the proffered ring. 'What about Faither?' she asked. 'What if he finds out?'

''E's nivver asked ti see it all t'years Aah've 'ad it,' Annie replied. 'Aah sh'll say Aah don't know where it is. An' that's true,' she added.

'Thanks, Mam.' Tamar slipped the ring onto her finger and held out her hand for her mother to see. 'Made to fit,' she smiled, as she picked up Victoria and went to the door.

Jonadab Oaks was working with his brother in the high field overlooking the farmstead. The farm-men's main occupation at this time of year was hedging and ditching and Jonadab and Uncle George were raking the hedge-slashings into small piles in order to burn them. Upon seeing Elizabeth's pony and trap come along the winding road that linked the two farms, Jonadab slowly straightened his back and leaned on his rake, screwing up his eyes to peer through the drifting wisps of wood-smoke. No emotion showed on his face as he watched Tamar and Victoria go in to make their farewell.

He sighed as he turned back to work alongside his brother, all the time keeping one eye on the door of the farmhouse. When the two women emerged, Tamar cradling Victoria in her arms, he paused once more to watch. His heart was heavy to see his daughter and her child leaving the valley, but he would not call out or wave to her. He was torn between sadness at the loss of yet another of his family and a stubborn refusal to hold out an olive branch. 'She gave me neither a look nor a wave,' he told himself bitterly, but it never occurred to him to make the gesture towards Tamar. 'Always defiant she was,' he brooded. He knew from Annie that Tamar was trying for a housekeeper's place, even though he had endeavoured to keep both her and her child down in Sleightholmedale. Now, as he watched her departure, he could only regard the move as a challenge to his authority.

The pony made heavy going up the hill which snaked up the steep incline out of the valley. Victoria had fallen asleep in Tamar's arms, so neither she nor Elizabeth could dismount to lighten the load. When they emerged from the canopy of trees at the summit Elizabeth halted Bella for a breather.

While the two women chatted, Elizabeth studied Tamar. Her cloak and bonnet were black, as was the gown which Elizabeth had altered slightly to fit her. Not only were they suitably sober for a young widow, but they bestowed on Tamar a look of demureness which, as Elizabeth knew only too well, was alien to her true nature. Her whole appearance was modest and unassuming so that Elizabeth was sure she would make a good impression on Stephen Lassiter. 'Shall we be long?' she asked now, as Elizabeth clicked her tongue and jerked the reins.

'No. I shan't go straight down Starfits Lane to the main Scarborough Road,' answered Elizabeth. 'We'll cut off and cross the ford at Kirkdale and join the main road further on.'

When at last they arrived in Helmsley, Tamar looked curiously around the little town. She could not help a feeling

97

of dismay as she took in the shabby cottages of Bondgate. The main street of Kirkbymoorside sloped steeply downwards, so that heavy rain washed the streets, carrying away any mud. Here there were no footpaths and the roads were coated with filth, so that those who walked them skidded and slithered, often landing in potholes filled with slush. Her eyes met Elizabeth's. 'Eeh, it's mucky!' she exclaimed, forgetting all the lessons Elizabeth had instilled into her.

'It is a mess,' the latter acknowledged, 'but perhaps this is the poorer part of the town. I can't see Church Street where Mr Lassiter lives being like this.'

'I only hope not,' said Tamar. 'Country muck is good honest muck, but this is disgusting.'

When they reached the market-place, conditions were even worse. There had obviously been a cattle market held a few days previously and the uncleared dung, wet with the morning's heavy rain, had been churned into the mud until the stench which rose from the water-logged ground was overpowering. With a grimace, Tamar drew her handkerchief from her sleeve and covered her nose, while turning Victoria's face into her shoulder in an effort to protect the little one from breathing in the offensive odour.

Seeing the gesture, Elizabeth felt a twinge of envy. Although she and George longed for children, there had been no sign of one since her miscarriage. She knew that he would miss Victoria as much as she herself would. 'We'd better try to find a tea-house,' she said. 'I told Mr Lassiter you'd be there in the afternoon.'

Although there were several inns, some of them looking most respectable, neither of them felt that it was correct or even safe for two unaccompanied females to venture inside such a place. Eventually they found a decent establishment run by two homely bodies, where they sat for half an hour over tea and scones, while Victoria had a basin of bread broken into warmed milk. Tamar nibbled her scone and sipped the tea with exasperating slowness, dawdling to put off the time when she must meet her prospective employer.

'Come along, lovey,' said Elizabeth to the baby. 'Finish up your pobs and we'll take your Mammy to see the gentleman.' Seeing the look of apprehension on Tamar's face, she rose to her feet with a smile. 'Come on, Tamar. You've two chances. He'll either set you on, or he won't. Don't forget – he wants a housekeeper as much as you want a job.' So saying, she picked up Victoria and led the way back to the trap. When they reached Church Street, they eyed the lawyer's house cautiously.

Although at each side there were terraces, it stood detached. It was larger than its neighbours, being double-fronted with handsome double doors. Tamar was relieved to see that the street was bordered by a footpath which was obviously swilled daily. 'At least I won't get my boots mucky . . . er – dirty.' She grinned at Elizabeth, although her expression was nervous.

'Don't forget all you've learned, and *smile*. You'll be fine,' urged Elizabeth. 'I'll come back in half an hour.' With that she laid the sleepy child in the cradle on the floor of the trap and drove away.

The door was answered to Tamar's pull on the bell by a little girl wearing a black dress and white apron. Although only about twelve years of age, she was bright and efficient. 'Yes, madam?' she piped, as she stood aside for Tamar to enter.

Tamar took a deep breath to steady her racing heart, and said, 'I have an appointment to see Mr Lassiter.'

'What name shall I say?' the girl asked.

After only a moment's hesitation, Tamar replied with a confidence she did not feel, 'Mrs Oaks.'

While she waited for the maid's return, Tamar looked round the house with interest. To her unsophisticated eyes, it was grander than she could ever have imagined. The hall was wide with a beautiful curved staircase leading upwards on the left. The spindles and sweeping banister gleamed with the patina of constant polishing. She only had time to take in the floor of patterned tiles, before the maid was back.

'T'master'll see you now,' she said. ''E's in his study.'

Tamar followed her down the hall and under the sweep of the stairs. Here she was surprised to see a door. At the maid's knock there came a call to enter, and the girl opened the door, motioning Tamar inside.

Once more, Tamar was impressed by the luxury of every-thing. Although fairly small, the room was expensively fur-nished. The floor was carpeted and the large oak desk and rich leather chairs all shone with a deep glow, only achieved through constant burnishing. The man at the desk rose as the door closed behind her and came forward, hand outstretched. Tamar had expected the solicitor to be elderly and this had been confirmed, at first sight, by the silvery sheen of his hair. As he approached to shake her hand, she looked up and caught her breath upon seeing the most handsome young man she had ever laid eyes on.

Stephen was equally startled. When he had agreed to interview Elizabeth Oaks' sister-in-law, he had held no preconceived ideas as to what to expect. He had been rather annoyed that there was a child, but if the mother were suitable, had determined to make it clear that his peace must not be disturbed. Seeing the slight, black-clothed figure enter his study, he had automatically risen in greeting without really noticing the woman in detail.

As he approached, and Tamar raised her eyes to his, he hesitated as he felt the impact of her beauty. The sombre clothing and the midnight blackness of her hair only served to highlight the exquisite face. She was pale with apprehen-sion and her dark-fringed eyes seemed to glow with amber light as they met his. Neither spoke for an instant but then he moved forward and clasped her hand. 'Good afternoon, Mrs Oaks. Please sit down,' he said, as he motioned her to a chair facing his desk.

Tamar felt as though her ribcage would not rise to allow her to draw breath. She felt, too, that when he spoke, she would be unable to answer. She kept her eyes downcast and tried to pass her tongue over her teeth, which had suddenly become dry, so that her lips clung to them. To her dismay her tongue was also so dry that she felt she could not moisten her mouth either.

Seeing the slight figure, her eyes lowered, Stephen felt an upsurge of sympathy. She looked so frail and nervous to be out in the world looking for employment, that he was filled with compassion.

Tamar's brain was in a whirl. *I must get the job.* The

thought went round in her mind. She was unaware that a similar determination was now spinning in Stephen's mind. '*She must come here. I must take care of her.*' All his lawyer's hard-headedness had gone. He saw only this slip of a girl, left to bring up a child alone and yet looking little more than a child herself. Tamar's appearance belied her twenty-two years, and she had an air of wistfulness and frailty which did not reflect her inner core of strength.

Afterwards, neither could have told what had been said but when the interview was over, Tamar knew that this was to be her home, and her daughter's home: this charming man was to be her employer and that she was to be paid a wage of eight shillings a week. She had never in her life had money of her own. Everything had been provided by her parents and she felt dazzled by the prospect which lay before her. 'What if I can't do the job?' she worried silently, but then thrust the thought away. She could only do her best and, whether it lasted or not, this new life would be an adventure.

'Will you take a glass of Madeira wine, to seal our agreement?' His voice broke into her reverie. Tamar hesitated, about to say that having been brought up a Methodist, she did not take strong drink but she might as well be hung for a sheep as a lamb, she thought, curiosity overcoming her scruples.

'Thank you, sir,' she answered. 'That would be very pleasant.' She was surprised to discover that she enjoyed the wine and as she sipped it, her cheeks became flushed with colour and she took on a vivacity she had not felt since before the scene when her father had found out that she was pregnant.

Stephen was enchanted. As she relaxed and became more animated, he realised how much he was looking forward to having her in his home. Although her speech was slow and deliberate, making it obvious that she was trying hard with her accent, there were times when she lapsed into the Dales brogue, which he found more attractive in her.

When Elizabeth arrived, the two were chatting and smiling like old friends: she was pleased, but not surprised to find that Lassiter intended to employ Tamar. At his suggestion that they should take a cup of tea before Elizabeth left, they all moved into the drawing room, a large, square room at the front of the house. Tamar had found the hall and the study impressive but now she was speechless. The ceiling was high with a beautifully moulded cornice and central rose, intricately modelled. Above the fireplace, the whole chimney breast was covered by a huge mirror, stretching from mantle to frieze, with a magnificently carved and gilded frame. As she and Elizabeth took their seats on a sofa, close to the fire, Tamar lifted Victoria to sit between them. Stephen Lassiter looked from the other side of the fireplace, where he was tugging the bell-pull.

'She seems to be a good little girl,' he observed.

'Well, she's only young, sir,' replied Tamar. 'I shall keep her out of your way as much as possible.'

He fingered his moustache for a moment, considering. 'It may be as well if we have a nursemaid,' he said. 'We'll go to the Union House and see if they have a suitable girl.'

Tamar could hardly believe her ears. She felt that it must all be a dream. Before she could answer, however, the door opened and the little maid came in carrying a silver tea service on a large silver tray. It was obvious that the combined weight was almost too much for her and she placed it carefully on a walnut pedestal table, with a release of pent-up breath.

'Thank you, Tempy. Is Mrs Judd about?'

'Yes, sir. She's in the hall, with the cakes,' answered Tempy.

'Ask her to come in, will you?' he ordered. When the cook appeared, carrying a three-tier wooden cake-stand, she was introduced to them. 'These ladies are both called Mrs Oaks,' said Stephen, 'and this one is going to take up her position here as housekeeper,' indicating Tamar. Noticing that Elizabeth did not attempt to shake hands, but merely nodded and smiled, Tamar did the same. The cook placed the cake-stand down close to the hearth rug and gave Tamar a calculating look. Tamar was disturbed to see hostility in her eyes.

'Mrs Judd is a treasure,' continued Stephen. 'All my friends envy me her skill. I know that you'll get on well together.' Tamar knew full well that they would not, but contented herself with outstaring the woman, who dropped her eyes and made for the door.

As Tamar slowly nibbled a piece of cake, which certainly lived up to Stephen's assessment of Mrs Judd's ability, she reflected on the cook's attitude. She realised with certainty that for some reason, the woman already disliked her. Perhaps her life in Helmsley was not to be as smooth as she had hoped. She was not to know, at this stage, that there was nothing personal in the woman's animosity. Mrs Judd wanted no interference in the way she ran the kitchen and did not feel well-disposed to having a child clutter up the house.

Tempy, however, had no such reservations. She made it obvious that she wanted to welcome Tamar and seemed happy to have a toddler in the house. Tamar found out, later, that she was the eldest of a large family and had missed them deeply when she came into service.

Now she led them upstairs to the bedroom which Tamar and Victoria were to share. 'Goodison will bring your things up,' she assured Tamar.

'Who's he?' asked Elizabeth.

'Mr Goodison drives the carriage, does the garden, brings coal in and things like that,' answered Tempy. 'Mrs Judd's the cook and I wait at table, answer the door and see to the beds and things. A woman called Mrs Robinson comes in mornings to do scrubbing and such.'

Tamar digested this information as she removed her bonnet and laid it on the bed. 'Everything seems well taken care of,' she commented.

Elizabeth nodded. 'The household certainly seems to run smoothly,' she agreed. 'Remember what I've taught you and you should be all right. I've no doubt you'll take your meals with Mr Lassiter and keep him company if he's at home in the evenings.'

As Tempy went to the door to open it for Goodison, Tamar's eyes met Elizabeth's. Neither spoke, however, while the manservant placed the cradle on the floor and the basket on the bed. As he went out, Tempy turned and eyed the one basket. 'Do you want me to unpack for you, ma'am?' she asked, recalling her position.

'No, thank you, Tempy. We'll manage,' smiled Elizabeth.

When the door closed, Tamar swung in a flurry of indecision towards her sister-in-law. 'It's no good! I can't do it,' she protested, her eyes filling. 'I'm worried about doing the accounts: and anyway, that cook doesn't like me.'

'Whether the cook likes you or not is of no consequence,' Elizabeth answered firmly. 'Pull yourself together, Tamar. You have the chance of a lifetime here. Ask Mr Lassiter if you may have the account book and then study it thoroughly – you'll soon see how to do it.'

'It's a lovely room.' Tamar looked round, appreciatively. Unlike the dark rich furniture of the downstairs rooms, the bedroom was daintier, having a wallpaper covered in blue flowers and long blue curtains at the window. A cheery blaze flickered in the grate. This in Tamar's eyes was the height of luxury. She had never before seen a fire in a bedroom. The fireplace was surrounded by a brass-topped fireguard. Although of oak, the furniture was golden in hue, giving the room an attractive lightness. 'I do hope I manage to keep the job.' Tamar looked more confident after Elizabeth's reassurance. 'He's paying me eight shillings a week.'

'Don't fritter it away,' warned Elizabeth. 'You'll have your keep, so try to put it in the bank. Both you and Victoria will need new clothes soon, but you should be able to put a good bit by.'

Before going downstairs to take her leave, Elizabeth had one last piece of advice. 'It's an odd position, being a housekeeper. You're neither fish, fowl nor good red meat. You're stuck in the middle really, without friends. Never forget, love, that you're above the servants, but you're below the master. You mustn't hobnob with them; don't expect him to hobnob with you.'

Standing in the drawing room doorway, Stephen watched Tamar wave goodbye to her sister-in-law. He noticed the slump of her shoulders as she turned from the door and then saw the way she squared them and lifted her chin, as she stepped purposefully down the hall.

'Mr Lassiter, perhaps I could have the account book to

study and if you've time, I'd like to know my duties.' She spoke with firmness and as she smiled up at him, Stephen felt his pulse quicken. Tamar was not what he had had in mind as his housekeeper but he was glad she had come. Already the house seemed brighter for her presence. As she passed before him into the study, Tamar thought with conviction, 'I am going to like living here!'

# CHAPTER TEN

Tamar Oaks found life in Helmsley a far cry from life on her father's farm. Although she was cat-like in her enjoyment of the comfort and luxury of the house, she found herself unable to settle to town life. Smaller than Kirkbymoorside, the town was more squalid than the neat little town, which was the only one she had known. The Borough Beck, which ran through the streets to join the River Rye at the far end of town, was little more than an open sewer which she had to cross if she ventured out on foot.

True to his word, Stephen had engaged a ten year old from the workhouse, to look after Victoria. Tamar had been rather nervous in the beginning, to leave the child in Gertie's care, but soon realised that the girl was not only strong, but dependable. She heaved the toddler about when her little legs grew tired and the two played happily and safely in the back garden whenever it was fine, where, more often than not, Goodison was there to keep a watchful eye on them.

Despite her early fears, Tamar found her duties undemanding. She was more than willing to fall in with the cook's suggestions for the meals, which resulted in the surly Mrs Judd gradually accepting her. The acceptance was grudging and the woman did not take the trouble to hide her dislike, but at least they managed to rub along with no open antagonism.

The Christmas period had been unseasonably mild, bringing to Tamar's mind a saying of her mother's: 'A green Christmas and a full churchyard.' True enough, January brought an epidemic of chest complaints and there were several deaths in the town.

One morning, as he read his paper at the breakfast table, Stephen looked across at Tamar. 'I hear that a client of mine, old Mrs Marshall of Canon's Garth, is ill. Would you take her a basket of food and see if she needs anything from the shops?' he asked.

When Tamar left Mrs Marshall's, she decided to cut through the churchyard to the apothecary's where she wanted to buy some medicine for Mrs Marshall and also something to rub on Victoria's chest – although it went against the grain to pay good money for such a thing when at home there was always a plentiful supply of goose-grease. As she walked along, deep in thought, she was aware of a figure standing on the path before her. Looking up, her throat constricted as her eyes met the mocking brown ones of the man who had attacked her at Cherry Tree Farm.

'Well . . . if it isn't the Widow Oaks,' he said, and touched his forehead in a sardonic salute.

Tamar stopped dead and then let out her breath in a long but silent sigh, determined not to let him guess the panic which had caused her heart to beat so strongly that she thought he must hear it. 'Get out of my way.' She spoke with a determination she did not feel.

The white teeth flashed, as he grinned impudently. 'Don't worry, *Mrs* Oaks. You're safe enough – and so is your secret,' he added. After a tantalising pause he continued almost casually, 'For the present, that is.'

Tamar thought she was going to faint. All feeling seemed to drain away from her body and she felt weak. She stared at him challengingly. 'If that's a threat, you can forget it!' she snapped, not bothering to deny that she was, indeed, unmarried.

As she moved forward down the path, he turned to walk beside her. 'No doubt you're as surprised to see me as I was to see you in the market place, a few weeks ago.' He spoke in a conversational tone, all menace gone.

Tamar listened to the lilting voice, describing how he had followed her back to Church Street and then made discreet enquiries to discover how it was that she was now in Helmsley. She was filled with dismay. Was her cosy niche in Stephen's household going to be jeopardised through this stranger? She turned to look at him through narrowed eyes, as they sauntered along the path, trying to assess how to deal with him.

As he caught the look, he stopped and catching her elbow, swung her to face him. 'There's no need to worry about me,' he promised. 'I mean you no harm. But mind,' he went on, 'you'll never be rid of me. Wherever you go and whatever you do, I shall follow.' As she twisted out of his grasp and made her way down through the churchyard, the mocking voice followed her. 'One day, Widow Oaks, you'll belong to Gareth Davis – make no mistake about that.'

During the weeks that followed, Tamar went about her business in the town in a state of near-panic. On one or two occasions, she caught a glimpse of Gareth Davis in the distance but gradually, she recovered her confidence and became her old spirited self.

Stephen Lassiter was becoming more and more captivated with her and made no attempt to hide the fact. As the spring progressed, Tamar could feel the tension in Stephen and was aware that he would soon be unable to contain his feelings. She could not believe that he would marry her and was determined to keep her head and not give in to him. 'Once bitten twice shy,' she told herself sternly. Each day, however, saw Stephen even more enthralled with her. At first it was her incredible beauty which had captured his interest. When they sat together in the evenings, her demure demeanour and eagerness to cater for his comfort delighted him, until he thought her the most perfect and attractive creature he had ever encountered.

Each new day saw Tamar wondering if Stephen would declare his feelings for her, wondering what exactly he did feel towards her and how she should react. She was unsure of her own feelings towards her employer. He was attentive and kind both to her and her child, and she was certain she could love him. More than anything, however, she needed the security of a stable relationship before she gave free rein to her emotions.

One evening in early May, he seemed ill at ease and restless. Tamar kept her eyes fixed on her needlework with such concentration and intensity that eventually the stitches became blurred and seemed to run into each other. Pushing the needle through the material, she closed her eyes to rest them from the fine work. When she opened them, it was to meet Stephen's, which were regarding her with deep intensity. 'Tamar.' As he breathed her name, he rose from his chair and crossed towards her. Taking her hand, he raised it to his lips and kissed it gently.

Tamar began to tremble. She did not speak, but her tawny eyes were lit with a golden glow as her lips parted slightly.

'Tamar, you must know that I love you.' He spoke now with more urgency. 'I can't go on without you.' Still there was no reply, as Tamar waited, breath caught and heart racing. Stephen became confused by her silence. He dropped her hands and seized her by the shoulders, looking into her face with desperation. 'I need you, Tamar. I want you!' By now his voice was filled with urgency, but still she made no answer. He took a deep breath. 'You must marry me, my darling.'

Tamar's pent-up breath was released in a shuddering sigh, as her heart soared in a delirium of thankfulness. He wanted to marry her! 'Oh, thank you, God,' she exulted. But no sooner had the thought passed through her mind, than it was overtaken by doubts. If she married Stephen Lassiter, he would expect to meet the family. Once this occurred, she realised that she could no longer keep the secret of Victoria's birth from him. It would be made obvious to him that she was no widow. She raised her hand to her forehead and sank back into her chair. There was also the problem of Gareth Davis, who seemed to be living in the town and had guessed, or ferreted out, her secret. Tamar's mind was in turmoil. She had just been presented with the chance of a life which was the answer to her dreams and, now, she could see it slipping away.

She made an instant decision. Raising tear-brimmed eyes to Stephen's, she slowly stood and faced him. His face was a picture of concern. He leaned forward and put an arm tenderly round her shoulders. 'Tamar, my dear. Whatever is wrong?'

The tears spilled over as she raised her hand to her throat in an unconsciously appealing gesture. 'I can't marry you. You won't want to marry me, when you know,' she faltered.

'Is it that you can't love me?' he demanded.

'Oh no! I do love you. Indeed I do,' she protested.

'What, then?'

'I'm not really a widow.' The words came spilling out, once she had decided to confess. 'I've never been married, Stephen. I – I . . .'

He placed a finger over her lips, stemming the flow. 'That's enough, Tamar. You've said the only thing I want to hear. Now tell me that you will marry me and you'll make me the happiest man alive.'

Tamar felt faint with relief. She would be Mrs Stephen Lassiter! She would never again live in the dale; never again be subject to her father's authority. As the wife of a successful lawyer, her future would be secure.

Now Stephen hesitated, feeling his way gingerly. 'Who is Victoria's father? I know it happened before we met, but I feel . . .' He paused, unwilling to raise a shadow between them, but anxious to know whom Tamar had loved before and why she had not married. 'I feel I should know,' he finished, rather lamely.

Tamar eyed the carpet and shifted her toes. Eventually she answered. 'I was taken against my will, by a member of the gentry,' she said in a low voice. 'He laughed when my father approached him about marrying me.'

'His loss is my gain.' The explanation satisfied Stephen's curiosity. He decided not to probe further. It was a common enough tale, and his heart went out to the girl.

The face which she raised to Stephen's was so radiant that his heart began to race as he gazed at the parted lips, showing even white teeth, and the amber eyes, fringed with night-black lashes on which the traces of tears still lingered. He swept her into his arms and covered her face and throat with fierce kisses. For a few ecstatic moments Tamar responded with a passion which took him by surprise, but then she began to struggle in his arms and pushed against his chest, until he released her.

As they drew apart, each slightly panting, Stephen took her hand. 'Forgive me, my dear,' he murmured, 'but I love you so much.' He paused and considered for a few seconds. 'Perhaps it would be as well if you returned to your brother's, or perhaps your father's home, until the marriage,' he suggested tentatively.

'No!' Tamar's reply came too sharply. She had no wish to change her life of comfort for the rigorous life at Aumery Park Farm, even for a few months. She smiled into his eyes and then looked downwards until her lashes lay like two black fans, veiling her eyes. 'I can't bear to be away from you, even for a few months. My time here with you has been the happiest in my life,' she told him with a winsome smile. Seeing the adoration in his eyes as he looked down into her face, she pressed on with a little more daring. 'I hope it will only be months – or even weeks – before we can be married?' The words were said with hesitation, but there was a question in her tone.

Stephen was enchanted that her ardour matched his own. 'As soon as it can be arranged,' he promised, to Tamar's delight. His keen lawyer's brain took over now. There could be no calling of the banns, for that would reveal Tamar's status as a widow to be false. He would have to get a special licence, he decided. That way, they could be married with the minimum of either fuss or delay. Once he had held Tamar and felt her answering passion, Stephen was determined that she must become his legal wife as soon as possible.

'I shall of course adopt Victoria and give her my name,' he announced. To Tamar this was the gilt on the gingerbread. Her darling child would be given a name and be removed for ever from the stigma of her birth. She realised that her marriage to Stephen would be a nine days' wonder in the little town, but the average person's memory was short and Victoria would soon be accepted as Stephen's natural daughter. 'We must visit our parents and tell them,' he suddenly recollected.

Tamar went cold. She had never met Stephen's parents, but knew that his father was titled and they lived on a large estate about twenty-five miles away, over towards Malton.

'Why have you turned pale, my darling?' he laughed.

'They won't want you to marry me,' she blurted out.

'Which ones are *they*? Do you mean your parents won't want me to marry you?' he teased.

'Of course not – I mean *your* parents. They'll object to you marrying a nobody.'

'Tamar,' he said quietly. 'Look at me.' As she dutifully did so, he caressed her cheek. 'You are not a nobody. You're a very beautiful and desirable woman who is going to be my wife.'

Nonetheless, Stephen had an uneasy feeling that Tamar was right. Remembering the eligible girls invited over by his mother whenever he was visiting, he appreciated that, without exception, they had been the daughters of wealthy families. He knew that his mother would oppose this marriage, yet he was determined to have Tamar, despite any opposition.

After writing to his parents the following day, Stephen told Tamar, 'I have to go to York on business and as I have some shopping to do, I shall take Goodison and the carriage. We shall be back tomorrow, so you'll be all right. Then we must arrange for you to go and break the news of our forthcoming marriage to your own family.'

While Stephen was away, Tamar tried to find a reason for not going back to Sleightholmedale. Although she longed to see her mother and missed Elizabeth and George, she had no desire to see her father again. Now that she had experienced another way of life, she realised what a martinet he was, always dominating every facet of his family's lives. The solution came to her quite suddenly: if she chose a Wednesday for her visit, she could see her mother and Elizabeth in Kirkby market and, in that way, avoid a meeting with her father.

Having settled this problem to her satisfaction, she ran to greet Stephen with a light heart upon his return from York. Goodison followed him into the hall carrying a great number of parcels, among which was a large dress box.

'Take this upstairs please, Tempy, into Mrs Oaks' bedroom,' commanded her master. Turning to Tamar, he added, 'Slip upstairs and try it on. Come down then to my study and let me see.'

When Tamar opened the box, both she and the maid gasped with incredulity as she lifted out the most beautiful gown she had ever seen. It was of heavy silk in a deep amber shade, almost the exact colour of her eyes. 'There, let me help, madam,' urged Tempy, as Tamar's shaking hands fumbled with the buttons of the black bodice and skirt she wore.

When the new gown was finally on and Tempy had fastened the last of the tiny buttons down the back, Tamar looked at herself in the full-length mirror which fronted the wardrobe.

'It's a bit on the roomy side,' said Tempy prosaically, 'but it can soon be altered.' Tamar was unable to reply. The reflection in the mirror was of a woman of outstanding beauty. The colour of the gown brought light to her face – light which had in some measure been dimmed by the sombre black she had worn in her guise as a young widow. Her eyes, enhanced by the shade of the dress, were lit by golden lights and shone out from her face like pieces of amber glowing in sunlight.

When she opened the study door, Stephen was standing behind the desk, studying something which lay before him on the desk-top. As he raised his eyes upon hearing the click of the door, he was unable to speak, so overwhelmed was he by her appearance. Seeing the effect it had upon him, Tamar was overcome by a sudden shyness. She was conscious of the transformation and felt unsure of herself, as though she had been metamorphosed into a different person. To hide her confusion and to give Stephen time to adjust to the new Tamar, she turned slowly round in front of him, arms outstretched, as though to show off the gown. When she once more faced him, she gave a mock curtsey. 'There, sir! Will I do?' she asked, with humility.

He sprang forward and took her in his arms. 'When I saw that gown, I knew it was ideal for you, but . . .' he paused. 'You were lovely enough before, but now! I just don't know how to express what I feel. You look like a princess.'

She gave him a little push. 'Don't crush my gown! Oh, Stephen, I can't thank you enough. I never knew that there were such lovely clothes to wear.'

'You'll have many more, my dearest. I shall have pleasure in showing off my wife to all the county,' he laughed.

Turning back to the desk, he took up the jewel-case on which his attention had been concentrated when she had entered. 'This will complete the picture,' he said, removing an exquisite golden necklace set with stones the colour of liquid honey when it catches the sun.

'What are they?' she whispered, as he fastened the jewels round her throat.

'Topaz. Tamar's gems, to match Tamar's eyes,' he answered teasingly. 'Wear them and your gown for dinner tonight, and they can be saved for special occasions.'

Tamar passed her hands over the silk of the skirt, which shimmered as though it had a life of its own. 'This'll be for better days than Sundays,' she promised as she made for the door.

'Wait! I was so stunned when you came through that door that the most important thing slipped my mind.'

Stephen's voice made her turn in surprise. 'More important than these?' Her voice was filled with surprise. 'Whatever can that be?'

Stephen smiled. He drew a little box from his pocket and flicked open the lid. 'Your betrothal ring. I hope it fits.' There against the white satin lining was a ruby which caught the firelight from the grate and glowed and flickered as though the flames were imprisoned within it. As he took her hand to slip it on to her finger, Tamar half-drew back. Once the ring was placed on her finger, had she taken an irrevocable step? Looking at Stephen, whose whole face shone with admiration, and noting the gifts with which he had showered her, she mentally shook herself and held out her hand, fingers spread, to receive the ring.

'There,' he said with satisfaction. 'Topaz for your eyes and a ruby for your lips.'

As she looked at the magnificent jewel gracing her finger, Tamar chided herself for her foolishness. She was the luckiest girl in the world!

A day or two later, Stephen was sipping his after-lunch cup of tea in the drawing-room when he heard a carriage draw up outside. Crossing to the window he saw a travelling coach with the Lassiter coat of arms emblazoned on the door. 'Damn!' he muttered as he strode swiftly across the room and tugged the bell-pull. Before the bell in the kitchen had time to stop, he was jerking it again. Tempy came scurrying quickly through the hall, drying her hands on her kitchen apron.

'Run upstairs quickly and help Mrs Oaks to put on her new gown. Ask her to come down as soon as possible to be presented to my mother,' he ordered.

Tamar's hands shook so much that she could not have managed without the little maid's help. Once she was into the gown, she looked into the mirror. She had no time to unpin her hair and re-dress it, but the strands which had escaped from her bun and framed her face in tendrils were quite becoming, she decided. 'Pass me the necklace,' she said, pointing to the dressing table.

Tempy hesitated. 'If you don't mind me saying, madam, I think they're a bit too much for morning,' she advised. 'I've noticed that ladies who call in the mornings don't usually wear fancy jewels – just chains or pearls.'

'Thank you, Tempy! Bring a tray to the drawing room with whatever Cook thinks is suitable.' As she made for the door, she paused. 'And tell Gertie to keep Victoria out of the way,' she added.

In the hall Tamar paused and took two or three deep breaths to recover her composure. There was a murmur of voices from the drawing room and she had her hand on the knob, ready to enter when Stephen's was suddenly raised in anger so that she could hear his words quite clearly. 'I am not the eldest son, Mother, so can make my choice where I wish. Hilary will inherit the title and estate and that will influence his choice of wife, but I shall marry whomsoever I like.'

Remembering that her position in the household was still that of housekeeper, Tamar gave a knock before opening the door. The woman who was seated in the high-backed chair usually occupied by Stephen, was dressed in a deep wine-coloured travelling costume of velvet. A matching hat had been removed and placed on her knee. She had opened her short jacket, showing a blouse of grey silk; her soft kid gloves and shoes were also of grey and, although obviously costly, the outfit only served to emphasise the uniform greyness of her appearance. Her beautifully dressed hair was grey; her complexion was of a greyish, putty hue, but her eyes were the greyest of all – a clear, cold grey, which regarded Tamar with an icy dislike.

Stephen moved forward and took Tamar's hand, leading her towards the fireplace. 'Mother, this is my fiancée, Tamar Oaks. Tamar, I'd like you to meet my mother, Lady Lassiter.'

Remembering the lessons instilled in her by Elizabeth, Tamar did not extend her hand first. If there were to be a shaking of hands, the other woman, being older and also higher in social rank, would instigate the move. So Tamar merely inclined her head and said, in a low, well-modulated voice, 'How do you do.'

Lady Lassiter merely nodded.

'She may not like me,' thought Tamar, 'but she's got me to put up with.' As she took her seat on the sofa, facing Stephen's mother, she turned on her sunniest smile. 'I've ordered refreshments, Stephen, so do sit down,' and she patted the sofa beside her. Seeing them seated together on the opposite side of the hearth, Stephen's mother bit her lip. Tamar had put her at a disadvantage by making them seem to be a team, with his mother opposing them.

Over a glass of wine and sandwiches they chatted in a desultory fashion, Lady Lassiter's probing questions being parried by Tamar in a guileless and seemingly innocent manner. All that her interrogator got from her was that her father was a farmer round Kirkbymoorside way and that her husband had been a farmer's son.

'How did your husband die?'

Tamar answered with no hesitation. 'He was killed by a bull.' Touching her handkerchief to her eyes, she went on to describe George's encounter with the bull on Butlers' farm. Clem Magson the cowman played the part of her hapless husband, who was gored before his rescuer could gain control over the bull. So vividly was the story told that Lady Lassiter had no hesitation in accepting it and even Stephen was impressed by the tale.

Feeling that she had acquitted herself well in the face of the opposition, Tamar said her farewells to Lady Lassiter, and left them. As she crossed the hall, she heard the thin voice raised petulantly. 'If you ask me, Stephen, the girl's an opportunist!' Tamar could not hear Stephen's answer, but was satisfied that she had not let him down.

Indeed, when his mother had departed, Stephen declared that his love for her was as unswerving as ever and explained that he had applied for a special licence.

'When it comes through, I want us to be married without delay,' he insisted. 'So you must go and see your parents.'

'Yes, I'll go next Wednesday,' Tamar promised, secure in the knowledge that with that arrangement she could avoid a meeting with her father.

# CHAPTER ELEVEN

The following Wednesday was a typical April day when Elizabeth Oaks set out for market. Although it was bright, the clouds were scudding across the sky and the tops of the highest trees in the valley were bowing before the fresh breeze. Glancing round as the pony stepped out briskly, she drew her cloak more closely round her, for the wind had begun to pick up. She could see the clouds piling up in dark ranks over the moors at the head of the dale.

The rain when it came was gossamer-fine, beading her lashes and the front of her hair with silvery droplets. It clung to her face like fine threads, which she brushed away with irritation. 'We can do without this on a market day,' she told herself, as she halted the pony outside Aumery Park Farm.

She entered the kitchen, where the table was covered with Annie Oaks' goods, ready to be sold at the market, and her mother-in-law exclaimed, 'Oh no! It's never begun to rain, has it?'

'Only mizzling,' answered Elizabeth, 'but the wind's getting up quite strong.'

Martha, the only daughter still living at home, came hurrying from the dairy carrying two large flat-bottomed baskets. She was followed by Lydia the maid, with two others. As they lined the baskets with snowy-white cloths, Annie supervised the packing of eggs, dressed chickens, jars of curd, cheeses and all kinds of country produce. 'Aah'm sorry Aah'm a bit late, love,' she apologised, 'but Aah seem ti 'ave a lot ti tek this week.'

'Good,' Elizabeth answered. 'The more we sell, the more money for us.' She continued, 'Don't mention it to anybody yet, Ma, but I've been making enquiries about renting a room to open as a tea-house.'

Annie looked at her in amazement. 'A tea-house?' she echoed incredulously.

'I'd only open it on Wednesdays and perhaps Saturdays,' Elizabeth added. 'Now Mother and Sarah are down at Cherry Tree, there's not enough to keep us all occupied, so I thought I could earn a bit more towards a farm of our own.'

Cherry Tree Farm was rented by Jonadab Oaks and run in conjunction with his own farm. Although George had his own sheep and reared a few pigs and hens, Elizabeth would not rest until he was his own boss instead of being, as she considered it, under his father's thumb.

When they bustled out to load Annie's trap, there was a pause in the rain, but the heavy clouds were making rapid progress across the sky towards them.

'It'll be a dowly day, standing t'market,' observed Annie as they started out, each in charge of her own pony and trap.

'Let's hope it takes up a bit,' Elizabeth replied, as she clicked her tongue and gave Bella a twitch with the driving-whip.

As they approached the steep and snaking hill, which climbed through a tunnel of overhanging trees out of the dale, the rushing wind drove the rooks before it, soaring like death-black tatters. Their hoarse cries rang out in a dirge as the rain began to hurl itself down in a torrential downpour. Both women sighed with relief as they reached the shelter of the trees. Although the leaf canopy was sparse, it being only April, the branches interlaced above their heads gave some shelter from the worst of the deluge.

By the time the ponies had wound their way slowly into the avenue of trees at the top of the ravine, the heavy shower had moved on and although the wind was still gusty, the sky was clear and bright. When they had reached the market, stabled their ponies in the Black Swan yard and arranged themselves on hired chairs, the weather appeared more settled. The cobbles were still rain-washed, but were drying quickly in the bright spring sunshine.

The improvement in the weather had brought out throngs of shoppers and the farmers' wives were soon doing a brisk trade, the townsfolk eager to purchase the fresh country produce. Elizabeth had a steady flow of customers for her

119

home-baking: over the past few weeks she had been sounding them out regarding the opening of a second tea-house. She realised that the only other one in the town could not really cope with the demand on market days and Saturdays.

Elizabeth was an intelligent and lively woman, intensely ambitious for George. Since her miscarriage on the day of her father's funeral there had still been no sign of another child. This was a source of sadness for both Elizabeth and George, but she was determined to channel her creativity in another direction and at the same time, earn more money to add to their nest egg.

During a lull in trading, as they sat relishing a couple of Elizabeth's pork pies, she was suddenly struck with an idea. 'Why don't we apply for the next two vacancies in the market-hall? After all, it only costs a penny a week to rent a stall and it cuts out the uncertainty of the weather.'

Annie hesitated. 'Aah allus thinks we'd miss t'passing trade,' she pointed out. 'Some folks never go into t'covered market.'

'Most of our customers are regulars,' Elizabeth argued, 'and if I can find some way of boiling a kettle – a brazier perhaps, I could serve teas in there. After all, a lot of farmers round here are Methodists and won't go into an ale-house. It means that they have to use Mrs Sleightholme's tea-house, which is so dainty that they feel out of place, or they remain thirsty while they're at the market. I'm sure they'd be glad of a mug of tea in the market-hall.'

They sat in silence for a few moments, each mulling over this new idea. Annie was a traditionalist and had never contemplated carrying on in any other way than the one begun more than thirty years before, when she had first attended the market as a young bride in her mother-in-law's company. 'T'Oaks 'as allus sat 'ere, opposite t'Black Swan,' she thought. 'Folks expect it.' However, the flow of customers started again and as the two women smiled and chatted while serving, each was contemplating the suggestion made by Elizabeth.

Faced with the steep pull up the main street of Kirkby-moorside, the covered carriage carrying Tamar and Victoria slowed down so that Tamar, leaning forward to look out of the window, could take it all in. How spruce and neat the town looked compared with Helmsley, she thought. Seeing the fine, stone-built houses lining both sides of the street and the cobbles, washed free of any clinging mud by the earlier heavy shower, she was unexpectedly overwhelmed by a feeling of homesickness. True, there were plenty of fine houses in Helmsley, one of which was her home, but there were also slums, and what dilapidated hovels they were . . .

As they drew level with the Black Swan, she called out for Goodison to stop the coach. She had bought herself a rich brown cloak, which she wore over the golden gown, as she thought of it. Knowing that, once married, she would have no more money worries, she had also invested in a cherry-red velvet coat and bonnet for Victoria, who at the age of twenty months was both walking and talking.

When the carriage stopped in the road opposite to where they sat, Annie and Elizabeth looked towards it with curiosity. Perhaps they were going to have some of the gentry as customers.

Having secured his pair of fine chestnuts, the coachman opened the door and lifted down a toddler, setting her on the edge of the road and then helping the other passenger down. Before turning towards the market women, she opened her reticule and took out some coins. 'Thank you, Goodison. Put the carriage in the yard at the back of the Black Swan, and ask the ostler to bring me a chair. When I want you again, I'll send word.'

As he remounted and turned the carriage towards the inn-yard, she took Victoria's hand and crossed towards her mother and Elizabeth. As Tamar approached, Annie felt faint and her usually rosy face blanched so that the veins in her cheeks stood out like a network of mottled threads. 'It is! It's Tamar,' she whispered. Not for the life of her could she have risen to her feet.

Elizabeth leaned over and began to chafe her hands. 'It's all right, Ma. It *is* Tamar and little Victoria,' she added, holding out her arms to the child, to give Tamar and Annie a chance to regain their composure. 'Come to Auntie Elizabeth. You remember me,' she smiled, as she bent down and lifted the child on to her lap.

Annie had resigned herself to never setting eyes on Tamar again. There were plenty of families who never saw their children any more, once they had been sent out to service. Elizabeth had told her that she intended to drive out to Helmsley one day and visit Tamar, and had invited Annie to accompany her, but she dared not go against Jonadab's wishes. Jonadab was steadfast in his refusal to speak Tamar's name, or to have her referred to by the rest of the family. Annie and her youngest daughter often talked about Tamar and her child, wondering how they were. These conversations, however, only took place when Jonadab was safely away from the house.

Although she loved her husband, Annie avoided doing or saying anything to upset him. While she was a tolerant and easygoing woman, marriage to Jonadab Oaks had caused her to look upon these traits in her character as weaknesses, rather than strengths. For Jonadab there were no grey areas of life; everything was black or white, right or wrong, sinful or virtuous. He could not accept that any child of his blood could be weak, and the fact that Tamar had borne a child out of wedlock was, to him, a slur on the name of Oaks, of which he was so proud.

By the time Annie and Tamar had wiped away their tears and begun to laugh instead of cry, the boy from the inn had brought out a chair, which Tamar drew up between her mother and sister-in-law. They were impressed by the way both she and Victoria were dressed. From Elizabeth's experience at her Uncle's big store in Leeds, she knew that Tamar's gown was pure silk.

When most of their goods had been sold and they could really settle down to talk, Tamar broke her news. 'I'm to be wed, Mam,' she announced proudly.

'Oh, lovey, that's grand!' exclaimed Annie. ''Tis ti someone thoo's met in Helmsley, then?'

'It's Stephen – Mr Lassiter,' answered Tamar. She felt half-shy and half-proud as she said his name.

There was a stunned silence from her listeners. Tamar

was stepping out of her class and they were not sure that the marriage would be a success under those circumstances.

'It's true,' she said, rather defiantly, sensing their disapproval. 'Look!' She held out her left hand. 'He's bought me this betrothal ring. It's a real ruby.' Recollecting, she opened her reticule and took out Grandmother Oaks' wedding ring. 'Thank you, Mam. I shan't need it again – I shall have my own in another week or two. I hope Faither didn't miss it.'

'A week or two? But thoo 'ardly knows each other! Marriage is a big step and a long engagement's for t'best.'

'Stephen wants it as soon as possible and it's to be in Helmsley. I'd be pleased if you and Martha could come, Mam. And you and George, of course,' she added, turning to Elizabeth. It was significant that she did not include her father in the invitation, nor indeed her younger brother Jonna. He and Tamar had always rubbed each other up the wrong way, when she was at home. This was only a personality clash, she saw, looking back from maturity, and her own abrasiveness was probably as much to blame as Jonna's cockiness. However, now that she had the luxury of pleasing herself, she had decided to invite whomsoever she liked to her wedding.

Annie hesitated, but Elizabeth replied immediately, 'Thank you. We'd love to come.'

'Aah can't really say yet, for me and Martha,' answered Annie apologetically. 'Eeh, Aah'd love ti be there, lass, but if as 'ow Aah can't get, thoo knows Aah'll be thinking about thi.'

'I know, Mam.' Tamar squeezed her mother's arm. 'I know it's difficult.'

Annie sprang to Jonadab's defence. 'There's nowt difficult atween me and thi faither! It's others as makes things difficult,' she said spiritedly.

The time passed all too quickly as Tamar described her life in Helmsley and did her best to convey to her mother what Stephen Lassiter's house was like. Suddenly she found Goodison beside her. 'I'm afraid it's time we went, madam,' he reminded.

'Yes, of course.' Tamar turned to Victoria. 'Kiss your

Gran and Auntie Elizabeth. You'll be seeing them again before long.'

Once this was done, Victoria turned to the more familiar manservant. 'Vickie's tired, Goody,' she said, as she lifted up her arms to him.

'Goody'll tuck you up with a rug and then we'll come back for your Mama,' he soothed. Turning to Tamar he said, 'She'll most likely be asleep, madam, before I get the carriage ʊack out here.'

Annie was dumbfounded by the coachman's deference to Tamar and by the way her daughter accepted his attitude. 'Like a real lady she was,' she confided later to Martha.

After Tamar's departure, Annie and Elizabeth made for home rather later than usual. Annie was so full of Tamar's visit that she gave no more thought to Elizabeth's suggestion about the indoor market. 'I wonder if she's told 'im t'truth about not being married?' she mused aloud. To her honest and innocent mind, deviousness was incomprehensible. She just hoped that Tamar had been open with Stephen Lassiter.

Elizabeth, however, was not too sure, 'I don't suppose we'll ever really know,' was her reply.

Lambing was in full swing. While Uncle George and young Jonna had been working with the sheep which were down at the farm, George and his father had been up on the high moor bringing down the flock which were due to lamb after the main herd. They had just got them into a field close to the farm, sub-divided with woven sheep-hurdles, when the two pony traps came into sight.

The sun was already sinking behind the gentle hills which faced the house and the shadows lengthened in the fields. After the blustery start to the day, the air was still, so that every sound of the afterglow was enhanced. The last bird calls were echoing across the dale as they settled down for the night and there was the occasional 'chuff' of a cock pheasant. Jonadab's ear was constantly tuned for the coughing bark of a dog-fox on the prowl, but this evening there was none.

'Thoo's late,' he accused as the ponies were halted at the door. If they had delayed their homecoming after they had sold all their goods, they must have been shopping he thought. 'Aah 'opes as 'ow thoo hasn't been wasting 'ard-earned brass,' he admonished.

When Martha and Lydia came out to unload Annie's empty baskets from her trap, Annie took advantage of the hustle to whisper to Elizabeth, 'Come in for a cup before thoo goes 'ome.'

Elizabeth hesitated. Her mother would have cooked a meal ready for when they reached Cherry Tree Farm, but she realised that Annie needed moral support. When she and her husband were seated at each side of the fire with the rest round the table, Annie took a long draught from her steaming mug and then set it down on the hob. Taking a deep breath, she glanced at Elizabeth, as though for reassurance. 'Our Tamar was in t'market,' she announced, rather too loudly. Nobody spoke. Only the ticking of the grandfather clock in the corner broke the breathless hush. Jonadab merely stared at her. 'She's ti be wed!' Annie sat back, satisfied that her announcement had broken the silence; even her husband's.

'*Wed*?' The black brows met and the vivid blue eyes flashed. 'Who to? Who's getting 'er, may I ask?'

'Mr Stephen Lassiter, her employer,' Elizabeth answered.

'A lawyer?' He usually prided himself on taking things in his stride, but was obviously astonished. 'Well, all Aah can say is – Aah 'opes as 'ow 'e knows what sort of a wife 'e's getting.' He sat forward in his Windsor chair and looked at each face in the room. When he was satisfied that he had everyone's attention, he continued, 'Aah'll tell thoo all now, and Aah sh'll not say it again. There's none from this family shall goo ti t'wedding.'

'Nay, Jonadab. Thoo can't say that. T'lass 'as been through enough,' gasped Annie.

'Aah've said it! And Aah means it. That's mi final word.' Whereupon he took a swig of tea from his mug.

Elizabeth opened her mouth to tell her father-in-law that she had already promised Tamar that she and George would go, but her husband had already risen to his feet. Although George was still the sensitive and caring man she had married, Elizabeth knew that deep down he was not as easygoing as he once had been. George had decided that no longer was he going to submit to anyone just for the sake of a quiet life. Now he stood up, so that he was above his father and could look down at him – a position he knew Jonadab hated. 'Nay, Faither! Me and Elizabeth will go to Tamar's wedding, even if none of the rest of you does.' He did not raise his voice, but spoke firmly and with a challenge in his tone.

Jonadab paused before giving his answer. This was a deliberate ploy, not only to give himself time to think but to draw the focus of his family's attention upon himself and away from George. 'Thoo'll be wanting a day off, then?' He raised his eyebrows and the startling blue eyes, unfaded with the passage of time, stared towards George.

George, however, was not to be intimidated. 'We all had a day off to go to our Joe's wedding and to Beth's. The rest of you all had a day off to come to my wedding to Elizabeth and I shall take the day off to go to our Tamar's. I'm sorry, Faither, but there you have it.'

'Aye, there Aah 'as it.' He paused for a moment and then went on, 'There Aah 'as it – from one who lives in a house provided by me and works at a job provided by me. This is all t'thanks Aah gets.'

George leaned forward, both hands on the table. 'Let's get the record straight, Faither. Don't forget who went up to the Towers to take t'letter to Sir Francis, asking to rent Cherry Tree Farm. Don't forget that it was rented to get extra land and that was why me and Elizabeth was offered it to live in. It wasn't to do us a favour – it was us doing you a favour.'

'*What?*' Jonadab jumped to his feet, the veins on his neck standing out like cords and his eyes flashing with rage. 'Is this the thanks Aah gets? Aah've raised thoo, fed and employed thoo and yet it's thoo that's doing me a favour.' He looked pugnaciously round the kitchen but no eye met his, apart from the steady brown ones of his son George.

'I've shown my thanks in my work, Faither. Let's not forget that Elizabeth and I could have stayed up at her mother's farm, where I was in charge, but you wanted me back down here.'

126

Jonadab settled back into his chair, with a look of disbelief. 'And Aah'm supposed ti be grateful, am I, for a son who works on the farm he'll one day run?' His voice was heavy with sarcasm and there was a sardonic twist to his lip. George was lost for words for a moment. Trust his father to take offence, when he'd only been putting his and Elizabeth's side.

Jonadab was now regretting his outburst; he had not spent his life battling against the elements without learning that patience was an essential component of success. He therefore settled himself in his chair, one hand on each knee and raised his eyes heavenwards in an attitude of exaggerated patience. This raised a titter from young Jonna – immediately quelled by a shaft from his father's glacial eyes.

George began again, willing his father to be fair and acknowledge that he had a point. 'There's nowhere else you'd get a man to work the hours I do, for as little money,' he reminded his father.

'Oh, it's brass we're after now, is it? There's a lot Aah'm finding out today.'

George felt stumped. The whole argument had taken an unexpected turn. All he wanted was to make clear his intention of attending Tamar's wedding, but his father's reaction had brought to the surface grievances which George had hardly known existed. He looked across the table and met Jonadab's eyes. Suddenly he felt his temper rising, as frustration overcame his normally placid temperament. 'I'll give him his name for nothing, and be blowed,' he thought defiantly.

Before he could hurl a reply at his father, however, Elizabeth forestalled him. 'We must get off. Mother will have a meal ready,' she said, rising to her feet. Taking George's arm, she turned him towards the door.

Just as they reached it, young Jonna spoke for the first time. 'Aah reckons it'll be a blessing for this family, when she changes 'er name,' he remarked.

George swung round, eyes blazing. 'Shut your gob,' he shouted. 'Nobody asked your opinion.'

'Take 'im home, Elizabeth,' Annie pleaded, 'afore he says summat he's sorry for.'

'I'm sorry for nowt I say,' was George's reply, as Elizabeth opened the door.

Just before the door closed, his father's voice reached him, heavy with irony. 'Thoo's a lucky man then, if thoo never says owt thoo regrets.'

# CHAPTER TWELVE

Jonadab's foresight in taking up heavy-horse breeding a few years earlier had proved to be a successful venture. Selling at first to breweries in the area, he had eventually acquired a contract to supply the army; their loss of horses in the Crimea meant that they would take all that he could supply. 'T'money's good and they pays prompt,' he often told Annie, with satisfaction.

So great was the demand that he frequently travelled the country, buying in stock to augment the home-bred horses. Although he was by now quite a wealthy man, none of his family would ever have realised the fact. The household was still run on the same frugal lines as it had always been and his regular advice to those of his family who were still at home was, 'Look after thi brass,' and 'thi best friend's thi pocket.'

Both sons had proved to have the knack of breaking-in horses, so that his stock were known for their gentleness and reliability, being able to work in any circumstances and showing no sign of skittishness.

The previous August had seen the Yorkshire Agricultural Society's show held at nearby Malton and this had fired all three of the Oaks men with the enthusiasm for entering the shows which were now being held throughout Ryedale. George and Jonna only saw the shows as a means of exhibiting their own particular pairs of matched greys, but Jonadab was sufficiently astute to realise that success would enhance the value of his stock.

The morning after the scene in his mother's kitchen, George was riding Violet up the lane to work. Seated sideways on her broad back, as the majestic animal ambled along the track he went over the events of the previous evening. When he and Elizabeth had left his parents, he had been all for handing in his notice and leaving the dale.

'There's plenty of farms to rent,' he had protested, in the face of Elizabeth's pleading for him to reconsider.

'We haven't enough put by yet to stock it, George,' she had reminded him.

'I've my own sheep and pigs and you've got your hens and geese,' he had answered mutinously. 'That'll do for a start.'

Before they entered the house, where the presence of Elizabeth's mother and sister prevented any privacy, they had stood in the cart-shed discussing their dilemma. Eventually he acknowledged that she was right. 'Starting out with too little capital is the road to ruin, George,' she pointed out.

'Aye, lass.' He bent to kiss her before going in. 'Of course you're right. You usually are.'

Now, as he made his way towards his father's farm he admitted that Elizabeth was indeed correct in her judgement. The dale was his home and he could not visualise living his life in any other surroundings.

The fitful showers and scudding clouds of the previous day were gone. The morning basked in a soft golden light, more like May than April. The dangling lamb's tails of the hazel catkins were over, but the silvery tufts of the goat willow caught the sun, lighting up the hedgerow. The lane linking the farms of the dale was a grass track, the only bare earth being the wheel ruts made by farm traffic and the occasional carriage of the well-to-do, who came down to visit the healing-spring beyond his own home.

The short grass of the track was starred with daisies and gleaming celandines while, among the hedges on the roadside, bloomed red and white dead-nettle, interspersed with the pale yellow of clumps of small, wild daffodils. As George looked around him at the freshness and beauty of the countryside and listened to the calls and songs of the birds which darted to and fro, busy with the business of nest-building, he decided that for good or ill, he was tied to the dale and could never be happy anywhere else.

Just as he arrived at his decision, another thought struck him. What if his father decided that he had gone too far and paid him off? George suspected that, as a younger replica of their father as well as bearing his name, Jonna was the favourite. Maybe Faither would be glad of the excuse to place Jonna in the favoured position of the son who would inherit. He grew cold at the thought and put it out of his mind. 'I sh'll not mention yesterday if he doesn't,' he thought, and determined to go on as if the argument had not taken place.

When he came into sight of Aumery Park Farm, however, it was to see his father riding down the lane towards the hill which led out of the dale. He looked at the ramrod-straight back disappearing round the curve in the road, and was overcome with a feeling of resentment. As he slid off the big shirehorse's back, his sister Martha came out of the kitchen door to shake the clip-mat which covered the flagged floor in front of the fire grate. George jerked his head towards the spot where their father had passed out of sight. 'I see he's taking the day off,' he said with a touch of sarcasm in his tone.

'Eeh, George, 'e's off on business, that's all 'e said,' answered Martha. 'You stood up to him good and proper last night. I'd like to go to Tamar's wedding an' all – and I know Mam would.'

'We'll see,' he promised, but without much conviction. He and Elizabeth were determined that they would go, but he could not for the life of him see his mother going against Jonadab's wishes. 'Tell our Mam and Jonna I'm up in t'woods, snigging fallen trees. That dappled colt's nicely broken, now, and it's time for him to work in double harness. Violet's nice and steady, so he'll learn a lot from her. If I'm wanted for owt, give me a call – I'll just be up above t'road.'

As George turned towards the stable, Jonadab was riding up the hill. Not even Annie knew of the sleepless night he had spent. He had been obsessive in his determination that Tamar and Victoria should remain hidden down in Sleightholmedale, so that no slur would touch the name of Oaks. He saw no difficulties in his plan and would have kept them secreted from the outside world, at least for his lifetime. When Tamar had left the dale he had been devastated to think that her name would become broadcast.

As time went by, he began to realise that her disgrace still appeared to remain unknown to his friends and neighbours. To Jonadab, no blame for Tamar's defiance could be attributed to Elizabeth. She could do no wrong in her father-in-law's eyes and he had convinced himself that in some way it was Tamar's influence that had persuaded Elizabeth to help her.

The news yesterday that not only had she escaped punishment for her immoral behaviour, but that she was to rise in the world by marrying above her station, seemed utterly wrong to Jonadab. She was to blame for the rift in his family. That George's uncharacteristic behaviour was brought about by Tamar, was only too clear to her father. George had defied him twice now: even raised his voice to him. This had upset Jonadab far more than he had shown. And it was all through Tamar. All night long he had swung between moral duty and family loyalty. What was he to do?

By dawn, he felt that his prayers had been answered. It was his duty to denounce the sinner, even though she was his own daughter. So it was that, after breakfast, he set out for Helmsley and an interview with Stephen Lassiter. Although his heart was heavy, he was certain that he was morally correct in his decision.

When Tempy opened the door to his ring, she was confronted by what seemed to her a frightening figure. Jonadab was about six feet in height, and still carried himself as erect as in his youth. His blue eyes held hers with a fierce gaze as he announced, 'Mr Jonadab Oaks, to see Mr Lassiter.'

Tempy's face did not show the surprise she felt. This must be a relative of young Mrs Oaks, she thought. 'The master's engaged at present,' she told him. 'Would you step inside and wait, sir?'

As she stood aside and motioned him to a seat in the hall, Jonadab took in his surroundings with interest. Tamar was certainly doing well for herself, he thought. It was luxuriously furnished, even for a lawyer. Before he could really get settled, the study door opened and Stephen Lassiter escorted his client to the front door. Jonadab regarded the lawyer with interest. Not to his taste, he decided. Too fair for a man and looked a bit of a namby-pamby.

As Stephen turned away from the door, Jonadab rose to his feet. 'Mr Jonadab Oaks from Sleightholmedale. Aah'd like a bit of a word, sir,' he said.

Stephen looked at him with curiosity. So this was Tamar's father. He certainly had the air of a tartar. No wonder the poor girl was afraid of him. He turned towards the drawing room. 'Do come and sit down in here.' He motioned the older man forward. 'I'll ring for Tamar to join us over a cup of tea.'

'No!' Jonadab spoke sharply. 'It's business – purely business.'

Stephen's forehead wrinkled in surprise, but he turned towards the study and ushered Jonadab inside. When they were seated, one each side of the desk, he placed his elbows on the desk-top, fingertips touching. 'What can I do for you, Mr Oaks?' he asked.

Jonadab took a breath. 'There's summat Aah thinks thoo should know,' he announced. Suddenly he was unsure of himself. However, he'd come thus far and would complete his errand. 'It's oor Tamar. She's not a widow. She's unwed.' He sat down and watched for Stephen's reaction.

To his surprise, the other man seemed unmoved. 'I know, Mr Oaks. Tamar has told me.' He spoke quietly, but with firmness, so that Jonadab had to revise his opinion of the lawyer. Perhaps he had more strength than was at first apparent.

He looked at Stephen in amazement. 'Thoo knows?' The jutting eyebrows rose in surprise.

'Yes.' Stephen could have laughed at Jonadab's expression but satisfied himself with continuing, 'Tamar has told me everything.' He was not really sure that this was so, but he loved her too much to care.

'Her reputation's tarnished. She's a fallen woman with a bastard child, and yet thoo's willing ti wed her?' Jonadab's face was a picture of disbelief and his voice rose at the end of the question.

'You are a Christian man, Mr Oaks. I know that from what Tamar has said. You must know it is possible to hate the sin but love the sinner. I do not condone wrong, but my love for Tamar outweighs what she has done. That is part of her previous life and she will start a clean slate as my wife.'

Jonadab did not really know what to make of his future son-in-law. He admitted to himself that he had underestimated him. He also had to confess that he had misjudged Tamar. He had been convinced that she must have deceived Lassiter, in order to get a proposal from him, but he had been wrong. A feeling of relief flooded through him. Although Tamar had strayed, she had finally been true to the teachings instilled by her father. 'Aah'm sorry, sir. Aah considered it mi Christian duty ti see that thoo was told, but if Tamar's done it, all the better.'

'Please don't call me sir. In a couple of weeks we shall be related – I shall be your son-in-law. Now, how about that cup of tea?'

They moved from the study to the drawing room, where Lassiter rang the bell. When Tempy came, he ordered tea and cakes and asked that Tamar should be invited to join them. When Tamar opened the drawing room door to see her father sitting there, she blanched and turned to retreat.

Stephen rose to his feet and held out a hand to her. 'Come in, my dear,' he said gently. 'We have an unexpected visitor.'

Tamar hesitated and then came forward, eyeing Jonadab warily. Her face had taken on a pinched look and her light golden eyes were remote. Why had her father come, she wondered. No doubt to make trouble for her!

Neither Tamar nor her father spoke as she took her place at the table and began to pour from the heavy silver teapot. Jonadab eyed his daughter impassively. She certainly paid for dressing, he thought. Seated in these surroundings, serving the tea as though born to it, she looked quite the lady, he admitted to himself.

As the silence stretched, Stephen began to feel the tension in the air. Clearing his throat, he addressed Tamar. 'I've been telling your father that we shall be pleased to see him at the wedding.'

Tamar put down the teapot, slowly and carefully. She sat

for a moment regarding it and then, taking a deep breath, almost spat out the word, '*No!*'

Stephen was taken aback. He had foolishly believed that bringing them face to face would heal the rift between them.

Tamar, however, although bearing no physical resemblance to her father had inherited his proud spirit and fiery nature. This time her voice was louder and firmer. 'No!' she said more strongly, as she rose to her feet. Jonadab's face was expressionless as he gazed at his daughter. She drew herself up and looked at him icily. 'I'm sorry, but things said can never be unspoken. Your door was closed against me and you're not welcome inside mine.'

Stephen looked from one to the other. He had never seen Tamar so cold and unyielding. 'Please, Tamar – ' he began, but she held up her hand and interrupted.

'No, Stephen. This man, for I cannot call him "Father", has said words that I can never forgive. To have him there would spoil my wedding day.' Her control faltered, tears sprang to her eyes and she swung round and hurried from the room.

Neither man knew what to say. Jonadab slowly stood up. 'Aah'll be off, then,' he said heavily. 'Aah'm sorry ti cause an upset.' He was rarely at a loss for words, but now he felt awkward and embarrassed. 'Mebbe Aah's been a bit hasty-like towards her, but my family's good name means a lot ti me.'

Stephen felt suddenly sorry for the old man. He sensed that he was struggling to maintain standards which were almost impossibly high. 'I'm afraid that the world is changing, Mr Oaks,' he said, 'and there are some ways in which we must change, too.'

Jonadab's slightly-sagging shoulders straightened. 'Nay! Aah'll not change. Aah does mi best ti walk in the Lord's ways and expects the same from mi children.' He spoke the words with dignity as he walked down the hall. At the front door, he turned. 'Aah wish thoo well. Aah knows thoo'll be good ti my lass.' With that, he went down the step, mounted his horse and rode down the street. Stephen watched him, until he turned the corner by the church and rode from his view.

# CHAPTER THIRTEEN

It was a sparkling, sun-drenched May morning when Tamar and Stephen Lassiter were married. Jonadab had told none of his family about his trip to Helmsley, merely insisting dourly that he would not attend the ceremony. Fiercely loyal to her husband, Annie also refused to go, even though she longed to do so. Jonadab, to their surprise, raised no further objection when George announced that he and Elizabeth would take Martha with them. The girl was delighted at this break in the daily routine of her humdrum existence. To the amazement of the whole family, Uncle George stated that he, too, intended to go to the wedding. During the period that he and his niece had lived at Cherry Tree Farm, a strong bond had been forged between them. Now, to his brother's ill-concealed annoyance, Uncle George was quietly insistent regarding his intention of seeing Tamar married.

When Tamar walked up the aisle on her brother George's arm, the small congregation was overwhelmed by her appearance. She wore a gown of heavy cream satin, quite simply cut, relying for its effect upon the richness of the fabric, which acted as a foil for her vivid colouring. The brim of her matching bonnet was underdrawn with georgette of the same hue as the topaz necklace which lay on her throat like pools of liquid gold.

Stephen had suggested that they should book a private room at the nearby Feversham Arms for the wedding breakfast but Tamar was reluctant to ask her staunchly Methodist family to enter an inn. Consequently Mrs Judd was to lay on a cold meal back at the house, before the Oaks returned to Sleightholmedale.

The cook still treated Tamar with a thinly-veiled hostility, although the rest of the staff were obviously fond of their new mistress and delighted by the marriage. Tamar had gone out of her way to be pleasant to Mrs Judd and was mystified by her attitude. She consoled herself with the thought that, once she was Stephen's wife, the cook would treat her more amiably. 'She can either change her tune, or put on her walking boots,' she told herself.

On this morning, however, there were no thoughts in her mind apart from the joy of her marriage to Stephen. No banns had been read and there were no guests invited, apart from a handful of Tamar's close kin. Lady Lassiter had made it only too clear that she was against the marriage, so that she and her husband found business in London to account for their absence. The couple were surprised, therefore, on coming out of the shade of the church into the dazzling brightness outside, to see that the path was lined with onlookers. Tempy and Gertie had slipped across from the house, each with a pocketful of rice with which to shower their master and mistress. As they laughingly ducked and dodged the handfuls of grain, Tamar suddenly hesitated and caught her breath sharply. There, a little way back from the path, leaning nonchalantly against a headstone watching her with a mocking smile, was Gareth Davis.

As Tamar paused, Stephen looked at her curiously. 'What is it? Are you all right?' he asked solicitously.

'Yes. Yes, it's nothing. It was just that a grain of rice caught my eye,' she answered, brushing her eye with the back of her hand. As she did so she glanced towards where the Welshman had stood, only to find that he had vanished.

She had been reluctant to mention her attacker to Stephen, fearing that, taken in conjunction with the circumstances of Victoria's birth, he would perhaps feel that she had encouraged the man's attentions. She was sensitive regarding her newfound status and dared not make any other revelation which might jeopardise his good opinion of her. Now she felt that the opportunity had passed forever. With a little breathy laugh, half-nervousness, half-relief, she took her husband's arm again and hurried down the church path.

When the little party crossed the road and reached the house, Martha was so impressed by the height of the rooms and the sumptuous furnishings, that she was unable at first to speak. She looked round in wide-eyed amazement, hardly able to grasp the fact that her sister lived in such luxury. Victoria, too, she noticed, accepted her surroundings with aplomb. For the first time in her fourteen years, Martha felt a niggle of dissatisfaction with her life. Now that she had seen Tamar's clothes, her home and the food served there, she realised that there were better lives than the one she lived. Tamar had been held up to her younger sister as an example not to be followed, yet here she was, dressed in satin and jewels, the mistress of what seemed to her sister to be a mansion and being waited on by maids.

Their father often read from the Bible that the wages of sin were death, but it occurred to Martha that Tamar had sinned and earned the good things in life – reward rather than punishment. She determined to ask her sister-in-law Elizabeth to explain this apparent contradiction. She looked avidly round, taking it all in, ready to describe everything to her mother upon their return.

Tamar and Stephen were to have only a brief honeymoon of three days in York. This was as exciting to Tamar as a visit to London or Paris would have been. She had never been to a larger town than Kirkbymoorside so that the thought of staying in an hotel, visiting the theatre and seeing the shops was a thrilling prospect.

When they had waved goodbye to the bride and groom, the Oaks drove home through the limpid glow of the afternoon. As they descended the precipitous track which led down into the valley, Martha drank in the heady scent of the bluebells which carpeted the broadleafed woodland, clothing the scarp which rose almost vertically on their right, and dropped away on the left in equal sheerness. Although the roadside grass was spangled with great drifts of primroses and dainty clumps of dog violets, it was the pervading odour of the bluebells which dominated the scene.

Martha sniffed appreciatively as she looked round and voiced everybody's sentiments. 'Eeh, it's grand ti get back. Tamar might live like quality, but Helmsley's not as good as t'dale.'

'Thoo's right at that, lass,' replied her Uncle George. 'Not many folks is as lucky as us.'

The warm and dry May was a foretaste of a glorious

summer. In early June, with the lambing well over, the sheep were sheared before most of them were returned to the moor for summer grazing. Although the hired men plodded on throughout the day at an even pace, George and Jonna tended to treat the shearing as a challenge, each trying to outdo the other.

They began the day in fine fettle, seizing a sheep in unison, flicking it into a sitting position with a dextrous twist and clipping rapidly until the fleece fell away like the peel from an orange, exposing the pithy-white underlayer of the wool. Gradually, throughout the day, the heaviness of the woolly bodies lolling against their legs and the heat of the fleece beneath their hands took its toll. Although their work rate slowed down, the brothers usually maintained a level pace, neither besting the other in the daily tally.

While he would not allow the men to bet, Jonadab encouraged this friendly rivalry, realising that it created interest throughout one of the hottest and dirtiest of the jobs on the farm.

As each animal was shorn, the womenfolk rolled up the fleece and put it aside to await the coming of the buyer from a woollen mill in the West Riding. To George's acute embarrassment, Sarah Butler had appointed herself as his helper and watched him with open admiration. When she and her mother had first come to live with them, her hero-worship had seemed to be amusing but now that she was turned sixteen and had put her hair up, he found her attentions irksome. She never missed an opportunity to be in his company and he considered that she was making fools of them both.

George admitted to himself that his sister-in-law had grown into an attractive girl. She shared with Elizabeth the quick, darting movements which had led him to think of his wife as his little sparrow. Sometimes in the evenings by the fire he would secretly eye Ann Butler and wonder how this woman with her cold, grey eyes could have produced these two sparkling and vivacious daughters. Like Elizabeth, Sarah's colouring was dark and her olive skin was flushed with an almost russet bloom along her cheekbones. Her eyes were large and luminous and when she laughed, her teeth gleamed, white and even. That she excited interest amongst the local youths was obvious and George wished fervently that she would transfer her admiration to one of them.

Before the flocks were driven up on to the moors, there was the task of washing them in the beck. This took place at a spot where the banks curved inwards and the gurgling brook had scooped out a pool of deeper water in its eagerness to push through the narrower gap. Here, generations of Oaks had dammed the stream with the same two tree trunks which were still used by Jonadab. They were rolled down the shallow bank and located so that they halted the flow of water just sufficiently to deepen the pool. Sheep hurdles, placed a few yards upstream, still allowed a current through, but created a passage of deeper water. Through this the sheep were ushered, with much shouting and stick-waving. Once washed, the herds were driven up on to the high moor where they grazed, until October saw them shepherded down to the valley to be salved.

In the shimmering heat of the summer, the petals fell early from the buttercups. This had always served as the signal for the start of haytime, which was soon in full swing. Annie sighed as she looked round the first field to be cut. Although the sweep of the scythe and the soft swish of the fragrant swathes as they fell beneath the blades were as hypnotic as ever, haytime lacked the joyousness which had been present when her family were all at home.

When the women went into the fields to rake up the newly-mown crop with large wooden rakes, she took note that young Sarah Butler had come along from Cherry Tree Farm with Elizabeth. Annie also noticed how Sarah was frequently to be seen close to George. 'Making sheep's eyes at 'im,' his mother told herself, with a glare at the girl. 'She needs a good dressing down.'

Not a drop of rain fell during the period of hay-making, bringing it soon to a successful close. The sweet-smelling herbage was forked up into the lofts above the stables and byres, while the excess was stacked near to the farm. Jonadab inspected it with satisfaction. 'That'll see us nicely through t'winter,' he remarked to his sons.

'Aye,' answered George. 'Harvest'll soon be on us. T'oats down in t'far field at Cherry Tree is turning colour.'

Jonadab reflected for a moment or two. 'Yon turfs that was cut in spring should be well dry by now. You two can start ti lead 'em in t'morn, while t'men get on with hoeing.'

This was an enjoyable task. The turves which had been set to dry, after having been cut earlier in the year, would be loaded and brought down to the farms. There they would be stacked, close to the houses, supplying both households with sufficient fuel for a whole year.

Dew still beaded the uncurled fronds of bracken and clung to the grass in shimmering droplets, when Jonna arrived at Cherry Tree Farm the following morning. George had just finished harnessing Violet, one of the two original grey shires which had been the foundation of Jonadab's stock.

Once across the stream, with George leading, they trundled their way slowly up the grassy track which led through the heather. This was an old drovers' road, used for as long as sheep had grazed on these moors and on the sheltered dales which ran between them. Upon reaching the turf-beds, the brothers dismounted and stood for a moment, unspeaking.

'By gum, but it's grand,' Jonna finally observed, taking in the view. They had left behind the sultry heat of the valley and on the moor top there was a refreshing breeze. So crystal clear was the air that the moors rolled away like the waves of an amethyst sea, until they reached the far horizon.

On his daily journeys between the two farms George had noticed how the heat of the sun had bleached the grasses of the hedgerows until they were now the colour of straw. He stooped and pulled up a clump of heather in which he stood ankle deep. Thoughtfully he rubbed it between his fingers. 'It's tinder-dry,' he remarked. 'We could do with a drop of rain, now we've got all t'hay made.'

Jonna laughed. 'Nay, it won't come to order,' he replied as his gaze took in the great blue dome of the sky. 'Not a cloud in sight. Anyway, don't forget t'corn'll soon be ready, and we've another eight acres of oats this year, on account of us 'aving built up t' 'osses. We don't want rain before that lot's cut.'

After this exchange the brothers began to work steadily, piling the turves high on the flat, four-wheeled carts. Being true sons of Jonadab, it never occurred to them to slacken their efforts just because their father was not present to oversee them. Jonadab was fiercely proud of the name of Oaks. He knew that, in the area, his family name was synonymous with integrity and hard work. From their earliest days, all his children had been taught that every waking minute must be filled with work. 'Satan finds work for idle hands to do,' was a favourite maxim of his and he also told them with great regularity, 'Honest toil brings its own reward.' As a consequence of having had these and various similar adages drilled into them with great frequency, each member of the family became filled with feelings of guilt if any part of the day was spent idly. Work was their life and was accepted as normal.

George and Jonna spent the best part of two weeks leading turves and then, one Friday evening, Jonadab rode down to Cherry Tree Farm. 'Noo then, lad,' he addressed George, after greeting the womenfolk. 'Let's 'ave a look at yon oats thoo thinks is about fit.' As father and son strolled round the fields, Jonadab looked about him with a sigh of satisfaction. 'Aah was lucky ti get this land. Poor James Waring 'ad neglected it but it's paid for mucking. It's a good crop of oats and we sh'll certainly need 'em all this year. Shire'osses is in demand and Aah wants ti keep more filly foals and build up mi breeding stock. You and Jonna's doing a good job at t'shows. Oor stock's getting well known through you and 'im winning rosettes. Let's 'ope you both does well wi' thi teams tomorrow.'

George heartily agreed. It was not only personal satisfaction that pleased him, when he and Jonna were usually placed in the first three in the heavy-horse class at local Agricultural Shows, but he was also well aware that success breeds success, and that the quality of their horses was becoming well-known beyond the boundaries of Ryedale. Enquiries for the purchase of their young stock came from breweries and railways all over the north, as well as from the army.

Jonadab was highly satisfied with the progress of his farming and looked now with pleasure at the sight of the fields of oats rippling in the faint breeze which came with the evening. A phrase from his Bible came into his mind. 'Lift up your eyes and look on the fields; for they are white already to the harvest.' He sighed with contentment. Things were certainly going well for him, he reflected. How proud his father would have been, to see how the family farm was developing and succeeding. With a conscious effort he brought himself back to the present. 'Aye, God willing, we sh'll start down 'ere come Monday,' he said aloud, as they turned away.

George's heart lifted. He loved the time of harvest. Although it lacked the almost carnival atmosphere of hay-making, harvest-time brought more personal pleasure to George than almost any other aspect of farming life. He enjoyed the bite of the blade into the crisp stalks, which made the actual cutting easier than the more pliable stems of grass. Although each swathe, when cut, fell more heavily across the blade of the scythe than did the crop of the hayfield, this presented a challenge to George's strength. The setting up of the sheaves in tens to form the stooks, which stood in regimented rows across the stubble, was more pleasing to George's orderly mind than the rather more haphazard haycocks which lacked any rigid uniformity – and finally, there was the stacking of the corn. To him the construction of a neat, round pike was far superior to the building of a haystack, with its blurred outlines. George was proud of his skill in the creation of these testimonies to the stacker's art, each neatly thatched with its conical roof of straw. Even his brother Jonna reluctantly admitted that George was his master when it came to stacking corn.

It was therefore with a light heart that George went out towards suppertime to visit the stock before bedtime. He had brought Rosie and Violet in from the pasture in prep-aration for the next day's Agricultural Show. To his sur-prise, when he entered the building where the mares were stabled, it was to find the great gentle beasts rather restive.

Normally placid and patient, tonight they turned their heads from side to side, ears pricked forward in a listening attitude.

George stroked the powerful necks and ran his hands down their flanks in a soothing movement. His presence did nothing to allay their fears; the whites of their eyes spoke of their alarm and they picked up their feet in turn, as though preparing to run from some unseen danger. George lifted the lantern high above his head and looked round to see if a rat had disturbed them. There was nothing to be seen, so he brought them a carrot each and with a final caress, left them.

As he closed the stable door, he was startled by a flash of lightning from the north. He stood, counting under his breath, until he heard the growl of distant thunder. 'It's far enough away, as yet,' he muttered to himself. 'It's to be hoped it doesn't get any nearer. We don't want them oats flattened.'

As he moved from building to building checking his animals, he was uneasily aware that the storm appeared to be drawing rapidly nearer. By the time George re-entered the kitchen, although the rain had not yet arrived, the ear-splitting crash of thunder and the violence of the lightning were so closely synchronised and so continuous that he concluded that the storm was directly overhead.

His mother-in-law was busy hanging a cloth over the wall-mirror. 'There! That won't draw t'lightning,' she stated with satisfaction. 'Leave the door open, George. If a thunderbolt comes down the chimney, it must have a way out.'

George nodded and did as she asked. He noted that there were no knives out on the table: they had all been put away in the table drawer to avoid attracting the lightning. There would be no bread cut for supper until the storm moved away.

It must have been half an hour before the tumult finally died down. During the time that the tempest had raged, George had positioned himself by the window, gazing into the night.

'What is it, love?' inquired Elizabeth.

'I'm waiting for the rain,' answered George. 'I can't

understand why it isn't pouring. Mind you, I'm thankful that it's kept dry, because we're starting to cut these oats on Monday and we don't want 'em laid. They're too good a crop to be damaged.'

'The lightning will just be to ripen the corn,' Ann Butler remarked.

'Nay. It's forked lightning, not sheet,' he replied. 'Anyway, the rain seems to have missed us. We'll have a bit of supper now and get to our beds.'

The next morning George set about the final grooming of his team, ready for the show. The previous day he had washed their manes and tails and the feathering on their pasterns and fetlocks. Now, after a night under cover deeply bedded down in clean fresh straw, all that he needed to do was a final burnishing of their coats, the plaiting of manes and tails with brightly coloured ribbons, and then they would be ready for the special, highly polished show harness.

Down at Aumery Park Farm, his brother would be busy at the same task. George was under no illusions: it was not the two Oaks against the opposition, it was Jonna against George. Their father did not care who was placed above the other, so long as their positions were winner and runner-up. George, however, realised that it was his brother's overwhelming ambition to beat him and his horses.

These thoughts were running through George's head as he worked on the shirehorses. Straightening his back to take a breather, he watched Sarah going back to the house with the egg baskets, while Elizabeth crossed the yard with two buckets of pig-swill. To their deep sorrow there was still no sign of another child and her figure was as neat and trim as a girl's. He noted again the great similarity between the two sisters, although there was such a difference in their ages.

As he looked, Elizabeth stopped and carefully set the buckets down in the yard. Thinking that she was finding them heavy, he took a step towards her. However, she had raised her head and was looking intently over towards the moors.

'What's up?' he called.

'I can smell something! What is it? Can you smell it?' came back her response.

George sniffed. There it was! His nostrils caught a faint but distinctive odour on the air, a musky smokiness which was vaguely familiar. It came to him in a flash – the smell of the burning ling, which he used as kindling to light the parlour fire. 'It's heather!' he gasped. 'T'moor must be on fire.' Even as he spoke, the first wisps of smoke curled upwards above the horizon.

Running back to the stable block, he quickly slipped a bridle on Elizabeth's pony, Bella. Leaping astride her, he urged the little mount out of the yard and down the lane towards his father's farm. As he approached the farm buildings, he could see Bert Weald the farm foreman and three of the men, hoeing turnips in one of the hillside fields to his left.

'Bert! Bert!' he shouted and beckoned him down. Alerted by the urgency of his voice, as well as the way he drove the fat little pony which carried him, the men dropped their hoes and began to run down towards the road.

George turned into the yard where, as he expected, Jonna was grooming Bonnie and Bluebell, watched by their father and helped by Tobias, the bonded lad from the Union House. 'Faither! Faither!' he called, as he slid down Bella's back. 'T'moors is alight beyond t'dale. It's blowing this way. If we don't dowse it, t'oats'll go up.'

His father swung round just as Bert Weald and the others came running into the yard.

'What's up?' asked Weald, seeing the consternation on his master's face.

Quickly George explained. His father rapidly issued instructions. 'We'll ride on ahead. You load a rulley with owt you can find ti beat it out – shovels, spades, besoms – owt at all. And bring everybody thoo can muster. T'women an' all.'

When they reached Cherry Tree Farm, it was to find that Elizabeth had already gathered together a supply of implements suitable for beating out the flames. As they made their way across Hodge Beck on their way up to the moor top Jonadab looked at the stream, which had dwindled to a mere trickle in the searing heat of the summer. 'We could do wi' some more water in t'beck, in case it's needed as a fire break,' he panted, as they splashed across the pebbly bed of the brook.

'Nay, we'll surely get it quenched before then,' protested George, his thoughts upon his home.

As they laboured up the hill they were conscious that what had been curling twists of smoke were now becoming thicker. Upon reaching the moor, however, the fire did not appear to have got too much of a hold.

'We'll soon put this out,' Jonadab grunted. 'Last night's lightning must have struck a tree.' He marshalled his forces with the skill of a general in the face of an oncoming foe. Under his direction, they spread out, each choosing a portion of the fire and beating it into submission. Just as it seemed that success was within their grasp and that they would triumph, out of the blue a wind arose, rekindling spurts of flame from wherever embers were still glowing.

As they concentrated on their task, they failed to notice how the fire was spreading. Gradually, the number of sheep running for their lives down from the moor and the whirring wings of the grouse which rose before the flames caused Jonadab to straighten his back and re-assess the situation. He went cold when he realised that his band of helpers were in danger of being surrounded. The hungry wind had soon whipped the flames into a frenzy of activity, so that the fire was like a roaring tide rushing over the moors in waves, engulfing all before it. It had advanced in an arc round them, until they were now in acute danger.

'Whoa! Whoa!' His stentorian voice rang out like a trumpet blast. As his fire-fighters halted their efforts and looked about them in dismay, he shouted again, 'Get thissens off t'moor,' beckoning them to run. Suddenly aware of the peril which surrounded them, they turned for the track which led down from the moor. George and Jonna fell back to give a helping hand to their mother and to Bert Weald's wife, Dorcas, who were breathless from their efforts against the fire, and now stumbled as they zigzagged with exhaustion.

'Come on, Mam,' urged George. 'At least t'bracken's still

green and won't burn well. Once we can get clear of the dry heather, we should be safe.'

Every little gorse bush in the fire's path went up in a shower of sparks which flew ahead, igniting spurts of flame. Each new flare-up ran along through the heather reaching before them like greedy fingers. As they reached the steep slope which led down from the moor, Jonadab stood urging them on and counting until he knew that all were safe.

Leaving Annie in his father's care, George hurried to catch up with Elizabeth and Sarah. 'Oh, George. Do you think Cherry Tree will be safe?' gasped his wife.

He looked back at the wall of flame high along the skyline at the moor's edge. 'Yes. The grass lower down is kept cropped short by the sheep and then there's t'beck.'

'But it's nearly dry!' Elizabeth loved their home and was apprehensive.

'The stream bed's wide enough to stop the flames,' he comforted.

As they splashed across the beck and trudged towards Cherry Tree Farm, George heard his father groan aloud. 'Oh, no! Dear God, no.' Jonadab pointed to the four-acre fields of oats ahead. The terrified sheep which had fled from the inferno on the moor had funnelled through a gap in the hedge and were now milling around in a stampede of terror, flattening the crop, which only an hour or so ago had stood erect ready for the reapers.

As they stood and watched the crop ruined before their eyes, there was a sudden whoosh as a clump of furze along the bank burst into flames as though spontaneously. As the seed pods burst open with a noise like the cracking of whips, showers of sparks were carried by the breeze over into the field of oats.

Jonadab looked round at his weary band of helpers. He must urge them into even greater effort. 'Come on! There's nowt we can do ti save t'crop, but we must dig a ditch for a fire break.' They realised that Cherry Tree Farm was now in real danger and the fire in the corn field must be contained. Bent backs suddenly straightened and they all broke into a run.

Elizabeth fell in alongside Annie Oaks and Dorcas Weald,

who were struggling along in the rear. 'Go into the house and help Mother. We shall all need a cup of tea when we've finished,' she said. Annie opened her mouth to argue, but Elizabeth held up her hand to stem her protests. 'Draw some water from the well and fill as many containers as you can in case we need it,' she pleaded as she ran after the others.

Bert Weald had sent Tobias to open the gate, to release the sheep which were massed near it and get them as far away from the approaching fire as possible. As the workers began to dig under Jonadab's direction, he looked at the house. 'It's a blessing there's a good stone wall round t'garden,' he observed. 'At least there'll not be sparks from t'oats and we should be able ti 'old it.'

By the time he was satisfied that the fire had burned itself out, in the dale if not on the moor, both fields of oats grown on Cherry Tree land were totally destroyed.

As the others trailed towards the farmhouse, where the older women had prepared mugs of steaming tea and a table full of food, Jonadab and his sons stood and surveyed the scene of devastation. 'Well, that's that.' Jonadab's tone was flat and emotionless, but sorrow was etched into every line of his face. As they walked across the farmyard he continued, 'Ah've allus said it and Aah'll say it again: pride goeth before a fall. Aah thought Aah could do nowt wrong in mi farming, but the Lord 'as taught me a lesson.'

George looked up towards the moor, now blackened and overhung with drifting clouds of smoke. 'It could burn for weeks below the surface,' he stated, 'and heaven knows how many sheep we've lost.'

When the farm-workers had gone back to Aumery Park, Jonadab and his family remained seated dispiritedly round George's table. Jonadab eventually spoke, his voice firm and decisive. 'Things'll be tight for a bit. Aah was thinking of buying mi own entire this year but that's not possible now.' His audience had had no idea he was contemplating buying a stallion of his own and were suitably impressed. 'As George says, there's no knowing how many sheep perished and we've lost eight acres of oats. Rather than buy in winter feed, I've decided ti sell some breeding mares.'

George and Jonna glanced across at each other and then spoke almost in unison. 'Not Rosy and Violet.' 'Not Bonnie and Bluebell.' Each pleaded for his own favourite team.

'No. They're too successful in t'show ring,' their father replied. 'Aah sh'll sell a couple of pairs of in-foal fillies.' He glanced round the table. 'It'll be a struggle and we must tighten our belts, but we sh'll come though, nivver fear.' His confidence in the future, despite the disasters of the day, heartened his family. 'After all,' he reminded them, 'we're all safe. We've got roofs over our heads and we've got health and strength. If we pull together, we shall overcome this. The Lord is testing us, ti see 'ow we stand up ti adversity and we sh'll show what Oaks is made of.'

With these words he rose from his chair and, followed by Annie and his younger son and daughter, strode out of the kitchen and back to his own home, supremely confident in his ability to weather this storm in his fortunes.

# CHAPTER FOURTEEN

Tamar had been married to Stephen Lassiter for over four years and there was still no sign of a child. True to his word, he had legally adopted Victoria, but Tamar knew that he longed for a child of his own. He was still as ardent in his love-making as he had been when he first made her his wife. Tamar too was eager as ever, and responded to him with tempestuous passion. She was at a loss to understand her failure to conceive.

Few of her friends either knew or remembered that Tamar had once been Stephen's housekeeper and Victoria was accepted as his child. Tamar's quick wits and natural intelligence had stood her in good stead in adapting to her new status: few would have recognised in the poised and gracious woman, the wilful girl who had rebelled against her father's discipline. Although she sometimes yearned for the little dale where she had spent her girlhood, Tamar knew that the quality of life she enjoyed as Stephen's wife far surpassed anything she had ever envisaged. Stephen was intensely proud of her beauty and never begrudged money spent on clothes to set off her appearance.

Victoria now attended a school for young ladies in Church Street, only a few doors from home. Gertie took her in the mornings and brought her back for lunch, then accompanied her charge once more on the afternoon journey. Since her arrival from the workhouse at the age of ten, Gertie had developed into a pretty and outgoing girl, devoted to Victoria. She and Tempy were best of friends and shared the household duties between them in an amicable fashion.

Only Mrs Judd the cook refused to be captivated by Tamar's charms. She was still barely civil, never going beyond the bounds into actual rudeness, but monosyllabic and uncooperative. Tamar countered this by leaving the woman to her own devices, merely giving her the numbers expected at each meal and usually agreeing when the menus were presented.

Stephen had bought Tamar a governess cart and a pony of her own, so that she was able to drive herself about. She usually drove to Kirkbymoorside every five or six weeks, to see her mother and sister-in-law on market day. No amount of pleading from either Annie or Elizabeth could persuade her to visit Sleightholmedale. Despite her veneer of sophistication, she would not face the possibility of meeting her father.

There was only one other cloud on Tamar's horizon and that was the Welshman, Gareth Davis. Months would pass with no encounter between them and then, just as she had begun to feel secure, he would dog her footsteps for a week or two. If she caught sight of him in the distance, he would sometimes raise a hand in an ironic salute. Once, when taking a short cut alone, he suddenly appeared from between two buildings, blocking her path, smiling as always. 'What do you want of me?' she had cried in desperation.

'That's for me to know and you to find out.' His lilting Welsh drawl had been teasing.

'Leave me alone!' she hissed at him, as she swung on her heel and went back to the throng of the market place. She rarely went out alone these days, usually making the excuse that she needed Tempy to carry her parcels. Since her arrival in Helmsley, she had to admit that the man had not put a foot wrong, but she was haunted by his attempted rape at Cherry Tree Farm. She could not decide whether their meeting in the churchyard had been accidental, or whether he had seen her somewhere in the town and kept watch on her. She consoled herself that she would ensure that she was never alone again, and then she would be safe from him, whatever his intentions.

At last, just before their fifth wedding anniversary, Tamar's hopes were confirmed and she knew that she was at long last carrying Stephen's child.

When she broke the news to him, he was delirious with joy. 'Oh, my darling!' he laughed, swinging her round in his arms. 'Thank God! I was sure that it was my fault that we were childless. You've already had Victoria, but I felt to blame that you had not conceived my child. Now everything is perfect.'

Tamar contained her impatience to tell her mother until the following Wednesday. Stephen was over-protective towards her and made it clear that he would not feel happy if she drove herself there in the governess cart. 'Go in the carriage with Goodison,' he pleaded. 'We've waited so long for this baby that we can't take any risks.'

Tamar was only too willing to do as he asked and decided that Victoria should take the day off school and go and see her Gran.

Elizabeth and Annie now had places in the indoor market, where Elizabeth had established a tea-stall. At one end of the market-hall was a cast iron stove and Elizabeth had pleaded and cajoled until the market superintendent had given in and allowed her to make use of it. She had bought two forms and a little table, and dispensed mugs of tea from a copper tea urn, using the stove to boil her kettles. As predicted she had built up a good clientèle of those who did not want to go to an inn for their refreshments. George was proud of his wife's business venture and her earnings were far more than they had expected. Ann Butler did not approve of her daughter going into trade, as she put it, but begrudgingly admitted that it was a profitable side-line.

Now, as Tamar sat at the end of one of the benches, close to where her mother was sitting, she sent Victoria off in Goodison's charge to look round the market. Once the excited child was out of earshot, she called Elizabeth over and told the two women, 'I'm expecting.'

Her mother's face lit up. 'Eeh lass! That's grand news,' she exclaimed. With a wry smile to herself, Tamar compared this reception of her news with the one when she was pregnant with Victoria.

Elizabeth kissed her on the cheek. 'I'm so happy for you,' she said, but though the words were heartfelt, Tamar noticed that a shadow passed over her face.

'I wish it could be you, as well,' she said.

Elizabeth turned away to serve a customer. 'We've given up hope, now.' came her reply. 'I'm afraid I'm too old.'

When Victoria returned, they had a mug of tea and one

of Elizabeth's pies, much to Victoria's delight who sat on the form, swinging her legs and drinking from a pint pot, thinking what an adventure it was. As she chatted to her grandmother, Annie found it hard to believe that this beautifully spoken and finely dressed child was her granddaughter.

When they reached home in mid-afternoon, Tamar found Stephen in an agitated mood. 'I've received a letter from my mother,' he said. 'My brother has been killed.'

Tamar felt no emotion at the news. She had never met Stephen's brother, Hilary, who had been with his regiment in India the whole of the time she had lived in Helmsley. She knew that Stephen's elder brother had gone against his parents' wishes in making the army his career: their father was in poor health and had wanted his eldest son to take over the running of the family estate.

'I must go over to Thorsbury immediately,' Stephen decided. 'My father is very frail and there will be a lot to discuss.' He looked across at his wife. 'You do realise, don't you, that this will change our lives?'

Tamar was surprised. 'In what way?' she asked.

Stephen considered for a moment before answering. 'Well, for one thing, I am now Father's heir and will one day inherit Thorsbury. Consequently, I think that it may be necessary for us to move to the Manor, so that I can take over the running of the estate.'

A wave of panic washed over Tamar and she felt quite faint. She had seen very little of Stephen's mother, but knew that Lady Lassiter disliked her intensely and did not make much effort to disguise her antipathy. She had to confess that the feeling was mutual: dismay rose within her at the thought of moving into the Lassiter home. 'But we're so happy here,' she protested, 'and you have your practice.'

Stephen shrugged. 'Our circumstances have now changed. Owing to my brother's absence and my father's state of health, the estate has been neglected. Now that it will one day be mine, and my son's after me,' he smiled as he leaned forward and kissed her, 'I must supervise the running of it.'

Stephen and Hilary Lassiter had never been particularly close, as his elder brother was considerably older. He had joined his regiment while Stephen was still at school so that, while saddened by his brother's death, no real grief was felt by the younger man. He had always believed that Hilary's duty had been to remain on the estate and protect his inheritance.

Tamar slowly sank on to the sofa and pressed a hand to her head. Her thoughts were in a turmoil. She had carved out a little niche for herself in Helmsley, having several friends who were about her own age and married to professional men. She was the mistress of a comfortable home and lived within easy reach of her own family. She felt that she possessed as much as life could offer. Suddenly, out of the blue, her whole way of life was threatened. She felt apprehensive and unsure as she realised that her unknown brother-in-law's death would bring about an upheaval in her life. The one consolation was that their move from Helmsley would remove her finally from the reach of Gareth Davis. 'Why did your brother never marry?' she inquired.

Stephen shook his head. 'He was only interested in the military life. He should have married and produced an heir but, though Mama paraded plenty of suitable girls before him when he was home on leave, he always returned to his regiment before he could be snared.'

Stephen then decided that, being only a couple of months into her pregnancy, Tamar should remain in Helmsley and not accompany him to Thorsbury. She put up no argument, only too pleased to keep out of her mother-in-law's way. 'I may be away a couple of weeks,' Stephen went on. 'As well as having Hilary's affairs to see to, as his executor, I want to look into the running of the estate. My father has a good agent, but there are three other farms as well as Home Farm and the woodlands are very extensive – the timber business brings in a good income. I feel that I must keep my finger on the pulse until such time as we move over there.'

Tamar once again felt her stomach lurch at the thought of living in the same house as Stephen's mother, the cold grey woman who did not bother to hide her dislike when they were alone. 'I can't live with her,' she thought in desperation, but knew deep in her heart that there was no way out of the situation.

Stephen was away for only ten days and then returned to say that his brother's death had been the final blow for his already weakened father. 'His heart is very bad,' he told Tamar, 'and the doctor doesn't give much hope for him.'

Tamar was sorry. What little she had seen of her father-in-law, she had liked. Stephen was very similar to his father, the two sharing the same gentle nature. Now she was dismayed to hear that the old man might die. His death would make their move to Thorsbury Manor a certainty. 'Has he seen another doctor?' she asked her husband.

'Yes. They've even had a man down from Wimpole Street in London,' he answered, 'but there's nothing can be done, I'm afraid.'

His fears were only too well justified. The following midday brought a messenger riding over from Thorsbury to bring the news of the death of Stephen's father.

'Well, Brown?' Stephen said, as Tempy showed the groom into the dining room, where her master and mistress were having lunch. The question in his voice was proof that Stephen anticipated his errand.

As he handed over the letter, the groom said, 'We are all so sorry, Sir Stephen,' and turning to Tamar, he gave a slight bow and said, 'Lady Lassiter.' Stephen observed the widening of Tamar's eyes. 'Take Brown to the kitchen, Tempy, and see that he gets a good meal before he takes my reply back to the Manor.'

When they were alone, Tamar raised tear-brimmed eyes to his. 'I'm so sorry, my darling,' she whispered.

'He has been ill for a long time, and really it's a blessed release,' he comforted her.

Tamar glanced at him. 'It gave me a shock to be called Lady Lassiter,' she admitted.

Stephen looked at her with tenderness. 'You were born to be a Lady, my darling,' he told her.

Tamar considered for a moment. 'What about your mother?' she asked.

'She will be the Dowager Lady Lassiter and will move

into the dower house, a smaller house on the estate,' he replied.

A glow of relief swept over Tamar. She was saved from sharing a house with Stephen's mother! Thank goodness for that, she thought. Events seemed to be moving swiftly and inexorably, bringing changes which they were powerless to stop as each generation made way for the next.

Stephen decided to accompany Brown on his journey back to Thorsbury that afternoon; Tamar would follow the next day in the big travelling coach. As Thorsbury was some seventeen miles or more from Sleightholmedale, she decided that first she must go and make her farewells at Aumery Park Farm. 'It will be the first time I've visited the dales since I arrived in Helmsley,' she said to her husband. 'I've avoided seeing my father since the day he came here, before we were married.'

'Yes, I think it's time to let bygones be bygones,' he answered soberly. 'Go and make your peace before we leave the district.'

Consequently, that very afternoon Goodison gingerly guided the carriage down the steep hill through the tunnel of trees into Sleightholmedale. Victoria chattered excitedly, exclaiming with delight at the sight of the deep purple bluebells which carpeted the woods. 'It's so lovely, Mama! Why haven't I been here before?' she demanded. 'You must have missed it.'

Tamar looked out of the coach window, which she had pulled down to drink in the heady aroma of the flowers. As she answered she reflected ruefully on how she had resented the valley when it had been her home. Taking a deep breath to steady her voice, she replied, 'I have missed it, pet. Indeed I have.' Leaning from the window, she called up to the coachman, 'Pull off the road into the quarry, please, Goodison.' When he opened the door and helped her down, she turned to Victoria. 'Now that your cousin Mollie Waind has gone to live in Bransdale with her parents, Grandma has no one to pick flowers for her. We used to take her lovely bunches when we were children. Let's go into the woods for a few minutes and pick her some.'

Watching her daughter dashing from clump to clump,

picking primroses and cowslips and parting the heart-shaped leaves to search out the pale fragrant violets hidden amongst them, it was brought home to Tamar with a pang that, despite a luxurious home, schooling and the refinements of life, Victoria's childhood was deprived. Seeing the child revelling in the colours and scents of the flowers which covered the roadside and woodland, she acknowledged that her childhood in this valley had been enriched in ways which were foreign to a town-raised girl.

'Come along, now,' she called, as she arranged sprays of tender green beech leaves behind the bluebells she had gathered. Their spring freshness was a perfect foil for the deep purple-blue of the flowers.

When they emerged from the sheltering trees and the valley widened out, Victoria was silent with wonder. The track meandered between hedges which frothed with the highly-scented cream foam of May blossom. The bright flits of yellowhammers as they flashed from one side of the road to the other, and the liquid notes of the blackbirds and song-thrushes from their perches in the hedgerows held her speechless. To her, the little dale was an enchanted valley.

When they reached the farm, Annie was astonished to see Tamar enter the kitchen, especially as her daughter was dressed in deepest mourning. 'Whatever's up, lass?' she queried, as she embraced Tamar and bent to kiss Victoria.

'Stephen's father has died and I'm afraid we're moving tomorrow,' answered her daughter.

'Tomorrow?' Annie flopped down in her rocking-chair and fanned her face with the corner of her apron in a vain effort to relieve her agitation.

Tamar turned to Lydia. 'Would you show Goodison the coachman where the stables are, please,' she directed the maid.

Lydia sniffed as she went out. It didn't seem long since Tamar was only too glad of her company, she reflected and here she was ordering her about like a skivvy. 'Lady Muck – that's who she is,' she told herself as she swung herself up beside Goodison.

When the coachman carefully manoeuvred his vehicle

into the yard, prior to feeding and watering his team, Jonadab Oaks was displaying a pair of shirehorses to a buyer from the army. He looked up with a frown. 'What's this then?' he demanded shortly.

Lydia opened her mouth to speak, anxious to be the one to bring the news of Tamar's arrival and witness her master's reaction. Before she could make her announcement, however, Goodison forestalled her. 'Good afternoon, sir. I am Sir Stephen Lassiter's man and Her Ladyship instructed me to attend to the horses here, if you don't mind.'

To Lydia's chagrin, her master's face showed no emotion at the news that after almost six years' absence, Tamar was back in the dale – and a Lady, to boot. He merely nodded to Goodison and turned back to his customer. What she could not know was that beneath his outward calmness, Jonadab's mind seethed with questions. What was Tamar doing here, when for years she had steadfastly refused to come home? Was the bairn with her? How had her husband suddenly come by the title?

As Lydia flounced out of the yard she was obviously in a huff about something, thought Jonadab. He was suddenly impatient to be rid of the prospective buyer, whose interest in his stock he had been nurturing all afternoon. 'Aye, well. What dost thoo think?' He was suddenly pushing for a quick decision, much to the other man's surprise.

'Well, now, Mr Oaks – I've others to see, before making a choice,' said the quarter-master.

'Please thissen! Thoo'll see nowt as good as mine,' came the swift retort, as Jonadab swung on his heel. 'When thoo's seen t'others, Aah've no doubt thoo'll be back,' he called over his shoulder, as he hurried away.

'Well!' The man was nonplussed.'He's a rum 'un, and no mistake,' and he looked towards Goodison. The coachman, however, was too diplomatic to express an opinion on his mistress's father, and kept his head turned towards his charges.

Upon seeing her father pass the kitchen window, Martha crossed towards where Victoria was playing with the cat on the rug. Holding out her hand, she spoke. 'Come along.

Would you like to come with Auntie Martha and see the farm? We've lots of animals for you to meet.'

'Oh, yes please. May I, Mama?' Victoria pleaded. This was the most exciting day of her life apart from Christmas, she had decided, and was savouring every new sight and sound.

'Of course.' Tamar smiled at her enthusiasm. At that moment the door was thrown open to reveal Jonadab on the doorstep. Victoria took a step back at the sight of this tall, fierce-looking man.

'Noo then! Who's this, then?' he queried, looking her up and down.

'Victoria Lassiter, sir,' she answered with her best curtsey.

Tamar intervened. 'This is your Granddad Oaks, my father,' she explained.

Victoria's face broke into a smile, then saddened. 'My Grandpa Lassiter's gone to live in Heaven,' she announced.

So that was where the title had come from, thought Jonadab. He had thought there was an elder brother. He looked at the little girl gravely. 'Aah'm sorry ti hear that,' he said, moving aside as she and Martha made for the door.

As Jonadab crossed the kitchen to take his place in his Windsor chair, he studied Tamar. She felt herself flushing under the sardonic gaze of his blue eyes, still as vivid as ever. He spoke to Lydia, who was seated at the table busy cleaning knife blades with powdered sandstone. 'Mash a pot o' tea and then find summat ti do outside,' he ordered. Lydia bristled. For years she had been treated like one of the family and now, twice this same afternoon, she had been ordered about. She banged the teapot and three mugs on to the plain deal table and took herself off, with a toss of her head.

As Annie bustled about, pouring out the tea and buttering scones, Tamar and her father eyed each other warily. He, it was, who broke the silence between them. 'So thoo got somebody who's made thoo a lady after all,' he remarked.

Tamar felt a glow staining her neck and creeping up her cheeks. This reference to her boast, when she had become pregnant with Victoria by Sir William Forster, was the last thing she had expected to hear. She had made a new life and the circumstances of Victoria's birth were buried deep in her memory. Her amber eyes flashed with the golden lights of temper and she drew a breath to retort. Her father, however, regretted the comment as soon as it was uttered. He held up a hand. 'Nay, lass. That was uncalled for and Aah'm sorry,' he sighed. 'Nowt can remove the past, but thoo's got a good man and made thicken a good life. Aah'm pleased for thoo.'

Tamar had never expected to hear an apology pass her father's lips and recognised the effort it must have cost him to admit being in the wrong. From that moment, the tension in the kitchen eased and the three of them were soon talking naturally together, as though the years of constraint between father and daughter had never existed.

Tamar glanced around at the kitchen. The stone-flagged floor was as spotless as ever, softened only by a clip-rug in front of the fire. The deal table was scrubbed white and she could almost swear that the bright red geraniums which graced the window-sill were the self-same plants that she had watered, years before. As she finished telling her parents of the death of Stephen's brother and father, she looked across at her own father with a wry smile. 'So you see, Father, I am indeed a lady – and would much rather not be,' she confessed.

'Whyever not?' exclaimed Annie. 'You'll mek a grand lady.'

Tamar described her life with Stephen. 'You've seen the house, Father. It's perfect for us and Stephen is happy in his work. Now we must leave all our friends and uproot ourselves to go to live in Thorsbury. It's a small village, about six miles from Malton. There is no school for Victoria and we cannot decide whether to have a governess, or send her to school daily with Goodison. I think we shall settle on a governess,' she concluded.

Annie found it difficult to grasp the calm way in which Tamar talked of manors, governesses and servants, as though she had been born to the life which she now lived. She often thought to herself that the two children who had sinned seemed to have had more success in life than the ones who had stuck to the straight and narrow path. Joseph, whose marriage to Mary Butler had been, as his mother put it, 'a rush job', had recently written from the Canadas to say that he now had his own farm of over two thousand acres. Tamar had not even worn a marriage band when her child was born and yet here she sat with a coachman awaiting her, shortly to live in a mansion and be a lady. Annie recognised that she could not discuss these thoughts with her husband, but felt that somehow, life was unfair.

While her father went to find Martha and Victoria, Tamar remarked, 'I'm not looking forward to tomorrow's journey. I'm just as sick in the mornings with this one, as I was with Victoria.' She took her mother by the shoulders and kissed her swiftly on the cheek. 'Oh, Mam! I wish you could deliver it, like you did her,' she said huskily. 'I'd feel much better about it.'

'Thoo can afford t'best now, lass,' her mother replied gently. 'Thoo'll be all right.'

'You are the best,' Tamar said, giving her another hug. Before she left, she looked steadily into her father's eyes, 'I'm glad I came, Father. I realise what a trial I was to you. I was wild and wilful, but I've settled down now and am pleased that things are all right between us.'

'Aye lass, and all the best ti thoo,' he said, as Goodison helped her into the coach. 'Give our regards to Stephen when you get home,' he added. When eventually they were out of sight, he sighed as he turned to his wife. 'That one'll never settle down,' he said. 'Looking out from yon pretty-pussy face is a wild tiger, waiting to get out. That's what them eyes reminds me of.'

Although Stephen had been insistent that once installed at Thorsbury Manor, Tamar should employ a French maid, she had dug in her heels and insisted Tempy should occupy that position.

'But she has no experience. She doesn't know what's what,' he protested.

Tamar's lips were pressed into a thin line and her eyes narrowed into an expression which he had come to recognize as brooking no argument. 'Neither do I, so we shall learn together,' was her uncompromising reply.

So it was that Tempy was installed in the travelling coach

162

beside her mistress and Victoria, while Gertie followed behind in a hired coach, with their luggage. 'At least I know I shall have two friends in that household,' Tamar told herself grimly.

Before departing, Tamar had scored a triumph over Mrs Judd the cook. Going into the kitchen, she had held out her hand in farewell, but the woman had pretended to be wiping her hands on her apron and so avoided the outstretched hand. Tamar had intended to reassure the cook that when Stephen sold the house and practice, he would recommend her to the new owner. Now, however, she held the woman's curranty eyes with hers and said coldly, 'Goodbye, Mrs Judd. No doubt my husband will give you a good reference,' and, swinging round, had walked from the kitchen leaving the cook with mouth agape.

As the coach bumped along the rough country roads, Tamar grew more nauseous. Her pallor became more noticeable and Tempy saw that her top lip was beaded with droplets of perspiration. She sat beside her mistress and, after chafing her hands, held a vinaigrette to her nose. Tamar took a deep breath of the smelling salts and then said faintly, 'Tell Goodison to stop. I must get out for some fresh air.'

When they resumed their journey, it seemed no time at all before they were crossing the four-arched bridge which led over the river to the front gates of Thorsbury Manor. Although the entrance was flanked by twin lodges, the huge wrought-iron gates were standing wide open. Tamar presumed that this was in readiness for her arrival, but found later that they had stood thus since her father-in-law's death, for the convenience of visitors calling to pay their respects to the newly-widowed Lady Lassiter.

As the coach swept round the wide drive towards the house, Victoria and Tempy looked out in wide-eyed amazement. Tamar's previous visits to the Manor had made her familiar with the view of the south front, but she could appreciate the impact made by the first sight of the mansion. The stone of which it was built was almost white, and sparkled in the rays of the midday sun. Together with the countless windows, this gave an appearance of lightness and delicacy which belied its size. The walls rose to crenellated battlements, so impressive that Victoria cried out, 'Oh, Mama! It's just like a fairy castle.'

'Indeed it is, darling,' replied her mother.

Descending shakily from the coach, she took the child's hand and together they went through the magnificent doors. Turning from the entrance hall, Tamar saw her mother-in-law standing by the ornate marble fireplace. The sombre black of her mourning dress exaggerated her pallor and, as she leaned forward to touch her cheek briefly to Tamar's, her eyes were chillingly aloof.

Tamar's heart sank. As she went to go upstairs, she thought of Victoria's remark. 'A fairy castle indeed,' she thought grimly, glancing back at the hostile figure by the fire.

# CHAPTER FIFTEEN

The village of Thorsbury was no more than a hamlet. The only street fell steeply down towards the secondary gateway to the Manor and had about fifteen cottages on the east side of the road. These were of a soft-hued golden sandstone topped by russet-toned pantiles. They huddled together in twos and threes, with the pretty little church standing back about halfway down the village.

The story was that there had once been houses on each side of the road but a century or so ago, those on the west had been demolished to add to the parkland. This strip had been laid out by the estate gardeners into what were known as Walks. Briar roses and honeysuckle had been cunningly trained to festoon the trees, until the whole effect there was one of enchantment. The only gateway from the Walks was directly opposite the church, so that the Lassiters rarely walked up the village itself. The Walks were forbidden to the villagers and in the final few weeks of pregnancy, Tamar spent much of her time strolling there, in such complete seclusion that she felt cut off from civilisation.

In the peaceful rural surroundings of Thorsbury, Tamar felt truly at home. She was only disturbed by the fact that, once the funeral was over, her mother-in-law made no attempt to leave the Manor and take up residence in the dower house. Tamar had little chance to talk to Stephen, who seemed to be occupied on estate business from morn till night. He was often away in the West Riding, where he now owned several woollen mills which had been the basis of his father's fortune. When he was back at Thorsbury, he had taken to sleeping in the dressing room now that her time was almost upon her.

This meant that the couple were virtually never alone. At dinner in the evenings, she and Stephen sat at the head and foot of the long dining table, with his mother between them, ignoring Tamar and monopolising her son's attention.

After the meal as they sat in the drawing room, Lady Lassiter did her best to make Tamar feel like an outsider by talking of people and circumstances of which Tamar knew nothing. If Tamar tried to sit up until her mother-in-law had retired to her bed, the other woman seemed determined that husband and wife should not be alone together, and Tamar's aching back would drive her up the stairs, miserably leaving Stephen and his mother chatting by the fire.

One night, as Tempy was helping her undress, she determined to tackle Stephen the next day. 'Wake me at half-past seven Tempy, please,' she instructed. When the maid woke her she sat up in bed and said, 'Ask Sir Stephen if he can spare me a few minutes.'

Stephen entered a short time later, looking anxious. 'There's nothing wrong is there, darling?' he asked in a worried tone. 'The baby isn't coming?'

'No,' she answered, 'but there is something we must discuss.' She hesitated, unsure exactly how to word what she wished to say.

'Yes?' He leaned forward from where he sat on the side of the bed and kissed her gently. Noting that Tamar did not smile he was concerned. 'You are happy at Thorsbury, aren't you, my darling?' he asked.

'Oh, yes.' Tamar's enthusiasm for the place momentarily brightened up her face. 'I love it here, Stephen.' Again she paused, but decided to press on. 'There's just one thing. I cannot feel that I am truly mistress here, while your mother is in residence. She gives the orders and the servants defer to her. I would like to know when your mother's going to move out.'

Stephen looked uncomfortable. 'She wants to stay here until after the baby is born,' he told her.

Tamar's lips tightened. She realised with a sinking heart that the longer her mother-in-law remained at the Manor, the more difficult it would be to dislodge her. There was, however, little she could do without appearing heartless in her husband's eyes. She settled back in her pillows and assessed him tenderly. 'You're looking tired, Stephen, and I see so little of you now. When will you be able to take things more easily?'

166

He smiled ruefully. 'Heaven knows. The estate and the businesses in Bradford have been allowed to run down during the last few years, while my father was not well. It means a lot of work at present, especially as I'm unfamiliar with the running of them. However, once our son arrives, I may have got things on an even keel and be able to take some time off.'

With this, Tamar had to be satisfied. At least, she thought, she had made clear to Stephen the fact that she was not happy living in his mother's shadow.

Owing to her advanced pregnancy and Stephen's frequent absences on business, no efforts had been made to appoint a governess for Victoria. Instead, the local curate, Selwyn Mathews, took over her instruction, until such time as other arrangements could be made. He was a merry young man and yet, quite firm in his discipline, so that the child was eager to please him and her education made rapid strides.

As Tamar's time drew closer, she remembered the difficult labour of Victoria's birth and grew more and more apprehensive. In this new life which had been thrust upon her, she felt that she must surround herself with a little group of servants whom she knew to be loyal to her. Although Walton the head coachman still drove her mother-in-law, the few times that Tamar had driven out, she had used their coach and pair from the days at Helmsley, with Goodison to drive her. Gertie still looked after Victoria, using the time that her charge spent in the schoolroom to attend to her clothes – washing, brushing and replacing buttons. Tempy was a friend, as well as her maid, the one person in whom Tamar felt that she could confide.

The girl realised that her mistress was dreading her confinement and insisted that Tamar spent the afternoons lying down. During this time of enforced idleness, she massaged Tamar's body with oil of almonds, not only to relieve her backache, but also to avoid unsightly stretchmarks on her body. 'I know Sir Stephen's too tired to come into your room at present and anyway, you're not fit,' she said confidingly. 'But you want to get your figure back after the bairn's born. You'll be as lovely as ever for him – I'll see to that.'

167

It was during one of these sessions, when she lay under Tempy's firm hands, that a thought occurred to Tamar. 'What's your real name, Tempy?' she asked. 'It can't surely be Temptation.'

Tempy threw back her head and laughed until she had to wipe away the tears. 'Lawks, ma'am,' she giggled, forgetting her carefully-cultivated veneer of refinement. 'It's Temperance. My family was Methodists.'

Tamar laughed with her and realised that she felt less depressed about the forthcoming confinement after this little spell of humour. As luck would have it, she had no time to build up her fears again, for her labour pains started that very night. Stephen was away, so she had passed a near-silent dinner in the company of his mother. The only words spoken had been to the butler and maid, who were waiting at table and when they rose, Tamar excused herself. 'I think I'll go up, Mama,' she said, pleading a backache which was not feigned.

By the time she reached her room, the old remembered pains were coming with great frequency. Tempy took one look at her mistress as she clung to the door handle, her back bent under the pain, and tugged on the bell-pull. She helped Tamar on to the bed and, as she removed her shoes, there was a tap on the door. The maid who came was a local girl. 'Is there a village midwife?' Tempy demanded. 'Her Ladyship's started in labour, though she's not due for another couple of weeks and there's no time to get the doctor and nurse from Malton, by the look of things.'

'Aye – Mrs Walton, t' 'ead groom's wife, delivers most bairns round 'ereabouts,' replied the girl.

'Go and get her then, and be quick about it,' urged Tempy. As the girl reached the door, she caught the additional command: 'And tell Cook to get some water on the boil.'

By the time Tempy had managed to strip Tamar and get her into her nightdress, the baby's head was in view. 'It's going to be quick,' Tempy cried. 'Don't push. Lie still and I'll run for Gertie.'

When the midwife arrived, flustered and overwhelmed to be called inside the Manor, it was all over. Helped by

Tempy and Gertie, neither of whom had experienced a birth before, Tamar had been delivered of a boy, quickly and with no trouble. While Mrs Walton washed the baby and dressed him in a layette far finer than she had ever imagined existed, Tempy attended to Tamar and put a fresh nightgown on her. The midwife laid the little scrap in Tamar's arms and said, "E's a lovely lad, Lady Lassiter. 'E's not big, but 'e's all the world ti grow in.'

Tamar looked down at the child, scarcely able to believe that it was all over so quickly. What little hair he had shone with a silver sheen in the lamplight and she could see in the crumpled, brick-red face, the likeness of Stephen. She closed her eyes briefly to say a silent prayer of thanks that, not only had Stephen received the son for whom he had so longed, but that the baby was the image of his father.

When she opened her eyes, it was to see Stephen's mother standing by the bed. For the first time since Tamar had met her, the putty-coloured cheeks were flushed and the hands which she held out for the child were shaking. As Tamar placed him in his grandmother's arms, tears rolled down the older woman's cheeks. 'Another Hilary Lassiter,' she whispered. 'The line will not die out.' Before Tamar could protest that she intended to call her son George, her mother-in-law looked up from the child. 'I must thank you for this, if for nothing else,' she said and, placing him back in Tamar's arms, turned and went from the room.

When Gertie brought Victoria to see her new brother, she leaned over the crib shaking with excitement. 'Oh,' she murmured. 'He's lovely – just like a real live doll.' With that she reached out a tentative hand and gently stroked the silver hair.

When Stephen returned the following day, the news was broken to him in the stable block by the groom who took his horse. 'Congratulations, sir,' the man beamed. 'Lady Lassiter gave birth to a son last night.'

Stephen took the stairs two at a time and threw open the bedroom door to see Tamar, sitting up in the big fourposter bed, nursing their son. Too excited at first to speak, he bent over to kiss her and then turned his attention to the

169

child. 'He's wonderful,' he gasped, as he gazed at the little face and held each tiny hand, studying the miniature nails in wonderment. 'And you're wonderful, too,' he added. While she had Stephen to herself, Tamar brought up the question of the name.

'It is the family name,' he explained. 'The eldest Lassiter son is always called Hilary, but why not make George his second name?'

With this Tamar had to be satisfied, but she felt mutinous. 'I had the confinement – I should choose the name,' she told Tempy. The maid, however, was noncommittal, not wishing to cross her mistress and yet seeing Stephen's point of view.

Although Stephen's trips to the mills became less frequent as he appointed capable managers, the farms on the estate and the timber business still took a great deal of his life and Tamar found that time hung heavily. Her mother-in-law's days were spent at her embroidery or visiting friends whom Tamar felt despised her as an outsider. She scarcely knew these women and told herself that she didn't wish to. One innovation she had brought to the village was that, unlike her predecessors, she made a point of visiting every house in the little community. She had introduced herself on the doorstep, often been invited in and asked the tenants to let her know if they had any problems with which she could help.

Tamar had been brought up on a tenanted farm and was sensitive to the diffidence felt when an approach to the landowner was necessary. She soon realised that Stephen's mother thought she was demeaning herself by 'hobnobbing with the peasantry' but Stephen was grateful for her interest and that was all that mattered to Tamar. Soon she knew the workers by name and could tell Stephen which man's wife kept a neat house and whose was a slut.

One evening as they sat round the fire after dinner, Stephen suggested to Tamar, 'Why don't you learn to ride? After all, your father is a farmer so you must be used to horses. You wouldn't be a real beginner and it would give you an interest when I'm busy.'

The more Tamar thought about the idea, the more she

170

liked it. She loved the country life of the estate and could have been entirely happy were it not for Stephen's habitual absences which only seemed to emphasise the constant presence of his mother. And now that she was free of the fear of encountering Gareth Davis on her walks, she revelled in exploring the grounds of her home. She often dawdled along the Walks and strolled on the banks of the river, which ran past the rear of the Manor. At this point, the river was swift: its swirling currents and dark menacing depths filled Tamar with dread for her children. Victoria was banned from the riverside and Gertie had been instructed never to take the baby anywhere near the water. The loss of her own younger sister Maria, who had been drowned in the Beck close to Aumery Park Farm, was ever-present at the back of Tamar's mind.

A week or two after Stephen's suggestion, he came home one day leading a pretty little mare on a halter. Upon entering the grand hall where Tamar sat, he gave her a quick teasing smile. 'Come and see what I've brought for you,' was his greeting.

Tamar jumped to her feet. 'What is it, Stephen?' she asked excitedly. He made no response, but just took her hand and led her towards the stable-block. These buildings were of a later date than the Manor house, being built of brick surrounding a large quadrangle. The ground floor consisted of stables, coach-houses, tackrooms and store-houses, while above, in addition to apartments occupied by unmarried male outdoor staff, was a room known as the Long Room. This ran the full length of one side and was used for village functions like the Mell or Harvest Supper, and the Christmas party.

As they entered the stable-yard, Tamar gasped with pleasure and ran forward to the mare, which stood tied up to a rail. 'Oh,' she breathed. 'Is she for me?'

Stephen smiled at her excitement. 'How lovely she is,' he thought for the thousandth time, as he looked at her fondly. She threw her arms round the horse's neck and in return, it flicked its ears and snickered with pleasure. It was almost pure white in colour, with mane and tail of silvery-grey.

'I shall call her Moonbeam,' Tamar decided.

'Why not go to Malton tomorrow and buy a riding habit?' her husband suggested as they walked back to the house.

Tamar took his arm and looked up at him. 'You're so good to me, Stephen,' she said seriously, 'but I would change all this to have more of your company.'

He gave a deep sigh. 'I know that, my darling and I only wish I could see more of you and the children. However, I am getting the business matters straightened out and I hope it won't be too long before I shall have more time to spend with you.'

While they were alone and could not be overheard by those inside the house, she once more broached the subject of his mother's continued presence at the Manor. 'I'm not the mistress here and never will be, as long as she remains,' she insisted.

'Be patient, Tamar,' he pleaded. 'It has been her home for well over thirty years and she needs some stability after losing Father. Besides,' he added, 'she's devoted to little Hilary and finds great comfort in him.'

Tamar bit back the retort which sprang to her lips. She had no wish to upset her husband, but she knew how much Stephen's mother hated her and felt that her mother-in-law was trying to usurp her place in the baby's affections. Tamar had been dismayed to discover that it was the custom, among the upper classes, to employ a wetnurse for babies. She not only missed the bond which breast-feeding had created between her and Victoria, but was made to feel most unwelcome when she visited the nursery. Search as she might, Tamar could find nothing of herself in Hilary. The child was entirely Lassiter in appearance so that, while she was pleased on Stephen's behalf, Tamar could not feel the deep love which she had for her daughter.

On her visit to Malton, she not only purchased a riding habit in deep, forest-green velvet, but ordered one to be made in a similar material of a light golden-brown colour, to match the shade of her eyes.

While she was still a novice, Stephen insisted that her daily rides should be accompanied by a groom. Although Jonadab Oaks had never encouraged his girls to ride, as he did his sons, they had all on several occasions had a go at riding the horses owned by their father. Tamar found the side-saddle strange at first, but her previous experience stood her in good stead. She rode out most afternoons and gradually built up a familiarity with most parts of the Lassiter lands.

In the July following Hilary's birth, which had taken place in February, Stephen announced at dinner, 'I think it's about time Seth Walton retired. He must be getting on for seventy, and we need a younger head groom.'

'Will you promote Charlie?' asked Tamar.

'No. I don't think it's a good idea to promote one of the workers. Charlie is too much one of the lads and won't hold their respect,' answered her husband. 'I don't want to wait until the Malton Hiring at Martinmas. I shall ask around and if I get no satisfaction I shall advertise.'

Tamar thought no more about this conversation and did not ask Stephen whether his quest for a new groom had been successful. She was blissfully unaware that Stephen's choice was the very man whom she was confident she had now eluded . . .

A couple of weeks later Stephen was called away to Bradford, where the manager of one of his mills had disappeared with the wages of the whole workforce. He sighed as he kissed Tamar goodbye. 'I'll get back as soon as I can,' he promised. 'So much seems to be going wrong since my father's death that it's unbelievable.'

Lunch was as dreary as it always was when Stephen's presence was lacking. His mother was her usual pale grey, silent self. Her sole topic of conversation nowadays was the baby and she seemed to resent the fact that Tamar was his mother.

When Tamar rose from the table, she remarked, 'I shall go out for a ride, Mama.'

Her mother-in-law raised dull eyes. 'I would wish that your deportment on a horse could be more that of a lady and less that of a farm waggoner,' she remarked spitefully.

Tamar bit her lip. She had had to learn to control her fiery temper in the face of her mother-in-law's insults. The woman was never offensive in Stephen's presence, but

Tamar knew that should she retaliate, as she was often tempted to, her conduct would immediately be reported to her husband. She was very sensitive to the fact that Stephen had enough worries at the moment without the antipathy between his wife and mother adding to them. 'You just wait, madam,' Tamar thought to herself, as she turned from the room and swept up the stairs. She was determined that her day would come.

When she reached the stable-yard, Moonbeam was saddled up and ready, tied up by the mounting block but there was no sign of Jonnie Medd, the young groom who usually accompanied her. As her eyes scanned the yard, she caught sight of him coming out of one of the stables. 'Come along, Jonnie – I'm ready,' she called sharply.

The lad ran over to her, touching his cap. 'T' new head groom's riding out with you today, m'Lady,' he told her.

Tamar's brows drew together in a frown. 'I didn't know Sir Stephen had set one on yet,' she observed.

'Yes, m'Lady. 'E started yesterday,' answered Jonnie.

As he spoke, a figure came from one of the stables leading a horse. Tamar glanced across curiously and as the man emerged from the shadow of the stable into the bright sunlight, her throat constricted and her heart gave a lurch. There was no mistaking that jaunty walk and the cocky tilt of the man's head. As the sun caught the coppery glint of the curls which clung closely to his head like a cap, the familiar Welsh lilt greeted her. 'Good afternoon, m'Lady. Which way are you wanting to ride, today?' asked Gareth Davis.

Tamar took a deep breath to steady her nerves before she replied. As he drew closer and they came face to face, she drew herself up and eyed him coldly. 'How dare you follow me?' she demanded icily.

He made no reply to her challenge, but his eyes were alight with devilish laughter as he unhitched her horse. 'Shall we mount, m'Lady and go where we shall not be overheard?' he suggested.

Tamar's eyes were cold. 'I'll not be alone with you,' she answered tightly.

'Come now.' His smile had gone as he led her horse

174

forward. 'The men are going to gossip if we stand here and argue. Mount up, and we'll talk as we ride.'

Tamar had no alternative but to do as he said, and they rode from the yard without another word. How bitterly she regretted now that she had not revealed the episode with Davis before her marriage to Stephen. If she had told him then, or even when the man had reappeared in her life at Helmsley she would now be on firmer ground. As her love for Stephen had grown, she had come to see clearly that she should have been more open with him at the beginning. She felt unable to marshal her thoughts into a semblance of logic. She was terrified that if she poured out the tale to her husband now, he would be filled with doubts as to the extent of her previous involvement with Davis.

Instead of choosing to ride through the woodland paths which she loved so much, Tamar turned up the village street, intent on keeping to the roads. Trotting past the houses, she was greeted with affection by those who saw her. 'Good day, m'Lady,' called more than one villager, so that Davis realised she had won the hearts of these people. When they reached the road which ran across the top of the village, the groom drew level and, with a nod of his head, indicated that they should take the righthand way which led to the river bridge. Upon reaching the bridge, he turned off the road and led the way through the trees, dismounting in a little clearing by the fast flowing water.

Tamar stood for few moments studying the turbulent river, which seemed to reflect the turmoil of her thoughts. Her tranquil life was threatened by the coming of a man whom she regarded as her deadly enemy. As she stood and contemplated the deep, rushing waters, she wondered whether she had the strength to push him in and be rid of him for ever.

As though reading her thoughts, Davis gave a low laugh. 'You have nothing to fear from me,' he said.

Tamar whirled round. 'Nothing to fear?' she demanded. 'You attacked me and tried to force yourself upon me, you wanted to blackmail me, you followed me around and spied on me in Helmsley – and you say I've nothing to fear!' She hurled the words at him with such violence that she paused in order to catch her breath.

Her face was ashen and her amber eyes glowed with the pent-up anger which was now released in a torrent of words. 'For six years you have dogged me wherever I went and now you have turned up here, where I thought I had found a safe haven.' Again she was silent for a moment or two, looking down at the carpet of tawny beech leaves, debris of the previous autumn, now shimmering in the dappled shafts of light which struggled through the tree canopy. Coming to a decision, she raised her head and her eyes met his. Leaning back against a tree trunk, as though to draw strength from it, she announced in a suddenly firm voice, 'I *will* be rid of you. I shall tell my husband of your attack on me at Cherry Tree Farm, and how you have pestered me all the years of my marriage.'

His smile was confident. 'And he'll believe you, will he?' he taunted. 'Won't he consider it odd that you've never said a word before?' Leaning towards her, he put a hand on each side of her face on the smooth tree bark, thus imprisoning her. 'I shall do you no harm,' he repeated quietly. 'My lesson has been learned. Once bitten twice shy, and a man only tackles a hell-cat once in his life.' He gently stroked her cheek with his finger. 'You will come to me, Tamar, before I come to you.'

'Don't call me Tamar,' she flashed. 'I am Lady Lassiter to you, and don't you ever forget it.'

With a swift movement, she dipped beneath the encompassing arms and was free of him. As she moved towards Moonbeam, however, he caught her arm and swung her to face him. 'What's it to be?' he challenged. 'I can go from this place today, and you'll see nothing of me again, or I can stay. If I stay, I can make you the best horsewoman in the district – one your husband will be proud of and one that the other ladies will envy when you ride to hounds.'

Tamar nibbled her bottom lip while she regarded the groom. Despite her previous fear of him, she took Gareth Davis at his word when he said he would not try to harm her. She recalled their encounter at Sleightholmedale, when she had almost killed him – and yet he still pursued her . . .

He must be a fine horseman since Stephen had chosen to employ him as head groom. Perhaps she could use his skills for her own advantage.

The man watched her face mirror her emotions, as she turned over his proposal in her mind. She had been dismayed to find that he must have made enquiries in Helmsley and tracked her down, but she'd become a much more confident and secure woman since the early days of her marriage. Conscious that if she accepted his presence at Thorsbury without protest, her chance to remove him was gone, nevertheless she felt that she could now handle the man. The simple fact that he was in her husband's employ gave her an advantage over him. Daring herself, Tamar came to a sudden decision. 'Yes! I want to be a good horsewoman, if only to show my mother-in-law I can do it.' Putting out a hand for him to shake, she added, 'It's a bargain, but I can tell you now, that I shall never belong to anyone but my husband.' Gareth smiled but did not speak, as he bent and clasped his hands together for her to mount her mare.

So it was that the two embarked upon a strange relationship. Before others his attitude was deferential and circumspect but when they rode alone, he treated her with the easy familiarity of an equal. True to his word, he schooled her in horsemanship and was a hard taskmaster. After hours of going round and round the stable yard, he was at last satisfied with her deportment in the saddle and she, herself, felt at one with her mount. Most days Victoria was allowed an hour from her lessons and joined Tamar, riding her own pony. At first the child was rather afraid of Davis, whose scar shone whitely against the tan of his face. However, his easy charm soon won her over and before long, she looked forward to her riding lesson as eagerly as her mother.

As Tamar progressed to facing easy jumps, her riding began to occupy more and more of her time and her thoughts. Davis was scrupulous in his treatment of her and only touched her when absolutely necessary. When she first began to have coaching in horsemanship, she was obsessed with her progress and it was her main topic of conversation whenever Stephen joined them for dinner. Eventually, however, as the tutor became more important to her than the tuition, she found herself reluctant to mention Davis to her husband.

When the summer ripened into the long hot days of harvest, Davis sought an audience with Stephen. As he entered the study, Stephen reflected on how fortunate he had been to obtain this man's services. Not only was he a good judge of horseflesh, but he was capable of treating most ailments which occured both in the hunters and the heavy farm animals. He was popular with the grooms and the coachmen and yet they respected him and his discipline was firm. As a final bonus, he could pass on his expertise in the saddle and both Tamar and Victoria had made rapid progress under his guidance.

'Yes?' he enquired pleasantly as he looked up.

'I thought you would wish to know, sir, that Her Ladyship is making good progress and I should like to take her further afield to tackle typical hunting country, so that she may get plenty of practice before she actually attends a meet.'

Stephen considered for a moment. He was longing to show off his beautiful wife to the County and what better introduction than in the hunting field, as an accomplished horsewoman? 'Yes. She must not take any risks, Davis, but she will need the experience before riding to hounds,' he agreed.

As Tamar rode further afield, she learned more about Gareth Davis and what she learned intrigued her. At the age of eleven he had driven a herd of Welsh ponies up to the West Riding, for use as pit ponies in the mines. Despite his youth he had travelled alone, sleeping in barns along the route, with which he had been familiar through previous trips in his father's company. Having reached Yorkshire, he had decided that enough was enough. He could see no future in the drover's life and had travelled around the north earning his living, usually with animals but often through casual farmwork.

She recognised him as a kindred spirit, with the same happy-go-lucky, questing attitude to life which she herself possessed. Although she had moulded herself into the demure and restrained wife suitable to Stephen's position, deep down she still possessed the wild spirits which had led her into Sir William Forster's arms.

The groom smiled to himself as he recognised where Tamar's interest in him was leading. He was playing her like an angler with a fish and knew that she would soon be netted. He noted how frequently she made excuses for their hands to touch or for him to lift her down from her horse. Upon each occasion the contact was only fleeting and he was careful to leave her longing for more.

As harvest time was drawing to a close and autumn would soon be upon them, Tamar admitted what she had tried to deny for the last few weeks. Her need of Gareth Davis constantly tugged at her and would no longer be denied. That day she dressed with extra care, choosing the brown velvet habit which set off her complexion and deepened the amber of her eyes. Tempy watched her silently. Although she had no suspicions of Tamar's interest in Gareth Davis, she had noticed a suppressed excitement in her mistress of late and worried as to what the cause could be.

They rode out from the stables in comparative silence, the groom a little way behind as befitted his position. Tamar turned along the track which led away from the village and the harvest fields, choosing instead the path through the thick woods which stretched down to the river bank.

Once they were a couple of miles from the Manor, where the woods were at their most impenetrable, she reined in Moonbeam and drew to a halt in a little glade. Turning to her companion, she held out her arms to be lifted from the saddle. As he clasped her waist, instead of jumping down she slid her body down his, so that his arms remained holding her and she was pressed close to him.

He caught his breath as the black fringes of her lashes swept upwards and the golden eyes met his. As his mouth descended hungrily upon hers and he swept her down among the bracken, Tamar succumbed to a passion far greater than she had ever known before. Her husband's lovemaking was gentle and restrained compared to the fierce passion which now engulfed all her senses as she gave herself utterly and completely in an explosion of abandonment.

When he rolled away from her, she idly pulled a frond of fern and stroked it down his cheek. He looked at her teasingly. 'Well, Lady Lassiter?' he smiled.

'Very well, thank you, Davis,' she laughed back.

# CHAPTER SIXTEEN

Tamar looked forward to the end of the harvest. During her years in Helmsley, she had missed life on the farm more than she would ever have thought possible. Now at Thorsbury she and Victoria often rode to the fields to watch the men labouring and when it was clear that the work of leading and stacking the corn would soon be at an end, she kept the child entranced with stories of the Harvest Suppers of her youth.

Towards the end of September there was a flurry in the Manor kitchens as hams and joints of beef were cooked and huge game pies baked, along with cakes and tarts of every kind. By the time the last load was led, dusk was falling and the scene was lit from the west by the orange glow of the sunset.

Tamar had allowed Victoria to stay up late to watch the leading in of the last load, which was a ritual joined in by all the estate workers. When the pair of huge horses made their way past the front of the Manor, where the family stood on the steps to watch, the glow of the setting sun was almost gone and in the eerie after-glow the scene took on an almost pagan air. Perched precariously on top of the load was the loader, holding aloft the corn-dolly for all to see. This was the creation of an old woman in the village and was the symbol of a successful harvest. Tradition had it that if the corn-dolly reached the following year's harvest intact, it augured well for the farm in the year to come. If, however, it was ravaged by rats and mice, it was an ill-omen for the farm and those who laboured there.

As the waggon trundled on its way towards the buildings, the loader swaying atop the load, the workers and villagers danced and sang around it. The Lassiters followed more circumspectly behind, reaching the stable-yard in time to see the previous year's corn-dolly being symbolically burnt. Those watching joined hands and danced round the bonfire

amid an air of frenzied excitement. As the flames died down
and the dancers stood back for the family to precede them
upstairs into the Long Room, there was a subtle change in
the atmosphere. The spontaneity of the dancers ebbed away
and they seemed almost shamefaced that their behaviour
had been witnessed by their employers.

While they all took their places along the tables, Tamar's
thoughts went back to similar evenings at Aumery Park
Farm. Her father's stern presence had prevented such
scenes of gay ebullience, but the weary harvesters had
always been welcomed with heartfelt gratitude and hospitality into her mother's kitchen, where the tables groaned
with an array of fare equally good as that now placed before
the workers of Thorsbury. At home, as she still thought of
it, the evening had been one of shared companionship and
merrymaking but here, once joined by the family, the workers were subdued, their voices muted.

Tamar occupied the seat where, for over thirty years,
Stephen's mother had sat. Although she no longer dominated the proceedings, Tamar was certain that it was the
older woman's presence which dampened the workers'
enthusiasm and made the meal and the dancing which
followed, restrained and formal. It was clear that the Dowager Lady Lassiter's attendance was an unwilling duty. She
showed no interest in the workers and indeed, apart from
the indoor staff, knew few of them by name. Tamar looked
at her mother-in-law's haughty face as she picked at her
food, exuding boredom. 'If only she'd clear off into the
dower house,' she told herself, 'I could really improve things
here.'

The end of harvest had also come to Sleightholmedale,
a couple of weeks earlier; despite Jonadab Oaks' reputation
as a stern man and a strict master, the workers surged into
the farmhouse kitchen, in answer to his invitation: 'Come
in, one and all. Make yourselves at home and praise the
Lord for a good bumper harvest.' He stood by the door
and called each worker by name, shaking hands with some,
inquiring about relatives of others, but thanking each one
for a job well done.

They had needed no second invitation. Mistress Oaks

was well known in the district for keeping a good table and now the snowy white cloths were spread with an abundance of good things, fulfilling all their expectations.

As the throng of workers laughed and joked, tucking into the vast amount of food laid out before them, Annie's mind went back to other Mell Suppers and not for the first time, she reflected on how her family had dwindled.

Martha, her youngest, was being courted by Sam Baldwin, the youngest son of the family at Cauldron Mill; although the lad had not yet spoken to Jonadab, Annie knew it would not be long before he asked for their daughter as his bride. Martha rarely went from the valley to where she could meet young men. She was a sweet-natured girl of a placid disposition, and considered herself fortunate to have found a suitor.

Young Jonadab, too, was now betrothed. He spent most of his spare time up at Skiplam, where the girl he courted was the only child of a wealthy farmer. ''E's got 'is feet under a good table,' his father often chuckled.

Annie looked down the table to where her son George sat next to his wife. She frowned to see that the seat at the other side was occupied by his sister-in-law, Sarah Butler. 'She still follows 'im about like a shadow,' Annie tutted. 'Why can't she leave 'im alone?' Although the girl's sister Christie was now engaged to be married and their Uncle Nathan in Leeds had tried to persuade Sarah to take over as his housekeeper, Sarah had dug in her heels and refused the invitation. Annie considered that Ann Butler should step in and make up Sarah's mind for her. 'Ruins that lass, she does,' she thought in disgust, as she glanced across at George's mother-in-law.

George and Elizabeth had come to terms with the fact that they would always be childless. It was a great blow to them, but Elizabeth was by now in her mid-thirties and there had been no hint of a pregnancy since her miscarriage in the early months of marriage. She had built up a good little business in the indoor market-hall and now she and George had amassed enough in the bank to set up on a farm of their own. Although they often discussed the possibility and even went to view farms that were advertised to let, they loved Cherry Tree Farm and had no real wish to leave it.

When the tables had been cleared and those who could do so had entertained the rest with songs and recitations, the whole company settled down for a sing-song. Accompanied by Bert Weald on his concertina, they sang a mixture of country songs and harvest hymns. At last the evening drew to a close and outdoor clothes were brought down from where they had been laid on beds.

'There'll be no need of a lantern, friends,' called Jonadab from the open doorway. 'It's as light as day tonight.'

Goodnights were exchanged and George set off down the lane with Elizabeth, Sarah and their mother. Jonadab was right: the harvest moon hung in the velvety blackness of the sky like a huge orb, casting such a radiance that the cart tracks in the road shone whitely, guiding their feet with no stumbling. The roadside foliage was touched with silver in the moon's rays, its brightness thrown into relief by the shadowy depths of the leaves behind.

Across the dale came the coughing bark of a dog-fox on the prowl and Elizabeth felt a shaft of worry for her poultry. She knew, however, that her mother could be relied upon to have fastened up the hens before coming up to the Oaks' farm for the supper, so she settled her fears. There was a nip in the air, and she pulled her cloak more closely round her. 'It's chilly,' she observed.

'Yes.' George glanced up at the clear sky. 'There could be a touch of frost – sounds are carrying clearly.' He hoped that an early frost was not the sign of a hard winter. For some years now he had shared the sheep herding with his Uncle George: the latter had never been particularly strong and now it was obvious that he was very ill. He had wasted away to an almost transparent frailness and was troubled by a rasping cough, which no amount of vinegar and black treacle could move. Most of his days were spent huddled round over the fire and George knew that his parents were worried about his Uncle's condition.

'Aah doubts but it's the galloping consumption,' his mother had confided tearfully. 'Aah can't see 'im lasting over t'winter.'

His Uncle's illness had placed the responsibility for all the sheep on George's shoulders. In addition to his father's considerable herds, he had built up a sizable flock of his own and dreaded the thought of a harsh winter. Before the start of harvest, the ewes had been returned to the high moorland pastures to fatten up and build up their strength before coming down for tupping. If there was to be a severe winter, George hoped that he would see the warning signs early enough to anticipate it. He had already seen to it that fodder had been stored in stone-built barns situated at strategic points on lower pastures. Before the heaviest snow-falls he would need to read the advance signals in the weather and move the sheep down into groups round the storage points, making them more accessible for feeding and, he hoped, cutting down losses in drifts. As the thoughts ran through his mind, he came to a conclusion. 'None of the farm lads really understand sheep. I wonder if Father would agree to getting a shepherd at t'Martinmas Hirings,' he mused.

'Handling all the sheep is certainly going to be too much for you on your own,' answered Elizabeth. 'You've plenty of other work as well as shepherding.'

As they turned into the yard of Cherry Tree Farm, George grinned. 'Aye! And handling mi father'll tek some doing an' all,' he retorted.

Although he was chary of broaching the subject of a full-time shepherd, when he did so, he found that his father had been giving some thought to the matter. After the disastrous moorland fire, it had taken Jonadab a few years to overcome the loss of both stock and crops. This spring, however, he had achieved his aim of owning his own stallion. 'General' was of a docile temperament so that, in addition to serving Jonadab's mares, he could also be used as a draught-horse for certain farm-work. Depending on this year's crop of foals, Jonadab was hoping to send him out on the road in the following spring. 'Aah sh'll advertise 'im in t'*Malton Messenger* and if we does well, Aah might try t'*Yorkshire Post* next year and send 'im further afield,' he had told his sons, adding, 'T'stud fees is a guinea and an 'alf, wi' a florin for t'lad, so it's not ti be sneezed at.'

Now, however, General was off-colour. Jonadab was in the depths of depression: he had kept the stallion in his stable and before going in for their midday meal, both father and sons were in consultation round the gentle grey. ''As 'e 'ad owt tiv eat?' Jonadab questioned the waggoner's lad, who had been given the job of keeping an eye on the horse.

'No, maister,' he answered, inwardly quaking lest he should be blamed if the horse died. He knew that his master must have paid dearly for such a magnificent beast and that he had deliberately chosen a grey stallion to breed more greys from his stock of grey shire-mares. Jonadab had an ambition, fired with a little conceit, to have any good quality grey shirehorses in the area attributed to himself. Upon seeing a good specimen, he wanted people to say, automatically, 'It's a Jonadab Oaks' breeding, is it?'

George went closer to the horse and inspected the straw underneath him. It was very wet and strong-smelling. 'Has he been making water a lot?' he asked.

The lad gulped. 'Yes. Aah thinks so.'

George looked at the other two. 'It could be an infection in his bladder,' he pronounced.

Jonadab turned to the lad. 'Go and bring some bottery leaves in from t'orchard hedge,' he instructed. As the boy ran from the stable, his master called after him, 'Bring plenty! Green, if there is any.'

Although Jonadab did not believe in the old country superstition that an elder bush planted by a house kept away witches, he was a firm believer that it deflected lightning during a storm. Consequently there were plenty of elders, or bottery bushes as they were known locally, around the farm. Not only did Annie make elderflower lemonade as a refreshing summer drink, but elderberry syrup was a warming and beneficial cordial in the winter. Jonadab always relied on the leaves for treating any horse which developed an infection or chill in the bladder. Now he could only hope that the heavy crop of elderberries, which heralded the end of summer, did not mean that all the leaves had fallen.

'We're in luck,' said Jonna, as Ned came panting in at the doorway with an armful of heavily-foliaged twigs.

'Shove 'em in t'manger,' Jonadab directed, 'and then get off for thi dinner.'

The three men watched the animal snuffling among the elder and then, satisfied that he would nibble at the leaves, they left the stable and turned towards the house.

'Is it possible for us to hire a shepherd at Martinmas?' George asked his father. He would have preferred to lead into the topic more subtly, but did not wish his Uncle to overhear the discussion.

Jonadab paused. 'It's crossed mi mind that thoo'll not be able ti manage all t'sheep this winter wi'oot some 'elp', he admitted. 'Aah dissent think thi Uncle'll mek old bones, Aah'm afeard, an' we mun come ti some arrangement.' George sighed with relief and Jonna grinned across at him. 'Mind thoo,' went on his father, 'it'll not be easy ti get a good man. A lot is leaving farming ti get more brass in t'mills in Leeds and Bradford and thereabouts. Why they should want ti work in them smelly places when they could be out in God's good air, Aah sh'll nivver know.'

Jonna looked at his fingerends, already cracked and sore from the outdoor work, even though winter had not begun. 'Nay, Faither, neither will I,' he said, with a grimace at George.

As George would be the one who would work most closely with the new shepherd, he went with his father to the Hirings in Kirkbymoorside to help choose a man. Whether they were going for a new place, or staying, the hired hands were all given the day off to attend the Hirings.

As soon as the basic tasks were finished, it was Jonadab's custom to seat himself at the parlour table with a ledger and a leather drawstring bag full of money. This was the only day of the year that the workers were ever allowed in the family parlour. Bert Weald was the first to enter and he put his cross to mark the receipt of his year's wages.

As each man drew his money and put his cross, Jonadab asked the same question. 'Art thoo goin' or art thoo stoppin'?' If the answer was 'stoppin'', the labourer would be given an extra shilling to fasten his contract for the next year, but he still had the rest of the day off to attend the merrymaking at the Hirings. Those returning for another year's work would be admonished by Jonadab: 'Don't be coming back in t'small hours. There's work ti be done in t'morn.' If the answer was 'gooin'', as the master counted out the money he would answer, 'Well goo, then! Thoo won't find a better place.' His expression made it clear that any man or boy unlucky enough not to find another situation need not expect any sympathy: his place would have been filled.

As he and George rode towards Kirkby, Jonadab grumbled loud and long about the money he had paid out that morning. 'Bert Weald's on twenty pounds a year now,' he complained. 'And 'is 'ouse, taties and milk.'

George thought grimly, 'That's twenty pounds more than I get, or our Jonna.' However he knew better than to put the thought into words.

When they reached the market place, he realised that his father had been right: there were nowhere near as many workers as there had been in previous Novembers. The little town was packed with milling crowds, but many of these were parents, come to collect their sons' wages before they either went back to work or moved on to another farm.

There was a carnival atmosphere, with stalls and side-shows to tempt the hired men and women to part with money handed over by new employers to seal the bargain. George pushed his way through the throng, looking for the spot where the shepherds were gathered. When he came to where the men were standing, identified by a tuft of wool in their hat-band or buttonhole, George hesitated. He felt embarrassed at the thought of walking among the men, assessing them as though they were cattle in an auction market. He stood by, watching as an elderly farmer and his wife went along the line, stopping before each man and commenting audibly to each other on his good and bad points. 'This'n looks good an' strong,' he heard the farmer's wife remark. 'A bit shifty round t'eyes,' came back the reply.

One man had attracted George's interest. He reminded him of his brother Joseph, who had emigrated to Canada. His hair had the chestnut glints of George's own and his brown eyes were steady with a touch of humour. As the couple approached him, George could not hear what remarks were passed but saw the dull flush of anger suffuse the shepherd's face, as the farmer picked up his wrist and spanned it, passing his hands up the man's arms to judge his muscles. His chin rose quickly in a proud gesture and George's heart warmed to him. As the couple passed on down the line, George quickly approached the man. Lapsing into the vernacular, as he smiled at his choice, he said, 'Thoo's not fastened yet, then?'

'No, maister,' came back the reply.

'Well thoo is noo, then,' answered George. The man held out his hand, which George seized and shook vigorously. Then fishing in his pocket, he held out a shilling which the man took. 'Oaks. Aumery Park Farm, Sleight-holmedale,' announced George. 'Sixteen pounds a year and general work, when needed, in addition to shepherding.'

'Aye, right, Mr Oaks,' the shepherd answered. 'My name's Bob Lamb.' He smiled. ''Appen that's why Aah become a shepherd – because o' t'name, like.'

Before George could reply, his father approached. Even now, Jonadab held himself as erect as in his youth and stood out from the crowd. Seeing that George was talking to one of the shepherds, he came forward to join them. 'Is this t'one thoo fancies, then?' he inquired, looking the man up and down.

'I've fastened him, Faither,' said George, a touch of defiance in his voice.

Jonadab's eyebrows drew together and the blue eyes hardened. 'Thoo's give 'im 'is shilling?' He was annoyed that George had acted without him. 'Where's 'e come from an' what's 'is experience?' he demanded, reproof in his tone.

Before George could answer, however, Bob Lamb took it upon himself to reply. His explanation that he had worked for several years for one master, until his employer had died, mollified Jonadab a little. 'Aah served a year at mi last place,' went on Lamb, 'but t'food was poor and a man can't work on an empty belly.'

Jonadab confirmed that the shepherd was not one for strong drink and was beginning to think that George had possibly made a good choice, when the old farmer and his

189

wife came back along the line. 'Thoo'll do,' the man said, approaching Bob Lamb.

'Aah'm spoke for,' the shepherd replied with a hint of satisfaction in his voice. As the couple turned away, the wife was grumbling that her husband had missed the chance of what they now considered to be the best prospect.

After giving Lamb directions to the farm and explaining that he would lodge at Bert Weald's cottage, Jonadab and George turned away. 'Will it be all right if Aah goes down after Aah've had a bite t'eat, maister?' asked Lamb. 'Aah've a few bits and pieces ti buy, but after that there's nowt much in my line 'ere.' Looking down at the black and white collie which crouched at his feet, he added, 'It'll be all right, will it, ti bring my own dog? Meg's used ti working with me, and she's well trained.'

The more the man talked, the higher he rose in Jonadab's estimation. 'Thoo's made a good choice there, Aah thinks,' he said grudgingly, as he and George walked across Crown Square. 'Mind thoo,' he added. 'Thoo should 'ave waited for me afore fastening 'im. Them as pays piper should call t'tune.'

'Aye, Faither,' George agreed, 'but we'd 'ave lost 'im if I'd left it any longer.'

Jonadab had already hired a new third lad, or 'thoddy' as they were known, and there was little more for them to do in the town: neither was interested in the attractions of sideshows or stalls. They both looked with disgust at the men who came rolling drunk from the inns and ale-houses. 'A silly waste of 'ard-earned brass,' Jonadab asserted and George could not help but agree. For most of the men, it was the only day of the year when they were able to visit a town, spending their days as they did working on the isolated farms of the moors and dales. Although they would regard it as the highlight of their year, many would make their way back with a sore head and a light pocket. Money not spent on ale would probably be stolen or gambled away as the Hirings attracted pickpockets and professional gamblers from the big towns.

It was late afternoon but not yet dusk when father and son began their homeward ride. The air was sharp with the promise of frost and George once again felt the premonition of a bleak winter ahead. 'It's a good job we managed to get a shepherd. I only 'opes he's as good as he seems,' he commented.

'Thoo picked 'im and thoo 'as 'im ti work wiv,' was his father's reply. 'It's thoo he mun suit.'

When they reached the base of the steep drop into the valley, they spotted Bob Lamb striding out ahead of them at a brisk pace. Over his shoulder was hung a canvas bag which contained all his worldly possessions, and close to his left heel trotted a black and white collie.

''E walks like a man as means business,' Jonadab remarked. 'There's nowt sloppy about 'im, so let's 'ope 'is work is as good as 'is stride.'

As they approached, they could hear that he was whistling merrily as he walked and, upon seeing them, he raised a hand and gave them a frank open smile.

George spent the next weeks showing Bob Lamb around the herds of sheep. Together they rode across Hodge Beck and gathered up the flocks to look them over before the onset of winter. Bob's dog Meg was a model of obedience and George knew that she would be as big an asset in the handling of the sheep as her master. Bob was taken round the various barns which held the winter fodder and together he and George rode the most advantageous trails, which would get the ewes down from the heights most speedily. George was impressed with the new man's knowledge of sheep, appreciating how quickly he spotted a sick or lame sheep and how neatly he and Meg could cut it out from the herd for attention.

In addition to his competence as a shepherd George liked him as a man. He discovered that Bob was twenty-five, four years his junior, and realised that it was the first time since his brother Joe's marriage, when they were seventeen and twenty, that he had had a companion of roughly his own age. He and his brother Jonna got on better now that Jonna had grown up, but George knew that his brother would always be jealous of him as the elder.

'I'm right pleased to get Bob,' he told Elizabeth. 'He's a

good man and I feel easier facing this winter with him working with me.'

She smiled at his enthusiasm, relieved that he now had help with the sheep. 'We may have a mild winter,' she reminded him. 'I don't know why you're so worried about the sheep.'

He stared into the fire. 'It's just a feeling I've got, that we're in for a hard winter. I only hope the snow doesn't come till after Christmas, though. The later it comes, the less time it stays.' So he continued to scan the sky for the massing of heavy clouds above the moorland, which would presage the coming of the snow.

# CHAPTER SEVENTEEN

Despite George's vigilance the snow, when it did come, took him unawares. One evening in late November, he did his usual round of the buildings to check his animals before going to bed. As he crossed the yard, he glanced round the skyline and was relieved to see no sign of cloud. The moon had set, but the sky was clear and lit by a sprinkling of stars. The silence of the night brought a feeling of unease; the normal rustlings of nocturnal creatures were absent and not even the hoot of an owl nor the choughing call of a pheasant disturbed the stillness. It was as though all Nature held its breath, but George standing on the doorstep for a last look round, could see nothing amiss.

While they slept, heavy clouds swirled over the valley in massed ranks and the snow began to fall. At first it came down almost lazily, in huge, silent flakes which soon blanketed the frozen ground. When George awoke, a couple of hours before dawn, it was to the rattle of the window frames and the moaning of the wind round the chimney pots, denoting a rising storm.

Dressing hurriedly, he dashed outside to find that, in just a few hours, the whole world had been transformed. Even in the farmyard, which was snugly sheltered with buildings on three sides, the snow lay deeply. He knew that the howling wind would be whipping up the downfall into deep drifts on the exposed high moor.

'I'll have my breakfast as soon as you can get it ready,' he told Elizabeth. 'You and Sarah'll have to see to all t'stock, as well as t'poultry and dairywork. I must go up onto t'moor and get the sheep down before they get buried.'

'Go down to your father's and fetch Bob,' urged Elizabeth. 'You'll manage better, two together.'

'Nay. It's drifted in the lane and I doubt if I'd get through. Besides, Rob and Tess are a couple of good dogs and I know t'moors better than Bob.' As he spoke, George was wrapping a clean sack round each leg over his trousers and criss-crossing them with bands to fasten them, giving greater protection for his legs. He wolfed down his breakfast and after buttoning up his overcoat, swathed a muffler round his neck, covering his mouth and nose. Draping another washed sack over his head to form a hood, he lit a lantern and then, seizing his crook from behind the door, set off to call his dogs. 'I should be back by dinner-time so get the stewpot on,' he said. 'No doubt I'll be frozen.'

'Do be careful, love,' said his wife, a frown on her forehead and a worried tone to her voice. 'I'd far rather you waited until it's light, or went down for Bob.'

'Nay, there's no knowing how long this lot's been coming down, nor how deep it is up yonder,' protested George. 'Anyroad, Bob'll already have set off and I may meet him up on t'tops.' So saying he set off with Rob and Tess at his heels to head for the high moor.

The path leading to the stepping stones which forded Hodge Beck wound narrowly between high sheltering hedges. Even so, the snow there was calf-deep, so that George needs must lift his legs at each step, making walking an effort. Once he had safely negotiated the slippery, ice-encrusted stepping stones, he was in the lee of the rising moor so that there was some protection from the swirling snow. Guided by a mournful bleating, he came across several groups of sheep, huddled together in the vain hope of safety. With the help of the dogs, who leapt silently through the snow, George managed to usher them to a barn, where they massed on the sheltered side. There he left them, knowing that they were safe, despite their plaintive cries. He spread out some fodder for them and then turned once again for the track to the moor-top.

The higher he climbed, the fiercer the wind. He realised that he had been foolish to risk the search alone, but there was no turning back. By the time he reached the high moor, visibility was restricted by a swirling mass as he was exposed to the full force of the blizzard. Half-blinded, his lashes and brows coated with a rim of snow, George was disorientated and unable to find a path which would lead him down to the shelter of the valley. There was no barrier against the elements and he was buffeted by the gale-force winds, which whipped across the open wastes of moorland. The dogs crouched at his heels for shelter, moving behind like grey ghosts in the stumbling tracks made by their master. Despite frequent pauses to listen for the doleful cries of lost sheep, the roaring wind was so loud that George was deafened to any other sounds. Realising that he was not only wasting his time until the storm abated but also endangering his life, George turned in what he hoped was the right direction for home. He was worried about Bob Lamb. If the shepherd had done as George feared and set off alone in search of Jonadab's flocks, he would never find his way across the unfamiliar moors.

The squalls of driven snow had now more than a hint of frost, so that the part of George's face that was uncovered was almost numb with cold and stung beneath the bombardment of icy slivers. If only he could come across a barn in which he could seek refuge from the full force of the gale . . . but visibility was limited to a few strides. As he tried to peer through the impenetrable veil of snow, searching in vain for some landmark or the vague outline of a barn, George's foot came unexpectedly into contact with a large stone, almost buried in the snow. He stumbled, and although he felt frantically with his crook for firm ground to steady himself and regain his balance, he pitched forward into a steep-sided dell, upon the edge of the moor.

He lay for a moment trying to recover his wind before rising again to his feet. Once down in the snow he was overtaken by a heavy lethargy. His eyelids drooped and his limbs no longer felt the bitter chill; they were merely numbed and heavy. His last thought before closing his eyes and succumbing to overwhelming tiredness was, 'I hope Elizabeth's got that stewpot on.' Looking down at their still and silent master, the two dogs began to slink nearer until they lay down beside him, noses resting on his body.

The feeding and cleaning-out took Elizabeth and Sarah all morning. Each in her turn looked frequently towards the moor but realised that no sign of George would be seen until he reached the yard. The wind seemed to drive all ways at once, so that whichever way they turned, as they struggled to and fro across the yard, and from building to building, the snow was always directly into their faces.

Before they had ventured out into the snowstorm, their mother had issued instructions: 'Pin up your skirts before you go out into that plother.' As the snow even in the yard was more than boot-deep, they were thankful that their skirts and petticoats were pinned well up out of the wet snow.

When they went in halfway through the morning for a warming mug of tea, Elizabeth opened the oven door and lifted the lid of the big brown earthenware stew-crock. 'Ooh, that smells lovely, Mother,' she smiled. 'Will you pop some dumplings in at about twenty to twelve? George'll want something warming when he gets back.'

'Aye! That'll stick to his ribs,' rejoined her mother.

'I could just eat some now,' Sarah said, sniffing appreciatively. 'I'm frozen.'

'Well, we've quite a bit more to do before dinner-time.' Elizabeth was uncompromising. 'Come along – the sooner we get on with it the sooner we shall finish.' So saying she bustled Sarah out again into the bitter cold.

It was noon before they had completed the morning's tasks, and as they came out from the buildings to go across to the house, the snow had ceased to fall. The sky was still grey and menacing and both sisters allowed their eyes to comb the white mantled slope of the moors for some evidence of life. There was no sign of either George or the sheep, and Elizabeth sighed as they entered the kitchen. 'I'm afraid the dumplings will be sad, before George gets here. Perhaps you can make another batch when we see him coming down from the moor-edge,' she suggested to her mother.

The meal was passed in comparative silence, each woman worrying in her own way because of George's failure to return. Elizabeth turned over in her mind the possibilities of what could have befallen George. She knew that her husband would take no risks and yet he should have been home by now. What was the best thing to do, she wondered. While acknowledging that Sarah seemed to be infatuated with George, her sister was so many years her junior that

196

she still thought of her as a child and dismissed her obvious affection for George as innocent admiration. For her part, Sarah's anxiety for his safety was almost too much to bear. She tried to mask her true feelings from her mother and sister, but her throat ached with tension and she felt desperate for some action to be taken, to try to search for him.

Although there was a break in the snowfall, the wind still blew fiercely from the north, moaning round the house and whipping up the fallen snow so that it skimmed across the fields like fine powder, piling up in deep drifts where its progress was interrupted by hedgerows. As she sipped her tea at the conclusion of the meal, Elizabeth reached a decision. 'He should have been here by now,' she announced. 'I shall take Rosie or Violet and try to get through the drifts and reach Aumery Park Farm.'

'Why don't we go up on the moor and look for George?' asked Sarah.

Elizabeth considered for a moment. She, too, was extremely worried, but tried to be practical. 'No,' she replied at last. 'We need to have more searchers. If he's lost, he should be able to get home while it's no longer snowing. If he's met with an accident, the moors are far too vast for the two of us to cover much of an area before dark.'

With this, she once more wrapped up warmly and made her way to the stable. When she came out leading Violet by the bridle, she went over to the mounting block and climbed up on to the horse. Then her mother, who had been watching from the kitchen window, ran to the back door. 'Do be careful,' she called from the step. Elizabeth raised a hand to indicate that she had heard, and guided the powerful beast into the lane. The drifts surely could not be more than chest-deep on the massive shire, she thought, and with a bit of luck she would get through. Since her marriage to George she had, in some measure, grown to share the family's belief in Jonadab's powers. She felt that if only she could reach her father-in-law and confront him with her fears for George's safety, he would somehow make everything all right.

Sarah finished the washing-up and, taking off her apron, folded it and placed it in one of the table drawers. Her mother sat by the fire, her knitting lying in her lap, eyes closed and spectacles slipped down her nose. Sarah touched Ann's hand. The older woman's eyes opened briefly and looked up at her in confusion. 'I'm just going out for a minute, Mam, I won't be long.' Sarah spoke in a low soothing tone, not wishing to rouse her mother fully.

'All right, love.' Almost before she had finished speaking, the eyelids had drooped and with a faint snore and a little wriggle, Ann Butler was once more asleep.

Sarah examined her boots. Stuffed with newspaper, they stood in the hearth. They were not yet dry but she had no others apart from her best ones, so she pulled them on over the warm, dry woollen stockings into which she had changed upon coming in from the buildings. She wrapped up warmly, winding a scarf round her neck, crossing it over her chest and pinning it at the back, as her mother had done in her childhood. Choosing a sturdy walking stick from those which stood behind the door, she quietly lifted the sneck and slipped out, so as not to waken her mother.

Looking northwards towards the end of the dale, she frowned to see the accumulation of heavy clouds above the moors. The windbreak of pine trees which sheltered the buildings on the north side, creaked and groaned in the piercing wind; the treetops whipped to and fro in a frightening manner. Sarah felt that their very height made them vulnerable and was afraid that the trunks would snap under the pressure.

Realising that there was more snow on the way, she clenched her teeth and set off for the moors. Relying heavily on the stick, she clambered upwards, stopping every now and again to call, 'George! George!' She wished that she had one of the dogs with her but both were with their master. Sarah believed that Tess and Rob were so devoted to George that they would be close to him, no matter where he was.

When she reached the summit, she was into the full brunt of the gale-force wind. Screwing up her eyes and looking round, it was with a sinking heart that she realised the enormity of her task. The moors stretched before her as far as the eye could see, in fold after fold of snow-covered dunes. There was no break in the uniformity; no landmark to help pinpoint her position. Sarah realised that if she struck inwards into the undulating tracts of snow-blanketed moorland, she would soon lose her way.

Consequently, she decided to walk northwards along the edge of the moor, safe in the knowledge that if the snow should begin to fall again before she found George, she only needed to make her way downwards and she would come across Hodge Beck, which she could follow southwards to safety.

By choosing to go northwards, she was walking directly into the driving wind but she pressed on, bent low over the walking stick to try to protect her face. Her eyes were half-closed and her cheeks were stiff with the numbing cold of the bitter wind. She counted every hundred paces, to give her something to cling on to and then, turning her head away from the gale, she shouted George's name, cocking her head this way and that to catch any reply.

Time ceased to have any meaning for Sarah. She was, by now, counting aloud almost mechanically. 'Ninety-nine, a hundred. *Stop! Turn! Shout!*' she intoned. Incredibly, this time, she heard a faint bark. Again she called out. This time the dogs answered. 'Rob! Tess!' She pursed her lips in a vain attempt to whistle, but they were too cold and dry. Again came the bark. Casting about for a sighting, she suddenly saw one of the dogs about a quarter of a mile away. It appeared so unexpectedly that it seemed to leap out of the ground. Sarah tried to run, lifting her feet high in the snow and stumbling over snow-encrusted tussocks of heather but suddenly, to her consternation, the dog disappeared.

Sarah stopped. Peering round, she was alarmed to see no sign of life in the empty wastes. So great was her disappointment that all life seemed to drain from her. Suddenly weak, she dropped to her knees and began to weep. Then, hearing a sound, she raised her head from her hands to see Rob creeping over the snow towards her, whimpering slightly. '*Rob!*' Sarah half-whispered, rising to her feet. 'Where's your boss?'

The dog's tail began to wag frantically and he ran round

her, barking shrilly. Sarah ran forward, and then stopped as the ground fell away before her. There at her feet was a shallow dell and huddled in the snow at the base of it was George, with Tess snuggled up to him, her head on his chest. With her heart thumping so hard that her ears were deaf to any other sounds, Sarah hurled herself down into the dip. 'Oh George, George,' she gasped. 'Oh, please God, don't let him be dead,' she prayed, as she sank to her knees in the snow and raised his head. Thankfully, she heard him groan, as she moved him. 'Wake up! Wake up!' she cried, as she rubbed his icy cheeks to warm them and try to bring him round.

George stirred and reluctantly opened his eyes. He longed to close them again in sleep, but Elizabeth was trying to keep him awake. Seeing that he had now regained consciousness, Sarah murmured, 'Thank God.' With a sound that was half-laugh and half-sob, she began to rain kisses on his ashen face. George's wits began to return and he realised that he would have soon passed from sleep to death, if Elizabeth had not found him.

'Thank you, my love,' he whispered, as he began to return her kisses. For a few moments, Sarah was lost in the ecstasy of feeling George's kisses on her lips, and his arms round her. She quickly pulled herself together, however, and rose to her feet. 'Come along! Get up!' she ordered. The insidious cold was once more creeping over George and he sank to the ground benumbed and unwilling to make an effort. Realising that she was too slight to lift him, Sarah was desperate. Kneeling beside him, she tried, unsuccessfully, to push him into an upright position. By now the light was fading and as the leaden clouds massed heavily on the horizon, the first flurries blew in the wind; heralds of another blizzard to come.

All her life Sarah Butler had been protected and cosseted by older members of her family but now, faced with Nature at its most pitiless, she knew that George's life depended on her. She must get him on to his feet and down from the high moor before the impending storm. Looking to the north, she could already see the curtains of snow which were sweeping towards them with terrifying speed. Lifting her foot, she aimed a kick at George, catching him under the ribs with her boot. 'Come on, damn you!' She hardly knew what she was saying; only knew that she must somehow rouse him to movement. As she raised her foot again, to aim another kick, George rolled over on to his knees and tried to rise.

'Elizabeth, help me.' His voice was so faint as to be almost inaudible. Swiftly she caught him under the armpits and heaved until she managed to persuade him from the ground. He was more himself now, shaking off the languor which the bone-chilling cold had brought.

Recognising that as movement caused him to return to his normal self, he would soon realise that it was not Elizabeth who had found him, Sarah took one last chance. Throwing her arms round George, she held him close and gave him a passionate kiss. As she pulled away, he studied her closely, through eyes which were still bleary. 'Sarah?' She was so much like Elizabeth in appearance, but he should have recognised her. She was a younger and, nowadays, a more vibrant version of Elizabeth. More like the Elizabeth he had married.

'Come along.' She took his arm and with her half-supporting him, they began to stumble towards the edge of the moor. As the blood began once more to course through George's legs, his muscles went into spasms of cramp, so that they needed to pause every few yards. Sarah glanced at the sky, noting how low were the heavy clouds which tumbled towards them in the rising wind. The snow was falling more steadily now and she was anxious to reach home before the weather closed in even more.

Elizabeth, meanwhile, had managed to get down the lane and had reached her father-in-law's farm, even though the narrow cart track was blocked in several places where the snow had drifted up against the hedge. Violet had moved slowly and cautiously but urged on by her rider, she had breasted the drifts and safely negotiated the lane. Elizabeth heaved a sigh of relief upon reaching Aumery Park Farm. Her main fear had been that the mare would stumble over an unseen obstacle and they would both be pitched headlong into the snow.

Quickly, she poured out her fears to Jonadab. He was half-annoyed and half-worried that George had gone up onto the moor in such fierce weather. 'Aah'm thunderstruck,' he said. 'Aah thowt as 'ow 'e'd 'ave more sense.' He, himself, had not allowed Bob Lamb to set out. 'Folks is more important than animals,' he added. 'Sheep can always be dug out when t'weather improves. They usually manage to survive a day or so buried in a snowdrift. Folks aren't so lucky.' He hurriedly mustered the farm-workers and explained the situation. 'Aah'll not wrap up 'ow grave it is,' he said heavily. 'George could 'ave died already up yonder. Finding 'im won't be easy.'

'I'd have expected him to have more sense,' said young Jonna tersely.

His father spun round on him. 'A man who puts 'is stock first is acting for what 'e thinks is t'best,' he snapped. Turning to Elizabeth, he asked more gently, 'Noo then, lass. 'Ow bad is t'lane?'

'Violet has made a path, of course,' she explained. 'If we have another couple of the big shires, they should be able to paddle down enough of the snow for the rest to follow on foot.'

They set off down the lane, Elizabeth, Jonna and Jonadab going ahead on three heavy horses and the men and dogs following, slipping and skidding on the hard-packed snow trodden down by the shires. Jonna looked up at the sky, now rapidly darkening. 'This is a fool's errand,' he observed. 'It's going to snow again before long and we sh'll all be lost.'

His father's brows drew together and his eyes flashed with anger. 'Is thoo willing ti abandon thi brother, then?' he demanded. 'As long as there's breath in mi body, we sh'll goo on searching.'

Jonna had the grace to look shamefaced, but made no reply.

When they reached Cherry Tree Farm, Jonadab led the way into the kitchen. 'Come inside.' He gathered them all together with a quick look round. When they had entered the house, he said, 'Noo then, we must 'ave a plan, and we must all keep within shouting distance. We want no more lost.'

Elizabeth looked round the room. 'Where's Sarah?' she asked her mother. Ann Butler was unwilling to admit that she had dozed away most of the afternoon by the fire.

'She said she was just popping out for a minute,' she replied. 'I expect she's looking round t'stock.'

Even as she spoke, however, the door was flung open and Sarah stumbled over the threshold, half-dragging and half-lifting George into the room. Once safe in the haven of the kitchen, she allowed George to slip from her grasp and ran, sobbing, to her mother. 'Oh, Mam, Mam!' she wept. 'I thought I'd never get home.'

Jonadab and Elizabeth bent over George, whose teeth were chattering uncontrollably and who, indeed, appeared more dead than alive. 'Get 'im ti bed, lass. 'E must be got warm.' Jonadab realised that the fact that George had reached home did not necessarily ensure that he would live. 'Tobias.' He spoke to the lad who had come from the workhouse at the same time as Lydia. 'Make a pot a tea.' Then to Ann Butler, 'Missus, put some oven shelves in t'bed ti get it warmed up afore we puts 'im in.'

Jonadab Oaks was at his most impressive when organisation was needed. Once everyone had drunk a mug of hot strong tea, he sent his own men out to feed and check the stock which was kept down at Cherry Tree Farm. George had been gently lifted by his father and Bob Lamb and placed on the rug before the fire. On top of the turves, which gave out a steady glow, they piled logs, until the blaze roared in the grate, filling the kitchen with life-giving heat.

As Ann Butler led Sarah towards the stairs, to help her out of her wet clothes and rub her down with dry towels, Jonadab seized her hand in both his. 'Aah can nivver thank thi enough, lass,' he said hoarsely. 'Thoo saved oor George's life and we shall nivver forget this day.' Sarah smiled but felt embarrassed, so made no reply as she followed her mother. Elizabeth came down to say that the bed was warm, so Jonadab and his younger son helped George upstairs. Once he was stripped and put into a clean dry shirt, he snuggled down with a sigh into the soft billows of the featherbed. Elizabeth had brought up a couple of hot bricks wrapped in pieces of blanket, which she popped into bed at each side of him.

'Give 'im plenty of warm drinks, lass,' instructed her father-in-law, 'and then a good night's sleep should see 'im all right.'

Elizabeth went to kiss George, as soon as they were alone. 'Try not to go to sleep yet, love,' she whispered. 'I'll bring you some hot milk and treacle.'

Down in the kitchen, Sarah sat by the fire, her feet in a bowl of mustard and hot water, her hands round a mug of tea. The colour had come back into her cheeks and Elizabeth thought how pretty she looked. It was obvious that Bob Lamb shared her opinion. Although ostensibly listening to what Jonadab was saying, he could not take his eyes off Sarah. Conscious that her feet were bare and her ankles in full view, she constantly tried to adjust her skirt to cover more of her ankles and yet keep the material out of the water.

Elizabeth studied the shepherd. They knew nothing about him, really, although she knew that her husband was impressed by him. He was certainly an attractive man, with bright, smiling eyes and a face which always seemed to be on the point of laughter. It was, she considered, time Sarah was married, but she never encountered anyone suitable.

She drew the pan of milk off the fire and carrying it over to the table, quickly poured it into a pint pot into which she had already spooned a generous measure of treacle. Giving it a brisk stir, she carried it carefully upstairs. Setting it down on the bedside table, she stooped over George. 'Come on, love. Sit up and drink this,' she urged, helping him into a sitting position. As he let the warm soothing potion trickle down his throat, Elizabeth sat on the edge of the bed and put her arm round his shoulders. 'Oh, love,' she whispered. 'I never thought to see you again. Our Sarah saved your life.'

'Aye. She did an' all,' he repeated. 'I shall always be grateful to her.' He thought for a moment, before going on. He tried to choose his words carefully, but there was no tactful way to phrase what he wanted to say. 'She'll have to go, Elizabeth.'

'Go? Whatever do you mean?' She thought at first that his ordeal had been too much for him and that his mind was wandering. 'She's just saved your life. How can you want her to go away?'

George looked at her, steadily and firmly. 'Your Uncle Nathan has wanted her with him in Leeds ever since Christie planned to be married. He wants his own about him, not strangers.' So saying, he sank back and closed his eyes.

Elizabeth felt troubled as she went back down the stairs. George could sometimes be almost mulish. Whatever had happened up on the moor to cause him to feel this way about Sarah, she wondered.

Jonadab was waiting for her at the stair bottom. 'Would you like either oor Jonna or Bob Lamb ti stop 'ere and see ti t'stock until George's is on 'is feet again?' he suggested.

'Why, yes. That would be a good idea,' she smiled. 'Perhaps it would be better if Bob stays and then he'll be nearer to the high moor if the weather clears. The sheep will have to be gathered up and brought down as soon as possible.'

Jonadab sent the men back to Aumery Park, noting that the snow had stopped and the coming evening was bright and crisp. 'It's too cold now for snow,' he told Bob. 'If it's clear tomorrow, see if thoo can gather t'sheep up and bring 'em down to t'lower slopes. 'Appen some'll be buried, but you've George's dogs as well as Meg.'

When he went out, Jonna was standing in the yard, holding Bonnie and Bluebell by their bridles. Approaching him, Jonadab stood and faced him. 'Thi brother's safe, thanks ti a bit of a lass. She 'ad t'backbone ti go up on ti t'moor in a blizzard ti find 'im, while you were willing ti let 'im lie up yonder and freeze ti death.' Jonna opened his mouth to speak but was stopped by his father's upraised hand. 'Aah'd give mi life ti save *my* brother,' he continued, 'yet you objected ti getting wet ti save yours.' He sighed deeply. 'Thoo's disappointed me,' was his final comment, as he climbed up on to Bluebell's back.

Jonna's lips tightened. His father always favoured George, he thought angrily as they plodded up the lane.

# CHAPTER EIGHTEEN

The early and severe blizzards gave way to an equally rapid thaw: the dale echoed to the sound of water. The melting snow dripped mournfully from the trees and the slope leading down from the moor was a mass of little rivulets, cascading down to run into Hodge Beck. The stream was in full spate, rushing over its stony bed with such force as to make the way across the stepping-stones hazardous for George and Bob. The two men combed the moors, squelching through the soggy ground until they were satisfied that all the sheep had been rounded up and brought down to the lower pastures to safety.

'At least it's given us a breather. If we get more bad weather later on we shan't lose many,' George told Elizabeth.

As soon as it was possible to get out of Sleightholmedale, he wrote to Tamar to tell her that their Uncle George's condition was worsening rapidly. He was not sure that she would come, but felt that she should be warned that the old man was close to death.

He waited for a fortnight after the heavy snowfall of late November and still nothing appeared to have been said with regard to Sarah's move to Leeds. One night, in the privacy of their own bedroom, he decided to take up the matter again with Elizabeth. 'Have you spoken to your mother or Sarah about her going to live at Uncle Nathan's?' he demanded.

Elizabeth hesitated. 'No. To be honest, George, I wasn't quite sure that you meant it. You were overwrought that night and after all, we do owe your life to Sarah.'

George was thoughtful for a moment. He knew that Elizabeth and her mother regarded Sarah's feelings for him as a girlish infatuation; something to be smiled about, with tolerant affection. What they failed to recognise was that Sarah had grown up. She was no longer the girl she had been when they had first come to live at Cherry Tree Farm. She was a vibrant and passionate woman who had revealed the intensity of her love for him up on the moors. He still loved Elizabeth deeply, as he had done ever since he was seventeen, but he had no wish to be the subject of Sarah's adoration day after day. 'A man can only stand so much,' he thought desperately, remembering how her kisses had awakened an answering reaction in him. 'It's time she's wed,' he answered his wife aloud. 'Bob Lamb makes it obvious he's keen on her, but she treats him like muck. She's not likely to meet anybody else down here. Not everybody falls on their feet, like our Tamar did.'

'She says she's not interested in men,' rejoined Elizabeth.

'No! "Men" she may not be, but "man" she's certainly interested in,' he said meaningfully, tapping himself on the chest.

Elizabeth began to laugh but seeing his expression, she stopped and studied his face. 'You mean she's throwing herself at you? My own sister?' she asked doubtfully.

George nodded. 'She's making a fool, both of herself and me,' he said.

Elizabeth could see that there was more to this than George would tell her, but she, too, came to the conclusion that Sarah must go to Leeds and that as soon as possible. As soon as she could she had a serious talk with her mother. 'She's no longer a child, Mother, and she's throwing herself at George. You must be firm with her. A few years in Leeds will broaden her horizons, even if she doesn't find a husband. Let's face it, she's a very attractive girl and it's time she was married.'

Ann Butler pressed her lips together. She realised that for George and Elizabeth to take such a firm line, Sarah must have made more of a nuisance of herself to George than she herself had noticed.

'Bob Lamb has shown an interest in her,' went on Elizabeth, 'but she'll have none of him.'

Her mother sniffed. 'I should think not,' she snapped. 'She's worth more than a shepherd.'

Elizabeth gave a sigh. She could rely upon her mother

to be firm with Sarah, even though it would deprive her of her youngest daughter's company.

While Bob Lamb was longing for Sarah Butler to pay him some attention, he was unaware that Martha Oaks felt the same way about him. Poor Martha's experience of suitors was limited to Sam Baldwin who, although hard-working and dependable, was not the type to turn a girl's head. When Martha compared Sam with Bob Lamb, it was to poor Sam's detriment. His homely features and shyness of manner contrasted sharply with Bob's attractive, open face and easy, merry demeanour.

Consequently, when Sam did screw up his courage to ask Jonadab for his permission to approach Martha with a proposal, Jonadab agreed, confident that he knew what Martha's reply would be. When he conveyed Sam's request to her as they sat around the table at tea-time, he was bewildered by his daughter's reaction. At first she sat in silence, stirring her tea as though to get it thoroughly stirred was of the utmost importance.

'Well?' demanded her father. "As t'cat got thi tongue?'

Martha made no reply. She still kept her eyes fixed on the swirling liquid; when she did speak it was part-defiance and part-apology. 'No.' She said the word clearly, but still did not raise her eyes to her father's.

'What?' He could not believe that he was hearing right. 'What does thoo mean – no?'

'No means no,' she answered. 'I'm not going to marry Sam Baldwin.'

There was a gasp of consternation from Annie. 'Nay, lass. Don't be 'asty,' she urged. 'It's been an understood thing for a year or two.'

'Well, it wasn't understood by me!' Martha's face was now flushed and she looked on the verge of tears. Annie glanced across at Jonadab. She could see the pulse beating in his temple: a sure sign of his mounting rage.

'Thoo's played fast and loose wiv 'im,' he stated. 'Thoo's walked 'ome from chapel together every Sunday for a couple o' years and now, when 'e does t'decent thing and asks me for thi 'and, thoo's refusing.'

Annie's mind cast back to the number of his children who

208

had defied Jonadab round this very table. Joseph, Tamar, sometimes even George had stood up to him; and now it was Martha, his youngest.

He looked at his wife. "Ad thoo any inkling o' this?' he demanded.

'No.' She was as taken aback as her husband. Like him she had taken for granted the fact that Martha would marry the miller's son. 'What's up, love?' she asked her daughter.

Martha made no answer. She could not tell them that she was desperately in love with Bob Lamb. She knew that Bob paid her no attention, but did not realise that his interest lay with Sarah Butler, down at Cherry Tree Farm.

Jonna looked up from his meal. 'Don't be so daft,' he advised. 'Grab him while you've the chance. You'll get nobody else, stuck down here.'

'Thank you very much,' she stormed. 'Then I'll stay an old maid.' So saying she ran from the kitchen and up to her bedroom, leaving those round the table confused and upset.

'That's all we needed,' Jonadab told his son. 'Your tongue wags afore your mind's thought.' Turning to his wife he instructed, "Ave a word wiv 'er, Mother. See what thoo can mek out.'

Lydia spoke now, for the first time. Although she had lived at the farm since she was ten and was accepted as one of the family, she rarely took part in family discussions. Now, however, she felt that she could be of some help. 'Aah'll 'ave a word,' she offered, having noticed the way Martha's eyes followed Bob Lamb and believing that he was the trouble. 'Aah'm t'nearest to 'er in age.' Looking round the table she added, 'While we're on about weddings, Aah might as well say that Aah'm going ti marry Tobias. That is, if thoo doesn't mind, missus,' looking across at Annie.

'Aah didn't know 'e'd asked thi,' Annie answered in surprise.

"E 'asn't. In fact 'e's no great cop, but there's not much choice hereabouts , as Jonna says. It'll mek no difference ti mi work 'ere, missus and after all, if a lass wants ti be wed, she must tek what the Good Lord offers.'

Before either her mother or Lydia had the opportunity for a quiet chat with Martha, the even tenor of life in the kitchen was disrupted the following day, by the arrival of Tamar. Annie and Jonadab were unaware that George had written to tell Tamar of their Uncle George's condition. It was therefore with surprise that they saw the coach draw up bearing the Lassiter coat of arms.

On the few occasions that Tamar had come down to the farm, or visited her mother and Elizabeth in the market, she had chosen Goody to drive her. She knew she could rely on his discretion for, although she was not ashamed of her background, she considered that the fewer people who knew of it, the better. She wanted to put no weapon into her mother-in-law's hands that could be used against her.

Now, as the coachman handed her down and she swept into the kitchen in her fur-lined velvet cloak, the difference in her life since her marriage was brought home to her as never before.

At Thorsbury Manor she never saw the inside of the kitchen yet here, it was the centre of family life. Her mother and the kitchen were the hub around which life revolved.

'Eh, lass, it's grand ti see thi!' Annie exclaimed, as she embraced Tamar. 'What brings thoo here? There's nowt wrong, is there?'

Although Tamar responded with a laugh, she had a feeling of guilt, deep within, to think that her visits were so infrequent that her mother feared she had brought bad news. 'Of course not,' she said, giving her mother a hug. 'I've come to see Uncle George. I understand he's ill.' Seating herself on one of the wooden chairs, she drew off her fine kid gloves and placed them on the table. 'I could do with a cup of tea, Lydia,' she smiled and when it was placed on the table before her, she wrapped both hands round it in a gesture which seemed natural, here in her mother's kitchen.

'How is Uncle George?' she asked, after having a deep draught of the hot liquid.

'Aah'm afraid 'e's badly, lass,' Annie answered sadly. ''E's not long ti go and indeed, it'll be a blessing. 'E's a terrible racking cough.'

Tamar thought of the gentle man who had shared part of her life at Cherry Tree Farm. His life had been spent in unquestioning subservience, first to his parents and then to his elder brother. He had never known the love of a woman, nor children of his own. Now he was slipping away from life as uncomplainingly as he had lived it. Tamar sighed and placed her cup on the table. 'I'll go up and have a word with him,' she said. 'I can't stay long. It's a long journey back and it grows dark early.'

As she mounted the ladder which led from the kitchen into what was still called 'the lads' room', she smiled at her awkwardness. Once she had skittled up and down these steps without a second thought. She bent over the bed and thought at first that she was too late. Her Uncle lay quite still, eyes closed and breathing so faintly that the bedclothes hardly stirred. There was a lump in her throat as she gazed down on the gaunt features. As though sensing her presence, he opened his eyes and focused them on her face. 'Tamar?' His voice was a whisper.

She sat on the chair by the bed and picked up his hand, stroking it gently. 'Yes, Uncle, it's me,' she smiled.

'It's grand ti see thoo, lass,' he breathed, and then after a ferocious bout of coughing, allowed his eyes to close again, as though the effort had been too great.

Tamar sat and talked quietly, telling her Uncle about her life and about Victoria, who had been only a small child when he had last seen her. Whether or not he could hear much of what she said, she did not know, but her heart was saddened that he should be here alone in his last hours. All those below were too busy and had not time to spare to comfort him with a few minutes' companionship.

When she returned to the kitchen, Annie was touched and surprised to see tears in Tamar's eyes. She knew that Tamar had a core of steel and, though she loved this daughter as devotedly as the rest of her offspring, recognised that there was a degree of hardness in her. 'Thoo's fond of 'im.' It was part-question and part-statement.

'Aye, Mam, I am. Uncle George was kind to me when there were others who were not.' Then she put into words what her brother George had thought several years before.

211

'I don't suppose he's ever done anything that *he's* really wanted to do. First it was Grandad Oaks who dominated his life and then it was Father. The life he's leaving really hasn't been worth living.'

Annie looked shocked. Unlike Tamar, her horizons were limited and in her opinion her daughter's remarks were almost blasphemous. George Oaks had been cared for and had work provided, first by his parents and later, by his elder brother. His life had been spent tending the land to which he'd been born and what more could any man want? He had not had the burden of responsibility which had been placed on Jonadab's shoulders.

Before she had time to remonstrate with Tamar, the door opened and Jonadab himself strode in, followed by his two sons. Tamar's eyes met George's and they smiled in mutual affection. Her father never seemed to change, she thought, noting the still-upright stance and piercing blue eyes. Her brother Jonna bore a startling likeness to their father; so much so that he looked like a younger version. Looking again, however, she saw a subtle difference, as though her father possessed some quality which had been omitted in the forming of his youngest son.

Tamar smiled within herself to witness the effect her father's presence had on those in the kitchen. One frowning look at the table where a pint pot of tea and a plate of scones or buns should have been awaiting his arrival, sent Martha and Lydia scurrying frantically about until his needs had been met. He took his seat at the fireside, mug in hand, and glanced across at her. 'This is an honour,' he said with sarcasm.

Tamar drew a breath, determined that he would not rouse her to anger. 'I've come to see poor old Uncle George,' she replied quietly.

'Aye.' Her father was instantly contrite and abandoned his attempt to bait her. 'Aah doubts but he's on 'is way ti' meet 'is Maker. It's good of thoo ti' come.'

'There's nothing good about it,' she replied. 'He is my Uncle; we've shared the same house for twenty years and I wanted to be with him. I only wish I'd known before that he was so ill. He could have had anything that money could buy to cure him, but I can see it's too late now.'

Jonadab's eyes flashed. 'We wants none o' thi money!' he exclaimed. ''E's 'ad every comfort and t' best treatment Dr Dawson could give.'

Tamar sighed and drew on her gloves. Would she never grow out of this knack of rubbing her father up the wrong way, she wondered. 'I'm sorry, Father. I didn't mean that the way it sounded,' she apologised. 'Please don't think I'm throwing money in your face. Money hasn't changed me,' she stated firmly. 'Stephen is a farmer, just as you are. We have the same worries and difficulties as you do here and, if there is more money involved, there are more wages to pay and more stock to buy.'

Jonadab nodded. 'Aye, lass. Aah see what thoo means. 'Appen Aah jumped too soon.'

Tamar looked round with affection. 'It's been lovely to see you all, even though it's a sad errand that's brought me.' She glanced out of the window, to see that the wintry sun was already low in the sky. 'I really must go. It will be dark long before I arrive home and I don't feel safe at night with only an old man like Goodison for company.' As she fastened her cloak, she looked earnestly at George. 'Give my love to Elizabeth. Let us know when the funeral is. Stephen will wish to come, too, if at all possible.' With that she was gone and a minute or so later, they heard the crack of a whip and the sound of horses' hooves as the coach pulled away.

There was silence in the kitchen for a moment, broken only by a sigh from Martha. 'By gum, she's got lovely clothes.' She felt that if only she could be dressed like Tamar she would win Bob Lamb.

'She scrapes 'er tongue,' sneered Jonna. 'You'd never think she was our sister.'

His mother frowned. 'Well, she *is* your sister,' she said shortly. 'She mixes wi' a different class now, but she's still one of us.'

Although the last days of the dying year were bitterly cold, there was no more snow. Christmas came and went, but there was no merriment for the Oaks of Sleightholmedale, where Jonadab's brother clung doggedly to life, although the rasping of his breath and his persistent cough brought sleepless nights for all in the house.

By mid-January, however, Tamar received the awaited letter to say that her Uncle had died quietly in his sleep. 'You will come with me, won't you?' she asked Stephen.

'Of course, darling,' he replied. 'I only wish we could see more of your family.' He admired his father-in-law's farming ability and had been given some worthwhile advice whenever they had met.

'Yes, so do I,' she answered. 'Even though Father always manages to rub me up the wrong way. Anyway, they have not really the transport for a journey as far as this and in any case, they could not spare the time from work.'

She looked at Stephen lovingly. He was so handsome and she did love him dearly, despite Gareth Davis. By some quirk in her moral fibre, Tamar found nothing incongruous in her tempestuous affair with the groom, caring for Stephen as deeply as she did. In her opinion, her love for her husband was not diminished at all just because another man could raise her to sexual satisfaction in a devastating fulfilment which was lacking in Stephen's love-making. Sometimes she admitted to herself that she hated Davis, but his passion was like a drug which she was unable to resist.

'Penny for your thoughts,' teased Stephen, coming to put his arms round her waist.

'I was just thinking how much I love you,' she answered truthfully, stretching up to kiss him.

They decided that Victoria would accompany them to the funeral, but that Hilary, who was a delicate child, should not be exposed to the January chill.

There was only a handful of mourners at Gillamoor Church, as Uncle George had rarely gone out of the little dale. The only people who really knew him were the labourers who helped out at the farm during the periods of sheep-shearing, haytime and harvest. As many of those were itinerant, following the seasons from farm to farm and from wold, to moor, to dale, there were few to mourn the passing of the gentle, self-effacing man.

Victoria was silent throughout the service and as they stood by the side of the grave where George was laid to rest beside his parents, she noticed in amazement that most of the women cried and that even her Grandad Oaks, who often appeared fierce and of whom she was a little afraid, took out a handkerchief and surreptitiously wiped his eyes. She had presumed that only children cried and was disturbed to see that grownups sometimes did so.

Once the funeral was over and they were back in the parlour of the cosy farmhouse, the atmosphere lightened and Victoria was passed from group to group, chattering like an enchanting little doll.

Stephen stood with Jonadab, looking out of the parlour window, watching the teams criss-crossing the fields, with ploughs behind them. 'You're nice and sheltered here,' he remarked. 'Most of our land at Home Farm is on exposed hillside and is too frozen to plough at present.'

Jonadab looked out with satisfaction. 'Aye. They're getting on wi' it,' he said. 'Mi ploughmen can't be idle. They knows as 'ow Aah can see 'em, if they stops.'

'Yes, they do stand out well. My fields are too far from the Manor for me to keep an eye on them. Either I or the manager of Home Farm must ride round the fields sometimes two or three times each day to check the men.'

Jonadab chuckled. 'What thoo wants, lad, is one or two pairs o' greys. Look and see 'ow they stands out against t'brown o' t'earth. If a team stops even for a minute Aah can tell – and t'men knows it!'

Stephen studied the fields, where the drab clothing of the workers blended into the deep rich brown of the arable land, but where each pair of greys was clearly visible, its progress across the field assessed instantly. He smiled in admiration at his father-in-law. He was a wise old bird and no mistake. 'Could I buy a couple of pairs of greys from you?' he asked, coming to a sudden decision.

Jonadab hesitated. 'Well, ti tell t'truth, all this year's broken foals is really spoke for. Aah can't breed 'em fast enough ti keep up wi' demand.' He considered for a moment. 'T'army'll tek all Aah've got, but Aah'm not too keen for 'em ti go for cannon-fodder.'

'I understand.' Stephen was disappointed at what he took to be a refusal.

After a moment's reflection, however, Jonadab went on, 'They'll never miss a couple o' pairs. Aah can just say they must tek what Aah've got and Aah'll let thoo 'ave a couple of pair.' Stephen opened his mouth to express his thanks but before he could get a word out, Jonadab spoke again. 'It goes against t'grain ti do business wi' friends or relatives. Aah've allus warned me lads against it, but Aah'll set t're-cord straight. Thoo'll pay t'full price – nowt knocked off, even if thoo is wed ti' oor Tamar.'

Stephen smiled. 'I wouldn't have it any other way,' he said, holding out his hand to seal the bargain. Once done, however, he gave a sudden grin. 'There'll be a bit off for luck?' he asked, proving that he still retained some of the guile he had picked up as a practising country lawyer.

Jonadab was nonplussed. As he told Annie later, 'And 'im wi' all 'is brass.' However, he put on a smile and replied, 'Of course. When t'time comes we'll come ti' some arrangement.'

The family had expected to feel strange in Stephen's company, but he put them at their ease and asked Jonadab's advice on farming matters, until they warmed to him. As Annie said later to Martha, 'Although 'e scrapes 'is tongue, there's nowt toffee-nosed about 'im.'

When at last Tamar and Stephen decided that they really must leave, Victoria pleaded for them to stay a little longer. 'No. We've a long way to go, pet, and you've had an exciting day', Tamar said firmly.

Annie took a breath. She had seen so little of this grand-child. She saw the children of her other daughters Ann and Beth most market days, but encountered Victoria so rarely that each time she had altered beyond recognition. She looked pleadingly at Tamar as she said, 'Mebbe when t'summer comes, your Mam'll let thoo come and stop wi' us for a few days.'

'Oh, may I, Mama?' Victoria clapped her hands and put her head on one side, smiling so winningly that everyone laughed.

Tamar looked at her fondly. 'Yes, I suppose so,' she

smiled. She tended to be over-indulgent with Victoria, partly because she could see herself in the child and partly too, in some perverse fashion, to make up for what she considered to be her own harsh upbringing under Jonadab's strict rules.

George studied his sisters. Ann and Beth had married into farming families and had the same careworn faces and workworn hands as had his wife and mother. Beside them, even in unrelieved black, Tamar shone out like a butterfly among moths. It was not only the cut of her clothes and the richness of the fabric which were distinctive but she herself possessed a bloom and glow over and above her personal beauty, which were absent from all the other women who were there. 'She's like the cat that's got the cream,' he thought, and indeed, there was an air of self-satisfied sleekness about Tamar.

When Martha brought Tamar's cloak, her sister noted how she stroked the cloth before handing it over. She looked at Martha with a fresh insight, noting the drabness of her clothes and the downward droop of her lips. As she kissed Martha, Tamar spoke in a low voice. 'Next time I come, I'll bring one or two gowns that I know will fit you.' Martha brightened and Tamar added, 'Nothing flashy, but not serviceable either.' They both laughed. Serviceable was a favourite word of their father's: everything from boots to clothes must be seen to be serviceable.

After they had gone, the others sat round the table and discussed them. It was evident to all the family that Stephen Lassiter still loved Tamar and that she, too, was happy. Jonna put it into words: 'It hardly seems right. There's us lot working and slaving from dawn till dusk for nowt, and the two who've not stuck to the straight and narrow as come off t'best. Our Joe's got 'is own farm in t'Canadas and there's our Tamar, no better than she should be, and living like a queen.'

Jonadab's brows drew together. No matter what Joe's and Tamar's earlier lives had been, both were respectably married now and their father had accepted them back into the fold. 'That's enough!' he snapped at his youngest son. 'We're a family and thoo'd best not forget it. We sticks

217

together no matter what. Aah've not forgotten yon mornin' in t'blizzard,' he added with a meaningful look and nod.

As Jonna rose to go and change back into his working clothes, he flushed with resentment. 'I'm not a child, Faither,' he remonstrated.

'Well, don't behave like one,' was his father's final word. Not for the first time in the past few months, Jonadab was disturbed to recognise envy and the seeds of discord in his youngest son.

# CHAPTER NINETEEN

The weather remained piercingly cold, so that whenever men or beasts had need to venture outdoors they were chilled to the bone. The snow did not return until early in February: this time, the Oaks were well prepared. All the sheep were on lower ground where they could be reached by men on horseback, and the womenfolk had laid in stocks of flour and yeast, so that there was no shortage of food. This enforced isolation was an accepted part of life in the dale, coming, as it did, every two or three years.

The townsfolk of Kirkbymoorside realised that while the snow lasted, the farm-wives would be unable to reach the market with their produce so Annie and Elizabeth were secure in the knowledge that whenever they were able to get out of the valley, their customers would be waiting.

The first couple of days brought a continuous heavy blizzard. The biting wind drove the snow before it, so that the whole dale seemed to be lost in a grey mist. On the third morning, they arose to find that the blizzard had died down, to be followed by keen frost as the temperature plummeted. The dale took on a crystalline magic; the sun climbed above the skyline of the moors, touching the snow-covered landscape with sparkling highlights. The trees stooped groundward under the weight of their snow-laden branches and the humans followed their daily work, once again pitting themselves against the inexorable forces of Nature.

Both Annie and Elizabeth were disturbed to find that each morning brought fresh fox tracks circling the hen huts. The snow gave them proof of what they always feared: the winter-hungry foxes were biding their time, ready to raid any hen-house which remained unfastened at dusk.

Ann Butler had written to Uncle Nathan in Leeds to say that when Sarah went there to act as bridesmaid to her sister Christiana, she would stay on to be his new housekeeper. She had not yet broken the news to her youngest daughter. Christie was to be married at Easter, but Ann planned to go over in late February to help with the wedding preparations and also, to take Sarah and see her settled in before she started her job.

At first, she had determined to tell her daughter of her decision after Christmas. However, she was beginning to feel her age and could not face an argument until it was unavoidable. Once they were snowbound she put the task off again and it was not until early March that the thaw began. Realising that before another couple of days had passed, she and Sarah would be able to make the journey to Leeds, Ann asked George if he had time to ride up to Kirkbymoorside and book them two inside seats on the Leeds coach. He was only too thankful that Sarah was to be removed from his home. Ever since she had saved him in the snowstorm, George had been uncomfortably aware of her presence. He would look up from his newspaper after supper to find her eyes fixed on him, in a way which brought back to him the passion with which she had kissed him upon the moor. He guiltily remembered the feel of her and felt acutely disloyal to Elizabeth ... Anyroad, he told himself, he'd be glad when she was gone.

While he was in the stable saddling up his horse, he did not realise that his mother-in-law was only now breaking the news to Sarah that she would be remaining in Leeds. He had the horse almost ready to take out, when the stable door was thrown open and Sarah rushed in. George looked up from tightening the girth as she banged the stable door behind her and stood, back pressed against it, glaring at him wildly. 'You're sending me away!' Her tone was bitter and tears streamed down her face.

George decided that he had better be diplomatic. 'We all think it's the best thing for you, to see something of life beyond the dale.' He spoke placatingly. 'Now dry your eyes, Sarah, and be sensible.'

Her expressive brown eyes flashed. 'Don't treat me as a child!' she cried scornfully. 'You know that I love you, and that's why I'm being packed off.'

George sighed. 'I'm a married man – your own sister's

husband.' He spoke firmly. 'Don't be silly. You only think you love me because I'm here in the same house and there's no one else.' He studied her for a moment. Her eyes were dark and luminous and her faintly olive skin normally carried a dusting of colour, high on her cheekbones. At this moment, however, her face was pale and set.

'It won't make any difference to my feelings for you,' she insisted. 'I've loved you ever since I was a child and I shall always love you. No matter how many young men I meet in Leeds, I shall never marry.' So saying, she once again burst into tears and, crossing rapidly to George, threw her arms around his neck and stretching up on her toes, began to kiss him with a fervour which shocked him.

Desperately, he unclasped her hands and pushed her away. 'That's enough, Sarah!' He spoke brusquely now, deciding that the time for tact was over. 'You should be ashamed to make advances to any man – but to your own brother-in-law is too much. Go and pack your things and leave me to go and book your seats.'

As he spoke Elizabeth entered the stable. Seeing her sister's tearstained cheeks and George's flushed face, she had some idea of the scene which she had interrupted.

'Oh, good! You haven't set off yet George. Here's a list of one or two things I'd like you to get for me while you're in Kirkby, if you don't mind,' she said matter-of-factly, passing him the paper.

'Right.' George placed the list in his pocket. Seeing Elizabeth's troubled expression, he gave her a kiss on the cheek and added, 'I won't be long, love.' This was not merely to reassure his wife, but to make clear to Sarah that his love for Elizabeth had never wavered.

When Elizabeth's mother and sister had gone to Leeds, Elizabeth and George had the house to themselves for the first time since the early days of their marriage. The complete absence of tension in their home and the privacy to talk in the evenings, just to each other, drove home to them as nothing else could have done, what a strain they had been under while Sarah and Ann Butler had lived with them.

Easter came and with it Christie's marriage. Apart from

221

an enthusiastic note from Sarah, describing the wedding and her gown, there was no sign of Ann Butler's return.

'She's always welcome here, as you know,' George earnestly told his wife, 'but it's grand to be on our own.' He hoped that Ann Butler would stay in Leeds, but felt he could not say so to Elizabeth. As his mother-in-law had come to know him better, she seemed to have accepted that he was the man for her daughter and even to have become quite fond of him, but he appreciated this new freedom.

Elizabeth sighed. 'Yes it is, my love, but I wonder how long it'll last? Mother won't be able to decide who needs her interference most, us or Sarah.'

George laughed. Elizabeth understood, though neither would have put it into words, that her mother was a thorn in George's flesh.

The blustery winds of March dried up the land so that when April arrived, with stronger sun and balmy air, the whole countryside sprang into new growth almost overnight. The last dull memory of winter faded and the hedges were a mass of silvery catkins of the pussy willow, while amongst them flourished cuckoo-flowers and Jack-by-the-hedge, attracting the early orange-tip butterflies.

One evening, as they worked happily together, feeding and attending to the livestock, George said, 'I'll just take a walk along the beck before we settle down, and check those sheep I've brought down for lambing.'

Elizabeth replied, 'And I'll just pour this milk into the skimming trays then take my apron off and come with you. It's a pleasant evening for a stroll.'

Crossing the stepping-stones, they strolled along the far side of the stream, mostly in silence, enjoying the peaceful spring evening. Suddenly, George placed a finger to his lips and, taking Elizabeth by the arm, gently pushed her down into the grass. She heard a shrill, penetrating whistle of a bird and trying to follow George's pointing finger, she caught a glimpse of brilliant blue-green plumage, with an orangey breast, as the bird flashed down into a deeper pool scooped out by the stream. Before she had time even to gasp, it flew back up and disappeared into a hole above the water.

'Was it a kingfisher?' Elizabeth asked in a whisper. George nodded and motioned her to silence again; although they waited for another quarter of an hour, it was a vain vigil. The bird did not reappear. 'I've never seen one before,' she said excitedly, when it was clear that that was to be their only sighting.

'I've not seen many,' answered George. 'It was just that I heard it call so I knew there must be one about.'

'It's strange we should see one this evening.' She looked up at him with a sideways, almost shy glance. 'They're supposed to bring good luck.'

'So I've heard,' answered George, rolling onto his back and looking up at the sky, while he chewed a stalk of grass.

'Well,' Elizabeth hesitated. 'I wasn't going to tell you yet but,' she paused. 'I think I'm expecting.'

George was utterly still for a moment, before rolling over on to his stomach. 'Oh, little love! Are you sure?' he whispered incredulously.

She nodded. 'Well, almost. I haven't dared to see the doctor yet, in case it's just my age or something. I am nearly certain, however.'

George was unable to speak for a moment or two. He was on the verge of tears and did not wish to appear unmanly. They knelt facing each other and to George, Elizabeth looked no older than her sister, Sarah. Her cheeks were flushed, her eyes shining and her lips were tremulous. 'I never thought to see this day,' he murmured, as he rose to his feet and gently pulled her up to him. He suddenly seized her under the armpits and swung her round and round, until she was breathless. As he put her back on her feet, George threw back his head and shouted at the top of his voice – 'Ya – ha! Ya – ha!'

Elizabeth gave him a push, which almost toppled him to the ground. 'George!' She was laughing at his antics, but anxious lest he should be heard. 'Be quiet! Someone'll hear and I don't want to tell anybody just yet.'

George looked round at the acre upon acre of emptiness. 'Who's going to hear, might I ask?' he said in a teasing voice.

'Well, sounds can carry on a quiet evening and you don't

want your father asking why you were acting daft. Or your Jonna,' she added as an afterthought.

As the freshness of spring gave way to the heat of summer, it became obvious that Elizabeth was indeed pregnant. Although she was by now in her late thirties, she recognised the same symptoms as in her previous pregnancy. Her breasts became tender, she endured a faint queasiness in the mornings but no actual sickness and finally, her figure began to thicken and take on a matronly look. After her miscarriage so long ago, Elizabeth met each change with apprehension, but she seemed well and in fact, bloomed in her pregnancy.

After the first few months, George was insistent that she give up the market stall. 'We can take no risks,' he pressed. 'Yon big kettle you use weighs a ton and anyway, I don't want you on your feet all day.'

Elizabeth knew that George was right: she could not take chances with this pregnancy. Both she and George had long ago given up all hope of a child. Now the opportunity had once again been given to them, she felt that they must do nothing to jeopardise the future. Before the next Wednesday, Elizabeth carefully made a notice to say that the tea-stall would close. This she took with her in the trap when she left to go to the market. As she set up her tables and put the big kettle on to boil, she made a point of taking Annie aside. 'I'm going to have to give up standing the market, Ma,' she announced quietly.

Annie was surprised. She looked at her daughter-in-law curiously. 'Why, lass, Aah thought as 'ow you enjoyed t'market,' she said.

'Oh, I do! Of course I do,' answered Elizabeth. 'It's just . . .' she hesitated, giving a little self-conscious laugh. 'I'm expecting a baby,' she said.

Annie was amazed. 'Aah'm fair flabbergasted!' she exclaimed. After a moment's pause, she went on, 'Art sure, lass? It's not t'change come early, is it?'

'No.' Elizabeth's voice was firm. 'Dr Dawson has confirmed it. After all these years and after the last time, I feel I must take things easy.'

Elizabeth's customers were disappointed to read her

notice, but although several of them asked the reason, she merely smiled and was noncommittal. After the lunch-time rush of customers, Annie and Elizabeth sat side by side with a cup of tea and a pie each. As they munched Annie placed her free hand on Elizabeth's arm. 'Eeh, Aah'm that glad, lass,' she smiled. 'Thoo must tek things easy, though, as thoo said.' She paused for a moment and then went on, 'Since thoo told me about t'baby, Aah've been thinking. Aah sh'll stop coming ti stand t'market, an' all.'

Elizabeth was surprised in her turn. 'But you love market-days, Ma! Why don't you bring either Martha or Lydia with you for company? It makes a change and gets you out of the house.'

'Nay, Aah dissent think so,' replied her mother-in-law. 'Aah'm feeling mi age, lately. Aah've only come this last couple o' years because we was indoors. Aah couldn't 'ave stood it outside in all weathers.'

They sat chatting together while Elizabeth waited for trade to pick up again. Many of the farmer's wives came in for a mug of tea and perhaps a piece of cake before they set off on the long drive for home. They became so engrossed in their chattering, that they did not notice a customer who came up behind them. 'Can Aah 'ave a cup o' tea an' a bun, missus?' came a voice. Jumping to her feet and crossing to the big teapot which was keeping warm, Elizabeth answered, 'Yes, certainly.' Turning, she saw her mother-in-law shaking with laughter.

'Eeh, lass! It's oor Tamar,' she smiled, wiping her eyes.

Tamar laughed. 'I haven't forgotten how the Dalesfolk talk, you see, Mam,' she teased, as she sat down on the bench next to her mother.

'We 'aven't seen thoo since t'funeral.' Annie tried not to sound reproachful.

'I'm sorry,' Tamar answered, 'but Hilary's delicate. He always seems to have a sore throat and a fever, so I don't like to leave him when he's not well. In any case, Stephen's mother uses Hilary as an excuse to stay on at the Manor and I want rid of her.'

'Eeh, lass! Don't say such things,' remonstrated Annie. The extended family was an accepted way of life in the dales and she had shared a home with her husband's parents and brother until their deaths.

Tamar sniffed. 'She hates me. She always has done – and most of the servants will never accept me as long as *she's* there.' She took a long drink of her tea and then continued, 'Anyway, she'll go before long, never fear.'

Elizabeth looked at her sister-in-law. Yes, she thought, if Tamar had set her mind on something she would never rest until it was accomplished.

After asking about various members of the family, Tamar eyed Elizabeth. 'You're looking particularly well,' she commented.

Elizabeth flushed with pleasure. 'Yes. I'm expecting a baby,' she replied.

There was a noticeable hesitation before Tamar rose and kissed her on the cheek. 'Oh, I'm so glad for you and George,' she said warmly, but when Elizabeth turned away to serve a customer, Tamar looked at Annie with a worried expression. 'She's getting on a bit for a first baby, isn't she?' she demanded. 'I do hope everything's all right this time.'

'Aye, lass. So do I,' replied her mother.' 'Anyroad, 'er and oor George is over t'moon, so don't put a damper on.' She went on to tell Tamar that she and Elizabeth would not come up to Kirkbymoorside to stand the market in the future. 'Except wi t'geese at Michaelmas and Christmas,' she qualified.

Tamar was disappointed. 'It's a long enough journey for me to come here to see you,' she said. 'The extra few miles each way will make it well nigh impossible.' Seeing her mother's face fall, she added hastily, 'I shall have to see what can be done.'

It seemed to Annie that no sooner had Tamar arrived in the market hall, than Goodison was by her side, suggesting that it was time they started off for home. As Tamar rose to her feet, she suddenly exclaimed, 'Oh! I'd almost forgotten why I came. I've brought some clothes for Martha.' As her mother began to speak, Tamar broke in. 'Don't worry – there's only a cloak, a couple of gowns and a few blouses. There's nothing too fancy or unsuitable.'

'Your father'll never let 'er wear 'em,' said Annie.

'He'll never notice. Anyway, if he does, tell him they came from Elizabeth. He'll let our Martha have them, if he thinks Elizabeth gave them to her.' Seeing the look of dismay on her mother's face, Tamar continued, 'You won't be telling a lie. I'll give them to Elizabeth and she can pass them on to Martha. Anyway,' she added blithely, 'you'll probably manage to smuggle them into the house without him seeing if you choose your time well.'

Leaving her mother-in-law in charge of the tea-stall for a few minutes, Elizabeth went back to the inn-yard with Tamar and the coachman. Here, Goodison lifted four large mantle-boxes from the coach and stowed them, as best he could, under the seat of Elizabeth's trap. 'However can we get them into the house without anyone seeing?' she demanded.

'You'll manage,' Tamar replied airily, as she collared a boy who was crossing the yard and slipped him a penny. 'Watch this lady's parcels until she gets back,' she instructed. Then with a kiss of Elizabeth's cheek, she was handed into the coach. While Goodison mounted and took the reins from the ostler, she called, 'Give my love to George!' and with that was gone, leaving Annie and Elizabeth with the task of smuggling the clothes into the house without arousing Jonadab's suspicions.

When they reached Aumery Park Farm, it was to discover that they had misjudged the time of their arrival. Jonadab and his two sons were just scraping their boots at the back door, prior to going in for a mug of tea. After this break, they would go out again to help with the evening tasks amonst the stock. Once his boots were satisfactorily freed of mud, Jonadab strode into the house, leaving the rest to follow. Annie looked at Elizabeth almost guiltily but Elizabeth just smiled and said, 'Leave the boxes in my trap and send Martha down to our house tomorrow. She can try them on then, so that I can do any alterations that are necessary. After that, we'll get them back up here one at a time. Don't worry,' she added. 'It'll be all right, you'll see.'

As they sat in the kitchen, Jonadab glanced across at George and remarked, 'While we're a bit slack afore haytime starts, Aah thought as 'ow thoo and me could deliver them two pairs of shires ti Stephen's.'

Annie saw the set of Jonna's lips and the mutinous expression which came over his face. She sighed – the older Jonna became, the more jealous of George he seemed to grow. Before he could protest, however, Elizabeth spoke. 'If you're going to be away all day tomorrow, George, perhaps Martha would come down and keep me company.' As she made the suggestion, she looked towards Annie.

'Why, aye. That's a good idea.' Annie was only too glad to cope with the clothes while her husband was out of the way.

When they reached home that evening, George said, 'After what happened to our Tamar, I don't like you being here on your own all day. Write and ask your mother to come back. If she doesn't, we'll go up to the Union Work-house, next week, and get a girl. After all, Lydia's been a big help and there must be others as good.'

'Aye – and there must be others as bad as Tobias,' laughed Elizabeth.

George sighed. Tobias had been a poor choice, as Jon-adab himself admitted. Now that he was a man he was no more capable of working unsupervised than when he had first come to the farm at the age of twelve. None of them could understand why a bright and hard-working girl like Lydia would wish to marry him.

The next morning George and his father set off for Thorsbury, each leading a pair of grey shirehorses. As soon as she knew that her husband was out of sight, Annie called Martha. 'Go down to Cherry Tree. Elizabeth's got some clothes for thoo, from oor Tamar.' Martha was so excited that she ran all the way down the lane, arriving flushed and breathless.

Elizabeth studied her afresh. She could be pretty, she decided, if her hair were not so tightly scraped back from her face and if her eyes shone with eagerness, as they did at this moment. Although one of the gowns sent by Tamar was quite deep brown in colour, the other was of a pretty shade of blue, which would set off Martha's eyes, which were the same deep blue as her father's. One of the bodices, or blouses as Tamar had called them, was of a deep rose pink and, although the other two were cream and white respectively, all were exquisitely trimmed with lace, embroidery or pintucks. As Martha tried on each garment in turn, Elizabeth could see that she was on the verge of tears. 'Eeh, I never thought I'd ever have any clothes like this,' she said, stroking the material of the blue dress.

'Nonsense!' answered Elizabeth briskly. 'There's no reason why Tamar shouldn't keep you in clothes. She can afford it, and they fit you a treat. They don't need altering at all.' She hesitated, not wishing to sow the seeds of rebellion in Martha. 'What a pity your father is so set against accepting what he might consider to be charity from Tamar. Anyway, we must be clever and change you gradually.'

Once they had cleared away and washed the dinner pots, she set to and washed Martha's hair. Putting strands from each side into curl rags, she said, 'Now sit by the fire and brush the rest dry, while I collect the eggs.'

When Martha was ready for home, she put on the pink bodice and Elizabeth dressed her hair. Instead of dragging it back into a tight knot in the nape of her neck, she twisted it into a more becoming coil, leaving the tendrils which had been twisted in the curl rags, to curl prettily round her face. As she stepped back to view the result, she realised that Martha was really a most attractive girl. Determined that she should not go the same way as her sister, Jonadab Oaks had ruled Martha with a rod of iron ever since Tamar's seduction by Sir William Forster. She had simply been given no encouragement to make the best of herself. Now when she pirouetted before the wardrobe mirror, Martha was transformed. Her cheeks were flushed and her eyes sparkled, while the deep rose pink of the bodice suited her to perfection.

Elizabeth had been unprepared for such a dramatic change. What on earth would her father-in-law say, she wondered. 'Oh, well,' she thought. 'It's done now – in for a penny, in for a pound. If you meet a young man,' she instructed, 'bite upon your lips and give your cheeks a rub to bring up the colour.'

Martha giggled. She was not likely to meet any young

man, she considered, but nobody had ever tutored her before on how to attract one. Looking out of the bedroom window, Elizabeth saw Bob Lamb the shepherd walking with his dog down the track from the high moor. 'Why don't you walk home along the beck?' she suggested. 'It'll be cooler and not so dusty along by the water.'

Martha waved to Elizabeth, as she ran down the side of the field of oats which lay between the farm and the beckside path. As she passed through the gate, to walk beside the stream, Bob Lamb caught sight of her from the other bank of the beck. 'Why, 'ello, Martha!' he exclaimed. Martha's cheeks became even pinker as she blushed to see him. For his part, he was amazed at the transformation. He had never before paid much attention to her. She was just the boss's daughter, a rather timid and drab little thing in his estimation. Now, he looked at her curiously, unable to decide what was different in her appearance. With a snap of his fingers to his dog, he gingerly crossed the stream, stepping carefully across the shallowest spots until he joined her.

'Be careful,' she said involuntarily.

He smiled. 'It's shallow enough. I just didn't want to get mi boots too wet.'

Looking at the water sadly, Martha answered quietly, 'I rarely cross it. When I was seven, my sister Maria was drowned in it.'

Lamb was at a loss for words. Looking at Martha, he could see that she was distressed. Putting a hand on her arm, he said gently, 'Would you like to sit for a while and tell me about it?'

As Martha raised her eyes to his, he felt suddenly protective towards her. For her part, she felt that he was someone to whom she could open her heart and who would understand. As they sat together on the grass, she looked at the tumbling waters of the beck and told him how Maria had slipped on the stepping-stones, down by the farm. 'She knocked her head on a stone and was drowned,' she concluded. There was a moment's silence and then she went on, 'I've always blamed myself. I was scared to cross the

230

stepping-stones and it was turning back to encourage me that caused her to slip.'

It was out: the heavy weight of guilt, which she had never confided in anyone before, was out in the open.

Rising to his feet, Bob Lamb reached down and taking Martha by the hands, pulled her up. Placing a hand on each of her shoulders, his steady brown eyes looked deep into her tear-filled blue ones. 'Look at me, Martha. Believe what I say. You were a child of seven when this happened.' He gave her a little shake. 'You were not to blame,' he said insistently. 'You were not to blame.' This time it was said more slowly and with powerful conviction.

Martha dissolved into tears and burst out, 'I've never dared to tell anyone until now, but I've felt guilty ever since.'

'Come now, Martha. Now you've told me, it will be all right,' he murmured. 'We bottle things up for years until they grow out of all proportion.' As her tears subsided, he smiled down at her. 'Now you've got it off your chest, you can see how silly you've been, can't you? It was just two little girls playing and one had an accident. Nobody was to blame.'

She smiled tremulously. 'Thank you, Bob. I feel better about it now than I have done since the accident,' she admitted.

As they resumed their stroll along the beckside, he stole a sideways glance at her, wondering why he had paid no attention to her before.

'You're looking very nice today,' he remarked.

Martha glowed. No one had ever told her this before – not even Sam Baldwin, who wanted to marry her. Thinking of Sam, she compared him with Bob. She had known Sam all her life and though he was a worthy and hard-working man, she knew why she had held back from agreeing to marry him. He was dull. Martha had been attracted to Bob Lamb since the shepherd first came to work on the farm the previous November. He had never appeared to notice her existence until today but now, strolling beside him in the warmth of the afternoon sun, Martha felt a heady excitement. Looking at him shyly, she confided, 'Sam Baldwin from t'mill wants to marry me. Faither wants it an' all.'

231

Bob glanced down at her. George had told him in private the reason for Sarah Butler being packed off to Leeds, and he had realised then that her infatuation for George was an obsession. Her mind was closed against any other man. As there was very little chance of her returning to the dale, except for occasional visits, Bob had succeeded, with a bit of self-discipline, in putting her out of his mind. Now he acknowledged to himself that his admiration for Sarah had caused him to overlook young Martha's attractions. He had a strong desire to get to know her better, and yet here she was talking of marriage! 'Do you love him?' he asked cautiously.

'No!' she answered vehemently. 'I neither love him, nor do I want to marry him.' Looking Bob straight in the eye, she added, 'There was a time when I could have drifted into marrying him, but no longer.'

'There's your answer then,' said Bob. 'It's better to remain a maid, than to wed the wrong man.' As they turned from the bank to approach the farm, round the edge of the Long Meadow, he took her hand, and drew her to a stand-still. 'Let's see how things go, shall we?' he said tentatively.

'Oh yes, Bob,' she replied, understanding the unspoken pledge.

In tacit agreement, they separated before reaching the farm. Martha felt that she was walking on air and when she entered the kitchen, Annie looked up. Noticing the flushed cheeks and sparkling eyes, she commented, 'By 'eck thoo looks bonny. That pink suits thoo a proper treat. Mind thoo,' she added, 'Aah don't know what thi faither'll say ti such a colour. It's not serviceable.'

Martha laughed. She did not care what her father thought. Bob Lamb had noticed her! Nay – more than that. He was interested in her and she felt on top of the world . . .

# CHAPTER TWENTY

The whole of the vale of Pickering lay spread out before the two riders, stretching as far as the eye could see. The fields were a chequerboard of shades, interspersed with large patches of broad-leaved woodland. 'What a view!' George exclaimed. 'I can see for miles.'

'Aye.' Jonadab glanced at the panorama outspread before them. 'But we aren't 'ere t'admire t'view, lad,' he chided. 'Keep moving, or we'll never get there.' As they drew nearer to Thorsbury village, however, each man leading a pair of two year old shires behind his horse, Jonadab looked with approval at the fields on either side of the road. 'These must be Stephen's,' he commented. 'We're approaching a bridge. 'E's got a good look on – it must be a bit o' good land.'

George smiled to himself. It was typical of his father, he thought. His own crops, if a good yield, were due to splendid husbandry, while any other farmer's were attributed to good land. He made no comment, however, as his father glanced over the parapet of the bridge.

'Aye, this is it. There's four arches.' As soon as they were over the bridge, a driveway cut off to the left and their way was barred by huge wrought-iron gates. 'Get down, and ask at t'lodge,' ordered Jonadab.

George dismounted and passed the reins to his father. He knocked on the door of the gatehouse, which was opened by an old man. 'Aye?' he queried shortly.

'We've got two pairs of horses for Sir Stephen Lassiter,' explained George.

'Not to t'front, thoo hasn't,' answered the gatekeeper sourly. 'Up yon 'ill. Turn left at t'top and go down t'village. When thoo gets to t'bottom, thoo'll see t'buildings and stable-yard. That's where thoo wants ti be.' So saying he went back inside and banged his door shut behind him.

'We're to go down t'village, to t'stables,' George told his father, as he retrieved the reins.

Jonadab's lips set in a straight line and his brows drew together in a frown. 'Dids't thoo tell 'im who we are?' he demanded. 'Dids't thoo say we're Lady Lassiter's faither and brother?' His voice was beginning to rise and it was obvious that his temper was on a short fuse.

George could have laughed aloud to think how, for years, their father had been ashamed of Tamar, but now he was proud to claim kinship. He kept his own council and merely answered, 'No, Faither. They won't want 'em at t'front door. We'd best go to t'stables, like he said.'

If the truth were told, Jonadab had had enough. The journey was the longest he had ridden for several years and he was feeling his age. It was he himself who had insisted upon a brisk pace and now all he wanted was to dismount and stretch his legs.

As they rode down the village, George noted how clean and tidy it was. The cottages were in good repair, showing Stephen to be a caring landlord. 'I couldn't live as close to other folk as they do,' he remarked to his father.

Jonadab, however, made no reply. He had just caught his first glimpse of Thorsbury Manor. 'By 'eck!' he ejaculated, pulling his mount to a standstill. They stood, looking in disbelief at Tamar's home. The sun was at its height, lighting up both the stone and the countless windows. It was an impressive sight. 'Yon lawn in t'front must be all on a couple o' acres,' stated Jonadab.

It was brought home to them, for the very first time, that Tamar had never once described her abode. Perhaps it was because her few visits to Sleightholmedale had been fleeting or was it perhaps, George wondered, because she knew how overwhelmed they would feel if they knew the truth.

'And they said they was just farmers, like us,' mused Jonadab, as they rode at a walk through the high arched entrance and into the stable-yard. Here they stood for a moment, looking round. Jonadab dismounted and trying his best not to sound too impressed, said with a nod of his head, 'They're even got their own farrier.' Looking in the direction indicated, George saw a smithy, with the black-smith and his striker hard at work.

A young stable lad led out another horse, and stood waiting for the one which the smith had almost finished shoeing. Jonadab hailed him. 'Now young man,' he called, as he handed his reins to George and approached the boy.

'Yes?' The boy was about twelve years of age and a little impudent in his attitude.

'We've some 'osses 'ere for Sir Stephen. Canst thoo tell me where 'e might be?'

'It's not 'im thoo wants,' answered the lad. 'It's Davis – t'ead groom.'

Jonadab was now standing over the boy. Stooping slightly to look down at him he said, very quietly but adamantly, 'Aah knows 'oo Aah wants ti see. Aah'm Sir Stephen's faither-in-law, so off thoo goes and tell 'im we're 'ere.'

The boy was in a quandary. If this stranger was who he claimed to be, he supposed he'd better do as he was told. To leave his work, on the other hand, would earn him a clout across his ears from Davis and perhaps, even from the smith as well. In addition, he had never been to the big house and had no idea where to go, or whom to see. All his working life had been spent in the buildings and the stable-yard.

Jonadab was used to implicit obedience. Raising his voice a little, so that it cracked out like a whiplash, he said tersely, 'Off wi' thoo.'

The boy dropped the halter he was holding and set off at a run through the gateway and towards the big house. As George bent to pick up the halter of the horse which the boy had been holding, he looked round the yard with interest, noting how his father's voice, though by no means a shout, had penetrated every corner. The men and boys who were working around the stables looked across curi-ously to see the strangers. Out of what appeared to be a tackroom emerged a man who walked with authority, stop-ping to have a word with one and another of the workers as he crossed towards Jonadab and George.

As he drew closer, walking with almost a swagger, George noted the way the sun glinted on a head of coppery curls.

It was not until he was practically up to them, that he turned his face directly towards them. George's disbelief and shock must have been mirrored in his face, as he saw the scar which marred the otherwise handsome features. It stood out whitely against the tanned skin, exactly as Tamar had described it, when telling of her attacker several years ago. George had never forgotten.

'What can I do for you? I'm the head groom.' The Welsh drawl was added proof that this was indeed the man who had attacked Tamar. George swallowed but was unable to reply. The groom smiled and put up his hand to stroke the scar. 'Gave you a shock, did it?' he asked. 'It's been with me so long that I forget it's there, but it can be a bit off-putting to strangers.'

Jonadab glowered at George. How could he be so offensive as to stare at the chap's disfigured face, he wondered. George still did not answer Davis. His thoughts were in turmoil and his open guileless face reflected the chaos in his mind. How could this man be here? Tamar obviously had no knowledge that the man who had attempted to rape her was working on her husband's estate. There was no doubt whatever in George's mind that this was the same man. Tamar's description, to him and Elizabeth, had been too vivid for him ever to confuse it. The man's presence here was no coincidence, he decided, and Tamar must be warned. Perhaps he was awaiting the chance of revenge for the crack on the head that had been given him . . .

With a start, George brought his thoughts back to the present, aware that both his father and the groom were looking at him curiously. He forced a smile. 'Sorry, mate,' he said. 'I was miles away. I though I'd seen you somewhere before.'

The groom grinned cockily and again stroked the scar. 'If you had, you'd hardly forget,' he chuckled.

'Just what I was thinking,' George replied.

Before any more could be said, Stephen came hurrying into the cobbled yard, hand outstretched, his face beaming with pleasure. 'How grand to see you!' he exclaimed, shaking hands with both men. 'So these are what you've brought me,' he said, as he moved round the four greys admiringly.

'Aye.' They were the pick of Jonadab's two year olds, but he would never admit it. 'They're noan so bad,' was his summing up. 'Two's geldings and two's filleys. In another couple o' year, if thoo wants General mi stallion ti call, just let me know. 'E's a fine specimen and good stock-getter and he's unrelated ti these two.'

When Gareth Davis had examined the greys thoroughly, running his hands over their muscles and looking at their teeth, Stephen said, 'They're in your charge now, Davis. Mr Oaks is a well-known breeder of greys and we're lucky to obtain some of his horses.'

As Stephen ushered his guests across the cobbled yard and into the drive which led to the house, George glanced back. Gareth Davis stood watching them, a thoughtful look on his face. He was intrigued and a little disturbed by George's attitude. It was obvious that the sight of him had been a shock to Tamar's brother, but Davis was convinced that he had never encountered George before. With a shrug, he turned away to give orders for the care of the greys, and the visitors' mounts.

Jonadab had presumed that George's silence was due to the size and luxury of his surroundings. After the first shock he was in no way abashed by the grandeur of Stephen's estate. 'Jonadab Oaks is as good as any man,' was an oft-repeated claim, and this he truly believed. He had held up his head in the most exalted company. Yet when Stephen threw open the front door and led the way through the entrance hall into a lofty and elegant room, graced with pillars and dominated by an ornate white marble fireplace, even Jonadab was taken aback.

As he and George hesitated by the doorway, Tamar rose from where she was seated by the fireplace. 'Father! George!' she exclaimed, as she came towards them, hands outstretched. 'How lovely to see you here at last.' She looked so relaxed and happy, smiling up at her husband, that George was convinced that she could have no idea that her attacker was employed by Stephen. He wondered how he could get a word, alone, to warn her.

When they went into the dining room, Stephen's mother joined them. 'Mother, may I present Mr Jonadab Oaks,

Tamar's father, and her brother, George,' Stephen said. Looking at the two men he completed the introduction. 'This is my mother.'

She held out a languid hand, which Jonadab seized and pumped up and down. 'Aah'm pleased ti meet thoo, ma'am,' he said.

George's eyes met Tamar's and they gave a mutual smile. In no way was their father going to be overwhelmed by this cold withdrawn woman.

The talk at the table was mainly about horses. Old Lady Lassiter took no part in it, pecking at her food in a listless fashion, eyes fixed on her plate. When Tamar began to tell her father and George about the children, however, her mother-in-law brightened up and looked quite animated. It was soon evident that she was besotted with little Hilary, and talked about him incessantly. 'Have you any family, Mr Oaks?' she inquired of George.

'My wife is expecting our first baby in January,' he replied shyly.

When the meal was over, Tamar led the way up the wide sweeping staircase to the nursery wing. Here, Gertie cared for Hilary, and Victoria now had a governess. She was excited to see her grandfather and uncle, running to hold up her face for a kiss. Jonadab was taken aback, not being a man given to overt affection. However, he bent down and kissed his little granddaughter on the cheek. 'Look, Hilary,' she said, leading the two year old forward by the hand. 'This is Grandad and Uncle George.'

Jonadab watched the child who toddled towards him. It was his first sight of his grandson and he felt a pang of anxiety as he looked down at him. Hilary had inherited his father's almost silver hair and fair colouring, but while in the father this in no way detracted from an appearance of strength, it accentuated the child's look of frailty. 'They're going ti 'ave a job ti rear yon lad,' he would tell Annie upon arriving home, and this was the thought that crossed his mind now.

Victoria's black hair and vibrant colouring, combined with her vivacity, served as a sharp contrast to her brother's apparent fragility. Jonadab looked at her fondly. The Oaks' blood was dominant there he thought; you couldn't beat good farming stock. It was a pity poor little Hilary hadn't inherited more of his mother. Anyway, he added to himself, as he looked with pity at the little boy, it was asking for trouble, giving him such a daft name. T'lad should 'ave 'ad a good, strong 'un.

When the time came for them to go, Stephen went with them to the buildings, to see where the greys were stabled. 'See that they are well looked after, Davis,' he instructed. 'They're rather special.'

'Yes, sir.' Davis touched his forelock and then glanced towards the Oaks, as though conscious that George's eyes were fixed on him with a disturbing intensity. He was puzzled by George's attitude, which appeared hostile, although he could think of no reason why.

George felt anxious that he had had no opportunity to be alone with Tamar, and so there had been no chance of warning her about the groom. He was certain that Tamar had told no one about the attack on her, apart from him and Elizabeth, so could not broach the subject in front of either his father or Stephen.

While the three of them stood by the pump in the stable-yard, waiting for their horses to be brought out, George nodded his head towards Gareth Davis, who was across the other side of the yard, well out of earshot. 'How long have you had your groom?' he asked his brother-in-law.

'Davis? Since just after we came to the Manor. Don't worry about those greys. He's an excellent chap with horses. I couldn't have a better head groom. He's as good, too, at handling men as he is horses.'

George, meanwhile, made no comment, but the thought that flashed through his mind was, 'Aye! *And* manhandling women!'

Having said their goodbyes, the pair rode along the semi-circular drive which passed in front of the Manor. Not only did this save the horses the pull up the hill through the village, but it gave them the occasion for one more glimpse of Tamar and the children, who stood on the steps, waving.

As they crossed the bridge and began their long ride home, Jonadab heaved a heavy sigh. 'Yon bairn's nobbut puny,' he commented. 'Aah could wish 'e looked a bit stronger.'

With an effort, George dragged his thoughts back from Davis. Surely Tamar must know he was there? After all, she had learned to ride and had her own horse. The whole problem was beyond him, he decided. 'What?' he asked.

'Yon lad of our Tamar's. Aah said as 'ow 'e 's only a poor little thing.'

'Aye. He is an' all,' answered George. 'He breathes good country air and must have t'best of everything, but 'e only looks frail.'

After a little more conversation, mainly expressing amazement at the splendour of Tamar's circumstances, they urged their horses to a brisk pace and had no further chance to speak. Upon arriving at Aumery Park Farm, when Jonadab dismounted, George remained on his horse. 'Is thoo coming in for a cup o' tea?' his father invited, but George shook his head.

'Nay, I'd best be getting back.'

His father gave a rare chuckle. 'Aah'll tell thoo what,' he grinned, 'yon owd woman were like death's 'ead at a feast. A real owd crabapple she is.'

'Aye,' George grinned back. 'There's no wonder our Tamar wants rid of her. She'd put the damper on anybody.' He swung his horse round and said over his shoulder, 'I'll be off then, Faither. See you tomorrow.'

Removing his hat, Jonadab stood staring after him, scratching his head in puzzlement. What was up with George, he wondered. He'd been a bit funny, quiet-like, ever since they'd arrived at Thorsbury Manor. Surely he couldn't be jealous of Tamar's grand lifestyle? Looking across the fields to the little beck, with the heronry beyond and the green sweep of the moors rising above, he drew a deep breath of satisfaction. What more could a man want, than this . . .

George made his way to his own home, shoulders slumped and mind disturbed. Now that he was away from his father, he could give full rein to his imagination as to what Gareth Davis was doing at Thorsbury. If the groom had been there for over two years, he must have had plenty of opportunity for revenge on Tamar, if that had been his motive.

When he rode into the yard of Cherry Tree Farm, Elizabeth was approaching the house with a pail of milk. Seeing her husband, she set it down by the back door and came across to the stable. While he unsaddled and fed his horse, she plied him with questions about his visit to Tamar's home. 'What's it like?' she asked.

George hesitated. He could picture the house and its setting, but was lost for words. 'It's big,' he said at last.

'How big?' she prompted.

'Well,' he paused for some means of comparison. 'It's bigger than t'Towers, where Sir James lives.' Sir James Sturdy was the Oaks' landlord, having inherited the estate upon the death of his father the previous year.

Elizabeth's eyes widened. 'It must be huge!'

George sought his memory for some of the facts given by Stephen and Tamar about their home. He felt guilty now for not having paid more attention, but his thoughts had been on the groom. He brightened as he recalled some of what they had been told. 'There's fifty-two stairs to t'staircase and three hundred and sixty-five windows.'

Elizabeth digested this information. 'Who cleans them?' she wanted to know.

'Faither asked that an' all,' vouchsafed George. 'There's a chap does nowt else. When he's finished, it's time to start again at t'beginning.' He could see that Elizabeth was pleased by his attempts to describe it all and continued, 'You should see t'stables, coach-houses and t'yard. I should think there's more folks live there than there is in t'village.'

As they walked back to the house, George managed to fill out his description by giving more details of the inside of the house. He told Elizabeth of the meal in the dining room, with the butler and maids serving on and made her giggle at his father's summing up of the Dowager Lady Lassiter. 'A real frosty-face she has an' all,' he added. He sank into his Windsor chair by the fire, while Elizabeth washed the eggs. 'It's grand to be back,' he sighed.

'You wouldn't swop, then?' Elizabeth smiled.

'That I would not,' he retorted. 'It's not like a home, not like this,' looking round with satisfaction.

'What about the little one?' Elizabeth asked. 'What's he like – Hilary?'

George frowned. 'To tell you the truth, Liz, I wouldn't give a lot for their chances of rearing him,' he said sadly.

'Oh, George! You can't mean it?' She was appalled.

'He's a poor little thing, wan and thin. He belies his pasture, because he'll have the best that money can buy. He just looks as if a puff of wind would blow him away,' George finished.

Elizabeth was silent for a moment. Her heart went out to Tamar. She felt a twinge of guilt, knowing that she had sometimes wondered whether or not Hilary's ill-health was an excuse invented by Tamar, because her visits were so infrequent. Now it appeared that the little boy was in reality a delicate child.

'Did our Martha come down?' George asked her.

Elizabeth's face lit up, as she told him of Martha's excitement over the clothes sent by Tamar. 'Oh, you should have seen her, George! She looked like a different person. I washed and curled her hair and she wore a lovely pink bodice to go home in. She looked really pretty!' She paused for a moment and then went on. 'Don't say anything, but I saw Bob Lamb going along the beck, so I sent her off that way, too. She's rather keen on him, you know.'

George looked surprised. 'Our Martha? Well, she's wasting her time. He's never looked twice at her.'

Elizabeth smiled. 'He's never seen her look the way she did this afternoon. No man could help but look at her more than twice.'

George could not imagine how a change of clothing could create such a transformation in his plain youngest sister, but passed no comment. Now that Elizabeth had exhausted the topic of Martha, they sat for a few moments in silence, one each side of the fire with a cup of tea. Back in his own home, it seemed incredible to George that he had actually seen Tamar's attacker at Thorsbury, and yet he was certain that the groom was the same man. Eventually, he decided to confide in Elizabeth. 'You know I said I'd like you to write and ask your mother to come back,' he began.

'Yes – why? Have you changed your mind?'

'No, of course not, but you remember why I don't want you to be alone?'

'Of course. It's because Tamar was attacked.'

'Well . . .' he drew out the word slowly, unsure now of what to say. It all sounded so impossible.

'Yes?' Elizabeth prompted.

'I've seen that chap! The man who tried to rape Tamar!'

Elizabeth placed her cup carefully on the hob by the fire and turned to look at George, who was leaning forward, looking at her earnestly. 'You can't have done,' she stated, but there was a question in her voice. 'Besides, you've never seen him, so you don't know what he looks like.'

'I've never forgotten Tamar's description,' he asserted. 'Ginger hair, tanned face and that scar, stretching from his right eye to his mouth. Well, that very same man is Stephen's head groom.'

He sat back to watch Elizabeth's reaction. It was eminently satisfying: she appeared to be what Jonadab would have termed 'gob-smacked'. 'I just can't understand what he can be doing there,' she said at last.

Although they sat up later than their normal bedtime, neither could find any explanation. George was insistent that Tamar must be ignorant of the man's presence. 'There'll be men working there that she never sets eyes on,' he declared. 'You can't imagine how big it is and how many men Stephen employs.'

Elizabeth was silent. She understood her husband's loyalty to his sister. There was only a year between their ages and there had always been a close bond between them. She recognised, however, that beneath Tamar's apparently circumspect exterior still lurked the reckless and tempestuous streak that had characterised her in her youth.

In the end, they came to the decision that whichever one of them saw Tamar first, would try to have a private word to tell her of Davis's presence, and then see how she reacted. 'Goodness knows when that will be,' Elizabeth sighed, 'now that I'm not going to stand the market any more.'

'How about writing to her?' queried George.

'No. Stephen may expect to read any letters she receives,' answered Elizabeth. 'We'd better leave it as we've arranged.'

Having reached this rather unsatisfactory conclusion, they went up to bed.

# CHAPTER TWENTY-ONE

The summer was tranquil and fairly uneventful; Jonadab Oaks felt that for once, Nature was working with him instead of against him.

Ann Butler had returned from Leeds in answer to Elizabeth's letter. Part of her journey, from Leeds to York, had been undertaken by train and afterwards she regaled anyone who would listen with stories of the noise, smoke and speed of the train, until they were heartily sick of the whole subject. What she never admitted was that in the beginning, she had been terrified of this new mode of travel and the first few miles had been passed with her eyes tightly closed and her lips moving in prayer. When she had eventually plucked up her courage and looked out of the window, she had been entranced by the views from the carriage and the speed of travel.

The new relationship between Martha and Bob Lamb was blossoming. As the summer progressed, their hesitant and tentative emotions became stronger. Bob had helped purge Martha of the terrible guilt that had haunted her since her sister Maria's death. Now, after years of self-doubt, she was growing in confidence and beginning to shed the tensions of her formative years. When the women went out into the fields to help their menfolk with the haymaking, it was noted, although no one passed a comment, that Bob sought her out and sat with her at 'lowance time.

'Doest thoo think there's owt in it?' Annie asked Jonadab one evening at bedtime.

'Aah'm not so sure,' he replied, 'but Aah reckons as 'ow there must be. After all, 'e chooses ti sit wi' 'er, when there's all t'men for 'im ti sit and talk ti.' As he climbed into bed he added, 'Anyroad, time'll tell. She could do a lot worse – 'e's a good, steady man and 'e's not given ti strong drink.'

Annie sighed. 'Aah could never understand why she wouldn't 'ave young Sam Baldwin. 'E's keen on 'er, and she seemed ti be fond of 'im till 'e asked for 'er in wedlock.'

A thought struck Jonadab and he hesitated on the point of blowing out the candle. 'Aah'll tell thi summat, Mother. She *were* keen on Baldwin's lad, till Bob Lamb come 'ere. That's when she went off Sam.'

Annie digested this piece of information and came to the conclusion that her husband was right. Poor Sam had been backwards at coming forwards, she told herself. He had missed his chance with Martha, as had his brother Will with their Beth. 'I expect he'll get over it,' she comforted herself sleepily.

Once the harvest was finished and the Mell Supper had been celebrated, Lydia approached Annie one morning in late September. ''Ave you thought any more about Tobias and me, missus?' she inquired.

Annie smiled. Lydia had been with them now for ten years or so and still persisted in calling her 'missus'. 'No, Lydia, 'Aah 'asn't,' she said. 'Aah wasn't sure thoo meant it.'

Lydia put her head on one side, reminding Annie of a little sparrow with her darting beady eyes. 'It's like Aah said, missus. There's not much chance of finding an 'usband down 'ere and Aah've no wish ti stop an old maid all me life. Anyroad, Aah've asked 'im and e's willing.' She looked pleadingly at her mistress. 'That is, of course, if it's all right by thoo. 'E'll be no bother. 'E'll share my room and 'e'll spend 'is evenings in t'stable out o' t'way, like 'e does now.'

Annie looked at her curiously. 'It doesn't seem much of a married life for thoo, Lydia,' she observed gently.

'It's better than nowt,' she was assured. 'We was in t'workhouse together and 'e'll do as 'e's told, which is more than a lot of 'usbands does.'

Annie smiled. 'Thoo's right there and yes, of course it's all right!'

Lydia beamed. 'We sh'll put t'banns in on Sunday, at Gillamoor. Can your Martha be mi bridesmaid?'

With a shock it was brought home to Annie Oaks that

they were the only family Lydia and Tobias had ever known, coming to Aumery Park Farm from the Union House as they had done at the ages of ten and twelve. 'Aah'll tell thoo what,' she said. 'We'll go into Kirkby next market day and Aah'll buy some stuff for t'frocks. Thoo can choose it and Elizabeth and me'll mek 'em.'

Lydia face split into a huge grin. 'Ooh thanks, missus! That'll be grand!' she exclaimed.

When the news was broken to Martha that Lydia wanted her for a bridesmaid, she was excited. 'I'll wear that blue gown of our Tamar's,' she decided.

'No, love,' Annie gently chided. 'It's Lydia's day. Thoo dissent want ti outshine t'bride.'

Martha agreed readily, although she was disappointed. She had not yet worn any of the gowns sent by Tamar and was longing for Bob to see her in the blue one. At her first appearance in the rose pink blouse, her father's eyebrows and icy glower had caused her to redden under his gaze but for once, her mother's slight head-shake had caused Jonadab to bite his tongue and he had made no comment to Martha.

When told of the forthcoming marriage between Lydia and Tobias, Jonadab expressed his amazement. 'She's a canny little thing, as bright as a button,' was his summing up of the maid. 'What she can see in 'im Aah dissent rightly know. 'E's as daft as a brush, and twice as wooden as t'shaft.'

Annie sighed. 'There comes a time Jonadab, in every woman's life, when she needs a man. Lydia's reached that point, and there's no one else. All our other men are either married or too young.'

'Aye, Aah expects thoo's right,' her husband rejoined. 'Toby's no great catch, but she's nowt better t'angle for, really.'

When the day of the wedding dawned in October, Elizabeth came up to the farm to help Lydia and Martha to prepare for the ceremony. She and Annie had made the gowns and, although they were of good strong material, befitting the bride's station and life-style, Lydia's chestnut-coloured material brought a touch of colour to her normally sallow cheeks, while Martha's deep maroon set off her fair colouring.

Annie was concerned to see that Elizabeth seemed to have lost much of her sparkle. The innate vivacity which had been one of her main attractions, seemed to have deserted her. 'Is thoo feeling all right, love?' she managed to ask, amid the excitement and chatter of Lydia and Martha.

Elizabeth smiled sheepishly. 'Of course, Ma. I've been waiting all this time for a baby, but I must admit the carrying of it is more tiring than I'd expected.'

Annie was a strong, wide-hipped woman who had carried and borne eight, with little discomfort. 'It's because you're smaller-framed,' was her comment.

After the ceremony Annie provided tea for the family and Tobias's workmates. It was with satisfaction that she noted how Bob Lamb's eyes continually strayed to Martha. As for Lydia, she was satisfied to have been the centre of attention for one day in her life. As she removed her wedding dress and put it away, she knew that it would only ever be worn at Christmas and other times of equal importance. On going back downstairs in her working clothes to do the washing up, she felt a quiet pride: not only had she now achieved the status of a married woman, but she had also had a proper wedding with a cake and an attendant – which was more than did most girls of her class.

Over at Thorsbury, the summer had also gone well for Stephen Lassiter. After more than three years at the Manor, he had managed to pull round the farms and get the timber business running smoothly. Although he was still away fairly often, visiting the mills in Leeds and Bradford which provided the bulk of his income, he was more relaxed now that he felt that he was mastering the intricacies of the various businesses which had been allowed to slip into low productivity during his father's ill-health.

During haytime and harvest, the four horses bought from his father-in-law had proved to be a boon. They were well-broken and when grazing in the fields, came to a call, taking no catching. Stephen was delighted with them and all his men knew that they were special to him.

Now that Hilary was three years old, Stephen had made

it clear to his own mother that the necessity for her to remain at the Manor was past. Tamar had left the persuasion to her husband, determined that there was no way in which her mother-in-law would be able to allege that Tamar had driven her out. She had to admit, however, both to herself and to Tempy, that she was delighted when old Lady Lassiter moved to the Dower House, taking with her not only her maid, but also one or two of the older servants. 'Thank goodness the old battle-axe has gone,' said Tamar. 'I can't tell you how much more at ease I feel, without her and her cronies snooping on me.'

She did not realise how much she had changed since becoming Lady Lassiter. Her riding ability had paved the way for her acceptance amongst the circles in which they now moved. When they had first come to live at Thorsbury, she had felt a little piqued by Stephen's neglect of her, while realising that his obsession with work was not really of his own choosing. In those days, too, she had been afraid of Gareth Davis, but her fear had been tinged with an awareness of his overt masculinity.

When she first felt herself swept away on the tide of desire, the risk of detection had added spice to the affair. Now, however, she had grown tired of Davis, and her excuses to avoid being alone with him became more frequent. Tamar would have been happy to finish the association, but Davis would not release his hold on her. She knew that the longer the relationship lasted, the more she courted disaster. She no longer needed the groom to accompany her when she rode out, since she was now a proficient horsewoman. This placed obstacles in the way of their meeting with any regularity, causing Davis resentment and bringing out the ugly side of his nature.

He had threatened on more than one occasion to reveal details of their love-making to Stephen. 'Then I'd clear off and leave you to face the music,' he had sneered. 'I can get work anywhere and am not tied here.'

No matter how Tamar used her wits, she could see no way out of the situation and was in a constant state of panic that he would carry out his threat. Even as she glanced out of the bedroom window, while changing into a riding habit,

Gareth Davis approached the front door leading Moonbeam and Stephen's magnificent black horse, Lightning.

'There's one I'd like to see the last of as well.' She said the words with such bitterness that Tempy glanced inquisitively from the window.

'Gareth?' Tempy was unable to fathom her mistress' desire to be rid of the groom, nor the depth of feeling behind the words.

'Aye, Gareth.' Tamar's tone was almost vindictive as she strode briskly from the room to join Stephen for a ride round the estate.

Her husband's brow furrowed as he noted the set of her face. Tamar always seemed to be in a bad mood recently and he was at a loss to discover the reason. During their ride, Stephen did his best to do so. 'Are you worried about anything, Tamar?' he asked.

'Of course not!' She put on a smile, but it was unconvincing.

'Perhaps you're bored,' he suggested. Suddenly struck by an idea, he said, 'What do you say to a week in London? We could take the travelling coach to York and then go up by train.'

The change in Tamar was dramatic. Her face lit up and her amber eyes danced with golden lights. This time, her smile was one of genuine joy. 'Oh, Stephen! How lovely!' she exclaimed. 'Perhaps I have been bored, without realising it.'

Not only was she exultant at the thought of a holiday in London, but she would also have a week removed from the constant worry of Gareth Davis. With Stephen away from the estate, she could relax in the assurance that there was no way that Davis could betray her.

The next couple of weeks were spent in a whirl of feverish activity. In answer to Tamar's claims that she had no clothes suitable for a visit to the capital, Stephen persuaded her to wait until they arrived and then she would be able to buy something. It was the first holiday since their short honeymoon in York so that Stephen, too, was eagerly anticipating the break from the routine of business.

'You've worked too hard since your father died,' Tamar told him. 'You're in need of a bit of relaxation.'

When Stephen's mother was told of their intended trip, she immediately offered to move back to the Manor, to oversee the children. Tamar offered up a silent prayer that Stephen would not be cajoled into agreeing to the step, but she need not have worried. He appreciated, as much as Tamar, the freer atmosphere in the house since his mother's departure.

'No, thank you, Mother,' he answered firmly. 'Gertie is quite capable of looking after Hilary and Victoria's governess is in charge of her, so there is no problem.'

While Stephen and Tamar were away, the weather remained crisp and dry. Hobson, the manager of Home Farm, kept the men hard at work, trying to get much of the land ploughed, before the coming of winter. On the day that his master and mistress were due back from London, he was determined to have as much as possible completed, in order to impress Stephen with the amount done during his absence. Having despatched the first and second waggoners with their teams, he turned to Ted Barlow, the third waggoner. 'Now, Ted. Thoo'd better mek a start on yon ten acre field down by t'river-side. It ought ti 'ave been done afore, really. It's a bit on t'spongy side, so Aah wants it finished afore t'rains come.'

Ted's team were Gracie and Daisy, the two grey fillies supplied by Jonadab. The sun had quite a lot of warmth in it and he set off, behind the back of the Manor and along the bank of the river, to the field where he was to work. He was a cheerful lad and interspersed his whistling with conversations with his team, having grown fond of the two gentle shires. Gracie and Daisy had already been broken to the plough while still down in Sleightholmedale and had been trained to plough together, Gracie walking in the furrow and Daisy being the land horse.

Ted peeled some sticks pulled from the hedge and used them as markers by which to guide his plough, in order to set his rigs. Once this was done he set about his task, quite happy to be in no other company that that of the two greys. Guiding the plough and following the team up and down the field over the uneven ground was very hard and tiring work. As he tramped behind the horses, he spoke to them constantly, in a caressing tone. 'Come on there, Daisy lass' or, 'Gee up a bit, Gracie'. Such phrases came in a constant stream of encouragement.

The two greys snickered in reply, blowing out their lips and twitching their ears upon hearing their names. Ted's monologue was kept up against the background sounds of the creaking of leather upon leather and the calls of the woodland birds. For all his enjoyment of the work and the companionship of his team the lad was not sorry when the ground covered, about half an acre, showed that it was time for his midday snack. Unhitching his horses from the plough, he fastened Gracie to a sapling on the bank of the river, before leading Daisy down for a drink. 'Come on, old lass,' he urged. 'Come and 'ave a nice drink afore Aah puts thi nose-bag on.'

His intention was to water both horses and while they had their nose-bags of oats, he would sit in the shade with his allowance and a bottle of cold tea. Slipping the bit out of Daisy's mouth, he led her by the halter to a gap in the belt of trees which clothed the river bank. Giving her the full length of the halter, he allowed her down to the bank, to drink her fill from the water. 'Go on, lass,' he murmured. Smelling the water, Daisy needed no further encouragement and put on a spurt to hurry down to the river.

To Ted's consternation, the soil of the slope suddenly gave way and the halter shank ran through his fingers as the terrified horse slipped down towards the water. Kicking and bucking to keep her balance, she managed to draw to a shuddering halt close to the rushing torrent about ten feet below where he was standing. 'Thank God,' he muttered, as he started to scramble down the last foot or two to seize the halter shank that dangled so near, and yet just out of his reach. He too felt the spongy soil drawing him downwards. With an effort, he heaved up first one foot and then the other and moved back onto firmer ground. One horrified look told him that Daisy had already sunk to her pasterns. Her eyes were rolling with terror as she began to struggle to free herself from the tenacious, sucking mud –

struggles that only served to hasten the process and cause her to sink at an even greater rate.

'Whoa! Whoa, old girl,' soothed Ted, when he saw that even with all his weight pulling on the halter, there was no hope of saving her that way. Casting a look at the frightened filly, he hauled himself by tufts of grass back to the top of the caved-in bank. From the crest, with a final 'Whoa!' to the horse, he ran and and seized Gracie's halter from the tree where he had tied her. Climbing on to her back, he used the halter shank to whip her into a lumbering unaccustomed trot, as he made his way back to the stable-yard.

Upon his arrival, he was nonplussed to find the yard and buildings deserted. 'Of course,' he muttered. 'It's dinnertime!' Jumping down, he ran up the stairs into the Long Room, where all the workforce were seated over the midday meal. 'Come quick! Come quick!' Ted shouted. 'Daisy's got into some sinking mud and she's going down fast.'

Knives and forks clattered down and forms were kicked over in the uproar which followed. Gareth Davis took a breath and shouted loudly, 'Whoa! Just wait.' All eyes were fixed on him as he held up his hand. 'The other heavy horses are all out on the land, so get to the riverside field as quick as you can, on horse or on foot. Jack and Harry, bring some traces. Hurry up, now. You know what Sir Stephen'll say if we lose her.'

Under his direction, the staff made their way with all speed to where the horse was trapped. Davis groaned as they came within sight of her. 'She's in up to her belly,' he exclaimed. 'We're going to have all on to get her out.' Quickly organising the men, he threaded a leading-rein through his belt, passing the free ends to a team of men. 'If I shout that I'm going down, haul me out as fast as you can,' he ordered. 'We don't want to lose Daisy but rather her than me.'

Some of the other men had been busy, tying together ropes and halters to make a long leash. Davis seized one end and started down the bank to where the horse was fast in the mud. Only her head was free to move by now and this she was tossing from side to side, her eyes rolling in panic, while her fear was further expressed in snorts and whimpers.

'If I can pass this under her belly and get it fastened,' he said, 'pull with all your might, and use the horses as well.' While he made his way swiftly but lightly across the boggy ground, giving his feet no time to be drawn down, the men higher up the bank were fastening the rest of the horses to the leash.

As he passed round the far side of Daisy, Gareth could feel the marshy ground clinging with each stride. He trod lightly, picking his feet up swiftly at each step in order to make as little contact as possible with the soft oozing mud. Quickly realising that it was an impossibility to tackle the rescue as he had hoped, he decided to fasten the makeshift leash to Daisy's collar. This would enable the men on the bank to keep her head up and give more time to spend on the attempts to raise her from the quagmire. Speaking softly to the horse, he came alongside her neck, anxious to attach the halter as quickly as possible and make his way back to firm ground.

One of the men on the bank called across to him, 'What's it like, Gareth?' As he began to shout his reply, he only managed the words, 'Bloody tacky,' when, at the sound of his raised voice close to her ear, Daisy swung her head towards him and caught him full in the chest with her nose. The blow caught him off-balance and he teetered for what seemed an age to the watchers, before falling into the rushing water with a hoarse scream. There was a loud crack as under the strain of the tearing current, the safety rope snapped and Davis was sucked under the surface of the swift-running river.

For a moment there was a stunned silence from his workmates and then pent-up breath was released in what seemed like a communal sigh, before the chief waggoner yelled, 'Come on! We might get 'im by t'bridge.' By the next field, the river curved in almost a right-angle so that by running diagonally across, they were able to cross the road and approach a place where, at the far side of the bridge, the ground shelved gently down to the water.

Although they spread along the bank and searched the

turbulence anxiously, there was no sign of the groom, either dead or alive. Ted had not gone with them. He sat above Daisy, talking gently to her, as she gradually sank into the bog. When, at last, the ground closed over her, he led Gracie back to the stables. The tears which coursed down his cheeks were not for the head groom. They were for the gentle grey shirehorse, whose death he blamed on himself.

When Tamar and Stephen crossed the bridge on their journey home from York, they passed the group of men, trailing up the hill towards the village. 'They're our workers,' said Stephen, looking from the window. 'Stop the coach, Goodison,' he called up to the coachman. As the horses were pulled to a halt, he jumped out of the coach and stood in front of the band of men who were trudging up the hill. 'What's wrong?' he demanded. 'What are you doing here? Why aren't you at your work?'

The men drew to a halt, removed their hats and caps but stood regarding him in silence. They moved their feet uncomfortably and avoided his eye, turning their caps in their hands. None wanted to be the one to break the news. At last, the head waggoner cleared his throat. 'We thinks as 'ow Gareth Davis is drownded, sir,' he stated.

'Davis – drowned?' Stephen was devastated.

Slowly Tamar stepped down from the coach, her face white and her eyes as dull as amber-coloured stones. 'What did he say?' she whispered. The men turned their attention to her. Now that the subject had been opened, each wanted to have his say.

'It's Davis, m'Lady.'

''E fell in t'river and was swept away, m'Lady.'

'We can't find 'im, but it's so deep and 'as such strong currents, 'e can't 'ave 'ad a chance.'

Tamar thought for a moment that she was going to faint. The group of men receded and their voices faded. She swayed slightly and Stephen took her arm and helped her back to the coach.

'I'll take Lady Lassiter home, men, and then I'll come down to the buildings. We've had a long and tiring journey and my wife is not well.'

Tempy was in the coach together with Stephen's manservant and had overheard the talk. As Tamar sank back into her seat, Tempy took out a bottle of smelling salts and held them under her nose. 'Are you all right, m'Lady?' she asked anxiously.

'Yes. Yes, I'm all right,' Tamar replied, opening her eyes and then veiling them with the black sweep of her lashes, but not before Tempy had seen the gleam of triumph in their topaz depths.

'She can't be glad 'e's dead . . .' the maid thought, but then recalled what Tamar had said about Davis before the holiday in London. What could she have had against the groom, she wondered.

After the initial shock, Tamar's reaction *was* one of elation. She had wanted some way of freeing herself from Gareth Davis and his demands and now, with no effort on her part, she was free of him for ever. A great weight was lifted from her mind. There was now no way in which Stephen could learn of her indiscretion. At last, she was safe. It did not feel unreasonable to her, that she felt no sorrow. Deep inside, Tamar loved her husband and her dalliance had been born out of boredom. It had not taken long for her to realise that it was not worth the risk of her position and Stephen's love. While they were in the travelling coach, she put on an outward appearance of sadness for a loyal employee, killed in an attempt to save his master's horse.

As they approached the buildings, Stephen called out, 'Stop here, Goodison, and I'll get out. You can go on up to the house.'

When they reached the Manor the children who had been watching from the window ran to greet Tamar. 'Oh, Mama! We've missed you,' cried Victoria, hurling herself into Tamar's arms.

'Missed you,' echoed Hilary, lifting up his arms to be picked up.

'And I've missed you as well,' she laughed, as she hugged them both. 'Come upstairs and you can see your presents.'

'Where's Papa?' asked Victoria, as the door closed when the final piece of luggage had been carried in.

Tamar hesitated. 'One of the workers has met with an

accident,' was all she said. The children were too excited at the thought of presents to ask any more details and the merry little group went laughing up the stairs, Tamar giving no further thought to the man who had died.

Stephen came in to change for dinner, thoughtful and brooding. He had organised a search of both sides of the river bank until dusk had closed in, but there was no sign of a body. He was upset that Daisy was gone, but the horse could be replaced. It was the loss of human life that lay heavy on him. 'Ted is not local,' he told Tamar, 'and knew nothing of the danger of that marsh. I didn't know myself,' he continued, 'but all the villagers know to keep away.'

'Thank goodness we've always warned the servants who have charge of the children, to keep away from the river bank.'

As Stephen talked of his intention of having the bog fenced off immediately, Tamar sat by her dressing table while Tempy brushed her hair. Her husband went through to his own dressing-room, and Tamar leaned forward, elbows on the dressing-table and looked at her reflection. It was only a week since, in this very room, she had wished to be rid of Gareth Davis; now he was dead. She gave a shudder. Had she some power unbeknown to herself, which smoothed her way through life, she wondered.

'Are you cold, m'lady?' Tempy asked solicitously.

'No.' Tamar smiled at the maid's reflection as she rose to her feet. 'It was just somebody walking over my grave.'

The following afternoon, Davis' body was found in a tangle of branches where the willows dipped their boughs into the river, close to Paradise Farm. This was well out of the village, although it was still part of the estate. Here the river took a wide right-angled bend, and the farmhouse and buildings snuggled there, protected, as though in the crook of an arm.

Tamar had just gone upstairs for her needlework when Jim Fairly, the tenant of Paradise Farm, drove down the village with the body under a blanket on a flat cart. Tempy who was by the window, remarked, 'I see he's surfaced, then.' Her mistress crossed to her and they stood in silence, side by side, while the rully was driven into the stable-yard.

Tempy sighed. 'There'll be plenty of lasses hereabouts who won't be dry-eyed when they hear that he's gone.'

'What do you mean?' asked Tamar in astonishment.

'T'was in more than t'colour of his hair that he was like a fox,' the maid replied. 'Like old Reynard, he didn't hunt at home. He went further afield for his sport. There's many a ginger-haired bairn in the villages round about who've lost their father this day; though they'll never know it, of course.'

Tamar went cold for a moment and then she was filled with a blinding rage. *How dared he?* She felt herself beginning to shake and grasped the back of a chair to steady herself. She suddenly felt the need to ride, to gallop at speed, her face into the wind and her mind filled with nothing but the rhythm of her mount. 'Get me a riding-habit out,' she said tersely. 'It doesn't matter which one. I want to go out for a ride in the open air.'

As Tempy helped her into her riding clothes, Tamar fidgeted and moved about until the maid was driven to distraction. When her mistress was dressed, Tempy handed her the riding hat which completed the outfit. Tamar gave it a flick, which sent it swirling across the room. 'I can't stand that on! I've a bad headache,' she snapped. Raising her hands, she snatched at the hairpins which controlled her hair, releasing black curls in a cascade down her back.

'Oh, m'Lady, no! It's not seemly,' cried Tempy.

'Who cares?' Tamar called back, as she almost ran from the room.

Upon her return, about an hour later, her mood was calm although this was belied by her appearance which Tempy described later to Gertie as 'like a witch on a windy day'. Her colour was heightened, her eyes bright and her hair was blown by the wind into a wild tangle.

Tamar never mentioned Gareth Davis again. Indeed, she rarely thought of him again. Three days later, dressed in the deepest black which suited her so well, she walked circumspectly by her husband's side to see the groom buried in the graveyard adjoining the pretty little village church. Tamar, Lady Lassiter's life was tidy and secure once again and she determined that it would now remain so. Her future would be devoted to her husband and children and no more would she be tempted into any indiscretions, she vowed.

# CHAPTER TWENTY-TWO

'It must be summat in t'air,' grunted Jonadab Oaks. No sooner was Lydia's wedding to Tobias over, than Bob Lamb had approached him for his permission to pay court to Martha, with a view to eventual marriage.

Jonna was still courting a girl from the neighbouring farm over the moor top at Skiplam. Maisie Brayton was the only child of a well-to-do farmer and his father viewed the forthcoming match with approval. On alternate Sundays, it was Jonna's habit to walk across the moor, having crossed Hodge Beck by the stepping-stones, and go to tea at the Braytons' house. This routine had been established for more than a year, so it was no surprise when one Sunday evening in early November, he announced at the supper table, 'Me and Maisie's set a date. We're ti be wed at Easter.'

'Eeh, Aah'm that glad!' his mother exclaimed. 'She's a nice lass and she'll fit in well 'ere. Thoo can 'ave yon front bedroom that was Gran and Grandad's. We made it ready for our George and Elizabeth, before they moved to Cherry Tree Farm.'

Jonna hesitated and took a sip of his tea, regarding his father warily over the rim of the mug. As he placed it slowly down on the table, he took a deep breath. 'Well,' he began, 'as Maisie's the only one, and there being no son ti tek over t'farm . . .' Again he paused.

'Well?' Jonadab could sense his son's reluctance to proceed.

'Well, Maisie's father wants us to live up yonder, so that I can get into t'road of running t'farm. After all, it'll be mine one day.' It was said with defiance, but even so Jonna was taken aback by the violence of his father's reaction.

'*What?*' he roared as he leapt to his feet. 'Trying ti tek thoo away from thi own land, is 'e?'

Jonna flinched back and Annie sighed as she looked from

father to son. Although so alike physically, she felt sure that Jonna would not stand up to his father's rage, as George would have done. To everyone's amazement, however, Jonna faced his father with a courage born of desperation. Rising slowly to his feet, he placed both hands on the table and leaned forward to face Jonadab. Blue eyes met blue eyes; each pair as cold and piercing as the other.

'It's not my land. It never will be my land. It'll pass ti George, and everything else with it.' The words were enunciated slowly and forcefully, underlining the bitterness and envy which had always tinged Jonna's feelings towards his brother.

The veins in Jonadab's neck stood out like whipcords, as he tried to control his voice. He knew that if he gave vent to his feelings and shouted at Jonna, it would upset Annie. Instead, his voice came out little above a whisper, cold and threatening. "Ow dare thoo defy me?' He paused, visibly shaking with anger. 'Aah'll tek a whip ti thi, if Aah dissent get an apology.'

Jonna suddenly lost all fear of his father. Once Jonadab had threatened physical violence, the son realised that he was more than a match for his ageing parent. Jonadab Oaks might be as lean and sinewy as ever, with muscles as firm and trim as in his youth, but age had taken its toll and he was not the equal of his son, who now faced him so challengingly. 'There's nowt for me ti apologise for,' he said firmly. 'Aah'll not be a slave ti this land, for no reward, like Uncle George was.'

Jonadab sank back in his chair, unable to believe what he was hearing. 'Us and ours 'as worked this land for generations,' he said heavily. 'Hast thoo no feeling for it?'

Jonna considered. 'No,' he said finally. 'You're a tenant-farmer, Faither. It's Sir James Sturdy's land and generations afore 'im. Us Oaks 'as paid for t'privilege o' working it and it means nowt ti me.' He nodded his head towards the west side of the house. 'Over yon moor is a farm that's mine for the taking. Lock, stock and barrel.' He emphasised the last four words. 'Aah'll not be anybody's tenant, Faither. Aah'll be responsible ti nobody but missen – mi own boss! Aah'll not give that chance up. Not for thoo – not for nobody.'

This declaration was greeted with a stunned silence. The eyes of those in the room shifted uneasily from father to son.

Jonadab's face was white, but his eyes blazed with icy light. His voice, when he eventually addressed his son, was cutting. 'So now we know.' This was yet another of his children to face him in defiance in this very kitchen. Jonna, who, despite his father's efforts to hide the fact, had always been his favourite, had followed the road first trodden by Joseph, his eldest son and then by Tamar.

The silence in the room stretched out, unbroken except by the heavy, deliberate ticking of the long-case clock in the corner. Annie felt that if no one spoke before long, she must get up and go out. She could think of no words to break the agonising tension. Before she actually rose to her feet, Jonadab spoke again.

'Can we tek it then that thoo'll be leaving us for this land of milk and honey?' He put the question with deceptive casualness.

Jonna's chin came up a fraction and he looked his father straight in the eye. 'Well, yes,' he answered. 'Eventually.'

'There's no eventually about it,' came back the answer with the speed of a striking snake. Jonadab's voice rose to a crescendo. 'If thoo intends ti go, thoo goes today.'

The shocked silence was broken by Annie. 'Oh, no! Don't be 'asty, Jonadab.'

He looked at his son. All colour had drained from Jonna's face. 'Disloyalty is disloyalty. Nowt can change that; and when it comes from t'family that a man 'as reared and cared for, it's far worse than from others.' Glancing round at those in the room, he gave a weary sigh. 'If a son of mine 'as no feeling for this land, it's better that 'e's off it.'

Annie and Martha began to cry, and Annie once again pleaded with her husband. 'Sleep on it, Jonadab. Don't say such things without further thought.'

'Aah needs no further thought, wife. Principles is principles and Aah sticks ti mine.'

It was plain for all to see that his father's ultimatum had come as a shock to Jonna. He pulled himself together with an effort and looked at his father. 'If that's how it's to be,

262

then that's that,' he said and turning away, climbed the ladder into what was still his room.

As he emptied his clothes out of the drawers, he glanced round the bedroom. This was another thing which had caused him to feel bitter. Even Tobias and Lydia were housed in better quarters, while he was still 'in the lads' room', where he had slept since leaving the cradle. He could not make out what was being said in the kitchen below. His mother was still sobbing and now and again he heard the low rumble of his father's voice, but no actual words. He put his few clothes in a neat pile on the bed and then looked round for something in which to carry them. Quickly he went down the ladder, crossed the kitchen and snatched up the top one of a pile of washed sacks from behind the kitchen door. As he strode back towards the stairs, his mother spoke, pleadingly.

'Son.' He neither spoke nor looked at her. As he disappeared once again into the bedroom, she turned to her husband. 'Say something, Faither,' she urged.

He shook his head with finality. 'All Aah've got ti say 'as been said,' was his response. 'If 'e puts another farm above this, then 'e's better away.'

Jonna placed his clothes in the sack, slowly descended the ladder and lifted his overcoat from its peg on the back door. As he struggled into it, he looked around. His mother and Martha were both crying softly, while his father's unblinking gaze was fixed on the fire. He cast his mind back to his homecoming earlier that evening. He had been so proud and happy to be returning to his family with the news of his impending marriage, yet now he was leaving home as an outcast. He kissed his mother and whispered, 'Goodbye, Mam. I'll be in touch.' Without even a glance at his father, he walked out into the night. Only when he had saddled and mounted Polly did he hesitate. The evening was misty and moist, with tendrils of thicker fog swirling around in the night air. He felt reluctant to tackle the journey back over the moors until daylight, and turned the horse instead down the lane to Cherry Tree Farm.

George and Elizabeth were on the point of going to bed

when they heard a knock on the door. 'Whoever can it be at this time of night?' asked Elizabeth.

When George opened the door, he was amazed to see Jonna on the step looking pale and distressed. 'Whatever's up?' he demanded. 'Come in, lad. Come in.'

Jonna slumped into a chair and poured out the events of the evening, while Elizabeth made another pot of tea.

'Will Maisie's father set you on, in the morning?' George questioned.

'Oh, aye. He's only too anixous to 'ave me there,' answered his brother.

'Well, then,' said George sensibly, 'stay here tonight, and go across t'moor to Skiplam tomorrow. Leave Faither to me. I'll work on him and try to bring him round. You'll be better working yonder, but we don't want a rift forever. He's come round to both our Joe and our Tamar and, heaven knows, he was bitter enough against them at the start.'

The winter drew on towards Christmas with the weather remaining unseasonably mild. The air was constantly heavy with moisture, few days being clear of the mists, which veiled the moor-tops and drifted among the valley trees in swathes, cloaking the bare branches.

For the first time in his life, Jonadab Oaks was the only man in the house. He refused to acknowledge Tobias, whom he had always labelled as 'stoddy'. This was a term of denigration, the meaning of which was obscure to everyone but himself. Left with no one with whom he could discuss the farm-work and stock when the day's toil was over, Jonadab became more and more morose, spending most evenings staring into the fire or wandering from building to building, checking his animals.

Annie and George meanwhile kept Jonna in the forefront of their conversations with Jonadab, behaving as though the rift had never occurred. If he regretted the outbursts which had led to Jonna's departure, Jonadab showed no sign. Rather did he wallow in a mood of self-pity, taking his son's desertion as a personal affront.

Christmas came and went, with Bob Lamb being invited to share the Oaks' family celebrations on Christmas Day, and all going down to Cherry Tree Farm on Boxing Day. There was still no word from Jonna, though, which cast a blight over Annie's mood. Once the holiday was over, George decided that he would ride over to Skiplam and satisfy himself that all was well with his brother. Before he could fit in a visit, he was forestalled by Len Brayton, Maisie's father, who rode down to Aumery Park Farm one Wednesday in mid-January, after attending the market at Kirkbymoorside.

When Lydia answered the door, he removed his hat and said, 'Would you tell Mr and Mrs Oaks that Mr Brayton of Skiplam Grange would like a word?'

Annie whipped off her apron and put it onto the table drawer, while calling out, 'Ask the gentleman in, Lydia.' She knew Maisie's mother from the days when she had stood the Wednesday market along with other farmers' wives, but had never met Len Brayton, the girl's father. As he entered she was impressed by his appearance. He was considerably younger than Jonadab, being about fifty years of age. He was a tall, distinguished-looking man, with an erect bearing. His hair was totally white, showing off his tanned face and humorous brown eyes. 'Come in, Mr Brayton and sit yourself down.' She was quite flustered to see him. 'Slip upstairs and tell t'maister that Maisie's dad's 'ere,' she instructed Lydia.

Jonadab was not to be hurried and methodically finished changing into his working clothes before putting in an appearance. When he did come into the kitchen, it was to see Annie and the visitor tucking into tea and jam tarts.

'Mr Brayton has come ti ask us ti tea next Sunday,' Annie explained. 'Aah've said as 'ow oor George's wife's time's nearly 'ere and Aah may be needed at t'confinement. Anyroad, what dost thoo think?' She deliberately placed the onus on him.

Lydia put a mug of tea in front of her master and then took herself off to the dairy, where she and Martha unashamedly listened at the door. There was silence in the kitchen as Jonadab sat stirring his tea. 'Thoo knows what's tekken place, Aah reckons,' he announced at last.

'Aye. Things get blown up out of all proportion,' Brayton replied.

The blue eyes which held his were glacial and unyielding. This man had taken his son, was the way it appeared to Jonadab Oaks. 'A son's place is on 'is family land,' he said unequivocably.

'Aye, Aah couldn't agree more,' answered the other man. 'But if a man has no son what then?' He glanced at them both. 'Then his son-in-law must act as a son and care for the land that'll one day be his.'

Jonadab digested this for a moment. Annie glanced at him for guidance, but receiving none, made no reply. After due consideration, Jonadab reluctantly contributed, 'Aye. Mebbe thoo's right.' After a pause he added, 'We'd be very pleased ti come ti tea. Thank Mrs Brayton for us.' He paused for a moment and then capitulated totally. 'Thoo and t'missus and Jonna and Maisie must come 'ere one Sunday, afore long.'

Annie uttered a silent but fervent prayer of gratitude and Len Brayton, his errand accomplished, took his leave. Annie crossed over to her husband then and kissed him on the cheek. 'Thanks, love,' she whispered.

Thus was the breach healed, before the chasm between father and son grew too wide. The two families began to exchange visits with more frequency and Jonadab and his youngest son were, on the surface at least, reconciled.

About two weeks after Len Brayton's visit to Sleight-holmedale, George rode up to work at Aumery Park Farm. 'Thoo's late,' was his father's greeting.

'Aye, Faither. I've had t'poultry to see to and t'milking to do,' he answered. Turning to his mother he went on, 'Mrs Butler says can you go down, Mam. Elizabeth's labour's begun.' At his mother's anxious look, he continued, 'I think all's well but she'd like you there, an' all.'

While Annie put on her cloak and bonnet, Jonadab called for the pony and trap to be brought round to the door. 'It's a blessing it's a mild winter up ti now,' he commented. 'It would've been a bad time for t'road between t'two farms ti be blocked wi' snow.' Eyeing George's face and noticing the beads of perspiration on his top lip he added, 'Aah expects as 'ow thoo'd like ti go back down home wi' thi mother.'

'Aye, I would an' all,' answered George gratefully.

The gratitude was short-lived, however, when his father replied, 'If thoo thinks Aah can spare thi, thoo's another think coming. There's plenty ti do now Jonna's gone and besides, it's not a man's place. Birthing is woman's work and thoo'd only be in t'road.'

Watching his mother ride down the valley towards Cherry Tree Farm, George felt a tide of resentment rising against his father. 'He never gives an inch,' he thought bitterly, not knowing that Jonadab was just as anxious over Elizabeth's labour as he was. The unending toil, which ground on at the pace of the changing seasons and the constant struggle against relentless Nature would be in vain, as far as Jonadab Oaks was concerned, unless there were others of his name to follow in his footsteps and work this land to which he had devoted his life. What concerned him more than it did George was that the child would be a boy. Several times during the morning he found himself consulting his watch, wondering how his daughter-in-law was progressing.

Just before noon George heard his mother's pony and trap coming down the road. He and his father had been horse-breaking in the roadside pasture and, urging the half-broken young colt to follow by jerking its leading-rein, George ran towards the gate. As he approached, his mother drew to a halt, her face beaming. 'It's a lad!' she called jubilantly.

George opened the gate and stood by the trap, full of eager questions. 'How's Elizabeth, Mam? Are they both all right?'

'Aye. It were an easy labour, if it's possible for one ti be so,' she answered.

Relief flooded through George. Until this moment he had not been aware of his own anxiety throughout Elizabeth's pregnancy.

Jonadab had followed at a more leisurely pace, not wishing to appear too eager to hear Annie's news. 'Is 'e a good strong lad?' he asked his wife gruffly.

'Aye. 'E's a good pair o' lungs,' she smiled, 'but 'e's not

very big.' Annie was broad-hipped and had given birth to overweight babies with no difficulty.

Jonadab grunted. 'Thoo can't breed cart 'osses out o' race 'osses,' was his reply.

'That's true enough,' answered his wife, thinking of Elizabeth's slight figure. 'If 'e'd been any bigger, she'd have had a bad time.'

Both his parents looked at George, whose face was a picture of delight. 'We'll get no sense nor work out o' thoo today,' his father remarked. 'Give me yon 'oss and get thissen 'ome.'

George needed no second telling. With heartfelt thanks he ran to the stable and, before his parents had gone more than a few yards, he had galloped past them towards his home.

Upon entering the kitchen, he found his mother-in-law dozing by the fire. He studied her for a moment, noting how she had aged. Her mouth was slightly open and the lines of her face were slack as she slumped in the rocking-chair. Looking back at the stormy relationship of a few years ago, he realised how much she had mellowed. Crossing the kitchen quietly, he went up the stairs and opened the bedroom door.

Elizabeth was propped up on the pillows, with the baby lying in the cradle by the bed. George's heart went out to his wife. Elizabeth's eyes held the key to her sparkle and now that they were closed, she looked so wan and frail that his throat constricted with fear. Tiptoeing over to the crib, he looked down at the red wrinkled face of the sleeping child. Try as he might, George could find nothing attractive in the frowning features and almost bald head. As he looked up, Elizabeth sighed and her eyes opened. Her face flooded with radiance as she saw him so that the impression of fragility was gone.

'Isn't he lovely, George?' she breathed.

George hesitated, unsure of what to say. 'Should he be so red?' he asked at last.

'He's had a hard time getting into the world,' Elizabeth replied. 'You'll be amazed what a difference a day or two will make. Pass him up to me, will you?'

Rather gingerly, George picked up the tiny bundle. As he handed the child to his mother, the little mouth opened in a yawn and George found himself looking into a pair of slate blue eyes. He put his finger towards one of the clenched fists and found it tightly grasped. At the same time, a swell of pride swept over George. This tiny scrap suddenly took on a personality. He was a real person! This was his son! 'Oh, love,' he whispered, as he sat on the side of the bed. 'Thank God. I never thought we'd see this day. We've waited so long, I'd given up all hope of ever having a bairn.'

'I know. I know.' She squeezed his hand as she spoke. 'Anyway, he's here now and who's to say there won't be a little brother or sister before long?'

When the time came for the baby's baptism, Elizabeth still had not recovered her former vivacity. She had decided to name the child Edward, after Prince Edward, and John in memory of her father. His godparents were to be her sister Sarah, young Jonna and Bob Lamb. Elizabeth was not altogether in favour of the last choice but as Lamb was now officially betrothed to Martha, she had given in.

It was Sarah's first visit to Sleightholmedale since she had moved to Leeds over a year before. When George met the York coach at the King's Head in Kirkbymoorside, relations were rather strained at first. Hardly a word was exchanged after the first greeting. As he drove up the main street and turned out of the town at the top, Sarah looked round her with pleasure and George studied her surreptitiously as she did so. Sarah was so much like the Elizabeth he had courted. She was wearing brown – a colour which had always suited Elizabeth. The rich shade of the material brought out the glow of her cheeks and her dark eyes shone and danced with pleasure to be home.

When he began the cautious descent down the almost sheer drop into the valley, Sarah clasped her hands together and leaned towards him. 'I didn't realise how much I'd missed it,' she said.

George swept a glance over the bare, grim-looking trees which clothed the sides of the escarpment. 'Nay. There's nowt attractive about it at this time of year,' he remonstrated. 'In the spring and summer it's lovely down here,

I'll grant you. Like paradise,' he added reflectively. 'But in early March it's dull and gloomy. It'll be better in a week or two when t'catkins are out and spring flowers begin to push through. Anyroad, there's no need to tell you this – you've lived down here long enough,' he continued.

As he spoke, they drew level with the quarry. This was where the stone had been hewn to build the farms of the dale. Sarah put a hand over his, as they held the reins. 'Pull off the road, George, just for a minute. It's the only chance I shall have to talk to you.' He hesitated, feeling a moment of disquiet. She smiled. 'It's all right, George. I'm not intending to embarrass you,' she assured him.

Bella was very old now and would probably be glad of a rest, George considered, so he drew the pony to a halt and walked her off the road and on to the quarry floor.

He looked expectantly at Sarah, but she sat for a few seconds before speaking. Then she looked across at him, grave-faced, all her sparkle quenched. 'You have no need to worry about me,' she said, with a faint smile. 'I've learnt my lesson. I realise what a fool I was, throwing myself at you the way I did.' George made a deprecating sound, but she held up her hand to silence him and then continued, 'I'm happy enough at Uncle Nathan's, although coming back has brought it home to me how much I miss country life. What I said when I left still holds good, George. I do love you – I shall always do so and no matter how many eligible young men my Uncle parades before me, I shall never marry.'

George felt uncomfortable at this declaration, especially as it was made in a steady and unemotional voice, far removed from the previous frantic outburst on the day she had left the farm.

'I just want you to know that I shall never change, but I also want you to allow me to come home now and again for a few days. I shall not act foolishly again.'

'Of course you can come home, Sarah,' he answered. 'It was never intended otherwise. We all just felt that you should have the chance of a different kind of life.'

When they arrived at Cherry Tree Farm, Sarah ran straight into the house. She stopped short just inside the kitchen door, startled and alarmed to see such a change in Elizabeth. Her sister sat in the rocking-chair by the side of the range, her eyes closed and her foot rhythmically working the rocker. She held the sleeping baby in her arms but the scene, which should have been one of contentment, was marred by her appearance. Her hair, once so dark and lustrous, had lost its sheen and was stranded here and there with grey. The rosy bloom of her cheeks had faded, leaving her sallow and drawn. Her whole attitude was one of mortal weariness and she slumped in the chair as though too tired to make the attempt to rise.

Sarah's eyes went to her mother, who was standing by the table, rolling pastry. Before either could speak, however, Elizabeth opened her eyes. Seeing her sister, her face lit up with some of its old gaiety. 'Oh, Sarah! How lovely to see you,' she cried, rising to her feet and kissing Sarah's cheek. She placed the baby in Sarah's arms. 'There! What do you think of your nephew?' she enquired.

Sarah looked down at the sleeping infant and made some suitable comment, but her mind was occupied with Elizabeth's obvious ill-health. 'What about you? she asked. 'Are you all right?'

Elizabeth hesitated, but smiled. 'I'm still rather tired after the birth,' she admitted, 'but I'm getting stronger.'

In the privacy of their bedroom that night, Sarah expressed her dismay to her mother. 'I've never seen anyone go downhill so quickly,' she said.

Ann Butler sighed. 'I know, lass,' she replied. 'The birth seems to have pulled her right down. She's not young for a first baby, of course, but she's getting plenty of good food, so should soon get built up.'

'She may be getting plenty of food, but she's putting it in a poor skin,' retorted Sarah. 'She's like a skeleton . . .'

Although George had written to Tamar to tell her of Edward's christening, he had not really expected her and Stephen to make the long journey from Thorsbury. He was gratified, therefore, when he saw them come into the church at Gillamoor, accompanied by Victoria, and the three year old Hilary.

When they returned to Elizabeth's parlour after the service, Jonadab and Annie looked round with satisfaction to see so many of their family gathered together under one roof.

While the baby was passed round the women of the family, Annie called little Hilary to her side. It was her first meeting with this grandchild, even though he had passed his third birthday, and she wanted to try to get to know him. Although she usually got on well with children, she found Hilary heavy going. Often her questions remained unanswered, with the child merely staring at her, wide-eyed. Poor Annie was not to know that Hilary found it difficult to understand her broad moorland dialect. His eyes swung round the room, but his mother and sister were sitting together on the sofa, playing with the baby, while his father, cup and saucer in hand, stood by the window with his uncles and the fierce-looking old man who was his grandfather. Gazing up at the kindly, apple-cheeked face smiling down at him, Hilary suddenly made up his mind. To Annie's delight, he climbed up on to her knee, put his thumb in his mouth and with a sigh, snuggled down and fell asleep.

For all his wealth, title and position, Stephen was still rather in awe of Tamar's father. Jonadab had made it clear that he had done his son-in-law a favour in allowing him to jump the queue and buy four of his grey shirehorses and now Stephen had to screw up his courage and confess that one was dead. He asked Jonadab if he could buy a replacement, explaining what had happened. 'It also cost me the life of my head groom, Davis, who was drowned trying to rescue the horse,' he said. 'You'll remember him – the chap with the scar.'

'Aye,' replied Jonadab. ''E seemed good at his job. 'E'll be a sad loss, poor fellow.'

George glanced across at Tamar. Stephen's remarks must have carried across the room, but his sister showed no reaction to the conversation. Elizabeth's eyes met her husband's. Turning to Tamar, she asked, 'What did Stephen say, Tamar? That your head groom had been drowned?'

Tamar's face was unruffled and serene, as she turned towards her sister-in-law. 'Yes, poor man,' was her reply.

'He gave his life to try to save one of the horses which Stephen bought from Father.' Showing no more emotion over the death of the man than that of the beast, she turned her attention once more to tickling Edward's toes.

Stephen arranged to buy a replacement for the lost horse and a further pair. 'You were right,' he acknowledged. 'They stand out well and make the overseeing of the men much easier.' He paused for a few seconds before proceeding. 'There's one thing you can be sure of, Mr Oaks. I shall find a different lad to look after them.'

Jonadab drained his cup and placed it on a table before answering. 'Will thoo tek notice of an old man wi' a bit more wool on 'is back?' he asked.

'Surely,' came Stephen's startled reply.

'Show thi faith in t'lad that lost Daisy. From what thoo's told me it was not his fault. If thoo moves 'em from 'is care, you'll breed resentment. Leave 'im in charge of 'em and he's your man for life. He'll repay you with faithful service.'

Stephen was quick to appreciate the sense of Jonadab's advice. 'Thank you. I'll do that,' he said.

Soon afterwards, the gathering broke up and the guests took their leave. Jonna was not slow to remind them that he and Maisie hoped to see them at their wedding, due in a few weeks' time at Easter. He had not realised how much he would miss his family and the work of breeding and breaking the shires with George. However, the realisation that he would eventually inherit the farm at Skiplam, when Maisie's father was too old to run it, sweetened the pill. He was thankful, too, that Len Brayton had healed the rift between him and his father, so that he was able once more to visit the family home.

When they had all departed, George looked anxiously at Elizabeth. During the visit, she had appeared to be her old vivacious self, laughing and joking, showing off the baby and exchanging news. Now she was suddenly drained of all energy, as though spent by the effort.

'Come on, lass,' he said gently. 'I'm off upstairs to change into my working clothes. I'll take you up with me and put you to bed.'

'Indeed you won't,' she retorted with a touch of her old

spirit. 'I shall be fine after a sit down. It's just that there were so many people that I feel a bit tired.'

'Sarah will see to the hens and the milking,' he replied, with a questioning look at his sister-in-law.

'Of course. It'll be a pleasure to do it, after a year of city-life. Take advantage of me while I'm here, Liz, and get some rest,' she urged.

Still Elizabeth hesitated.

'Go on, love.' Her mother added her voice. 'You've probably got a bit of cold coming on. George's mother's going to give him a bottle of coltsfoot linctus for that cough of yours. She's made a lot this year.'

Although Elizabeth felt reluctant, she was thankful to settle down in bed, knowing that her mother would see to Edward and that her sister would gladly take on her share of the farm-work.

She only awoke when George came to bed, bringing the baby for his last feed of the day. While Elizabeth sat and nursed little Edward, they discussed the events of the day.

'It all went well, love,' George said with satisfaction. 'I think they all enjoyed it.'

'Yes.' Elizabeth looked thoughtful. 'Did you see Tamar's face when Stephen told us about the groom – Davis, was it?'

'I didn't notice anything.' George sounded surprised.

'That's just it,' Elizabeth said. 'There was nothing to notice. She never turned a hair. In fact, she seemed more bothered about the horse than about him.' She paused before continuing, 'You are sure it was the same man?'

'Positive!' said George emphatically. 'He was distinctive enough, but that scar settled it. He was the man who attacked our Tamar.'

Although they discussed the mystery at length, it was clear that they would never reach a solution to the puzzle of the man's presence at Thorsbury and whether or not it was with Tamar's knowledge.

'She's a dark one, is our Tamar,' concluded George. 'You'll know what she wants you to know and no more. She'll see to that . . .'

# CHAPTER TWENTY-THREE

Just as there had been no real winter, so there was no fine spring. The icy grip of winter had never clutched the valley, so that the arable land was not made friable by the action of frost. The drying winds of March also failed to arrive, so that the soil was sticky and would not polish to the ploughshare. It clung tenaciously to the boots of the men who tried to prepare for the sowing of spring corn.

'What's it like?' called Jonadab to Bert Weald the foreman, who was ploughing in a field along the roadside.

'Nobbut tacky, maister,' he answered, lifting one foot to show the weight of mud sticking to his boot.

As he grew older, Jonadab Oaks was becoming even more tetchy and impatient. 'We must force it dry,' he told George at their mid-morning break. 'It'll 'ave ti be turned time and time again ti get t'sun on it as much as possible. It'll mek us late all t'year.'

'There's one drawback,' George answered. 'T'lambing will be on time, so everything will come at once.'

'Aye.' Jonadab was disgruntled. 'Nature never seems ti work with us – allus against. There's been no frost ti kill t'pests and this warm weather will set rubbish seed sprouting, so that when we do get t'seeds sown, t'weeds'll be stronger and choke 'em.'

He drove his men every daylight hour to ploughing and reploughing the fields, turning the earth over to the sunshine as often as was humanly possible. It was through the increasing power of the sun that the land eventually became workable. The moisture was drawn up until the ground steamed, filling the air with dampness which sapped the workers' energy. 'There thoo is,' Jonadab commented. 'Give Nature time, and she manages ti get things right in t'end. Read t'Bible and thoo'll see it all there: "Seed time and 'arvest shall not cease".'

George glanced at Bert Weald, who winked slyly behind

his master's back. George grinned but felt a mild resentment. His father's demands meant that he saw little of his wife and practically nothing of his son.

Easter Saturday, the day of Jonna's wedding to Maisie Brayton, proved a welcome break for the whole family. The service was to take place in the tiny Anglo-Saxon church of St Gregory, which nestled in the picturesque valley of Kirkdale on the banks of Hodge Beck a few miles further downstream from Sleightholmedale. The church was far removed from any habitation and was cradled in its own little niche, surrounded on all sides by heavily-wooded hills. The spot was off the beaten track and approached by means of a ford, which added to the appeal of its position. The magnificent yew trees outside the church were so large that they appeared to be as ancient as the building itself.

When the ceremony was over, the wedding party piled once more into the traps for the journey to Skiplam Grange. Jonadab and Annie had visited there previously so that it came as no surprise to them, but the rest of the family were most impressed with the solid buildings and general air of prosperity at the Braytons' farm.

'By gum, our Jonna's done well for himself,' George commented.

Bob Lamb glanced around to make sure that his employer was out of earshot. 'Aye. He always fancied himself as t'cock of t'midden, but he's good reason to now.'

So that was the workforce's opinion of his brother, George reflected. Lamb was in a difficult position. He was soon to become one of the family, but still had the status at present of a hired man. George was also aware that with lambing so near, his father was resentful that the shepherd had been invited along at all: his place was among the flocks. Set against that was the fact that Martha was Maisie's bridesmaid. As her 'intended', Lamb's invitation was only to be expected.

Martha was wearing the blue gown passed on to her by Tamar: to her family and Lamb she looked as pretty as a picture. Elizabeth had dressed her hair, which had spent the night in curl-rags, and Bob Lamb was not the only young man who could not take his eyes from her.

'Aah could 'ave wished she'd looked farther afield,' Jonadab grumbled that night, as he prepared for bed.

'But thoo likes him, Jonadab.' Annie was amazed at this turn-round. 'Thoo said 'e was a good man.'

'Aye, and so 'e is,' he replied testily. 'But 'e 'asn't a penny ti bless 'isself with. My daughter could do better. After all, he's nowt but what 'e stands up in – and what Aah pays 'im,' he added as an afterthought.

'All Aah ask is that 'e makes her happy,' his wife replied. 'Thoo only 'as ti look at 'em, ti see they think t'world of each other.'

Her only reply from Jonadab was a sniff as he blew out the candle.

The summer followed the pattern of the opening months of the year. 'Neither nowt nor summat', as Jonadab termed it. George gave a hand to Bob with the shepherding at the height of the lambing season, but hay-making was snatched between showers and stretched out for weeks.

'If only we could get a week of fine weather,' wished Jonadab. 'We could be finished in no time.'

'Aye,' George replied. 'The hay's been tedded and turned so often, there'll be no goodness left in it.'

Although Ann Butler was willing to look after Edward, Elizabeth did not help with hay harvest. 'I don't feel fit, love,' she apologised to George. 'The least bit of effort tires me out.' Her husband studied her with concern. She had never recovered fully from Edward's birth. As much as he had longed for a son, and loved the boy, he would never have placed fatherhood before Elizabeth's health.

Martha's marriage to Bob Lamb was planned for the end of harvest, so she and Annie were relieved when, once the hay was all safely led, there was a long spell of hot and sunny weather.

'There's one thing to be thankful for,' George said to Elizabeth. 'We're not likely to lose *this* harvest through fire on the moor-land. The damp spring will have been good for something, at any rate.'

Edward was now sitting up well, and Elizabeth took him on her knee and began to feed him porridge from a spoon.

'I shouldn't try to wean 'im yet if I were you,' Ann Butler

observed. 'The longer you breastfeed, the less chance there is of another baby.'

'Oh, but I want another baby, Mother,' she protested and then, with a smile at George, 'as soon as possible.'

George was dismayed. While realising that Elizabeth had had quite an easy labour with Edward, he could see the decline in her health since the birth and dreaded to think what effect another child might have upon her. He had no time to think any more on the subject, however, as no sooner was hay-making over than harvest was upon them. Despite the lateness of the sunny period, Jonadab's prophecy was proved correct and the harvest looked likely to be a bumper one.

As he led the reapers out on the first day, it was brought home to George how much he missed the camaraderie and even rivalry with Jonna. In previous years his brother had been present, so that each spurred the other to greater effort. Now, glancing round the men who swung their scythes alongside him in the field, he recognised the gap which yawned between him and them. When the women came out with the morning allowance, Bob Lamb threw himself down beside George and as he relaxed, exchanging jokes and banter with the shepherd, George appreciated that, in Bob, he had gained a real friend.

Uncle Nathan in Leeds had agreed to allow Sarah Butler a week off during harvest, so that she could come home to help her mother and Elizabeth with the all-important baking while the fields of oats down at Cherry Tree Farm were being cut. When Sarah and Elizabeth came out to the men with the savoury and fruit pies and pasties, hot from the oven, their faces were flushed from the heat of the kitchen. Bob eyed the younger sister, remembering how he had wanted her the previous year. He still admired her vivacious appearance and sparkling good looks, but knew that, although Martha Oaks was not as flashy in her appearance, nor as outgoing in temperament, she was the one for him.

Now that Sarah had ceased to embarrass him, George was more at ease in her company. Elizabeth, too, was brighter and appeared at last to be improving in health. Once the fields down at Cherry Tree Farm were stooked and, before the corn at his father's farm was ready for leading, George took Sarah up to Kirkbymoorside to catch the coach. 'Thank you, Sarah,' he said sincerely, as he handed her out of the trap. 'Elizabeth and your mother couldn't have managed without you.'

'I'll come any time I'm needed,' she promised. 'Uncle Nathan is talking of selling the business and retiring. If he does so, he may not need me in a smaller establishment and I may come home.' She looked at him anxiously. 'If that's all right, George,' she added quietly.

Considering for a moment, George admitted to himself that he had enjoyed Sarah's company. Her presence had brought a lighter atmosphere than his home had possessed of late. 'You're always welcome, Sarah,' he assured her, blocking from his mind the original reason for her move to Leeds. 'I think Elizabeth seems a little better, don't you? Your visit's cheered her up.'

She ignored this comment, unable to bring herself to agree. She knew how Elizabeth's desperate attempts to put on a show of good health for George's sake waned when he left the house. She was deeply worried about her sister's condition, but Elizabeth had dismissed her fears, insisting that she was merely run down. Catching her mother's eye Sarah had known that their concern for Elizabeth's health was mutual. At this point, she contented herself by saying earnestly, 'If I'm needed, George, for *any* reason, just write and tell me. I'm sure Uncle Nathan can manage for a time without me.'

As she held out her hand to shake his before boarding the coach, George suddenly gave into an impulse and bent and kissed her cheek. When he saw the flush which began in her throat and spread up her cheeks, he regretted the gesture. Raising a hand to touch the place, she looked into his eyes. 'You still think of me as a child,' she half-stated, half-questioned.

'No.' He exchanged stare for stare. 'I think of you as a younger sister.'

As quickly as it had come, the colour receded from her face, leaving it stark white. 'Thank you, George!' The words were almost a hiss and her eyes blazed. 'You certainly know how to please a lady!'

'Oh, heck! Nay, Sarah! Don't tek on so,' he pleaded. 'I meant nowt to cause annoyance.'

With a swish of her skirts, she turned from him and mounted the steps into the vehicle. As the driver slammed the door, she leaned towards the window. 'I'd hate to be there when you *do* mean to annoy me,' she snapped.

As the driver cracked his whip and the coach rumbled away out of the innyard and down the street, George was left looking after it with a dumbfounded expression. 'Now what have I said?' he wondered as he went to his pony-trap, troubled both by Sarah's reaction and to the fact that he had kissed her.

Once all the harvest was in and the Mell Supper had been held, Annie began to prepare for Martha's wedding. Tamar had written to say that she and Stephen could not attend, but that she would like to buy Martha's outfit as a wedding present.

'As long as it's serviceable,' was Jonadab's grudging reply. 'We wants none o' them daft white outfits that's no use afterwards.'

Martha was only too happy to accept Tamar's proffered gift. She admired her sister's taste and knew that Tamar would do her best to fulfil their father's stipulation and yet provide an attractive outfit. She was not disappointed. Tamar was driven down the valley by Goodison, who was now the head coachman at Thorsbury. When he had carried in the boxes, Jonadab took him round the fields where the horses were grazing. Although Goodison was Tamar's servant, Jonadab always treated him like any other visitor to the farm, taking him on a conducted tour of the stock. He had in fact, elicited something which even his daughter did not know. Unwilling to call the manservant by his surname, Jonadab had asked him his first name and had addressed him as Albert for years.

While the two men examined and discussed the merits of Jonadab's horses, Annie, Martha and Lydia gathered eagerly round the kitchen table as Tamar opened the boxes and displayed their contents. 'Aah 'opes as 'ow they're hard-wearing and serviceable,' observed Annie.

Tamar smiled, remembering her delight and disbelief at the sight of the first gown ever bought for her by Stephen, when she was his housekeeper. She had spent more than she had intended on Martha's trousseau, buying not only the wedding outfit but also the undergarments to wear with it and a beautifully embroidered and pin-tucked nightgown in the finest lawn.

When she opened the largest box and lifted out the jacket and skirt of heavy dove-grey silk, Martha was speechless, stroking the material with little gasps of pleasure. The whole outfit was spread out on the spotless table-top, to exclamations of admiration from all. The gloves and dainty buttoned boots were of identical shades of grey kid, while the blouse was matched exactly by the deep rose pink of the bonnet. Tamar had chosen carefully: the heavy silk and exquisite workmanship, while not flashy, had an aura of richness. 'Slip upstairs and try them on, love. I'd like to see you in them since we shall be in London when you're wedded,' instructed Tamar. 'Give her a hand, will you?' she added to Lydia.

When they were alone, she looked at her mother fondly. 'I was a great trial to you, I know,' she said. 'But everything has worked out better than I ever deserved. Stephen and I are very happy together, Mother, and Victoria is accepted by everybody as his daughter. In fact, to be honest, I think he's even forgotten himself that he isn't her real father. I wish Hilary was not so delicate, but there isn't anything really wrong – he's just not a strong child.'

Annie made sympathetic noises but before she could really develop this conversation with Tamar, the door opened and Martha stood before them. The deep pink of bodice and bonnet brought a rosy glow to her cheeks which was most becoming. The skirt swayed as she moved, the heavy silk catching the light so that it gleamed as though alive.

'Eeh, love,' Annie's voice trembled with emotion. 'Thoo looks a treat – a proper treat.'

'We can do better than that,' laughed Tamar. 'You look

really lovely, Martha. I wasn't too sure about the grey. I would have preferred cream, but it isn't "serviceable".' As she said the word they all laughed. 'However, it suits you and even Father can't find fault with the colour. If you keep your figure it should last a lifetime.'

'Thank you, Tamar,' Martha breathed. 'I can never thank you enough. There's all these, too.' She swept her hand to indicate all the other garments on the table.

'Well, let's get them out of the way,' suggested Tamar in a brisk voice. 'We don't want Father to see them and stop you accepting them.'

'Oh, no! Don't say things like that.' Martha and Lydia scurried round the table, picking up boxes, paper and clothes, then ran from the kitchen.

'Thi faither means well, Tamar. It's just that 'e's a bit set in 'is ways.' Annie was eager to excuse Jonadab.

'You needn't explain Father to me.' Tamar's tone was caustic. 'There was a time when I never expected to see the inside of this house again. I know a lot of the fault was mine, but he can be harsh. That you can't deny.'

Before Annie had time to reply, Jonadab walked in through the back door. 'Where's all t'finery, then?' he asked, looking round.

'It's packed away until the wedding day,' answered Tamar. 'It's to be a surprise to you all.'

Her father's brows drew together in one of his sudden frowns. 'Aah 'opes as 'ow it's not a lot of fancy fol-de-rals,' he said suspiciously.

'I've just told her that if she doesn't put weight on, it will last her her lifetime,' answered Tamar calmly.

'That's all right, then,' he grunted. 'We've no time for flipperies 'ere.' Looking round, he asked, 'Is Lydia busy?' Without waiting for a reply, he looked across to where Tamar sat by the table. 'Mash a pot 'o tea. Aah 'aven't all afternoon ti waste and oor George'll be in for a drink an' all, in a minute.' Smiling wryly, Tamar did as directed. The fact that she was now a titled lady with a houseful of servants carried no weight with her father. His children were expected to help their parents, no matter how rich or highly-placed they became.

After Tamar had departed, Annie cleared her throat and said nervously to her husband, 'Aah thought Aah might get summat new ti wear for t'wedding.'

Jonadab's forehead furrowed, as his brows shot up in incredulity. 'Summat new?' He could not believe his ears. 'What's up with what thoo's got? Thi best clothes is still smart.'

Annie could almost count on the fingers of one hand the number of times in over forty years of marriage that she had gone against her husband's wishes. Now she braced herself. 'They're black,' she stated flatly.

'Of course they're black,' came back his reply. 'It's a good serviceable colour.'

'Aye – and Aah'm a good serviceable woman,' she answered spiritedly. 'Well, Aah wants a change.' To Jonadab's utter amazement and consternation, she was in full flow. 'They wasn't even new for our Joseph's wedding seventeen years ago and Aah've worn 'em for every wedding, funeral and christening since.' Taking a deep breath, she folded her arms in a defiant gesture and continued, 'Aah'm not asking thoo ti pay for owt. Aah've money of mi own and Aah sh'll go into Kirkby next Wednesday and get summat new.'

Jonadab capitulated. He could not imagine where Annie had obtained enough money to buy them, nor why she wanted new clothes, but her outburst was so uncharacteristic that he put it down to women's funniness. A favourite saying of his was 'There's nowt so funny as folks' and it was his belief that this summing up applied to every one except himself.

Since Elizabeth and her mother-in-law had stopped attending the Wednesday market, Annie had arranged for a huckster to call at both farms every two weeks and buy their surplus eggs and dairy produce. The man would buy any farm produce the women had to sell and, although his prices were not as high as they could have obtained in the market-hall, they had neither the waste of a day nor the worry of unsold goods. Like most farm-wives, Annie's earnings had been used to clothe herself and her girls. Now that Martha was the only one of her daughters left at home,

Annie had been pleasantly surprised at the rate at which her savings had grown. This gave her a sense of independence which she had not previously experienced. Once she had put forward the idea of a new outfit, she was seized with enthusiasm. When Wednesday arrived she and Martha set out for Kirkbymoorside, not only to visit the dressmaker, but also to take the wedding cake to be professionally iced. 'Aah could do it missen,' she had told Martha, 'but why should Aah? Aah've t'brass ti pay for it ti be done at t'baker's, so Aah shall!'

The marriage was set to take place on the first Saturday in October. The wedding day dawned bright and clear. George had driven up from Cherry Tree Farm and gone ahead with the bridegroom, leaving Elizabeth, her mother and the baby to follow on with Annie. 'Best man again,' he had laughed. 'I sh'll know that job backwards.'

When the two men had left, Martha and Annie came downstairs, their appearance bringing exclamations of admiration from Elizabeth and her mother. Jonadab, on the other hand, said not a word. While acknowledging to himself that Martha was a lovely bride, as all his daughters had been, and that Annie was still a fine-looking woman, their choice of clothes met with his disapproval. Martha's was too light-coloured to be truly utilitarian, but as it had been bought and paid for by Tamar, he could make no objection. Annie's outfit, however, was a different matter. He glowered when she asked artlessly, 'What dost thoo think, Jonadab?'

He eyed her up and down, taking in the plum-coloured jacket and skirt, with matching bonnet. 'It's red!' He uttered the words in an accusing tone. In Jonadab Oaks' eyes the colour red ranked with strong drink and playing cards as symbolic of the devil.

'Nay.' Annie was too pleased with her outfit to take offence. She stroked her new skirt caressingly. 'It's not red at all. It's plum-coloured – a nice, deep, serviceable shade,' she added, as she led the way out to her trap.

Jonadab's grim face softened as he looked at his youngest child when they were left alone together. He had always had a soft spot for Martha, remembering what a bright little thing she had been in childhood. The drowning of her

284

sister, Maria, had quenched Martha's effervescent, bubbling personality, changing her into an introspective and self-contained girl. That it was the shepherd who had rekindled Martha's sense of fun could not be doubted. 'Come on then, lass,' he said gently. 'Thoo mustn't keep 'em waiting.'

There was not as large a congregation in Gillamoor Church as there had been for previous Oaks' weddings, largely due to the fact that Bob had no relatives in the district. This confirmed Jonadab's fears about the man's background. A groom who had no one to come to his wedding was odd, to say the least. In his estimation, Bob Lamb was a 'box o' mystery'.

To George's consternation, the ceremony was punctuated by Elizabeth's coughs. He had been vaguely aware of her cough for some months now, but here, caught and amplified by the height of the church, he realised that it was persistent and frightening. At the meal that followed, although he sat next to Elizabeth, he had no time for conversation. His brother Jonna, and his sisters' husbands were all demanding of his attention with farming talk. Even so, he was not too occupied to notice that his wife ate little, chasing the food around her plate with the fork although she talked animatedly with the other women, comparing notes about their children and discussing Martha's outfit.

Again, when they reached home, George noted how his mother-in-law immediately took the baby from Elizabeth and carried him in. Although a finely-boned child, Edward was now ten months old and Elizabeth obviously found his weight too heavy to carry for long.

'Sit yourself down, love,' George insisted. 'Mek her a cup of tea, Ma, while I go and see to the stock.'

'I'll do the hens and milking, George,' Elizabeth protested.

'Nay, you've had a tiring day and no doubt you two'll want to talk over t'wedding and what everybody was wearing,' he joked. 'I'll not be long.'

It had become their custom that while he went round the farm last thing at night, to check the stock and buildings, Elizabeth went up to give Edward his last feed of the day.

Although he was now weaned, he still had a breastfeed at night. When George went into the bedroom, Elizabeth was sitting up in bed sipping elderberry syrup. 'I think I've got a bit of a cold,' she remarked, allowing the hot, soothing liquid to trickle down her throat.

'You've had it for far too long. I'd like you to go into Kirkby and see Dr Dawson,' was his answer. As she drew a breath to reply, he held up a hand to silence her. 'Now, Elizabeth. It's not often I insist, but the beginning of winter is a bad time to start with a cold. You coughed all through the wedding.'

'It was chilly in the church,' she said defensively.

'Anyroad, it won't hurt to call and have a word with the doctor.' George could be stubborn when necessary.

When Elizabeth called at the surgery the following week, Dr Dawson said very little. His face was grave and he questioned her closely about her cough. 'Do you find yourself easily tired?' he enquired.

'Oh, yes – but then of course the baby is demanding, although I've finished feeding him myself.'

With a caution not to work too hard and to keep warm during the coming winter, Dr Dawson asked her to call in a month's time and let her go. When she had left the surgery, he stood for a moment thoughtfully tapping his teeth with his spectacles. He must have a word with young Oaks the next time he saw him in town, he decided.

Elizabeth, meanwhile, returned home in a cheerful frame of mind. 'There's nothing wrong with me,' she assured her mother and husband. 'In fact I got the impression that he felt I was wasting his time. I'm just run down with feeding Edward.'

With this they had to be satisfied, although whenever Sarah came to stay for a few days, it was brought home to George even more forcibly how drawn and thin Elizabeth had become. Sarah resembled so much the Elizabeth whom he had married, that the contrast with her present appearance was even more dramatic.

It was at Christmas that Edward took his first steps, just before his first birthday. 'Oh, I'm so glad he's walking early,' Elizabeth cried. 'That makes things easier.' Turning to

George she confided, 'I'm expecting again, George. Isn't it wonderful?'

George was devastated. How could Elizabeth cope with another pregnancy when she had not yet recovered from the first, he wondered. Once Edward was toddling, he became such a handful that both his mother and his grandmother found that he demanded all their time and energy. 'I'll go up to the workhouse and get a girl to look after him,' George suggested. 'Look how good Lydia has been to Mam.'

'No, George.' A shadow passed over Elizabeth's face. 'I don't want a stranger here. I want to look after my son and my house myself. I can do it, with Mother's help.'

George looked across to where Ann Butler was dozing by the fire. Seen thus, slumped in the chair, she was an old woman. As he took the pail to go out and do the milking he could not help but wonder what was to become of them all. He had his own demanding job toiling from dawn to dusk, working for his father, and more often than not when he did happen to be at home, he did Elizabeth's farmwork, too.

Catching Edward under the arms, he held him aloft and swung him until he chuckled. 'Now that you're walking, you'll soon be gathering t'eggs for your mammy,' he said, as he plonked him onto Elizabeth's knee and went out. And, 'By 'eck,' he thought gloomily to himself as he walked across the yard and entered the cow-shed. 'It's all bed and work.'

# CHAPTER TWENTY-FOUR

The third week in January saw the snow clouds massing to the north of the dale. It had become routine now for George to attend to his own cows, pigs and poultry, before going off to work on his father's farm.

Elizabeth seemed to have no energy for even the simplest of tasks. She spent most of her days in the rocking-chair by the range, mending and knitting, getting to her feet to pretend to be busy whenever George was present. He discussed her condition anxiously both with Ann Butler and his own parents, but they could only assume that a second pregnancy was sapping her strength.

When he brought in the eggs to be washed he said, 'It's going to snow by the look of it. Is there owt you want from Kirkby love, before we're snowed in?'

'Oh, yes. I need some yeast – get the best German. It's a bit dearer, but I find it better. We need a pound of tea, as well. Anyway, I'll make a list, if you're going in.'

When George came downstairs, changed and ready for town, Ann Butler said, 'We're getting low on flour. If there's a chance that we shall be snowed up, could you take a couple of sacks of wheat to Cauldron Mill on your way in, and pick up the flour as you come home?'

George did not really wish to take the pony-trap. He had intended to go on horseback to speed the journey. However, the flour was essential if they were likely to be cut off by deep drifts, so taking Elizabeth's list, he loaded two sacks of wheat and set off down the lane towards Aumery Park Farm. Although by now it was almost mid-morning, the visibility resembled the twilight hour. The lowering clouds were leaden and dark, piling up from the north before a piercing wind which chilled George to the bone.

Jonadab was surprised to see him in the trap. As he led his own horse from the buildings to the road, he called, 'What's up? Aah thought as 'ow we'd ride in together.'

George drew the pony to a halt. 'I've a couple of sacks of corn to drop off at Cauldron Mill first. If this lot begins to fall,' with a nod at the sky, 'there's no knowing how long we shall be cut off.'

'Aye,' agreed his father. 'It's not looking good. Anyroad, Aah'll see you in Kirkby.' He jerked the reins and went on his way.

Upon arriving at the little market town, George put his pony in the charge of the ostler at the Black Swan before setting out to do his errands. As he came out of the York Union Bank, he heard a shout from across the street. 'George! George Oaks.'

Looking round, he was surprised to see Dr Dawson pushing his way through the crowds which thronged the busy market place. As the two met, the doctor asked, 'How's your wife?'

George looked at him blankly for a second or two. How could the doctor know of Elizabeth's pregnancy? 'She's not too good, Doctor. Always tired,' was his reply. 'You know of course that she's expecting another baby.'

Dr Dawson's normally genial face darkened with anger. 'Good God, man,' he barked. 'What on earth are you thinking of to get a woman in her condition in the family way?'

George was taken aback by the doctor's reaction and answered defensively. 'I know she's not well, but she's forty now Doctor and doesn't want Edward to be an only child. After all,' he added, 'you examined her just before Christmas and found nothing wrong.'

The doctor's anger subsided. He took George by the elbow and led him through the crowds into the comparative peace of Crown Square. 'What did your wife tell you, when she had called to see me?' he asked quietly.

'She said that she got the impression you felt she was wasting your time.' George had begun to feel uneasy.

Dawson sighed. 'Elizabeth is gravely ill.' He spoke gently. 'I did not say it to her in so many words, but she is an intelligent woman and must have known what the symptoms indicate.'

George looked at him blankly. 'We thought she was just run down after having Edward.' His voice was questioning.

'I'm afraid it's her lungs.' The doctor looked him straight in the eyes. 'Elizabeth has consumption, George.'

George was quite still. His normally ruddy complexion took on a grey tinge and he felt for a moment as though the breath was being squeezed from his body . The sounds from the market place began first to recede and then to be almost deafening. Just as the doctor put a hand on his arm, with a look of concern on his face, Jonadab Oaks came towards them. 'Good morning, Dr Dawson. So here thoo is, George. Aah've been looking for thoo.' When George made no reply, Jonadab looked at his companion. 'Is summat wrong?'

'I'm afraid he's had a nasty shock,' explained the physician. 'I felt that I must tell him that Elizabeth has consumption. To be quite frank, I cannot see her living long enough to have this baby.'

George turned to his father with relief. He felt as he had done as a child: his father would sort things out. 'Tell him he's made a mistake, Faither,' he pleaded.

'Nay, lad.' Jonadab spoke sadly. 'Now it's put into words, it should have been obvious to us all. Weight's dropped off 'er and that cough is bad enough ti tear 'er lungs out.' George looked stricken. 'Come and 'ave a cup of strong tea, lad.' Jonadab's voice was full of compassion.

'I know you're teetotallers, Oaks,' said Dr Dawson, 'but this calls for something stronger than tea. As a medical man, I prescribe a noggin of brandy. It's purely medicinal and there's no need for either him or you to feel guilty about it.' He led the way into the Black Swan, which was only a yard or two away and after pushing George down onto a settle by the roaring fire, went to the bar, returning with a brandy for George and a whisky for himself.

'What about you, Mr Oaks?' he asked. Jonadab shook his head. It was bad enough to be seen in such a place, but he would not allow strong drink to pass his lips. He did not really approve of alcohol being given to his son, but felt unable to refuse the doctor.

George sat huddled in a corner of the settle, a picture of dejection and hopelessness. Jonadab was concerned to see his son begin to shake uncontrollably and his teeth to chatter.

'It's shock,' explained the doctor. 'Here – get this down you, man.' George took a sip of the brandy, gasping a little as the fiery liquid trickled down his throat.

'Give me thi list and Aah'll finish t'shopping,' suggested Jonadab. He was uncomfortable in the inn, even in the doctor's company and realised also that George was in no fit state to go trailing round the shops.

The brandy did its work and George began to take a grip on himself. The colour returned to his cheeks and he stopped shaking.

'That's better,' approved the doctor. 'You must pull yourself together. You've a hard row to plough, I'm afraid, and you must keep cheerful in front of your wife.'

'Cheerful?' George made a bitter sound, half-laugh, half-groan. 'You tell a man that his wife's going to die, that his son is to be left motherless and a new baby's life may be lost – and you tell him to keep cheerful!' His brown eyes were dark with pain as he looked at his companion. 'I feel that I shall never smile again,' he protested.

'It's essential that you put on a brave face for your wife's sake,' was the response. 'All that you can do for her is keep her happy, keep her warm and try to ease the cough. It's difficult, I realise, but you're not the first man to find himself in this position and you won't be the last.'

'That's no consolation to me,' George answered grimly as they rose to go.

'I'm sorry, George. If you need me, send one of the men up and I'll come down straight away.'

As he turned to leave, Jonadab re-entered the inn. 'All's done, lad,' he said gently, noting with relief that George appeared to be more composed. 'We'll be off.'

They made for home, Jonadab riding beside the trap, keeping pace with his son. Although few words were exchanged, George was grateful for his father's unspoken support.

Relations between the Oaks and the Baldwins at Cauldron Mill had been rather strained since Martha had refused Sam Baldwin's proposal and married Bob Lamb.

This had widened the rift already caused by George's older sister Beth, who had chosen someone else before Will Baldwin had plucked up enough courage to propose to her. Normally George felt embarrassed during his visits to the Mill but today, he was only too pleased that conversation was kept to a minimum.

As he loaded the bags of flour the first snowflakes began to fall. Although they had not much more than a mile to go to Aumery Park Farm, the wind began to pick up, driving the snow into their faces. George screwed up his eyes and lowered his head to gain some protection from the stinging sleet, reflecting morosely that the weather was well-suited to his mood of desolation and despair.

'Come in for a minute,' his father urged as they pulled up at the family home.

'Nay, I'll push on home before the weather gets any worse.' George was anxious to get back to Elizabeth.

Jonadab, however, was insistent. 'This is a family problem and must be put to t'family,' he said.

When they entered the kitchen, Annie bustled forward to take her husband's overcoat. 'Mek a pot o' tea, Lydia,' she said. 'Come to t'fire, George. Thoo looks frozen.' George pulled out a wooden chair from the side of the table nearest to the fire, and to the consternation of those in the room, placed his arms on the table and laying his head on them, burst into a paroxysm of grief.

For a few moments his sobs were the only sound and then his mother bent over and placed an arm round his shoulders. 'Nay, nay, lad, whativver's up?' she asked. 'Nowt can be as bad as this.' George turned in his chair and putting his arms round his mother, buried his face in her apron and continued to sob uncontrollably. She patted the heaving shoulders and looked across at her husband, a query on her face. Martha and Lydia stood by helplessly, at a loss to understand what could be wrong.

'It's Elizabeth.' Jonadab's voice was husky with emotion. 'Dr Dawson's told George that she's got consumption.'

This news only confirmed what Annie had secretly feared for some months. She had watched the change in her daughter-in-law's appearance and knew what the weight-

292

loss, combined with the persistent cough, had presaged. To Martha and Lydia, however, the news came as a complete shock. Martha burst into tears, but her father swung towards her. "Old thi noise,' he said sternly. 'It's oor strength George needs now, not oor tears. There'll be enough time for weeping when t'lass is gone.'

Martha hiccupped into silence, although tears still coursed down her cheeks. Under his mother's patting, George's sobs eventually subsided. 'I'm sorry, Mam,' he apologised. 'It won't happen again. I must put on a brave face, for Elizabeth's sake.'

While he sipped his tea, Jonadab laid out his plan to help George to spend most of his time down at Cherry Tree Farm. 'Thoo'll 'ave all t'stock down there ti see to,' he said. 'There's no knowing 'ow long this lot'll go on,' nodding towards the window where the snow could be seen swirling past. 'If thoo gets cut off and thoo needs owt, thoo must try ti get through on one of t'shire'orses that's stabled down yonder. When t'snow's gone, there's plenty of hedge-laying and ditching ti keep thoo busy round 'ome. Bob'll tek one of t'other men at lambing time, unless 'e can't manage without thoo.'

'Thank you.' George was too upset to express his gratitude at any greater length, but the fact that it came from his heart was plain to see.

As he strode towards the door, his mother handed him a scarf from a peg on the back of the door. "Ere lad, thoo'll need a muffler,' she said. He wound it round his neck, covering his nose and mouth as he went out into what was now a blizzard.

The sleet had turned to snow which totally blotted out the landscape, so that all George could do was to give the pony her head, to find her own way home. When she turned into the yard, the ground had already quite a covering and it was a relief to lead the pony into her stall, where the stable steamed with the heat from the warm bodies of the other horses. Once he had given the pony a rubdown, George shouldered one of the sacks of flour and trudged across the yard towards the house.

Like the rest of his family George accepted the hardships

of life down in the dale. Both summer and winter brought long days of toil, all through the daylight hours. Under normal circumstances, a few days of isolation, cut off by the snows of winter, brought a period of ease from the unremitting struggle. George took pleasure in the feeling of being cocooned in a silent white world, safe with his family and stock. This time, however, as he stumbled through the snow which blanketed the surface of the yard with deceptive smoothness, he felt no relief at the prospect of respite from his labour. His heart was filled with dread at the thought of being cut off from civilisation, with no hope of reaching the doctor if Elizabeth grew worse.

He kicked the snow off his boots, before carrying the flour into the kitchen. Since the doctor's disclosure that morning George's thoughts had been in turmoil. His instinct had been to reach his wife as soon as possible and he had resented his father's request to stop off at the main farm for a few minutes. He had half-convinced himself that Elizabeth was likely to have collapsed and died during his absence. Looking round the kitchen now, his heart swelled with relief. There was a cheerful fire blazing in the grate, its flames reflected with dancing tongues in the copper saucepans which stood on the dresser. From the beams hung bunches of herbs, put there in the autumn to dry, so that the kitchen was fragrant with the scent of sage, rosemary and marjoram.

Elizabeth was seated in her rocking-chair, telling a story to Edward and her mother had obviously been dozing at the other side of the fire. When the door was snatched from George's hand and flung open by the wind, sending a flurry of snowflakes into the room, both women started.

'Oh George! Thank goodness you're back,' Elizabeth exclaimed. 'I've been so worried. What's the lane like? This wind will cause some drifting.'

George put his shoulder to the door to bar it against the wind. 'We shall be cut off before morning,' he prophesied. 'The wind's gale force and the snow's coming down so thick, it's a job to see through it.'

Before going into the dry-goods store with the flour, he looked once again round the kitchen. It appeared so normal and reassuring that his fears of the morning seemed without foundation. His eyes then went to his wife. Although it was only early afternoon, the sky was so dark that it was more like dusk, and the kitchen was only illuminated by the firelight. As the flickering flames played on the contours of Elizabeth's face, it was apparent to George how much weight she had lost. Although the glow from the fire imbued her cheeks with a rosiness which was not really there, it also brought into relief the lines which overlaid her skin in a fine network.

He felt the tears pricking behind his lids and when she became aware of his scrutiny and looked up enquiringly, he hid the despair in his face by bending over the sack. 'What is it, George?' she smiled.

'I could do with a mug of hot strong tea, when I've put this away,' he said, as he carried the sack to the store.

The blizzard raged for three days without any lessening of its ferocity. Although George fretted about the sheep, he knew that he could rely on his brother-in-law to get to them as soon as was humanly possible and that he himself could have done no more for them than Bob would. Apart from that he savoured the days spent at home with Elizabeth and Edward.

Before the arrival of the worst of the winter, he had dragged the hen-houses on skids, using the shirehorses, and placed them close by the yard. He managed to keep a path open between the back door and the buildings, so that the essential work with the animals could be done. Other than the morning and evening work, his days were spent in Elizabeth's company and in getting to know little Edward.

Ann Butler had needed no telling that her daughter had not long to live. She had seen the lung infection too often to mistake it. Now she was sensitive to the couple's desire to be together and when George joined Elizabeth in the parlour each afternoon, she found excuses to busy herself in the kitchen and leave them in privacy. Although he had occasional twinges of guilt, knowing that his father would be finding tasks for those down at Aumery Park Farm and driving them just as hard as usual, George felt that these few precious days were a gift for him to treasure and dwell upon for the rest of his life.

The thaw came quite rapidly. During the period spent in the house, it was brought to George's notice that Elizabeth had hidden from him just how weak she had become. Her mother was now in her sixties and was taking on not only the whole burden of the housework but, also, the care of little Edward. 'He's too much for you, Ma,' commented George.

'Bless him,' she replied. 'He's as bright as a button, but I must admit he's a bit of a handful.'

'Next time I go into Kirkbymoorside, I'll see if I can get a girl to take him off your hands,' he promised.

George kept the parlour fire banked up with peat all night, so that it was soon stirred into flame each morning with a supply of wood, after a good riddling with the poker. Thus the room was always warm for Elizabeth, who now spent much of her time lying on the sofa which George had drawn up before the fire.

Upon hearing his proposal, she stirred and turned towards them. 'Oh, no, George. I want my boy all to myself. I don't want a nursemaid for him.'

George took her hand, stroking it gently. 'He's bright and lively and he's getting to be too much, both for you and your mother. No one is trying to take him from you, only to give you a bit of a rest from his demands. I'll try to choose a nice strong girl who'd used to children and you'll find her a great help, I'm sure.'

If Elizabeth noticed that George's work kept him busy at Cherry Tree Farm she made no mention of the fact, but Ann Butler made it clear that she was pleased to have him within call. The antagonism she had felt towards him both before and in the early days of his marriage to Elizabeth was gone, its place taken by a genuine affection. She recognised in George a strength and dependability which had been lacking in her own son.

When George was able to get into market, he took the pony-trap, determined to call at the workhouse on his way home. Passing the Post Office, he was struck by an idea: he would write to Sarah, saying that Elizabeth's condition had worsened somewhat, and ask her to come home for a couple of days. Her visit would be a welcome change both for Elizabeth and her mother and it would also prepare Sarah for what he had now come to accept as inevitable but did not wish to put in writing. Elizabeth's cough was persistent and she had become so weak that George carried her up and downstairs.

Once the letter was written, addressed and left with Mr Cooper at the Post Office, George made his way up the main street. The workhouse was a large, handsome building standing on rising ground a short distance out of town. Although he had not previously visited the place himself, he had often heard Lydia talk of the years spent in the institution, so he knew that conditions there were humane compared with many such places in other towns.

When George explained his needs to the matron she was thoughful for a while. 'What a pity you didn't come a couple of weeks earlier, Mr Oaks. We'd a good strong girl went out to service last Wednesday, who would have just suited you.' She went on to explain that of the sixty or so inmates, half were still children. 'We do have more girls than boys at present, but we don't put them out to work until after their tenth birthday,' she continued. 'So there's only three to choose from.' Ringing a small hand-bell on her desk, she asked the woman who answered it, 'Fetch Mary, Lizzie and Kitty, will you please?'

When the three little girls were pushed through the door, George was struck by their smallness. He had forgotten how tiny Lydia had been, when she had first come to work for his mother. The girls all wore identical gingham dresses, covered with hessian aprons. They were much of a height and were all thin, scrawny even. As George looked at them, they eyed him with a mixture of eagerness and apprehension. There did not seem a lot to choose between them, but the smallest of the three seemed to stand out from the others. The anxious eyes which were fixed on George were hazel, large and black-lash fringed, seeming too big for the pinched pale face.

George felt, once again, the embarrassment which had overcome him when he had hired Bob Lamb at the Martinmas Fair. He was anxious to finish the business as soon as possible and yet the choice he made was important. The chosen girl would share his home, tend his wife and bring up his son. He glanced at the other two, but was drawn once more to the smallest child. He hesitated, unsure of what to say. The whole transaction made him feel like a customer in a shop.

'This is the one, I think,' he said to the matron, indicating the girl.

'Thank you, girls.' She addressed them briskly. 'Go and get your things, Kitty.'

Kitty hesitated. 'Can Aah 'ave a word wi oor Freddie afore Aah goes?' She made the plea with a hopeless little droop of her shoulders.

'We-ll.' The matron paused. 'I've no doubt Mr Oaks is in a hurry,' looking at him with raised eyebrows.

'Of course she can have a word with Freddie, whoever he is,' George replied. The little face was suddenly radiant.

'It's mi brother and ta, Mr Oaks,' she smiled as she left the room.

'Freddie is seven,' explained the matron. 'They lost both parents and a younger sister two years ago with diphtheria and have been here ever since.'

George pondered for a moment. 'Will you write to me, Matron, when Freddie is ready to go to work? I'll take him as well. It would be a pity to split them up.'

As Kitty clambered into the trap and pushed her bundle under the seat, George asked her her second name. 'Parker, sir,' she replied, smiling shyly. George had never been addressed as 'sir' before and found it a little strange. In Kirkbymoorside and amongst the farms around he was known as George or even 'Jonadab's lad'. His life had been lived in the shadow of his dominant father but here was someone who did not know his father and regarded him as a person in his own right.

He told the little girl all about Elizabeth's illness. 'So you see, Kitty,' he concluded, 'your main job will be to look after Edward, but you must be willing to give my mother-in-law, Mrs Butler, a helping hand whenever she needs one.'

'Don't worry, sir. You can depend on me,' was the cheery response. Despite himself, George felt his spirits lift a little and felt that he had made a good choice.

They drove on in silence until the road turned out of the avenue of trees and began to drop away amid the dramatic scenery of the escarpment. Although it was still only mid-March, the trees bore a canopy of opening leaves in varying shades of tender green. Kitty looked around with pleasure. 'Oh, sir, isn't it lovely?' she cried.

George looked at the familiar scene as though seeing it afresh through the child's eyes. 'Yes, it is, Kitty. It is lovely,' he agreed.

Both Elizabeth and her mother were delighted with Kitty. She immediately took complete charge of Edward and proved herself extremely competent in coping with the strong-willed little boy. Once Elizabeth's mind was at ease and she knew that her mother was relieved of the strain of dealing with Edward, she gave up the struggle of trying to rise from her bed and get dressed. By now, she was almost seven months pregnant and it soon became apparent that she was unlikely to live long enough to give birth to the child.

Sarah's reply to George's letter was a disappointment. Her Uncle had a business associate staying at the house and could not spare her until just before Easter, which was still three weeks away in early April. She would arrive on the Wednesday coach from York on the day before Maundy Thursday. Could George please meet her in the Black Swan yard.

Ann Butler looked at George. 'I can't understand Nathan not letting her come,' she said. 'Did you explain how bad she is?' with a nod towards the ceiling.

'No,' he admitted. 'I didn't want to upset her too much. Anyway,' he looked away so that she would not see the tears which sprang to his eyes, 'I still thought she might get better. She hadn't taken to her bed then.'

'I know, lad.' She pressed his shoulder while wiping away a tear with the corner of her apron. 'I don't know which is worse, the shock of them going sudden like John did, or the strain of watching them fade away.'

Three weeks later, George was waiting in the Black Swan yard when his sister-in-law's coach arrived from Leeds. As Sarah descended, he moved forward swiftly to greet her. 'How's Elizabeth?' she asked, as he bent to kiss her cheek.

For a few seconds George was unable to speak. It took a great effort to keep his voice steady when he did reply. 'I'm afraid she's bad. Very bad.' He almost whispered the words.

To his consternation, Sarah burst into tears. 'She's going to get better, isn't she?' she sobbed.

Without speaking, George took her arm and led her to the trap. Once away from the town, he drew the pony to a halt and turned to face his sister-in-law. He was now in control of his feelings and spoke levelly, but gently. 'She has not long to live, Sarah,' he said sadly. 'The baby is due in a month or so, but I can't see her living long enough to have it.'

Sarah was stunned. 'I didn't realise that she was so ill,' she sobbed. They remained by the roadside until George was satisfied that she had regained her composure. He told her about Kitty Parker and what a boon the girl was, and gradually managed to calm her grief.

When Sarah entered the bedroom at Cherry Tree Farm, the sight of Elizabeth's frailty and waxen pallor almost reduced her to tears again. She knew with a feeling of despair that Elizabeth was indeed dying. She bent over and kissed the burning cheek. 'Now, love. I've come to give you and Mother a hand for a few days,' she whispered.

Elizabeth's eyes fluttered open, but her reply was almost inaudible. Then, with a deep sigh, her lashes closed once more.

Taking advantage of Sarah's presence in the house, George crossed the stream and went up to the high moor, to give Bob Lamb a hand to check the sheep and bring down the ewes which were due to lamb first. Although he loved the sheltered little valley which was the only home he had ever known, George was pleased to get up on to the moor-top. Before he reached the rising ground he noticed, on the banks of the beck, furry catkins on the willow trees. The water's edge was studded with clumps of small, pale wild daffodils or Lenten Lilies, as his mother often called them. He decided that on his way back, he would pick some of the flowers and twigs of pussy willow to set them off. 'They'll cheer Elizabeth up no end,' he told himself. He breathed deeply, appreciating the crispness of the air up on the moor, his glance taking in the fresh growth of the heather, pushing through the blackened remnants of the previous year's flowers. Among the heather uncurled the upright fronds of new bracken, while the close-cropped turf between gave easy access to the sheep which were spread across the moor. Seeing Bob Lamb in the distance, George raised a hand and began to move among the sheep, checking them as he went.

As they passed among the animals, which were scattered across the moor, sometimes they were a mile or so apart, at others they worked their way towards each other, until they were quite close. It was at one of these periods that Bob straightened his back and looked across at George. His tone was almost apologetic as he said, 'Martha's going to 'ave a bairn.' He need not have worried about George's reaction. His generosity of spirit was such that he walked across and shook Bob's hand.

'Eeh, I'm glad, Bob. Give our Martha our congratulations.' Although he smiled as he spoke, his brother-in-law noted that the smile never reached his eyes, which remained sad and brooding. As George turned away, his eye was caught by a small figure stumbling towards them through the tufts of fresh green heather. His heart seemed to stop for a second, when he recognised Kitty. 'What is it?' he cried, and began to run towards her.

Tears were streaming down the child's face. 'Oh, sir, sir,' she cried. 'Mrs Butler says to come at once. T'missus is worse, she's proper badly.'

Leaving her to follow, George set off at full speed towards the farmhouse. He found the kitchen empty and rushed towards the stairs, taking them two at a time. When he entered the bedroom, he thought at first that Elizabeth had gone. Her eyes were closed and the face on the pillows was almost translucent. Little Edward was asleep on the bed, curled in the crook of his mother's arm, while Ann and

Sarah Butler stood, one on either side of the bed, weeping quietly.

George stopped just inside the door and drew in his breath in a sharp gasp. To his relief Elizabeth's eyes opened and he went towards the bed. Kneeling beside it, he took her hand and softly kissed her cheek.

'Thank God Kitty managed to find you in time,' she whispered. Looking over his shoulder to her sister, she murmured, 'Look after him, Sarah.'

Leaving Sarah in doubt as to whether she meant George or Edward, Elizabeth's eyes drooped once more and they realised that at last, her suffering was over.

# CHAPTER TWENTY-FIVE

Between Elizabeth's death and her funeral, George was grateful for the way Sarah took charge of everything. She was decisive and efficient, shouldering the responsibility of all the arrangements. 'You and Mother have been under a great strain,' she told George. 'Anything that I can do to help, I'll do only too willingly.'

The day of the funeral in April was one of mixed sunshine and light showers. Little Edward and Kitty were left in the care of Dorcas Weald, Jonadab's foreman's wife, while the rest of the family followed the hearse up to Gillamoor Church. Members of both the Oaks and the Butler families had gathered from the dales villages and outlying farms of the North Yorkshire moors and George was touched to see several tradesmen from Kirkbymoorside who had come to pay their respects.

Afterwards, close friends and relatives gathered in his father's house to chat in sombre mood over funeral cakes and tea. All George's tears had been spent weeks before and he was now able to move among his family, chatting quietly, in apparent control of his emotions. As he drew near to where Tamar sat nursing Edward who had been brought along by Kitty, she said, 'Would you like us to take him back to Thorsbury with us for a few weeks, George? Kitty could come, too, so that he won't feel strange.'

George looked at the child sleeping peacefully in Tamar's arms. 'No!' He spoke sharply and then, recovering his innate good manners, added, 'Thanks all the same.'

Sarah had heard the offer and the response and came over to them. 'Mother is quite run down you know, George after all that nursing. Uncle Nathan and I would like to take her back to Leeds with us for a complete change. It would make it easier for you if Tamar took Edward. You could come back to your mother's for a short time.'

George looked from one to the other. How neatly they

were disposing of his future he thought bitterly, as though his feelings did not count. *'No!'* Conscious of the crowded room, he kept his voice low but bent and snatched the sleeping child from his sister. Holding him close in a fiercely protective gesture, he glowered from Tamar to Sarah. 'I've lost my wife and baby – am I to be robbed of my child and home?' he demanded in a shaking voice. 'Just to make things all neat and tidy?'

Neither spoke and the suggestions were not raised again.

The year that followed was the unhappiest period of George's life. Since the age of seventeen, Elizabeth had meant more to him than anything in the world and he found life without her to be bleak and empty. Unable to face his evenings in the company of his mother-in-law and the little housemaid, he threw himself into his work, always finding something to occupy himself with away from Cherry Tree Farm. He took to going to his mother's for his midday meal and there were many days when he did not arrive back home until after Ann Butler and Kitty were in bed.

With feelings of guilt, he realised that he was treating them badly and that, although he had clung so tenaciously to Edward, his son hardly knew him. However, he just could not bring himself to sit in the house, knowing that Elizabeth would never again be there.

Every two or three months, Sarah came over from Leeds and cleaned the house thoroughly. George was grateful, although he knew that her visits were an endeavour to spare her mother the extra work. Whenever Sarah came to stay, he made the effort to spend his evenings in the house rather than finding jobs outside which needed his attention.

A few weeks after Elizabeth's death, George had an encounter in Kirkbymoorside which left him deeply disturbed. Striding up the middle of the road between the rows of market stalls, he saw his father's landlord, Sir James Sturdy. To his dismay, walking beside Sir James and chatting to him was a tall figure whom George immediately recognised. It was Sir William Forster, Tamar's seducer and the father of Victoria.

'How dare he show his face here?' George half-whispered the words aloud. He felt the colour rise in his cheeks as he remembered the night spent in prison for his attack on Sir William in this very market place. He made to move between the stalls on to the pavement, to avoid coming face to face with the man for whom he felt an implacable hatred. Sir James had seen him, however, and raised his cane.

'Oaks,' he called. 'Just a minute.' George paused and turned slowly round to face the landowner. James Sturdy suddenly recollected the feud between his brother-in-law and the young farmer, although he had no notion of the extent of Sir William's involvement with the Oaks. 'Wait a moment, William,' he said, as he hurried towards George. 'I just wish to say how sorry I was to hear of the death of your wife.' He shook George's hand as he spoke.

'Thank you, sir,' George responded, touching his cap. With that he turned away, thankful that he had avoided coming face to face with his enemy.

When he told his father of the encounter George expressed his surprise at Sir William Forster's presence in the town. 'He's married to Sir James' sister,' Jonadab replied. 'They often stay at the Towers with their little lad. There's no reason why not.'

'I'd have thought he'd be ashamed,' George protested.

'Nay, lad, men like 'im cast their seed widely, wi' no thought of t'consequences,' answered his father. 'What seemed a tragedy to us at the time would mean nowt to such a blackguard.'

The year passed its peak and the warm days of summer slipped into autumn unnoticed by George, who still drove himself in an effort to submerge his grief and loneliness in hard work.

Martha's baby was due in mid-December and Annie Oaks was hoping that the birth would not be delayed into the busy Christmas period. Her worries were unfounded. Martha gave birth to a little girl with no fuss and no complications. When the labour began, Annie sent Tobias down to Cherry Tree Farm to ask Ann Butler to assist at the birth.

When Martha was safely delivered of the child, the two women sat before the fire drinking tea. 'Aah wonder if thoo'd come and give me a hand wi' t'Christmas geese,'

Annie asked diffidently. 'Martha'll be in bed until near Christmas and although t'huckster will tek most geese in their feathers, Aah've a goodly number ordered to be plucked and dressed.'

To her relief Ann Butler agreed. 'I shall be only too glad of the company,' she confessed. 'I get lonely down yonder with only two bairns.' She nodded towards Edward and Kitty, who were playing with the cat before the fire.

'Thoo must all come and 'ave Christmas dinner with us.' Annie felt sorry for the woman, realising how solitary her life must be now.

When the men came in for a mug of tea before going to attend to the animals, Bob looked anxiously at Annie. 'Well?' he queried.

'It's a little lass,' Annie answered with a smile.

Swiftly he unlaced his boots and as he pulled them off, asked anxiously, 'Are they all right?'

'Aye,' answered Annie. 'Martha's tired, of course, but they're both fine.'

When Bob had left the kitchen, heading for the stairs, Annie glanced at her husband who sat by the fire warming his hands round the pint pot of tea. 'She wants to call t'bairn Maria!' she told him.

'That's a nice thought,' he answered. 'She and oor Maria was very close, afore the lassie was took from us.'

Annie looked uneasy. 'Aah feel it's tempting fate ti call t'bairn after somebody who's died.' She was rather shame-faced to put forward this argument, knowing that Jonadab had no time for superstition.

His reaction was as she had expected. 'We'll have no superstitions, Mother,' he said in an uncompromising tone. 'Those who trust in the Lord should 'ave no room for such devilish thoughts.'

Annie turned away, hurt by Jonadab's scorn. As she bent over and spoke to Edward, George looked up. He rarely referred to his wife, but now he said, 'If our bairn had been born, we'd decided that if it was a girl, we'd call it after our Maria. After all, Mam, if you look at it one way, we're all called after somebody who's dead.'

'Aye, thoo's right Aah suppose.' Annie was comforted by this way of looking at things.

Although none of those present in the kitchen realised it, this marked the beginning of George's climb back to normality. Of his own free will, he had spoken of Elizabeth. Not only of Elizabeth, but also of the child which had died with her. He felt as though a block of ice which had encrusted his heart since Easter, had begun to melt. He looked from his mother-in-law to his son and then to poor little Kitty, and admitted to himself that he had neglected them while wallowing in self-pity. 'Has Edward seen his little cousin?' he asked, picking up the boy.

'No.' Both grandmothers spoke in unison.

'Come on, Kitty. You'd like to see the baby as well, I'm sure.' George led the way through the parlour towards the stairs.

When they had left the kitchen, there was a short silence which was broken by Ann Butler. 'That's the best he's been since our Elizabeth died,' she commented.

Jonadab took a swig of his tea and then spoke reflectively. 'Aah thinks George is coming ti terms with 'is loss,' he said.

'Thank God,' Annie breathed. 'Aah feared for 'is sanity at one point.'

The Christmas period helped George's rehabilitation in progress. Sarah came home for the holiday and Christmas Day was spent at Aumery Park Farm.

Annie looked round the dinner table with a beam of contentment. It was like the old days, before her family was scattered. The table was laden with an assortment of food, the crowning glory of which were two plump geese roasted to golden perfection. They had been the pick of Annie's flock, cosseted and fattened especially to grace the Christmas table.

When everyone was replete and not another crumb of plum pudding could be forced down, Annie was pevailed upon to go and sit in the parlour with Ann Butler and the men.

While Martha sat by the kitchen fire in her mother's rocking-chair feeding baby Maria, Sarah organised Lydia and Kitty to take tea through to the others. 'Set one on the hob for Martha,' she instructed, 'and then we'll have ours when we've finished the washing up.'

At bedtime, when Jonadab came back from his final check of the stock, Annie gave a sigh of pure satisfaction. 'Aah was dreading this Christmas with Elizabeth having gone, but it's been t'best for a long time.' Jonadab merely grunted as she continued, 'Aah've said quite a few harsh things about Sarah Butler when she was younger, but she's been a real 'elp today. Aah couldn't 'ave managed without 'er, really.'

'Aye, she's not a bad lass,' Jonadab admitted, as he climbed into bed. 'And, by 'eck, she's t'spitting image o' their Elizabeth.'

In addition to Christmas Day, Jonadab Oaks also gave his workers a holiday on Boxing Day, apart from the necessary work of attending to the animals. This meant that George spent Boxing Day at home with Sarah and her mother. When the day drew to a close and he, Sarah and his mother-in-law sat in the lamplight round the parlour fire, he admitted to himself that he had enjoyed the time spent in their company. It was true that, deep down, he felt he was being disloyal to Elizabeth's memory, but he was conscious that a barrier had been overcome and he could once again begin to live his life normally.

When Sarah went back to Leeds, George was surprised to find that he missed her. Ever since her childhood, he had found Sarah's open admiration and affection for him an irritant. Now, with the sophistication acquired in Leeds, she had apparently outgrown her infatuation for him. George told himself that he was pleased by this but in reality, he was rather piqued.

As Easter drew nearer, and the time of Sarah's next visit approached, George found himself looking forward to her coming. Earlier in the week Ann Butler had remarked, 'I shall be pleased to see our Sarah. I know it's another two weeks to the anniversary of Elizabeth's death, but I shall always think of it at Easter. Sarah being here will make things easier.'

'Aye.' George thought deeply. This, of course, must be why he was so looking forward to meeting Sarah's coach on Wednesday. Her presence in the house would lighten the atmosphere when their minds were filled with memories of Elizabeth.

They had escaped being snowed-in this winter, although there had been several light snowfalls and weeks of keen frosts, making the ground rock-hard and difficult to work. Easter fell early, coming at the end of March. Although there was still a chill in the air, with traces of snow on the hills and in the northern lee of the hedges, there was the undoubted promise of spring abroad when George harnessed the pony into the trap, to start out to meet Sarah. He found himself whistling as he worked so that Kitty, running out to tell him what was needed from town, was surprised to hear him so cheerful.

'Oh, sir. It's grand to 'ear thoo whistling,' she smiled. 'Mi dad used to whistle a lot when 'e were alive.'

'Poor little mite,' George thought. He had not forgotten the vow he had made to bring her younger brother to live with them as soon as he was ten.

As the pony trotted along the track between his home and that of his parents, George looked with appreciation at the valley. The familiar scenes seemed fresh to his eyes, as though he saw them for the first time. He pondered on how it would seem to Sarah. Would she look upon it, as she usually did, as a welcome change from the scenes of the city – or would it seem boring and humdrum to her? His reflective and thoughtful mood affected the pony who sensed his lack of urgency and slowed to a saunter. Coming back to the present, George fished his watch out of his waistcoat pocket. 'Oh, blow!' he exclaimed aloud. 'If t'coach is owt like on time, I sh'll be late.' He flicked the pony's back with the whip, causing her to start and break into a trot.

When George arrived at the market place he found Sarah standing by her luggage outside the inn, looking around anxiously. As he approached, her face lit up and when he dismounted, she clutched his arm. 'Oh, George! I thought there'd been an accident. I didn't know what to do,' she cried.

'I'm sorry, Sarah. I lost track of time,' he apologised.

'Would you like to go for a cup of tea before we set off? I've one or two things to get for your mother, but I'll join you in the tea-house in a few minutes.'

When he went to meet Sarah, he stood in the doorway studying her for a short space of time before going over to join her at the table. He was startled at the first sight of her across the room. It could have been Elizabeth as she had looked in her prime and he felt his heart give a sudden lurch.

There were few words exchanged on the drive home, but when George turned out of the avenue of trees and drew the pony to a cautious walk before beginning the steep descent into the dale, he glanced across at Sarah. 'I'm glad that you've come, Sarah,' he said.

'I'm glad to be here, George,' was her reply, as she smiled up at him.

Heartened by her response, George came to a sudden decision. As they drew level with the quarry, he steered the pony off the road and came to a halt on the quarry floor. Once they were off the road, surrounded on three sides by the towering stones of the quarry walls, he was seized by a sudden diffidence. He recalled the incident when Sarah had saved him in the blizzard, remembering how she had declared her love for him. Perhaps she had changed since she had seen more of the world. Nervously he cleared his throat. 'Sarah,' he began. 'I want to talk to you before we reach home.'

She looked at him in some surprise. 'Yes?' She had no means of knowing what was to come.

'I know it's early days,' he blurted out, 'but will you marry me?'

This was the last thing that Sarah had expected. She looked at him with incredulity. Then, to George's consternation, her eyes flashed and the colour rose in her cheeks. 'Why, may I ask?' Her tone was cutting. 'You've made it clear for years that I mean nothing to you, and yet here, out of the blue, comes a proposal. Am I to take it that I'm merely a convenience? It would cause tongues to wag if I came back here to live, to give my mother a hand, would it – so you're willing to marry me to make it look respectable!'

310

George was taken aback by her reaction. In the three months which had passed since Sarah's return to Leeds, she had filled his thoughts and his feelings for her had ripened into love. The idea that she should doubt his love came as a shock to him. She had no realisation of the way his feelings had developed in the period that they had been apart.

As she paused in her tirade, in order to recover her breath, George found his voice. 'Nay, Sarah,' he began, but before he could say any more she burst forth in another torrent.

'Don't "nay Sarah" me!' she stormed. 'Perhaps it's not only a convenience you see me as, but just a pale shadow of our Elizabeth. Now you've lost her, you think you can replace her with me.'

Normally placid and easygoing, George had suddenly had enough. A refusal was half-expected and could have been borne, but Sarah's outburst suddenly proved too much. Seizing the weeping woman by her shoulders, he began to shake her vigorously. 'Stop it!' he shouted. 'Shut up! I love you, you silly woman. I love you.'

The words echoed round the walls of the quarry and combined with the violence of the shaking, quelled Sarah's outburst in full flow. Her eyes widened and her lips parted in amazement. 'George?' She spoke his name in a questioning tone, unbelieving of what she had heard.

Disturbed by the raised voices and the movement in the trap, the pony began to paw the ground restively, causing the vehicle to rock. Climbing down, George held up his arms to help Sarah down. When they stood on the stone floor he still held her, lightly. 'I love you, Sarah.' The words were spoken tenderly this time. 'Once you said that you loved me. Is it too much to hope that you still do?'

Although the tears were still wet on her cheeks, the happiness that flooded her face was answer enough for George. As he tightened his arms to draw her close, the passion with which she responded shattered George. Realising how easy it would be to lose his senses in the ecstasy which swept over him, he drew back and gently disengaged himself from her arms. 'Come along, love, let's get home,' he said. 'Your mother will wonder what's become of us.'

Before reaching Cherry Tree Farm, they agreed to say nothing as yet to their families. 'For one thing,' George decided, 'it isn't really seemly, yet. It's not quite a year since Elizabeth died and anyway,' he continued, 'let's have it as our secret for a while.'

Over the Easter period they discussed their plans in the evenings after Ann Butler had retired to bed. 'Uncle Nathan is going to sell the store in Briggate,' Sarah told George, 'and has already one or two people interested. He wants to buy a private house, perhaps in Headingly, and retire from business entirely.'

She decided that it would be for the best if they arranged for the wedding to coincide with the closing of the store. 'Then he can start with a new housekeeper in a new house,' she added. On one point she was adamant. 'I have no wish to be married at Gillamoor,' she insisted.

This floored George completely. 'Where, then?' he asked. 'Down in Kirkbymoorside?'

'No. Neither of us lives in that parish – it would perhaps be difficult to arrange.' After a long discussion, Sarah put forward the proposal that they should be married in Leeds.

'Leeds?' George was astounded at this suggestion.

'It is where I live,' she reminded him. After a brief hesitation she looked at him, a hint of tears in her eyes. 'I don't want our wedding to be in any way like your wedding to Elizabeth,' she said wistfully. 'I know I look like her, but I'm an entirely different person and I want this to be clear to everybody from the beginning.'

By the time Sarah returned to Leeds they had decided that George should write to his brother-in-law, Stephen Lassiter, for advice on how to obtain a Special Licence. 'Then we can be married whenever is convenient, without waiting for the banns to be called,' Sarah stated. George looked at her with a tender smile. No matter how much she tried to stress the difference between herself and Elizabeth, not only did she resemble her sister in looks, but she possessed the same organising ability and, once she felt the security of George's love, she glowed with Elizabeth's sparkle.

When Stephen opened George's letter he looked up at Tamar. 'This is from George,' he told her. 'He and Sarah are to be married in the autumn and he wants to obtain a Special Licence.'

'So she's got him at last,' Tamar remarked.

'I think he's very lucky to get a second bite of the cherry,' her husband chided.

'Yes,' Tamar agreed quickly. 'I'm pleased for them both. After all, I had a second chance through meeting you, didn't I?'

Both George's parents and his mother-in-law were pleased when George broke the news.

'A man needs a woman, lad,' observed Jonadab.

'Aye, and a woman needs a man,' put in his mother. 'Aah'm pleased for thi, George.'

Upon learning that the wedding was to take place in Leeds, Jonadab was insistent that he would accompany his son. 'Aah sh'll stand for thi as a witness,' he declared.

George's heart sank at this statement. He had expected to slip away alone on the coach to York. From there he would go on the railway to Leeds and after a quiet wedding, attended only by Sarah's Uncle and perhaps a friend of hers, he and his new wife would return home the following day. He felt obliged to demur, although knowing his father's obstinacy once he had made up his mind, George's attempted objection was only half-hearted. 'Nay, Father. I know how busy you are. Uncle Nathan'll be a witness. After all, he's on the spot and it would only be a waste of your time, going all that way.'

Jonadab's chin jutted forward at a determined angle, while his eyes flashed shafts of ice-blue light. 'Nonsense!' His voice was beginning to rise. 'Dost think Aah'd let a stranger stand as a witness at thi wedding, instead of thi own flesh and blood?'

'No, Father. I just didn't want to put you to any trouble.' George spoke apologetically, hiding his resentment. Even though he was now in his thirties he felt that at times his father still treated him as though he were a child.

'We sh'll have finished harvest and there'll be nowt urgent that needs me,' was his father's answer. 'Of course Aah sh'll go, so there's an end to it.'

As it turned out, George was glad of his father's presence, especially on York station. It was George's first encounter with trains and he found the engines, the steam and noise quite alarming. To his surprise, Jonadab appeared to accept what George regarded as the turmoil of the station, with composure. Jonadab's only loss of poise came when their train drew in and a porter picked up his overnight case and started to walk towards a carriage. 'Ay thoo! Put that down!' Jonadab's voice cracked out above the rattle of wheels and the shunting of engines. His long legs covered the distance to the porter and, upon reaching the man, he seized back his luggage.

The porter was startled. 'I was going to put it in a carriage for you, sir,' he explained.

'Aah'm quite capable of carrying it missen. Aah'm not in mi dotage.' Jonadab was offended and outraged, grumbling at length to George as they boarded the train.

Sarah was waiting to meet them and the journey by cab from the station to her Uncle's shop was a revelation to both George and Jonadab. Never in their lives had they seen such crowds, traffic and so many shops. Although both Elizabeth and Sarah had told him that Uncle Nathan's shop was a large store, George's knowledge of the world was so limited that it had been beyond his imagination to envisage such a place as was revealed when they arrived.

His mind was in a whirl and he was relieved that Sarah had organised everything. They were to be married in the parish church the following morning, and Sarah's Uncle had booked the wedding breakfast at a nearby hotel. The only other guest was Betty Barker, a friend of Sarah's who seemed to be a pleasant and friendly young woman.

When the meal was over, they collected Sarah's belongings from her Uncle's and began the journey back to Sleightholmedale. Originally, it had been George's intention for them to spend their wedding night in a guesthouse in York but when his father had decided to attend the wedding, this plan had to be scrapped. Both in the railway carriage and in the coach from York, Sarah and George sat side by side, their fingers secretly intertwined under Sarah's voluminous skirts while Jonadab, sitting opposite, either dominated the conversation with his plans for his horses and his farm or lapsed into silences, his eyes looking at but not really seeing his son and new daughter-in-law. That they would have preferred to be without his company never occurred to Jonadab. Indeed, he had no doubt but that George was glad to have him there.

When, at last, they reached Aumery Park Farm and he dismounted from George's trap, Jonadab urged them to go in. 'Just for a cup o' tea and ti tell thi mother about t'wedding,' he persisted.

George, however, was firm. 'No thank you, Father. We've had a long day and Sarah's mother will be anxious,' he said. When they finally managed to drive off, as soon as they rounded the next bend, George pulled the pony to a halt and drew Sarah into his arms. 'We've been married all day and I haven't had a kiss yet, Mrs Oaks,' he murmured into her hair.

As he drew away and looked at her at arm's length, their eyes met and both burst into laughter. 'What a wedding day!' she said, wiping her eyes.

'Well,' he replied. 'You said you wanted it to be different: you only need my father along to make anything different.' He kissed her again, his lips harder and more demanding. 'Let's get home,' he whispered. 'The wedding day may be nearly over, but the wedding night hasn't yet begun.'

# CHAPTER TWENTY-SIX

Sarah slipped back into life at Cherry Tree Farm as smoothly as a hand into a glove. With her arrival, the atmosphere in the house became brighter and more cheerful. To Ann Butler and to George, it was as though Elizabeth had never left them, although neither would have hurt Sarah by putting this thought into words. His home ran smoothly and George sang and whistled now as he went about his daily work.

Jonadab and Annie remarked at the change in their son. 'Thank God he's back to his old self,' his mother said fervently. With Martha, her husband Bob and the baby Maria present, the family was more like it had been when the children were young. When the opportunity arose, she gently questioned Lydia about the chances of a child.

'The Lord knows what He's doing,' Lydia answered, cheerfully enough. 'We wouldn't want another Toby, would we?' Although Tobias was grown up and married, he still remained as slow-witted and dull as he had been as a child.

'Lydia's bright enough for both of them,' Annie often told her husband. She was relieved in a way that Lydia did not produce any children and did not seem unduly worried by the fact.

Young Jonna was back in his father's favour, Maisie having produced a son. 'Another Oaks ti carry on t'name,' his father had said in a smug and self-satisfied tone, as though taking the credit for the child. 'There'll be Oaks up at Skiplam Grange for years to come.'

To George's joy, Sarah had a baby girl less than a year after the wedding. Little Edward was now out of petticoats, having been breeched and his long curls cut off on his fourth birthday. Although both his grandparents bewailed the change, George was proud. 'He looks a real lad now,' he said, and took the boy with him whenever he could.

'I've heard of a little pony for sale,' he told Sarah one

morning. 'If it's owt like, I'll buy it for our Edward. It's time he learned to ride.'

When George returned from market, Edward was dancing up and down in the yard with Kitty doing her best to keep him calm. However, when he turned into the farmyard, with the pony on a leading rein behind the horse, Kitty was just as excited as Edward, for astride the pony, looking rather apprehensive, was her young brother Freddie.

'Oh, sir, sir!' she cried, running forward to help her brother down. 'You didn't forget! You've brought our Freddie.'

Edward looked from one to the other. 'Is the lad for me, too? Have you bought him for me to play with?'

George threw back his head and laughed. 'Nay, you silly goose,' he answered, lifting Edward on to the pony. 'Freddie is Kitty's brother and he's come to live with us and work here. I've no doubt he will play with you, though.'

Although George and Sarah's daughter, Ann, put in an appearance well before Christmas, it was not until the following spring that Tamar managed to come down into Sleightholmedale to visit them. She had usually seen to it that Goodison drove her whenever she visited her family. She knew that his discretion and loyalty could be relied upon and, although not ashamed of her family, she realised that her background was unusual for one of her position. Goodison was, however, retired by now and she felt rather nervous when the young coachman Robert took the unfamiliar, steep road which led down into the dale. 'Slow right down, Robert,' she called anxiously. 'This hill is very steep and dangerous.'

'Yes, m'Lady,' he replied obediently. He knew his mistress to be a fearless rider, not balking at any fence and recognised that if she recommended caution, he must heed what she said.

As he began his cautious descent, Victoria pulled down the window and cried, 'There's a little quarry just off the road on the righthand side. Pull into it for a few minutes, Robert.'

When the coach had stopped Victoria and Hilary got out, exclaiming over the wild flowers which grew in profusion among the honey-coloured stones. Every crack on the quarry floor was a mass of creamy primroses and delicate violets, while the steep, rocky walls were clothed with ferns and here and there, an early wallflower.

'We'll each pick a little posy,' Victoria told Hilary. 'One for Grandma and one for Auntie Sarah.'

Tamar dismounted from the coach. 'Come along, Victoria. You're a young lady now. You're no longer a little girl to go picking wild flowers.'

Her daughter looked round, savouring the beauty of the place. 'I suppose you're right, Mama,' she replied. 'It's just that this is one of my most favourite places. It's like a secret garden.'

Tamar looked round. Surely Victoria's love of the place could not stem from the fact that this was where she had been conceived? She pushed the thought to the back of her mind, for these days she rarely thought of Sir William Forster. It was far more comforting to accept that her husband was Victoria's father, as did almost everyone else.

When they returned to Thorsbury Manor that evening, Stephen was curious. 'How is George's second bite of the cherry?' he asked.

Tamar hesitated. 'It's like going back in time. It's just as though Elizabeth had never died.'

'Do they seem to be happy?' Stephen was fond of George and had been distressed for him when Elizabeth had died.

'Deliriously.' She absent-mindedly crumbled a piece of bread. 'I feel mean,' she confessed. 'I never really liked Sarah. She's thrown herself at our George ever since she was a child. However, now she's got him, I must admit that they are ideally suited and they are both utterly content.'

Stephen looked across at her fondly. His wife had kept her figure and was still a striking-looking woman. He knew nothing of her period of unfaithfulness, but was aware that there were many men in their social circle who envied him his wife. 'I'm pleased for them both,' he smiled. 'I only hope they are as content as we are.'

Tamar was indeed content. Since the death of Stephen's mother, she had blossomed in the role of lady of the manor. She was keenly interested in the welfare of their tenants, most of whom were estate workers, and was, at the presnt time, consulting with the vicar on establishing a school in the village.

Hilary was not to be sent away to school. Both Tamar and Stephen felt that he was too delicate to be educated away from home. Consequently he shared his sister's governess, with coaching in the classics from the curate, Selwyn Mathews. All in all, thought Tamar, she was fortunate in the way her life had unfolded.

By the time Victoria reached the age of eighteen she was an acknowledged beauty. She had inherited the same curling black hair and glowing amber eyes which had given Tamar her outstanding attractiveness. Her appearance was not the only feature passed down from her mother, however. On the rare occasions that Jonadab and Annie saw Victoria, they were disturbed to recognise the wilfulness and inner turbulence which had dominated Tamar's character at the same age. They had attributed Tamar's wildness of spirit to her frustration with what she saw as the dullness of life in the dale. By contrast their granddaughter was petted and indulged to an extent which earned their disapproval, and yet she chafed and fretted against any form of restriction. 'Aah'm afraid they'll 'ave trouble wi' yon lass,' Jonadab gloomily forecast after one of Victoria's infrequent visits.

'She wants summat nobody sells,' was Annie's summing up. 'She 'as everything money can buy and yet she's not 'alf as satisfied wi' life as oor Molly.'

Molly Waind, their eldest daughter's girl, had spent the first five years living with her grandparents and although now grown up, often stayed for a few weeks with them. She was a quiet, placid girl, always eager to please and not afraid of hard work. The difference between her and her cousin Victoria could not have been greater.

'Mindst thoo,' Jonadab continued. 'Oor Tamar was allus different from t'rest. They 'as t'same breeding and t'same rearing, yet they grows up as different as chalk and cheese.'

Victoria had set her heart on a season in London, with a coming-out ball and a busy social calendar. Neither Tamar nor Stephen were in favour of this suggestion, partly because of the expense involved and partly because they saw no need. Although they had still kept the London house which had belonged to Stephen's brother, they rarely visited the capital and were not particularly interested in life there.

'I am only a country squire,' Stephen protested. 'There are plenty of young men in the County for you to be able to find a husband here.'

'I've known them all since I was a child and there isn't one who is interesting.' Victoria could be mulish when crossed. Nevertheless, both her mother and father were adamant that her entry into adult society should take place in their own area.

Tamar studied Victoria, before taking her into Malton to have two ball-gowns made. One, of course, must be white but although tradition demanded that the other should be of a pastel shade, she still remembered the rich gold silk of the first gown which Stephen had bought for her. The colour would do so much for Victoria . . . but Tamar finally decided against the gold, not wishing to fly in the face of convention. No sooner were the gowns delivered, one virginal white and the other the palest duck-egg blue, than the first invitation of the season arrived.

'It's a May Ball at Lambston Castle,' Tamar told Victoria. 'It will be a very grand affair for your début.'

As the date of the ball drew closer, so Victoria's excitement grew. Poor Gertie, who was still with them, was plagued daily to try out various hair ornaments and styles.

To Tamar's consternation, on the morning before the ball, Hilary awoke with a raging temperature and a troublesome cough. A messenger was immediately sent to fetch the doctor from the next village. He confirmed Tamar's fears that it was a severe attack of bronchitis. 'I will leave him a draught and call again tomorrow,' he promised. 'Keep him in bed with hot bricks to try and break the fever and see that he isn't left alone. Sit up all night with him, if he's no better this evening.'

Victoria was disbelieving. 'You mean that we can't go?' she demanded.

'There are plenty of other invitations, and we will give a ball for you here,' Tamar assured her.

Victoria's face set. 'It's not the same! This was to be my

very first ball and I've looked forward to it for weeks,' she retorted. 'Now stupid Hilary's spoilt everything.'

'Don't talk nonsense,' Tamar replied shortly. 'He can't help being ill and I must not leave him tonight, so there's no more to be said.'

As Victoria turned to flounce from the room, Tamar saw her eyes fill with tears. Whether this was from frustration or rage, she had no way of knowing but realised that, in her anxiety over Hilary, she had underestimated the intensity of Victoria's disappointment. 'Wait a minute!' she called, just before the door closed upon her daughter. When the girl came reluctantly back into the room, dabbing at her eyes with a balled-up handkerchief, Tamar smiled. 'I know your father is not too fond of social gatherings,' she said, 'but go and see if you can wheedle him into taking you on his own. You'll find him in his study, so go and plead your case.'

Victoria could twist Stephen round her little finger and soon persuaded him to take her to the ball that evening, even though Tamar would not leave Hilary.

'Don't get yourself settled in the card-room and forget about Victoria,' Tamar instructed him. 'You must keep an eye on her – and don't forget to dance with her if she doesn't get many partners,' she added.

When they were ready to leave, she quickly realised that Victoria would not lack partners. Gertie had tamed the unruly mass of black curls into ringlets while the gown of white lace was a perfect foil for Victoria's creamy skin and delicately-flushed cheeks. 'Have a lovely time, darling,' Tamar said, kissing her daughter.

Stephen sighed as he kissed his wife. 'I hope the laddie soon improves,' he said. 'Look after yourself, my dear.' With that, they were gone and Tamar returned to the sick room. She was relieved to see Tempy sitting by the bed, bathing Hilary's burning face with a cloth wrung out in cold water. The maid had married one of the footmen a few years previously and lived halfway up the village in a small cottage next to the church. She was more like a friend to Tamar than a servant and came to the Manor whenever she was needed, although she had two young children of her own.

Gertie had run to tell her about Hilary as soon as she could be spared from dressing Victoria, and Tempy had lost no time in coming to share her mistress' vigil. It was the early hours of the morning before Hilary's fever broke. As soon as he began to sweat, they washed him down and put on a clean nightshirt. Before long, he fell into a deep, natural sleep.

'Thank you, Tempy,' Tamar smiled across the bed. 'You're a true friend.'

Tempy was embarrassed. 'I'll go down to the kitchen and bring you something to eat,' she answered, changing the subject.

Tamar was still eating her belated supper when she heard the coach return. Not wishing Victoria to burst into the bedroom when Hilary had just gone to sleep, she went downstairs to meet her husband and daughter in the grand hall. Victoria was muffled in her black velvet cloak, leaning sleepily against Stephen, whose supporting arm was round her shoulders. 'Here we are,' he said. 'Safely delivered home, the belle of the ball.'

Looking at her daughter's face, sleepy and contented, Tamar knew there was no need to enquire whether she had enjoyed her first ball.

As she left them, trailing tiredly up the stairs, Tamar looked at Stephen. 'She knocked them sideways,' he stated proudly. 'The young pups were almost fighting to sign up for a dance and the girls were green with envy. Her poor old father never managed even one dance.'

Hilary was still in a sound sleep and Tamar was satisfied that the following day would see a great improvement in his condition. It was, indeed, a good thing that he was much better the next morning as, from rising at midday, Victoria regaled Tamar with an account of every minute of the ball, from the start to the finish.

'Did you meet anyone special?' Tamar asked, as soon as she could get a word in.

'Yes. There were two young men that I thought especially nice.' Victoria had turned pink. 'They are cousins, but I did like one a little more than the other. They have asked leave to call on me and Papa has met them and given his permission.'

With his background of legal training, Stephen was an astute judge of character: Tamar was happy that Victoria appeared to have met two eligible suitors at her very first ball.

A few days later, Tamar was going downstairs early in the afternoon, when she saw Hodgetts, the butler, admit two young men. As he made his way to announce their arrival to Stephen, Tamar turned back and went to warn Victoria, whom she knew to be changing into a riding habit. 'Don't bother to change,' she teased. 'Two very personable young men have arrived and I think it's you they've come to visit.'

Leaving Victoria rushing round in a frenzy of excitement, choosing and discarding afternoon gowns, Tamar went downstairs to join her husband in the drawing room. 'Ah, there you are, my dear,' he said as she entered. 'These are the two young men I mentioned after the May Ball. This is Francis and this is Tom – and this is my wife, Lady Lassiter.' He completed the introductions.

As they shook hands, Tamar smiled at them. She could see which one was Victoria's preference. Although Francis was reasonably good-looking, Tom was outstandingly handsome. Standing just over six feet in height, he had clear, light blue eyes and hair of an almost flaxen shade. For a moment Tamar thought that she had met him before; there was something vaguely familiar about him. However, as she turned away to ring for tea and cakes she knew that it could not be so.

When Victoria joined them, it was obvious that both young men were captivated by her, but she gave no indication of preference, dividing her time and attention equally betweeen them, as she charmingly offered them their cups and plates of cakes.

'You are not from Yorkshire, I believe, Mr . . . ?' Tamar paused, leaving the remark on a question, as she looked into the pale blue eyes.

'Forster, ma'am. Thomas Forster,' he replied.

323

Tamar felt the blood drain from her face, leaving it cold and pinched. The eyes which were looking into his widened and she saw parallel frownlines appear between his brows as he took in her look of horror and disbelief. 'Is anything wrong, Lady Lassiter?' She heard his voice as though from a great distance.

Unable to speak she shook her head and then placed the other hand on top of her cup, which had begun to rattle on its saucer. Using both hands, she replaced her cup and saucer on the side table. Passing her tongue over her lips, she managed to get some words out. 'I'm sorry, Mr Forster, but I don't feel well. I've come over quite faint.' Collecting herself sufficiently to mutter an 'Excuse me,' to the room in general, she made her way blindly for the door. Once outside, she leaned against it feeling too dizzy and ill to move.

After several deep, shuddering gasps, she went slowly up to her bedroom, hardly aware that she was moving. Her head was a whirl of tumultuous thoughts. What cruel fate had dragged this man into Victoria's life? He could only be on a chance visit to Yorkshire and yet their meeting seemed preordained. When Tamar reached the privacy of her bedroom, she threw herself down on the bed in a torrent of tears. Was this God's punishment on her for her unfaithfulness with Gareth Davis, she asked herself.

Eventually, she cried herself into a sleep of utter mental exhaustion and this was how Stephen found her when the visitors had gone. As he looked down on her rumpled gown and tear-swollen face, he felt a wave of concern sweep over him. Rarely had he seen his wife appear so defenceless. Tamar was normally so resolute and full of determination that he could not but feel anxiety to see her in this state. Leaning over the bed, he placed a hand on her brow.

At his touch, Tamar's eyes swept open and, with an exclamation she sprang to her feet. 'Stephen! Stephen!' she cried wildly. 'She must not see him again. You must stop him coming here.'

'Now, now, my dear,' he soothed, leading her to a chair. 'Take a deep breath and pull yourself together. You aren't making sense. Who must not see whom again?'

Tamar took a breath and tried to marshal her thoughts. How much should she tell Stephen, she wondered. He believed that she had been taken against her will by Victoria's father and there was no need to disillusion him, even if she had to reveal the man's name. Stephen's logical mind would find a way out of this mess, without the necessity of telling the truth to Victoria. She hesitated only a moment and then looked up at her husband, her tawny eyes awash with tears. 'Thomas Forster must not see Victoria again.' Her voice was low but determined. 'Their association is impossible.'

'I know he's young,' answered Stephen in puzzlement. 'Almost a year younger than her, but he's mature for his years and comes of a good family. No shortage of money there, either – a large estate in Leicestershire, I gather. If their friendship developed, there could be a long betrothal period.'

'Look at me, Stephen.' She tugged at his arm as she looked deep into his eyes. 'Listen to what I say. Thomas Forster must not meet Victoria again. They are brother and sister.' The words were spoken with such intensity of feeling that he knew instinctively that there could be no mistake.

Over the years, Stephen had grown to accept Victoria as his own child and never thought of her now in any other way. Tamar's words reminded him forcibly that this was not the case. He felt almost winded, as though he had been dealt a body blow. Feeling behind him for a chair he slowly sank into it. 'Who else knows?' he stammered.

'Only my own family. My father had thought of telling Sir Francis Sturdy, Sir James' late father, but William Forster was betrothed to Rowena Sturdy and he didn't wish to distress them.' She gave a tight little smile, which was more a grimace. 'There was enough distress in our house, without causing more,' she added with a trace of bitterness.

Stephen rose to his feet and drew her up into his arms. 'My poor darling,' he whispered, stroking her hair. 'No wonder you felt ill.'

'I thought it was all water under the bridge,' she told him brokenly. 'I never expected to meet William Forster nor any of his family again. What a cruel stroke of fate, to throw him and Victoria together.'

Stephen found himself engulfed with a rage so powerful that he began to shake. 'I could kill Forster,' he stated. 'I hate the man and yet I've never even set eyes upon him.'

Although they talked at length, the pair arrived at no definite decision. 'Both young men are leaving in the summer to do the Grand Tour,' Stephen ruminated. 'They are travelling together, so we can ensure that Victoria meets plenty of eligible young men while they're abroad. After all, they will take at least a year, perhaps even two, over the trip.'

With this conclusion they took a little comfort in the hope that things would turn out as they wished. Victoria's incessant chatter about Thomas Forster during the next few days was a constant source of annoyance to Tamar, although she tried to hide this. 'He is rather young,' she reminded her daughter. 'A young lady is far better to choose a husband who is a few years her senior.'

Victoria tossed her head. 'Nonsense! Aunt Elizabeth was seven years older than Uncle George and look how happy they were.' She spoke defiantly but Tamar made no reply, not even to chide her for her rudeness. She realised that Victoria was anxiously waiting for Thomas Forster to get in touch with her.

The letter arrived the following week, addressed to Stephen. In it Thomas thanked them both for their hospitality to him and his cousin. After sending his hopes that Tamar was fully recovered, he asked permission to call upon Victoria while he was staying in Yorkshire. After he had read it, Stephen rang for the butler. 'Ask her ladyship if she can spare me a few moments please, Hodgetts,' he instructed.

When Tamar arrived, he passed the letter to her. 'He must not come,' she categorically declared, as she put it down on the desk.

'No,' replied Stephen. 'I shall write back and say that we consider that he is too young to pay court to Victoria. I can always suggest that he should approach us again upon his return from Europe. That way there can be no offence taken and no one but ourselves need know the truth.'

Tamar thought for a moment. 'We can always arrange a short London season for her. She's bound to meet a suitable beau.'

So it was settled: the letter was written and despatched. All that remained was to see that Victoria and Thomas had no further opportunity for their feelings to develop. If they chanced to meet socially, Tamar was determined that they would have no chance to be together without supervision.

Victoria became more moody and fretful as the days passed. She took to waylaying Hodgetts on his way to her father's study with the post, and rifling anxiously through the letters. One lunch-time, after another disappointment, she burst out, at the table, 'I can't understand why Thomas Forster has not asked to call on me. I know he liked me and we got on so well. We had so much in common.'

Tamar looked swiftly across at her husband, who finished chewing his mouthful then answered in a carefully noncommittal tone, 'Actually, he wrote last week, but your mother and I decided he was too young to be paying court to anyone yet. I asked him not to call.'

She looked at Stephen in disbelief. 'You asked him not to call?' she echoed. As she rose to her feet, colour flooded her face and her eyes glowed vividly with anger. 'How dare you?' The words came out quietly at first, as though expelled on a breath. Inhaling deeply, she reiterated the words. *'How dare you!'* Hands on the table and leaning towards him, the question was repeated in a crescendo, ending almost in a shriek.

Stephen was taken aback, unaware of the depth of passion which lurked within the usually carefree girl. Tamar, however, was her father's daughter. Rising abruptly, she swiftly went round the table to where Victoria had now begun to scream. Seizing her daughter's wrist in a vice-like grip, she spoke in a tone like the crack of a whip. *'Control yourself!'* The words came out in what was almost a hiss, as she propelled the hysterical girl to the dining room door, which was hurriedly opened by Hodgetts.

When they reached Victoria's room, Tamar released the

weeping girl. 'Don't ever show yourself up in front of the servants again.' Her tone was almost cold. 'Your father and I have made the decision and there is no more to be said. You have only met Forster twice, so put him out of your mind. There are plenty more fish in the sea.'

Victoria had dried her tears. 'You don't understand,' she protested. 'We had so much in common. We felt a mutual attraction from first meeting.'

Tamar put an arm round her daughter and gave her a squeeze. 'I understand more than you will ever know,' she said sadly, 'but you must put this young man out of your mind.'

# CHAPTER TWENTY-SEVEN

For several days after Victoria's outburst, the atmosphere at Thorsbury Manor remained strained and tense. She had no memory of her life before going to Helmsley as a toddler and could only remember being petted and indulged by doting parents all her life. She could not comprehend what she regarded as their harshness and retaliated by a withdrawal into mulish silence. She did not come down to meals for the rest of that day and all of the next, instructing the servants to take hers up on a tray.

'The longer this behaviour is allowed to continue, the harder it will be for us to win her over,' Stephen commented to Tamar, as they took a leisurely ride round the estate.

'Don't worry, I'll put a stop to it,' she replied firmly. When they arrived home, she rang for the butler. 'Miss Victoria is to be served no more meals in her room, Hodgetts,' were her orders. 'See that a place is laid for her at the table as usual.'

'Yes, m'Lady.' The butler knew that the younger servants were sympathetic to Victoria and that he must impress upon them that no food was to be smuggled up to her, not even by Gertie, who idolised her young mistress.

Although Victoria declared to Gertie that she would starve to death, when she had endured a half day without food she took her place at the dining table, albeit with a set face and stubborn silence. Her parents conversed as though noticing nothing amiss and she gradually began to take some part, although remaining downcast and quiet. Within a day or two, to their relief, she was once again her normal vivacious self.

What they had no means of knowing was that one of the young grooms had come to the back door, asking for Gertie. When the maid joined him outside, he whispered urgently, 'There's a young toff in t'Walks. He asked me to get a

329

message to Miss Victoria to meet him in t'summer-house up at t'far end.'

'Shush!' Gertie glanced hastily round, but there was no one in earshot. 'Thanks, Clary, but for God's sake don't tell a soul. Go back and say I'll tell Miss Victoria.'

Victoria set off for her stroll up the Walks with studied casualness, taking Gertie with her. Halfway up, she instructed her companion, 'Stay here and keep watch. If Mama should come for a walk, or the tutor should bring Hilary to study Nature, run up to the summer-house and warn us.'

Thus was laid the pattern of the next few weeks. Each time they met, Thomas would pre-arrange with Victoria their next rendezvous. He and Francis Sturdy would ride over to Thorsbury and leaving his cousin to while away his time in the inn at Appleby, a nearby village, Thomas would wait in the summer-house until Victoria could join him there.

Gertie was terrified. She knew that they had become lovers and realised that one day, the liaison must be discovered. What if she were dismissed? Where would she go and what would become of her, she wondered. It was almost a relief to her when, one afternoon, Tempy came through the gate which led into the Walks from the village street, opposite the church.

'What's going on here?' she demanded, as she came along the path through the trees towards where Gertie was standing. The maid was facing the Manor, on the lookout for someone coming from that direction.

'Oh!' Gertie's hand went to her chest. 'You made me jump. What are you doing in t'Walks, Tempy?'

'I've come to see why *you're* always hanging about here. I can see you from my window, you know.' Gertie's involuntary glance up towards the summer-house and the look of guilt on her face told Tempy all she needed to know. 'You silly bitch!' she said harshly. 'You're covering up for Miss Victoria while she meets yon chap. Have you no more sense?'

Gertie began to cry – noisy, gulping sobs. 'Don't say owt!

Don't tell anybody, Tempy,' she pleaded. 'You'll get me into trouble.'

'Aye, and what if he gets *her* into trouble – what then?' Tempy challenged. 'If the master and mistress aren't in favour of him, there must be a reason. Haven't you thought of that?'

Gertie was now sobbing hysterically. 'Don't tell on me, Tempy,' she begged.

But Tempy was back through the gate and running down the village street. She knew that there was no real need for haste, but wanted Tamar to know what was going on, as soon as possible. Although she no longer worked at the Manor, she was still close to Tamar and had free access to the house. Upon entering the kitchen, she asked if the mistress were in.

'Yes. She and the master are in his study,' answered a footman.

Tempy hesitated. Although anxious to talk to Tamar, she felt that to disclose her news to Stephen put it on a more formal footing. Deciding that Victoria's parents must be told, however, she braced herself and tapped on the study door. When she entered they looked up, surprised.

'Is there something wrong, Tempy?' asked Stephen, noticing her anxious manner.

'Yes, sir. I'm afraid there is,' she replied, 'I feel like a tell-tale, but I think that you should know.' She glanced from one to the other and then blurted out, 'Miss Victoria's meeting that young man you've forbidden her to see. They're up in the summer-house at the top of the Walks at this very moment.'

Her mistress' reaction puzzled her. Anger she had expected – even sorrow – but Tamar turned ashen and the expression upon her face could only be described as one of horror. 'You must go up there and send him away, Stephen,' she gasped. 'Thrash him if needs be.'

Stephen looked across. 'Thank you, Tempy,' he said. 'I know we can rely upon your discretion.' When she had left them, he came round the desk and put his arm on Tamar's shoulder. 'If I thrash him, as you put it, he may retaliate – don't forget what a big chap he is. It may end up with *him* thrashing *me*. This thing must be carefully considered, if we are to avoid the whole County hearing the entire sorry tale. Think of the consequences for Victoria if the truth came out.'

Tamar's brows drew together as her mind worked at full speed, choosing and discarding a variety of possible actions. 'I have it!' she exclaimed at last. 'You must write to William Forster and ask him to call on us.'

'And when he does, what then?'

'Then I shall see him,' was her reply. 'I shall tell him who I am and insist that he puts a stop to this association.'

Stephen could think of no better solution, so he wrote immediately to Sir William Forster and sent the letter by one of the grooms, rather than wait another day and let it go by post.

Gertie was too frightened to tell Victoria that her clandestine meetings with Thomas had been discovered and went about her duties inwardly quaking, waiting for her master's wrath to break on both her and Victoria. When there were apparently no repercussions, she heaved a sigh of relief. Her tears must have had an effect on Tempy and she had had second thoughts about reporting her, she decided.

When Sir William Forster received Stephen's letter, he puzzled about it. He sent back a message by the groom that he would call on him the following afternoon, but to his knowledge, he had never heard of either Stephen Lassiter or Thorsbury Manor. It was probably some business proposition, he presumed.

When he was shown into the drawing room at Thorsbury, Stephen rose to meet him. Before shaking hands, he spoke to the butler. 'Would you tell her ladyship that our guest has arrived please, Hodgetts, and ask if she would join us.' As he greeted his guest and offered him a drink, Stephen regarded him with curiosity. So this was Victoria's natural father. He dropped his eyes, unwilling for the man to see the revulsion and dislike in them. The other man was obviously curious as to why Stephen had asked him to call.

'You wished to see me?' he said.

'Yes.' Stephen realised that he could not wait for Tamar's

appearance. 'I believe that your son has been meeting our daughter.'

'Yes?' William recalled the well-farmed lands, the neat village and the magnificent south front of the house. Thomas seemed to have chosen well, he thought with satisfaction, taking in the furniture and decorations of the room. There was obviously no shortage of money.

Stephen paused, as the door opened to admit Tamar. Both men rose as she crossed the room. Stephen looked at her with admiration and affection. She was wearing a gown of deep gold silk, very similar in colour to the first gown he had ever bought her. The shade echoed the amber of her eyes, lighting them with shafts of gold. She looked incredibly lovely and bore herself with poise and dignity. A quick glance at Forster told Stephen that the man was gazing at Tamar with fascination, but not recognition. 'This is my wife,' he said.

Tamar inclined her head and saying, 'Please sit down,' took her seat in a chair by the fireplace.

Stephen continued, 'Your son Thomas asked our permission to pay court to our daughter Victoria. We refused, but he has been meeting her secretly in our own gardens. We must ask you to speak to him: this association must be stopped.'

William Forster looked from one to the other. 'Stopped?' He echoed the word in disbelief. 'My son is a handsome lad. His prospects are good. Why must it be stopped? Many parents would be pleased to have Thomas as a suitor for their daughters.'

Tamar looked across at him. How could she ever have imagined herself to be in love with this man? His formerly handsome face was now bloated and blotchy. The once-golden hair had greyed and thinned. He had grown stout and breathless and was the epitome of excess. Comparing him with her husband, still slim and handsome, she felt an onrush of affection for Stephen. 'You don't remember me, William?' She raised her eyes to his, as she asked the question.

Surely he would have remembered this woman, if he had ever met her, he thought. And yet as his eyes met the distinctive amber ones, now fixed intently on him, he felt that he *should* know her. He delved into his past. There had been so many women in his life, but he would not have forgotten one like this, he told himself.

Seeing the blank look upon his face, Tamar felt slighted and deeply humiliated. She had borne this man's child and in her youth had flattered herself that she had made a lasting impression upon him. Now, as he sat so obviously searching his mind for some recollection of her, the distaste which the sight of him had aroused turned into cold fury. She was incensed to think that in the years since Victoria's birth, William Forster had apparently forgotten her existence. 'My name was Tamar Oaks, of Sleightholmedale.' Her voice was icy as she made the announcement

Feeling the first stirrings of recognition, he searched her face. How could it be, he wondered. This woman was a lady while the tempestuous girl he had known all those years ago had been of peasant stock.

'Yes!' The amber eyes blazed, as she struggled to maintain her composure. 'Your life was spent in total disregard of those whom you used and hurt, while indulging in your own pleasures.' Seeing his eyes swivel uneasily towards Stephen, she went on, 'My husband has given his name to your child, although he was unaware until now that you are in fact her father.'

'Her?' Again his eyes went from one to the other. 'A daughter.'

Tamar nodded and gave a deep sigh. 'This is the reason why Thomas and Victoria must not meet again. My daughter is your daughter. They are brother and sister.'

'Oh, my God.' He was obviously shaken. There was silence in the room, as he put his hands over his eyes and sat unmoving. Eventually, he looked across at them. 'What can we do?' were his first words.

Tamar's lip curled scornfully. '*We* shall do nothing. *You* will tell your son the facts. He must know the truth and he must swear that Victoria will never know. There can be no shuffling out of your responsibilities, this time. This incestuous relationship must be stopped and you are the one who can bring it to an end.'

Stephen looked at his wife in amazement. He was seeing a different Tamar from the one he had presumed he knew so well. He had never seen her so hard and unrelenting. Looking at the stricken man opposite, although Stephen felt a deep hatred towards him at this moment he also had a twinge of pity for Forster.

'No,' he remonstrated. 'I cannot tell Thomas. He's my only son. I can't risk losing his affection.' After a brief pause he added, 'After all, he's due to go to Europe with his cousin in a few weeks. While he's there, your daughter will meet other eligible young men.'

Tamar was exasperated. '*Our* daughter! This is the whole point of your being here. She is your daughter; as much as Thomas is your son. You will tell him, have no doubt. If you don't, I shall make the matter known to your wife.' Her eyes blazed and her face was contemptuous. 'Your past actions have caught up with you and you will suffer, as I once suffered.'

The eyes that Forster raised to hers were tortured. His face was grey and his cheeks sagged slackly. 'For pity's sake, there must be some other way.'

Tamar, however, would not yield an inch. 'I don't remember that you felt any pity for me in my time of terrible distress. Anyway, you have my final warning: you must tell your son as soon as you return. I don't wish to set eyes on either you or him again.' She tugged the bell-pull and when the butler appeared, announced, 'Sir William Forster is leaving, Hodgetts. Show him out, please.'

The manservant's face was impassive, but underneath he was bursting with curiosity as to what could have taken place to bring about such a dramatic change in the visitor. He had shown into the drawing room a person almost strutting with self-confidence and arrogance of manner. The man now dismissed by Lady Lassiter so disdainfully had a beaten look.

William Forster rode back to his brother-in-law's home, head pounding; he found difficulty even in thinking logically. As he passed through the next village, he dismounted and went into the inn. Slouching over a table, sipping a glass of whiskey, he tried to find an alternative means of ending the friendship between the two young people, but was convinced that Tamar would carry out her threat to tell his wife unless he did as she had demanded. He found it difficult to believe that the tempestuous girl with whom he had enjoyed what he regarded as a bit of fun, could have developed into such a poised and dignified woman.

He was devastated by her insistence that he should reveal the truth to Thomas. There were no other children. Rowena had been an unsatisfactory wife, he considered. When she had discovered her husband's way of life – his fondness for women, drink and gambling – she had withdrawn herself from him. All the affection of which he was capable had therefore been lavished upon his son. He was reluctant to let the boy know the truth about Tamar Lassiter's girl, but could see no other way of nipping their romance in the bud.

When he arrived back at the Towers, he had still not decided how to tackle the problem. To his relief, Thomas and Francis were out shooting and not expected back until early evening. By the time Thomas received his father's message and sought him out, Forster had decided to treat the whole thing lightly. 'Ah, Thomas,' was his greeting when his son entered the room. 'I've been over to Thorsbury Manor today.'

Thomas looked surprised. 'I wasn't aware that you knew the Lassiters,' he remarked.

'I didn't. It was Sir Stephen who asked me to call,' his father answered. 'Well,' he paused for a moment. 'That's not strictly true. I didn't know Lassiter, but I used to know his wife.'

There was a silence between them, as he debated with himself exactly how to go on. For his part, Thomas watched his father warily, certain that the visit was to do with Victoria. In the end it was he who broke the silence. 'Did you see their daughter, Victoria?' he asked.

'No, I didn't,' came the reply.

'I asked permission to call on her, but they turned me down,' Thomas said indignantly. 'They say that I'm too young, but surely they can't think that I'm not good enough for her?'

Forster hesitated. He was well aware that his son knew

nothing of his way of life. In the years of Thomas' school-days, Forster had curbed his drinking and philandering during the boy's vacations, always striving for his son's approbation and respect. Now, his judgement clouded by alcohol, he decided to abandon any attempts to cover up his relationship with Tamar. After all, Thomas was now a man and must be shown life through a man's eyes. Never-theless, as he came to his decision, he could not help but feel uneasy. 'No, it isn't that.' Forster had broken out in a cold sweat. 'It's an odd coincidence, actually,' he continued, trying to smile. 'When I said I'd known the Lassiter woman, it was, as you might say, in the Biblical sense.'

Thomas was perplexed for a second or two and then realisation dawned. 'You mean that you and Lady Lassiter were lovers?' he asked, looking at his father in disbelief. 'I can't imagine her having an affair – she and her husband seem to be so happy together. According to Victoria, theirs is a perfect marriage.'

Forster's chuckle was genuine this time. 'Oh, this was before she married Lassiter. He didn't get a lily-white virgin as a bride. I'd trodden that path before him.'

Thomas was aghast. 'But she is such a lady – so . . .' he searched for a word, '. . . so composed and fastidious.'

It was significant that Thomas expressed no doubts as to his father's part in the affair. Despite William's efforts, Thomas *had* discovered a little of his father's reputation and was sensitive to its effect on his mother.

'She was a little trollop – a tenant-farmer's daughter over on your Grandfather Sturdy's land,' Forster growled. 'Free with her favours, too, she was.' He was reflective for a time. 'I wonder how she managed to snare Lassiter? It can't have been easy for her. After all, there was the child. He must have known what she was.'

'You mean that Victoria was born before the Lassiters were married?' Thomas was finding all these revelations difficult to accept. 'If this is true, why do they consider that I'm not good enough for her?'

Forster took a last deep draught of the whiskey which he had been drinking steadily since his homecoming. He looked at his son pityingly. 'Surely I've made it clear. The woman claims that I'm the girl's father.'

Thomas stood as though transfixed. He groped for a chair and lowered himself down into it, his eyes upon his father's face. William had been so engrossed in blackening Tamar's character that his tone had become almost gloating. He was oblivious to the effect of his revelations upon his son.

Thomas thought for a moment that he was going to be sick. He looked at his father in horror. 'You can't mean it! I don't believe it!' He whispered the words in a tone of desperation.

'The girl's your half-sister – a by-blow of mine,' sneered Forster.

Thomas put his head in his hands and rocked it back and forth. Gradually, the rocking increased, until his whole body was moving rhythmically to and fro in the chair. He pushed his knuckles into his eyes, but could neither control nor conceal the tears which flowed through his fingers.

His father rose to his feet. 'What have you done?' he demanded, crossing to Thomas and gripping his shoulder. 'You haven't been lovers?' His son nodded wildly. 'My God,' said William. 'It's to be hoped she isn't pregnant. Why can't you take your pleasures among the lower classes?'

Thomas sprang to his feet, knocking his father's hand away. 'Like you, do you mean?' he said harshly. 'If you had lived a better life none of this would have happened. I love Victoria. I wanted to marry her. I was not merely "taking my pleasures", as you term it.' As his father advanced towards him, Thomas took a step back and held up his hand. 'Don't come near me, Father. You have ruined my life and I'll never forgive you. Never!' With that, he pushed past his father and dashed from the room. His eyes were blurred with tears as he ran from the house and round to the stable-block.

'Saddle up my horse,' he ordered one of the lads. While this was being done he paced up and down, flicking his leg with his crop and staring ahead unseeingly. He had no idea of where he was to go, nor what he was to do. He only knew that he could not bear to be under the same roof as his father.

When the horse was ready, he leapt into the saddle and gave the mare a vicious swipe with his crop, raising a weal. 'Come on, damn you! Let's have some speed out of you.'

With a startled whinny the mare was off down the drive and out into the road at full gallop, leaving the stable-lad aghast. Young Mr Thomas was not usually given to ill-treating his horse. Thomas gave the mare her head. His mind was benumbed to the sights and sounds of the June evening as he cut across country, through fields and over hedges, at a pace which matched the turmoil in his mind. As horse and rider raced through the gathering dusk, he knew only that he needed to put as much distance as possible between him and his father.

When his place at the dinner-table remained vacant that evening, Rowena looked at Francis. 'Where's Thomas?' she inquired.

'I've no idea, Aunt,' was his reply. 'I haven't seen him since we came back from shooting this afternoon.'

His father glanced across at them. 'He said he had a headache and was going for a good long ride,' he told them.

'How odd,' commented his cousin. 'I would have ridden out with him if I'd known.'

'He said he wished to be alone,' observed Forster. 'I think he was the wrong side out, for some reason.'

No more was said and only his cousin realised that he had not returned by bedtime. He presumed that Thomas had ridden over to Thorsbury in an attempt to see Victoria.

# CHAPTER TWENTY-EIGHT

In the valley of Sleightholmedale, the Oaks were in the middle of hay-making. Nowadays Jonadab took little part in the everyday work of the farm, considering that his age had earned him the privilege of semi-retirement. He still gave the orders. It was not in his nature to relinquish this right, but most of his time was taken up with his heavy horses. They were his pride and joy and he found the breeding and training absorbing.

However, as soon as the dew was off the sweet-smelling crop, he was out in the hayfields, leaning heavily upon the walking stick which was increasingly becoming a necessity to him, moving from group to group, 'geeing them up', as he put it. Haytime, this year, had not been the longed-for period of unbroken sunshine. Showery spells had meant that hay that had already been piled into cocks had, of necessity, been spread out to dry again, before once more being made into haycocks.

When they were blessed with a fine spell, Jonadab drove the men hard, keeping them at work until the fall of dusk made their toil an impossibility. The previous evening it had been almost ten o'clock when Jonadab gave the order to knock off work. As they trudged wearily home, the harsh scream of a horse in terror had rung through the silence of the night. 'Get off home, t'rest on thoo,' Jonadab had instructed. 'George, 'ave a look at t'hosses we've been working today, then if they're all right, get thissen down 'ome.' Turning to his son-in-law, he said, 'Come wi' me, Bob. We'll go down to t'far field and see if that lot's all right. Aah couldn't rightly tell which direction it came from.'

Finding all the horses there, and nothing wrong, they made their way home, perplexed as to what the sound had been. 'Mebbe somebody's horse has got loose and is up on t'moors,' suggested Bob.

'Aye, 'appen so,' replied Jonadab heavily. 'Sound carries

a long way on a still night like this. Anyroad, it's not one of ours.'

The pearly morning sky fulfilled the promise of the rosy sunset of the night before and Jonadab was eager to get the workers into the hayfield. The sun gained strength early in the day, drying up the dew and allowing work to begin fairly early. When the women came out with the midday meal, moving among the men, giving out meat and potato pasties and mugs of tea from a steaming bucket, Jonadab pulled out his watch. He screwed up his eyes and squinted to see it in the sunshine. 'Right, men,' he bawled, his voice carrying to all corners of the field. 'See if thoo can get finished in three-quarters, instead of t'usual hour.'

By moving from group to group as he ate, having a word here and a dry joke there, Jonadab communicated his sense of urgency to the workers without causing any resentment that their dinner-hour was being curtailed. When the women collected up the mugs and went back to the house to prepare the mid-afternoon 'lowance, the men set to work with a will, fired with enthusiasm. 'He certainly knows how to handle men,' George remarked to Bob Lamb.

They had just broken off for the afternoon snack when a horseman came riding down the track from the entrance to the dale. Upon seeing him stop by the field gate and dismount, Jonadab walked over towards him.

'Mr Oaks?' the man enquired.

'Aye,' was Jonadab's laconic reply.

'Sir James Sturdy has sent me round to all his farms. His nephew Thomas has disappeared and he would like you to search your land.'

'A child is he, then?' asked Jonadab.

'No. He's a young man, about the same age as Mr Francis. He went out for a ride yesterday and hasn't come back. His mother, Sir James' sister, is getting anxious.'

'Aye, we'll 'ave a look round,' promised Jonadab.

'I expect 'e's visiting some wench,' laughed the groom, 'but you know how women worry about their sons.'

When his father came back across the field George looked at him curiously. Passing his forearm across his dripping brow, he asked, 'What did yon chap want?'

'There's a lad missing. It'll be Miss Rowena's son. Thoo'd better come wi' me and we'll ride through t'woods and along t'beck.'

Jonadab looked with pleasure at the scene in the field. Men, women and even children were busy raking, tedding and putting the hay into cocks. While Edward and little Maria Lamb played among the fragrant crop, they were unknowingly imbibing the ethos of work which would dominate their lives. Already they had begun to recognise that life was a constant struggle against the elements. 'We could start leading this field tonight, if all goes well.' He looked at the cloudless sky as he spoke with a feeling of satisfaction that the weather appeared to be more settled.

While George went off to saddle their horses, Jonadab explained to Bert Weald where they were going. 'Aah dissent expect we sh'll be long, Bert, but keep 'em at it,' with a nod towards the workers.

'Aye, maister,' came the reply.

'Do you think we should split up?' George asked, as they set off.

'No. If we do find 'im, it may need both of us if there's been an accident,' replied his father.

'I don't think it's likely, do you?' Although George knew that neither he nor his brothers would have stayed out all night, he felt that the gentry lived by different standards.

His father, however, appeared thoughtful before replying. 'Aah can't 'elp but remember that scream last night. Aah'm convinced it was a horse. It sounded terrified and Aah can only 'ope it hadn't taken a tumble.'

As if by mutual consent, they rode off the road into the woods which clothed the hillside on the left. Once out of the brightness of the sunlight and into the deep shade of the broad-leafed woodland, they paused to give their eyes time to adjust to the change of light.

'If we keep to t'clearings,' advised Jonadab, 'we shall see easy enough if an animal 'as been blundering through the undergrowth. T'bushes and bracken'll be trampled down, so we'll be able to follow its trail.'

They found no signs of a rider and as the way became steeper, climbing up the brink of the escarpment Jonadab, who was in the lead, held up his hand. 'We'll go to t'top, through t'woods and come out on t'road. Then we'll ride down t'hill and cut across towards t'beck.'

'We'd better walk the horses until we get past the quarry,' George suggested.

'Aye,' Jonadab looked round. 'It's years since Aah've been up 'ere,' he commented. 'We could do with snigging some of these fallen trees out this autumn, after 'arvest. There's enough fire wood 'ere ti last us years.'

As they approached the quarry edge, George's eyes were caught by something across the other side of the abyss. 'Father! Look!' he exclaimed, pointing to a trail of broken bracken leading to the very lip of the quarry. Together they gingerly approached the edge and peered over.

'Oh, my good Lord,' whispered Jonadab, in a muted voice. There, way below them on the quarry floor, lay the crumpled remains of horse and rider.

'He can't have known it was here and has ridden over it in the dusk.' George was overwhelmed with sadness at the sight. Although he did not know the young man, the tableau of this violent and sudden death was deeply disturbing.

'Aah'll go round t'top and down into t'quarry and stop with 'im. Thoo must go t'Towers and take 'em t'news,' his father said solemnly.

When they reached the road, George spurred his horse into a gallop and set off towards Sir James Sturdy's home. He had only gone about a mile when he caught sight of two riders ahead of him. Recognising the distinctive piebald mount of the estate manager, he let out a shout. 'Mr Watson! Mr Watson!' They halted and waited for his approach. 'I'm afraid we've found him,' said George, only too grateful that he had seen these men and was spared breaking the news to any relatives of the dead man.

'Found him? You can't mean that he's met with an accident?' The manager was dumbfounded. Like most of the searchers, he had supposed that they were on a wild goose chase to placate an over-anxious mother.

George was silent for a moment, considering. He had not seen the body close to. They had presumed that the man was dead. Upon reflection, however, he was certain that neither man nor horse could have survived the drop on to the stones of the quarry floor. 'I fear he's dead, Mr Watson,' he said gravely.

'Oh, my God.' The man took off his cap and mopped his brow. 'Lady Rowena will lose her wits. She dotes on the lad.' Turning to his companion he instructed, 'Make your way back to the Towers, Ted. See if you can find Sir James or Sir William. You know where the quarry is, do you?'

'No, sir,' came the reply.

George explained how he would find the spot. 'Although I think Sir William knows the way,' he finished.

The three men made their way back towards Sleight-holmedale in silence. As the road turned to climb down the almost sheer side of the escarpment, George pointed out the flattened vegetation where the rider had chosen to go through the woods, rather than ride down the road. 'He maybe didn't want to meet anybody. 'Appen he had a lot of thinking to do and wanted to be alone,' George suggested.

'It was odd for him to be by himself,' came the reply. 'Mr Francis and him were inseparable – more like brothers than cousins. When the Forsters came to stay you never saw one without the other.'

By now they had reached the quarry. Jonadab was seated on a large outcrop of stone in his shirtsleeves, having draped his coat over the head and shoulders of the dead youth. The body was lying a few yards from that of the horse, having evidently been thrown off during the fall.

Watson said, 'It's certainly Mr Thomas' horse. It can't have been stolen. There's no mistake about the rider?'

Jonadab shook his head. 'Aah've no idea, Mr Watson. Aah've never seen the young man as far as Aah knows.'

The estate manager walked across and lifted the coat. 'It's him.' He dropped the jacket once more over the broken body. 'The poor devil knew what was coming, by the look of horror on his face.'

They had no time to say more, for they heard the sound of hooves coming down the road. A minute or two later, William Forster rode into the quarry accompanied by his brother-in-law and nephew.

'Well?' Sir James Sturdy addressed Watson.

'I'm sorry, sir. It is Mr Thomas,' he replied heavily. 'It must have happened some time yesterday.'

'It were just about twilight.' Jonadab spoke directly to the father. 'We 'eard t'horse cry out, but couldn't tell from where.'

Forster was now kneeling by his son's body, a corner of the coat in his hand and his face contorted with grief. Looking up, he realised for the first time who it was that had discovered the body. 'You two!' He looked from George to Jonadab. 'I've lost my son, my only son, and you have to be here to intrude on my grief.'

'Nay, sir.' Jonadab's voice was almost gentle. 'Aah've lost a child missen, and mi 'eart bleeds for you and Lady Rowena. No man should outlive his child! 'Tis the worst thing in the world.' Turning to James Sturdy, who could make nothing of this exchange, he said, 'We'll be off now, sir. No doubt the sergeant will want to 'ave a word wi' us. Dust want me to send a cart and waggoner up?'

'No thank you, Oaks. I will arrange everything,' was the reply.

As they rode back down into the valley, George was wrapped in thought. During her pregnancy, Tamar had confided in him that the quarry was where she and Sir William had been in the habit of meeting. What a strange and macabre chance, he thought, that the very place in which Forster's daughter had been conceived was the same place that had brought about the death of his son.

When they reached the hayfield, he turned to his father. 'I'm sorry, Father, I've no stomach for work. If you can manage without me, I'll take Edward back home. Keep Kitty and Freddie here and I'll probably be back when I've milked and foddered up at home. Sarah's not too good today.' Sarah was well on in pregnancy with a second child and had her hands full with little Annie, who was just walking and Ann Butler who was nowadays quite frail.

'Aye, lad. It's been a nasty shock. Aah wouldn't wish such a thing on any man, even 'im,' Jonadab replied sadly.

In the quarry, the sombre group awaited the arrival of the police sergeant and a conveyance from the Towers, to take the body back. Sir William Forster, although utterly self-centred, had idolised his son. Thomas had been the only person in the world for whom he had any feeling, apart from himself. Now he was distraught in his grief. 'If only I could go back,' he said wildly. 'The last words we spoke were in anger.'

James Sturdy looked at him curiously. 'You mean you'd quarrelled?' he asked.

'No! No, of course not.' Even in the depths of grief, he knew that no one must gain an inkling of the truth about Victoria.

Francis Sturdy suddenly thought of her. 'Father,' he whispered urgently. 'I can do no good here. There is someone who needs to know about poor Thomas and I must be the one to tell her.'

Not really taking in what he had said, his father nodded. Quickly mounting up, Francis rode out of the quarry and set off on the long journey to Thorsbury. Tragedy had never touched his life until now and the suddenness with which his cousin's life had been snatched from him had left Francis numb with shock and grief. Despite his own feelings, however, he felt an obligation to break the news to Victoria, rather than let her hear it from someone else.

When he and Thomas had first met Victoria, he had fallen in love with her too. Not possessing his cousin's good looks, striking height and dominating personality, he had not been surprised that she had preferred Thomas. Now he was anxious that she should learn of the accident from the only person who knew how close she and Thomas had been. Francis had no way of knowing that others knew her secret, too.

By the time he reached Thorsbury, he had still not decided what to say. His schooldays were only just behind him and nothing in his life before had prepared him for this situation. It was only when he dismounted at the front door of the Manor that he felt the first twinges of doubt. He knew that, for some inexplicable reason, the Lassiters had barred Thomas from seeing Victoria. What if this ban applied to him, too?

Screwing up his courage, he rang the bell and told the

butler who answered it, 'Francis Sturdy. May I see Sir Stephen and Lady Lassiter, please?' He had no thought that they might not be at home and in this he was fortunate. The butler showed him into the grand hall and he had not long to wait before Stephen and Tamar put in an appearance. Tamar was obviously perturbed to see him, as though expecting to see Thomas with him. The shock of his cousin's death suddenly overwhelmed Francis and the colour drained from his face, while he began to shake.

'Whatever is wrong?' Stephen asked, noticing his sudden pallor.

'May I speak to your daughter, please? It is very urgent.'

Tamar rang the bell and then, struck by a feeling of disquiet, looked across at him with narrowed eyes. 'This is not to deliver a message from Thomas Forster, I hope?' Her voice was challenging.

'No. Thomas is dead. He has been killed.' The terrible words seemed to hang on the air. The Lassiters looked shocked and incredulous, while Francis was unable to say any more. As they heard Victoria's footsteps coming down the wide oaken staircase, he suddenly found his voice. 'Please let me tell her,' he murmured.

When Victoria swept in she was amazed to see Francis there. 'Why, Francis! What a surprise,' she said, with a quick glance around the hall as if hoping that Thomas was there.

Swiftly, he crossed over to her. 'Please sit down,' he said, pressing her into a chair.

Registering the gravity on their faces, she looked from one to the other in growing alarm. 'Whatever is the matter? Is something wrong?'

'Thomas has met with an accident.' Francis' voice was low and full of misery. He felt unable to meet her eyes.

'An accident?' The fact that he was speaking openly in front of her parents was lost on her for the moment. 'You mean he's been hurt?' Her voice trembled as he raised his eyes to hers and she read the pity and compassion in them. 'No! No!' Her face was a mask of horror and disbelief. 'It can't be true.' She looked wildly and pleadingly from one to the other. 'Tell me it isn't true?' she beseeched him.

He shook his head, slowly. 'I'm sorry, Victoria. He was out riding and his horse went over the edge of a quarry. He was killed instantly.'

Tamar was stunned. Victoria's screams made little impression on her as she digested Francis' revelation. 'Do you mean the quarry on the way down to Sleightholmedale?' When Francis replied that it was so, she shivered uncontrollably. Then, recovering herself, Tamar bent over the weeping girl and raised her to her feet. Taking her in her arms, she looked at her husband over Victoria's head. 'Give him a good stiff drink, Stephen. He looks all in,' she said quietly, nodding towards Francis Sturdy. 'Come along, Victoria.'

She led her hysterical daughter gently towards the stairs, a cold sick feeling in the pit of her stomach as she recalled Victoria's protective gesture of placing a hand across her body as the news of Thomas' death had been broken to her. 'Oh, God. Let it not be so,' she prayed as she led Victoria to her room.

'Whatever's up, madam?' asked Gertie, who was busy putting away Victoria's day-gown.

'Mr Forster has been killed,' Tamar answered brusquely. The maid's eyes opened wide as she clapped a hand over her mouth in shock. 'You may well look shocked.' Tamar's voice was like a lash. 'You've been covering for them! Don't bother to deny it.' Gertie's sobs joined Victoria's as her young mistress threw herself on the bed in a torrent of tears. Tamar was cold with fear and she unleashed her anguish and apprehension on Gertie.

'I took you from the workhouse as a child, gave you a good home and this is the thanks I get. You have plotted with my daughter and helped her to sin.' With a shuddering sigh she added, almost to herself, 'And such a sin as you can never know.' She took a deep breath to steady herself then, sitting down on the bed, she shook Victoria gently. 'Victoria! Shut up! Listen to me.'

Eventually she managed to break through to her daughter and Victoria raised her swollen and blotched face in enquiry. 'Answer me, truthfully. You are carrying his child, aren't you?' When she hesitated, her mother went on, 'The truth will come out eventually, so I must know now.' Victoria nodded mutely. 'How long?' asked her mother.

'I only just know,' she answered in a whisper. 'I hoped you would allow us to marry.' Her eyes once again over-flowed with tears.

Tamar felt that she had reached the depths of bitterness and despair at that moment. Her child was suffering through her mother's sin and yet she could never reveal the truth to her. Turning to Gertie, who was still gazing at her with a terrified expression, Tamar rapped out, 'Go and get her a cup of tea!' As the maid scuttled towards the door, her mistress clutched her by the shoulder and swung her round. Tamar's eyes were blazing, almost cat-like. 'Tell no one what you know. Not now – not ever!'

Gertie nodded, unable to speak. When she returned with the tea, Tamar seemed calmer. 'Miss Victoria must not be left alone, do you hear me?'

'Yes, m'Lady,' whispered Gertie. 'I'll look after her, don't worry.'

'If you'd looked after her before this I'd have no need to worry now,' Tamar retorted. When she closed the bedroom door behind her, she stood on the landing, her burning forehead pressed against the cool wood of the door jamb. Her eyes were tightly closed as her brain teemed with alternatives. *What were they to do?* Thinking back, for the first time she could appreciate her father's vain attempts to keep the news of Victoria's birth hidden from the outside world. If only there was a similar secure haven where Victoria and the coming child could be hidden . . .

How proud she had been of her daughter! Thanks to Stephen, the girl had been brought up with every advantage which money and position could provide. Tamar contemplated her own early years of toil down in Sleightholmedale, when every waking hour had been filled with work, either inside or outside the house. In addition to her striking physical resemblance to her mother, Victoria had inherited her turbulent and passionate nature, her life taking the same path. The thought that George and Sarah would give Victoria a home until the baby was born crossed Tamar's mind, but she shrank at her father's reaction when he learned of her daughter's disgrace. She could hear his voice now: 'What's bred in t'blood will out in t'flesh.'

Although Tamar was soft and feminine in appearance, she had Jonadab's inner core of toughness. There was no use crying over spilt milk, nor in harking back to the past. She must apply herself to dealing with the present crisis. *Of course!* Joseph and Mary had been in the same position. They would understand.

Eventually she took a breath to steady herself and then made her way downstairs. The two men sat in the hall, talking in solemn tones about the accident. She was pleased to see that young Sturdy was now in command of himself.

As he rose, he looked from one to the other. 'Before I go, there is something I would like to say, Sir Stephen, Lady Lassiter,' he announced.'I know that Victoria loved Thomas, as he loved her. From the moment I first saw her, I fell in love with your daughter too, but of course, my cousin was such an outstanding chap that I had no chance.' He stood for a moment, trying to choose his words. 'This may seem presumptuous at a time like this, but I don't know when I shall see you again. When a reasonable interval has passed and Victoria has had the chance to recover, may I have your permission to call on her?'

Tamar looked at his open face and spaniel-like eyes as he declared his love for Victoria. Glancing at Stephen as though for his approval, she suddenly saw a way out. 'I have thought that we may send Victoria to visit my brother in Canada, perhaps for a year, to help her to get over the shock,' she said. 'When she is back in England, I am sure that my husband agrees that we should be delighted for you to call, if you still wish.'

Francis managed a faint smile. 'Thank you, Lady Lassiter. I will wait a year – I will wait for eternity if it means that I get a chance to court Victoria.' With that he bowed to them both and made for the door.

Tamar heaved a sigh of relief. She would write to her brother Joseph immediately. At last she could see a path to the future . . .

# ROWAN BESTSELLERS

### OLD SINS
*Penny Vincenzi*

An unputdownable saga of mystery, passion and glamour, exploring the intrigue which results when Julian Morrell, head of a vast cosmetics empire, leaves part of his huge legacy to an unknown young man. The most desirable novel of the decade, *Old Sins* is about money, ambition, greed and love... a blockbuster for the nineties.

### GREAT POSSESSIONS
*Kate Alexander*

A wonderful saga set in glamorous between-the-wars London that tells the story of Eleanor Dunwell, an illegitimate working-class girl who comes quite unexpectedly into a great inheritance. Her wealth will attract a dashing American spendthrift husband – and separate her from the man she truly loves.

### THE WIND IN THE EAST
*Pamela Pope*

There were two things Joshua Kerrick wanted in the world: one was money to buy a fleet of drifters; the other was Poppy Ludlow. But Poppy and Joshua are natural rivals. This vivid historical drama traces their passionate story among an East Anglian community struggling to make its living from the sea.

### LOVERS AND SINNERS
*Linda Sole*

A dramatic and powerful novel of the darker side of love, set in fifties London. Betty Cantrel, former housemaid and now a famous night-club singer, is to hang for the murder of her lover. As she sits in her cell she reminisces over the two very different men who have shaped her life. Which of them does she truly love and why does she kill him?

### FRIENDS AND OTHER ENEMIES
*Diana Stainforth*

Set in the sixties and seventies, the rich, fast-moving story of a girl called Ryder Harding who loses *everything* – family, lover, money and friends. But Ryder claws her way back and turns misfortune into gold.

# THE FLIGHT OF FLAMINGO
## *Elizabeth Darrell*

A strong saga unfolds against a backdrop of marine aviation in its heady pioneering days before the Second World War. When Leone Kirkland inherits her autocratic father's aviation business, she also inherits his murky past, and Kit Anson, his ace test pilot. She needs him; she could love him, but he has every reason to hate her.

# THE QUIET EARTH
## *Margaret Sunley*

Set in the Yorkshire Dales during the nineteenth century this rural saga captures both the spirit and warmth of working life in an isolated farming community, where three generations of the Oaks family are packed under the same roof. It tells of their struggle for survival as farmers, despite scandal, upheaval and tragedy, under the patriarchal rule of Jonadab Oaks.

# A BOWL OF CHERRIES
## *Anna King*

A heartwarming East End novel of family life set in post-war London. It is the story of Marie Cowley's working class upbringing, her fight against a debilitating disease which overshadows her childhood, and her passionate determination to survive and find happiness despite everything.

# THE SINS OF EDEN
## *Iris Gower*

Handsome, charismatic and iron-willed, Eden Lamb has an incalculable effect on the lives of three very different women in Swansea during the Second World War that is to introduce them both to passion and heartbreak. Once again, bestselling author Iris Gower has spun a tender and truthful story out of the background she knows and loves so well.

# ELITE
## *Helen Liddell*

Anne Clarke was a ruthless, politically ambitious, beautiful and brilliant woman... passionately committed to the underground workers militia of Scotland. But did her seemingly easy rise to the post of Deputy Prime Minister and her brilliantly orchestrated, perfectly lip-glossed public face conceal a sinister secret?

## THE DIPLOMAT'S WIFE
### Louise Pennington

Elizabeth Thornton, beautiful and elegant wife of distinguished diplomat, John, has everything. Until Karl – dangerous, ruthless and passionate – turns up in her life again. Under the glittering chandeliers of Vienna, 'City of Dreams', her past returns with a vengeance and she must choose between safe love she shares with John and heady passion she feels for Karl.

## THE ITALIANS
### Jane Nottage

A contemporary international novel capturing the very essence of the fabulously rich D'Orsi family. Wealthy, passionate ex-playboy Alberto D'Orsi has everything – including the memory of the only woman he loved and lost during the Second World War. Now an old man, he must decide who will inherit his vast fortune: his aristocratic wife or wayward son and daughter? His decision shocks everyone.

## THE RICH PASS BY
### Pamela Pope

A moving story of endurance and love, set against the harsh realities of Victorian London. When Sara surrenders her illegitimate child to the Foundling hospital she vows one day to reclaim her. Poor and destitute, she survives everything the hostile world can throw at her – fighting to remain true to her promise and to hide the passion she feels for the father of her child.

## ANGEL
### Belle Grey

Silvie Lazar, successful actress of Victorian London and notorious as the model for *The Angel*, painted by Pre-Raphaelite artist Will Mackenzie, is still haunted by her father's death in a duel many years ago. With Will's help and her own financial skill she returns at last to Budapest to confront the ghosts of her past – and her father's murderer.

# OTHER ROWAN BOOKS

Prices and other details are liable to change.

ARROW BOOKS, BOOKSERVICE BY POST, PO BOX 29, DOUGLAS, ISLE OF MAN, BRITISH ISLES

NAME _____

ADDRESS _____

_____

Please enclose a cheque or postal order made out to Arrow Books Ltd. for the amount due and allow the following for postage and packing.

U.K. CUSTOMERS: Please allow 22p per book to a maximum of £3.00

B.F.P.O. & EIRE: Please allow 22p per book to a maximum of £3.00

OVERSEAS CUSTOMERS: Please allow 22p per book.

Whilst every effort is made to keep prices low it is sometimes necessary to increase cover prices at short notice. Arrow Books reserve the right to show new retail prices on covers which may differ from those previously advertised in the text or elsewhere.